The
Missing
Treasures
of
Amy Ashton

The
Missing
Treasures
of
Amy Ashton

Eleanor Ray

Gallery Books

New York   London   Toronto   Sydney   New Delhi

G

Gallery Books
An Imprint of Simon & Schuster, Inc.
1230 Avenue of the Americas
New York, NY 10020

First Gallery Books hardcover edition June 2021

GALLERY BOOKS and colophon are registered trademarks of Simon & Schuster, Inc.

For information about special discounts for bulk purchases, please contact Simon & Schuster Special Sales at 1-866-506-1949 or business@simonandschuster.com.

The Simon & Schuster Speakers Bureau can bring authors to your live event. For more information or to book an event, contact the Simon & Schuster Speakers Bureau at 1-866-248-3049 or visit our website at www.simonspeakers.com.

Interior design by Jaime Putorti
Illustrations by Laura Levatino

Manufactured in the United States of America

10 9 8 7 6 5 4 3 2 1

Library of Congress Cataloging-in-Publication Data has been applied for.

ISBN 978-1-9821-6352-5
ISBN 978-1-9821-6354-9 (ebook)

For Susan, Teddy, and Violet

The

Missing
Treasures
of
Amy Ashton

Chapter One

It really was too much. Amy's colleagues were nice enough, in their way, but she'd spent all the working week with them. Surely on Friday evening she should be free to go home, take off her shoes, and relax on her sofa. Alone.

But here she was. Standing in a cloud of cigarette smoke outside a crowded pub, shoes cutting into her feet, being jostled by people pushing past her struggling to carry a round of three pints in two hands.

Something was bound to get broken. Amy felt her body tense in anticipation, and she clutched her warm glass of Prosecco closer to her chest.

"It's a lovely change to have you out with us, Amy," said Mr. Trapper, one of the eponymous partners in Trapper, Lemon, and Hughes, the medium and not-at-all-growing firm of financial advisers where Amy ran the admin team. "Good to let our hair down once in a while." He laughed, tapping his balding head to signal it was a joke at his own expense. Amy's dark hair stayed tightly pulled back in a ponytail. "Builds morale," he added. He had a Prosecco bottle in hand and proceeded to refill Amy's glass.

"I couldn't miss Emma's leaving drinks," said Amy. She'd tried. When five o'clock came, she'd stood up, shaken Emma's hand, and wished her all the best for the future. Duty done. But Emma had clung to her, insisting that she come to the drinks. Amy couldn't for the life of her work out why Emma seemed to think they were friends; Amy had been nothing but businesslike. She'd given Emma adequate instruction on what her role was to be and what was expected of her. She'd declined all the meeting requests for awful-sounding "girls' lunches," and she'd certainly ignored all of the little messages with smiley-face emojis on the office instant messaging system that some of the team used to waste their time.

Thinking about it, she had made the mistake of once making Emma a cup of tea when she found her crying in the toilets, presumably the result of a boyfriend's actions. She'd even patted her gently on the back. And now in return she could see her plans for a comfortable evening dissolving like the Alka-Seltzer poor Emma would need the next morning.

Mr. Trapper moved on to refill more glasses, and Amy was left on her own for a moment. She glanced at her watch. She'd been here forty-five minutes. Now was the perfect time to make her escape. "Hey, Amy," said a voice. Amy spun around and found herself face-to-face with Liam, the new head of marketing. "I haven't seen you out for drinks before," he said, smiling at her.

"I'm usually busy," she replied, stepping backwards. "And actually I need to—"

An arm snaked round her waist from behind. Before Amy had time to react, she felt a wet warmth by her ear. She spun round again: people from the office kept sneaking up on her. Thank goodness at work she had a desk with its back to the wall.

"I'll miss you," said Emma, her voice already a little slurred as she leaned into Amy. Amy smelled Red Bull and Jägermeister on

Emma's breath and was suddenly reminded of the 2017 Christmas party she'd been forced into attending two years ago. Emma looked at Amy's expression and laughed, giving her a wet kiss on the cheek. "You're special."

"Yes," said Amy, disentangling herself. "Indeed." Carthika appeared, and Amy successfully transferred Emma across. The two of them swayed together in what Amy assumed was meant to be some kind of dance. "Just nipping to the loo," she said, as she saw Liam approaching her once more.

The swarm around the bar was four people deep, but the rest of the pub was quiet. It was a warm day in early July and people had chosen the pavement rather than the dark pub room. An abandoned wine bottle sat on a sticky round table, with two empty glasses for company. Amy paused and glanced at the bottle. It looked almost black in the dim light of the pub, but Amy could tell it would have a beautiful green translucence if held to the light: like the lime-flavored hard candies Tim used to enjoy.

Amy climbed the steps to the loo and sat down in the cubicle, thankful for a few moments to herself with the weight off her feet. She thought about the bottle again. It had a perfect shape to it: a long, elegant neck and straight body. Symmetrical. Perfect. It couldn't just go in the bin. It wouldn't be right.

She went back downstairs and discovered that the bottle still sat there. Empty. Forlorn. Amy made sure no one was watching. Thankful for her large handbag, she grabbed the bottle and popped it inside. The neck peeped out like a little lapdog, but Amy didn't think anyone would notice. She fought the urge to take the glasses too—they looked so sad, sitting there. No. That would be stealing.

But the bottle wasn't stealing. No one wanted it.

She'd make sure it was taken care of.

Amy found she was glad she'd come after all.

*   *   *

NORMALLY THE TRAIN home on Fridays was less busy than the rest of the week. People paused for drinks after work, spreading the usual 5 p.m. commuters thinly as butter across the evening.

Not today.

Two trains in a row were canceled. Amy joined the throngs of people staring up at the departures board as if it were a movie screen. Every once in a while a new number appeared, and a portion of the throng separated and rushed to their platform. A collective sigh of disappointment was released by those left behind.

Finally Amy's train was announced and Amy allowed herself to be carried along in the commuter current. She boarded, spotted a single seat in a group of four, made her way towards it gratefully, and sank down. As the train filled up, she noticed a man near her. He was standing a little awkwardly, and Amy looked at him more closely.

His arm was in a sling.

Of course, there was only one right thing to do. Amy immediately stood up, stepped to one side and gestured with a silent half bow that he should take the seat. It was only fair. Before he could, a young woman with a nose ring pushed past him and hurled herself into the new vacancy. Somewhere a whistle blew, and the train started to move.

Amy looked at the man. He was maybe in his late forties, about ten years older than Amy herself, and he seemed tired. She noticed that his shirt was wrinkled and she felt a little flicker of recognition in her heart. He had no one to iron it for him while his arm was out of action.

The man caught her gaze and gave Amy a good-natured shrug, accompanied by a little *the youth of today* eye roll. He stoically held on to a pole with his good hand.

Perhaps it was the warm Prosecco. Perhaps the blister developing on her heel. Perhaps the way the wrinkled-shirt man just accepted his fate. Amy found she just couldn't bear it.

"Excuse me," said Amy, her voice polite. The woman was peering at her phone, completely engrossed. She didn't look up. Amy coughed. "Excuse me," she said more loudly. Some of the other commuters glanced at her. Still the woman ignored her. Amy stepped forwards, entering the sacrosanct space between the facing seats. Knees on both sides of her recoiled as if they were snails retreating into their shells.

"She can't hear you," said a man sitting next to the nose-ring girl. He was wearing a pretty floral shirt. "She's got earphones in."

Amy looked. Sure enough, the woman had bright-white wireless earphones nestling snugly in her ears. Feeling bold, Amy reached forwards and tapped the woman on the shoulder. Finally she looked up.

"What?" the woman asked. She removed one of the earphones and frowned at Amy.

"That man has a broken arm," said Amy. "I gave up my seat for him. And you sat down." She waited for the woman to jump up and apologize.

"This isn't a disabled seat," said the woman, not moving.

"I'm not disabled," ventured the man with the sling. "I just fell down some stairs."

"That's not the point," said Amy. "It was his seat. I gave it to him because he needed it."

"I don't see his name on it," said the woman. The other commuters, sensing the start of some unexpected drama, looked up to watch.

"But he's got a broken arm," said Amy.

"It's actually my wrist that's broken," said the man. Both women ignored him.

"He can have my seat," said the man in the floral shirt. He made to get up.

"She should stand," insisted Amy.

"Make me," said the woman, a latent threat lacing her voice. Amy stepped back, alarmed by the escalation.

"Calm down, love," said a suited man sitting by the window, glancing up from his paper. Amy looked at him, and to her surprise, he was looking back at her. He was telling *her* to calm down, after that woman had clearly threatened her.

"I'm not the one who needs to calm down," she said, realizing her voice was starting to crescendo. "That woman stole a seat from a man who needed it and now she's threatening me. You all heard her." She looked around the train carriage. A silence took hold, as if people had suddenly remembered that no one was meant to speak to strangers in the city. Certainly not on public transport. "Didn't you?" she asked. Her voice sounded too loud, even in her own head.

"I'm fine to stand," said the injured man, looking embarrassed for his part in the drama.

"What's wrong with you?" the seat thief asked Amy.

As if complicit with the commuters, the train jolted. Amy was thrown forwards. She clutched a pole and regained her balance, but her bag swung from her shoulder and the empty wine bottle fell out. It hit the floor of the carriage with a thump and rolled under a seat.

"She's drunk," declared the seat thief, as if that justified her own actions.

"I am not drunk," said Amy. "I just . . ." She saw everyone staring at her.

It was none of their business why she had that bottle. It was none of anyone's business.

Amy bent down to escape their gaze and retrieve the bottle. It rolled farther away from her, and Amy found herself on her hands and knees on the sticky floor, surrounded by shoes. She saw a blue M&M, an empty Coke can, and a half-eaten burger under the seats. It smelled of pickle. The bottle had gone, rolled out of sight as if it were embarrassed by her too.

It was too much.

The train came to a halt, the doors opened, and Amy felt fresh air rush into the carriage. It was three stops early, but Amy knew she had to get into that air. Away from these people. Away from the bottle that had abandoned her.

Maybe it didn't deserve to be rescued after all.

She straightened up, pushed her way off the train, and stepped out into the July evening.

IT HAD TAKEN three full trains going by before Amy was finally ready to reboard. A ten-minute walk from the station later, and here she was.

Home.

Amy felt better just seeing her front garden. Her beautiful pots guarded the house faithfully. She held her key ring tightly in her hand as she finally slid her key into the lock. Amy went in and closed the door behind her, ready to forget that the evening had ever happened.

She stepped forwards into her hallway and tripped. Damn. One of her giant stacks of newspapers had fallen over. Again. Newspapers were mingling with unopened mail and dried petals. The debris lined the floor like autumn leaves. She shuffled through; she couldn't face clearing up the mess. Not this evening. Some of the other towers of newspapers looked precarious too, reaching floor to ceiling like Doric columns. Her hallway reminded her of the Acropolis.

The Acropolis after a party, she thought, stumbling over an empty wine bottle. She used to store her collection of green bottles in the kitchen, but she'd had to move some so she could get into the fridge. Ten or twenty privileged bottles sat neatly on her hallway shelves; a couple had even been transformed into vases with stems of honeysuckle. But that had been some time ago, and the flowers had dehydrated into crunchy brown husks.

Many of the bottles lounged empty on the floor, still waiting for a purpose.

A second chance.

*   *   *

MOST OF AMY'S clothes were in a wardrobe that she could no longer access. Tim's clothes would be in there too—he hadn't taken any of them. After it happened, Amy had used the base of the wardrobe for extra storage, then a few things had accumulated in front of it: mirrors, bottles, a couple of indoor pots. She'd tried to get an outfit out one morning a few years ago, and realized it wasn't worth the effort. She didn't really want to wear bright colors now in any case, so she'd just left their old clothes in the wardrobe and replaced them with an assortment of gray and black essentials; some smart for work, others comfy for home. She kept her "active wardrobe," as she called it, spread on top of one of her boxes, and made sure that she could always still get to the washing machine and the iron. She didn't want to waste more money on clothes than she had to, not when there were so many beautiful things that she wanted to buy.

It was Saturday morning, so Amy picked up her jeans and a black T-shirt. She made a special effort not to catch a glimpse of herself as she dressed. It was a challenge, as many mirrors lined the room. She knew that mirrors were meant to make a room feel spacious, but today it felt as if they were making the room smaller. Piles of boxes were reflected back at her, towering up and reaching for the ceiling. But even so, many things could not fit in a box and instead littered the room: vases, unopened bottles of hand lotion, stacks of ashtrays. And the mirrors themselves, of course, mocking her with infinite reflections.

Amy swore under her breath as a shot of pain flew up through her foot. She looked down; she'd merely trodden on a cigarette lighter. Good. Nothing damaged. She sat down again to pull her slippers on. Slippers seemed to be the thing that took the most delight in hiding from her in the house, so she'd taken to buying several pairs at a time.

She was very careful with her vases and bottles, of course she was. But every now and again, one decided that it had had enough of life and flung itself to the floor. Shards of broken glass had embedded themselves in Amy's feet a number of times, until she made the wise choice to invest in rubber-soled slippers.

She made her way down the stairs, holding tight to the handrail to make sure she didn't lose her footing over the boxes and crates that had somehow ended up squatting on the staircase. Edging through the hallway and sighing at the sight of the newspapers littering the floor, Amy went into the kitchen to make herself a cup of tea.

The choice of mugs was a favorite moment in her day. So many beautiful options lined her counters. She'd just decided that today was a china teacup with a gold rim sort of day, when the doorbell rang.

It gave her a bit of a fright. It didn't ring often and was never who she hoped for. It didn't help that the bell delivered an ungainly rendition of the first bars of Beethoven's Fifth, which would make the great man turn in his grave. Amy added a new doorbell to her mental shopping list and decided to wait it out and hope whoever it was went away.

The person outside, finding the bell ineffective, started pounding on the door.

Then silence.

Amy peered into the hallway in hope that whoever it was had given up. A pair of brown eyes stared back at her, framed by her letter box. There was a clatter as the eyes disappeared and a mouth adorned with a peachy shade of lipstick came into her rectangular field of vision.

"I can see you," said the mouth. Of course it was all a lie; mouths can't see. "Please open the door."

Amy debated opening the door only to the extent that the chain would allow, but that always made her feel like a paranoid old lady. She hadn't yet turned forty. Instead she extracted her keys from her handbag, opened the door just enough to squeeze outside, then deftly swung it closed behind her before her visitor could see any more of her hallway.

Her next-door neighbor, Rachel, was still crouching with her mouth pressed to where the letter box had just been, and it left the women awkwardly close, Rachel at crotch height to Amy. It was a position neither relished, and Rachel stood up and stepped backwards, looking put out.

"Can I help you?" enquired Amy, with the least helpful tone she could muster.

Rachel made a sighing sound that reminded Amy of a horse. "Smudge found another mouse," she said. "He dragged it across our new ivory carpet last night and left a trail of blood. I can't get it off."

Amy glanced at her front garden, deciding that it was time to water her potted geraniums again. The plants had grown leggy and the flowers, once postbox red, were rather brown, but the glazed pots they lived in were still a beautiful shade of crimson. Her rose had little green buds of promise that matched its own green pot, and she could smell her honeysuckle, clinging to the front of her house as it snaked up from the large deep-blue pot that reminded her of the ocean.

"Amy!" said Rachel. Amy looked back at her neighbor. "Are you even listening to me?"

"I'm sorry for the mouse, poor little thing," Amy replied eventually. "But Smudge is your cat. I really don't know why it's got anything to do with me."

"You know why."

"Of course I don't," replied Amy, wondering why Rachel blamed her problems on Amy. Too much time on her hands, she suspected.

"I've had enough. It's the final straw. Things have to change."

"You're getting rid of Smudge?" suggested Amy.

"No," said Rachel. "I'm going to call the council. The mice are coming from your house. I know they are."

Amy was sure Rachel could know no such thing, unless she spent her evenings tracking mice through the cellars of Ivydale Close. The walls were thin enough for Amy to know that was not what she did of an evening. She argued with her husband, watched *EastEnders*, and then had noisy sex, presumably with said husband. The smell of cigarette smoke used to follow all three activities, but recently Amy had smelled something sweeter. She'd wondered briefly if Rachel had made the unlikely transition from smoking to baking, until she realized it was the saccharine flavor of a vanilla vape wafting through the air.

"I've never seen a mouse in my house," Amy replied.

"They'll be hiding under all your rubbish."

"There is no rubbish in my house," said Amy with pride. Her house was fairly full, of course, but that was because it was filled to the brim with treasures.

"We both know that's not true," replied Rachel.

"And I'd thank you to keep that cat away from my property," continued Amy. "I hate to think of the damage he could do to my birds."

Rachel rolled her eyes at the mention of Amy's birds and opened her mouth, but her words remained unspoken as both women were distracted by the growl of a large engine. Their little street of suburban terraced two-up two-downs rarely saw much traffic, and they both turned to watch as a large moving van pulled in.

"Old Mrs. Hill's place. It must be," said Rachel. The women enjoyed a temporary truce as they watched the van attempt to park.

Amy missed Mrs. Hill. She'd been a perfect neighbor, quiet and undemanding. Even when Amy had shared the house with Tim and Chantel, they'd never made it beyond a gentle nod of greeting and an occasional muttered "hello" if either was feeling particularly gregarious. In fact, she hadn't even noticed that Mrs. Hill was gone until her grown-up children turned up one day to fill up their cars with her possessions. Sad as Amy had been, there followed a glorious time with no neighbors at all on that side, a luxury rarely afforded in the area. Then the FOR SALE sign was replaced with a triumphant boast from the estate agent. SOLD.

And now, here they were. Her new neighbors.

Well, not exactly. Two men in bright-blue overalls emerged from the truck and opened it up. "I'm going to see if they'd like a cuppa," said Rachel, trotting over to the van. She turned back to Amy as she went. "Sort out the mice or I will be forced to report you. I mean it this time."

She watched Rachel smiling at the removals men while trying to get a good peek inside the truck. Amy went back into her house. She couldn't help but want to nose too, but she decided to take a subtler tack and headed to her living room.

Even she had to admit, this room was at capacity. Boxes were piled up like pyramids. Some had mirrors leaning on them; some had vases still waiting for flowers. There were several clocks that had long since ceased to tick. Lighters were scattered like confetti on what little floor space there was.

Many boxes were adorned with birds.

Amy kept as many of her birds out as she could. It seemed cruel to have them cooped up in darkness when they loved the sunlight, but Amy couldn't make space for them all to be free at once. She'd kept the sofa mostly clear to give herself a rather indulgent place to sit, and she'd also made sure she had a thin walkway to the window. She traversed her miniature ravine, then turned back to admire the room.

Hundreds of little china eyes peered back at her. She'd quite a collection in her aviary, as she liked to call it. Inquisitive blue tits, exotic parakeets, diving swifts, angry jays, proud kingfishers. Perched on shelves, on boxes, on the windowsill.

Exquisite.

She felt she shouldn't have favorites, but she couldn't help herself. She approached the windowsill and placed a gentle hand on Scarlett's back. Amy still remembered the moment she'd found her in the bargain bin of Amy's favorite charity shop. The china body of a robin, her breast bright red and her eyes gleaming. Full of hope.

But her delicate legs were broken and her feet were nowhere to be seen.

Amy had frantically rummaged through the bin, to the amusement of the volunteer staff, until she emerged triumphant with the robin's china perch, complete with spindly feet still tightly gripping the branch. She'd bought the bird at once and rushed home. Some glue and a nervous wait later, and the robin was whole again, albeit with legs that would forever be crooked.

That didn't matter to Amy, of course. She loved her all the more for her imperfections. She pulled the curtain to one side, and they looked out of the window together.

Rachel was flicking her hair around and laughing at something the younger of the two removals men had said, and the older man was unloading chairs from the van alone. He had a round belly and a nasty cough. Amy peered at the chairs. There were four, wooden and nondescript. Not much to be gleaned about the new neighbors from that.

Amy had barely noticed it at first, but the area, once having rather a grimy edge, had gradually become desirable. Laundromats had been replaced by artisan bakeries, and the price of a cup of coffee had gone up fourfold. Couples and young families were snapping up properties like organic croissants. The row houses were small but came with gardens and an easy commute into the city. Amy supposed that she should be pleased that her house, which she had scrimped and saved for when her landlord wanted to sell it, had gone up in value. But the truth was it made no difference to her. She couldn't imagine ever moving.

What if Tim came back?

She watched Rachel walk past Amy's house and back to her own. Amy was pleased to see that the older man had the help of his companion again. They lifted a table out of the van, then unloaded something garish: bright yellow and plastic. Amy strained her eyes, trying to work out what it was.

A car. She looked again. No, a bed in the shape of a car. A child's bed.

Damn.

It was inevitable, she supposed, and there were other children on the street. But right next door? Her hand found Scarlett again, and for a moment she imagined the robin to be quivering with fear. Children were breakers. They both knew that. Silently she promised Scarlett that she would keep her safe.

She watched more furniture as it was paraded past her window. A futon. Beanbags. A number of houseplants at various stages of dehydration. Numerous boxes, their contents a mystery.

Rachel emerged from her house clutching a large plate with what looked to be a Victoria sponge sitting on top. She certainly hadn't had time to bake it—she must have run to the local shop. Amy leaned forwards, pressing her forehead against the window-pane. Sure enough, Rachel was panting as she made her way past Amy's house to old Mrs. Hill's place. Amy couldn't see the door from her perspective, but she heard the bell ring and a woman answer. Not one but two children emerged from the house and into her field of vision.

Both were boys. Amy couldn't help but feel that was even worse news. A nursery rhyme about slugs and snails and puppy-dog tails started to play in her mind.

The older child might have been eight or nine and began kicking a black-and-white ball at the side of the removals van. Balls could cause a lot of damage. Amy watched him kick, wondering if he had enough power to get it through her window. The younger child was perhaps three, and was watching his brother and sucking his thumb, every once in a while throwing a little air kick.

"Charles Frederick, stop kicking that ball at once," commanded a woman's voice from inside the house. "You'll break something."

It was exactly what Amy had been thinking, and she was pleased to see that the boy obeyed her. He nestled the ball under his arm and bent down to pet Smudge, who'd left Amy's front garden to entwine himself around the boy's legs.

The men left a pile of boxes on the pavement and all the adults disappeared inside the house. The voices stopped. Presumably Rachel and the men had been invited in for tea and maybe a piece of the cake. Amy found she was hungry herself and almost wished she'd been friendlier and could join them all. She decided to prepare a snack. She was pretty sure she still had a lump of cheddar in the fridge, and some crackers somewhere. She'd eat with Scarlett. She watched the elder boy attempt to pick up Smudge, but the cat made a run for it.

She heard a thud. The heartbreaking sound of something being smashed. Amy closed her eyes and put her hand to her head, fearing the worst. A sob broke out.

It all came from outside, she told herself. Not her house. She opened her eyes and looked. Sure enough, one of the boxes had fallen. The smaller child was on top of it, his face crimson and his mouth bellowing in anguish. He must have tried to climb the boxes and had knocked one over.

Amy hated the thought of anything at all being broken, but at least it was nothing of hers. The larger boy abandoned the cat and the ball and grabbed his brother in a big hug. The little boy held out his hands, and his brother inspected them and dusted them off. The ball rolled away, making its escape from the scene of the crime.

"Charles Frederick!" Amy watched as their mother charged out of the house, ignoring the small crying child and starting to lambaste his older brother. "What did I tell you about kicking your ball here?"

The boy muttered something inaudible, but Amy could tell from the hang of his head that he was taking the blame.

"It's the last straw," the woman continued. "I warned you. Didn't I?" Amy listened. There was something in the tone of voice that she didn't like at all. For a moment she hesitated, wanting to keep the neighbors at arm's length. Then she rushed out of her house, forgetting to close the door behind her.

"It wasn't him!" she declared to the woman, who scowled at her for a moment before turning her gaze to the smaller child. He was holding his brother's leg and had a little scrape on his knee that attested to his guilt. Amy found herself temporarily distracted by his T-shirt—a dinosaur sniffing anachronistically at a lighthouse.

"Daniel Joseph!" said the woman. "Was it you?" The smaller child cowered and started to cry again. Amy felt terrible. This little boy getting in trouble wasn't what she'd intended, even if he was to blame. A trickle of clear snot joined forces with the tears on his face. He paused from his crying to lick it up, and Amy found herself feeling a little nauseated.

His mother looked momentarily sickened too. "Get your brother a tissue," she said to the older boy.

"It was me," said Charles Frederick, wiping his brother's nose with his sleeve. "I knocked over the boxes. That woman is lying."

"You mustn't accuse strange women of lying," said his mother. She turned to Amy and squeezed out a smile. "I'm so sorry about that. I don't know where he gets his manners from." She wiped her hands on her jeans and reached one hand out to Amy, who was wondering what to feel about the "strange woman" comment. "I'm Nina. These two are my partner's children." She shrugged a little, looking as though she was feeling better now Amy knew that they were not her offspring.

Inspiration struck Amy. "It was Smudge," she said.

"Excuse me?" said Nina.

"Smudge knocked over the boxes," she said triumphantly. "Rachel's cat," she added in explanation, seeing Rachel emerge from the house at the commotion, with a little cream at the corner of her mouth.

"Oh gosh, I'm so sorry," said Rachel. "Of course I'll pay for any damage."

"No need, I'm sure it's nothing," said Nina pleasantly. Amy looked at the two women, uncomprehending. How could they be so relaxed when something could be damaged? "Let's go back inside."

"Don't you want to check the box?" asked Amy. "What if one of your things is broken? A bottle, maybe, or a glass? You might need to repair it."

"What if it's one of my diggers?" asked Charles, looking anxious.

"That's not going to be urgent, is it?" Nina said with a laugh. She looked at Amy. "Will you join us for cake?"

Amy's stomach rumbled, but she declined. "I'd really feel better if you checked in the box," she said. Rachel gave Nina a knowing look, and Amy had the impression that she'd already been a topic of conversation.

"This is your new neighbor, Amy Ashton," said Rachel, sounding apologetic.

"Can I look in the box?" Amy was feeling increasingly sick. "I have some glue. . . ."

Nina shrugged and walked to the box. "A few mugs and some toys were all that was in here," she said dismissively as she opened it. "Nothing valuable." Amy followed her, peering over her shoulder. A jumble of little yellow cars looked back at her. No, not cars. Diggers.

"Are my JCB construction machines okay?" asked Charles, rushing over to the box and leaning in so far it seemed he might tumble inside. "My remote-controlled metal die-cast excavator was in there!" He began to take out the toys one by one, including several still in their original boxes. He lined them up on the pavement. Smudge came over and gave them a curious sniff.

"We're trying to move into the house, not onto the curb," said Nina. "Take those inside."

"They're all okay," said Charles, looking relieved. "Tough machines, JCBs." He smiled at Amy.

Amy looked at what remained in the box: an assortment of mugs, one clearly damaged. Nina followed her gaze. "Only one mug broken," said Nina cheerfully. "No real harm done."

It was no wonder a mug had been broken. The packaging was a couple of sheets of loose bubble wrap, woefully inadequate. Amy looked at the casualty. It was a beautiful shade of yellow with a pretty sheen, like butter melting on a summer's day. The handle had come off and the mug itself was broken in two. It would always have a hairline scar down the middle, but all the pieces were there. Amy was sure she could fix it.

"Stop," she exclaimed, as Nina went to toss the pieces into a large wheelie bin. "I can repair it."

"It's just a cheap mug," said Nina. "Don't bother."

"Let her," said Rachel. "It's easier."

"Fine." Nina passed her the broken pieces, and Amy cradled them carefully. "Thanks," Nina added, clearly not meaning it.

Amy hurried back to her house. The door was still open, which was lucky as she'd not brought her key. It still made her uncomfortable: What if Smudge had crept inside? It could have been carnage for her birds. She vowed not to forget herself like that again.

But despite her hurry, she could hear Rachel talking to Nina. "She didn't used to be like this, apparently," she said, the excitement of gossip audible in her voice. "Poor Amy. It's tragic, really, what she's been through."

Amy had no desire to hear her story told by Rachel. She closed her door with a thud.

October 1998

"Who put the Spice Girls on?" asked Amy, looking around the room.
The house party was in full swing and no one answered, though she
suspected the two girls dressed as cats, busy touching up their whis-
kers with eyeliner as they peered into a small mirror. Amy shuffled
through the CDs and selected the new Garbage album. "Dance?" she
suggested, skipping to the second track.

Chantel pulled herself up from the sofa and joined her. Amy
lifted her arm and Chantel twirled out and then back again, her
black skirt swirling up to reveal her stripy yellow-and-black leggings.
It was their signature dance move, so of course it came out at every
opportunity, even shoeless on the carpet at this party Seb had thrown
for Halloween while his parents were out of town.

"Take a break?" asked Chantel, as the CD came to an end and
someone replaced it with the Verve. Her voice was already a little
breathless and her face sweaty. "It's hot work being a bumblebee."

"Sure," said Amy, and they both sank back into the sofa. "You
must be roasting in those leggings."

"True, but they're the best bit of the costume," said Chantel. "If I take them off, I'd just look like a naff fairy." She gestured to her small wings, designed for a fairy costume.

"Or a fly for my web," said Amy, wiggling her fingers at Chantel in a not very convincing spider impression. She was pretty pleased with the costume she'd pulled together. She'd had inspiration from a black vest top she'd had already, with silver cobwebs printed over it. She'd added a black woven skirt, fishnet tights, and as many plastic spiders as she could sew to her clothes.

"I can tell you're an artist," said Chantel, surveying the costume. "You've got that eye."

"I can't wait to start my foundation course."

"Your costume is freaking me out," said Chantel. "I keep thinking you're crawling with real spiders." She shuddered and passed Amy the plastic Coke bottle they'd topped up with Malibu. Amy took a deep swig and handed it back, feeling the room spin a little. A whiff of cannabis floated through the air. Amy knew that Chantel was bound to sniff it out and befriend whoever'd brought it.

"It would have been better if you'd come as a flower," said Chantel. "You'd match my costume and you wouldn't be quite so terrifying."

"Or a jar of honey," mused Amy. "Not very Halloween-y though."

"I smell the good stuff," interrupted Chantel inevitably, sitting up and eyeing the room like a meerkat. "Want some?"

"No," said Amy. "I'm fine with the Malibu."

"Probably a good idea. You'd terrify yourself, wearing those insects stoned."

"Spiders aren't insects," she started, but Chantel was gone. Amy looked around the party. Seb, dressed as a cowboy, was fervently snogging a witch on the sofa. The two girls with cat ears and black noses had put *Five* on the CD player and had taken her and Chantel's place dancing. She briefly watched them bouncing up and down while counting to the music on their fingers. She took another swig of her drink.

"I've always liked spiders," said a boy wearing a bright-orange T-shirt and black jeans. "And Garbage." Amy felt he was slightly familiar, but she didn't think she'd spoken to him before. He had an apologetic slope to his shoulders typical of the very tall and a Noel Gallagher haircut, and he was, Amy realized, excessively handsome. "Mind if I join you?"

"Sure," said Amy, trying to sound nonchalant. Foggily she felt as if he were someone she'd admired at one time. Perhaps he'd been a couple of years above her in school. Or maybe he'd even been on telly.

"What's that?" she exclaimed, the admiration dissipating as she caught sight of something orange and mushy hanging from his earlobe.

"Damn, is there more?" he said, his hand reaching for his ear. "I thought I'd got it all."

"What on earth . . . ?"

"I've blown my cool, haven't I?" he said with a grimace. "Maybe this will help explain." He rummaged through a plastic bag, the ubiquitous royal-blue kind that came from every corner shop. Amy heard a bottle clink against something; then he produced a shard of pumpkin and a small hammer. Amy took the pumpkin piece, turning it over in her hand. It was wet and sticky.

"I was trying to be authentic," he said. "But instead I'm just pumpkin-flavored."

"Smashing Pumpkins," said Amy. "That's who you've come as."

He grinned back at her. "You're the first person to get that. Turns out it was a terrible idea."

Amy laughed. "Plastic spiders seem like genius now," she said. He smiled back at her, and Amy noticed his eyes crinkling in the corners. "I know you from somewhere."

He bit his lip. "I am famous round these parts."

"Really?"

"No," he said with a laugh. "But my band did have our first-ever gig last week, even if it was in the back room of a pub." He sounded proud and a little embarrassed all at once.

"Of course," said Amy, the pieces falling into place like a reassembled pumpkin. "You played at the Firkin!"

His mouth fell open. "You saw us?" he asked. "Maybe I'm more famous than I think."

Amy laughed again. "You did have to tell me before I recognized you." She paused. "You were pretty good though."

"You're my first groupie!" he declared. "You can be my Yoko."

Amy felt herself coloring a little. The band had been good. Really good. She'd loved them.

"I don't suppose you have a corkscrew?" he asked. He lifted a bottle of wine from his bag. "I think we should celebrate."

"Sorry," said Amy, wishing desperately that she did have a corkscrew. Suddenly her plastic bottle of Malibu and Coke seemed terribly uncool. She gave it a gentle flick with her heel, and it rolled under the sofa out of sight. She glanced around the room. A few boys were gulping from beer cans, and a bottle of overproof rum was doing the rounds. "I don't think anyone else here is drinking wine," she said, getting to her feet. "I'll check the kitchen."

"I'm too sophisticated for my own good," he said.

Amy laughed. "That would be more convincing if you didn't have butternut squash in your ear."

"Pumpkin," he corrected. "Give me some credit." He followed her into the kitchen. "Listen," he said. "If we can't find a corkscrew here, how about we take a walk and try to hunt one down? I could do with the fresh air."

Quietly Amy opened a drawer and pushed away the corkscrew she'd just found. She closed it again.

"Nothing here," she said, knowing she was a terrible liar. "We'll have to."

"Great." He smiled at her, and she smiled back.

"I'll just let Chantel know. . . ." She looked around the party and saw Chantel kissing Dean Chapman again, who she insisted was not her boyfriend but who she always snogged when she'd had a couple of drinks. "Oh," said Amy. "She's busy."

"I'll get my coat," he said. "My name's Tim, by the way."

"I'm Amy," she told him. "Amy Ashton."

IT FELT COLD but fresh outside after the smoky haze of the party, and Amy breathed in deeply. "It's good to be outdoors," said Tim, as if reading her mind. "But you must be cold." He took off his jacket, a heavy leather affair, and draped it round her shoulders. Amy had seen guys do that in the movies, but it had never happened to her in her seventeen years. The boys at school were not that gentlemanly, and she suddenly felt as if she were in a proper love story. With a rock star. She shivered a little.

"If you're still too cold, we can head back inside?" he said.

"No," she said quickly, pulling the coat closer round her. "I'm fine." She smiled at him. "Thank you."

"I hope there's no pumpkin on that," he said.

"Me too," she agreed. "Spiders hate pumpkins."

"Really?"

"I've no idea," she confessed. They both laughed, and walked on. This bit of Amy's hometown was new, sprung up in response to the railway extension that suddenly made it possible to live here and commute to work in London. The houses were almost identical for miles, and it was easy to get lost or think you were walking in circles.

"So are you a full-time rock star?" teased Amy.

"Sort of," said Tim. "I finished my A levels last year and my dad wanted to pack me off to university to study law, but I'm taking a break instead to try to make a go of the band."

"A rebel," said Amy, calculating that he must be two years older than her, itself rather exciting. "Very rock and roll."

"Yes," said Tim. He paused. "So you liked the band," he prompted.

"It was awesome," said Amy honestly. "I loved that song about missed sunsets."

"'Already Dark'?" exclaimed Tim. "I wrote that." Amy noticed his back was a little straighter. She was tall, but he towered above her. He must be well over six feet. And handsome and funny and talented and his leather jacket smelled like her favorite chair at her grandmother's house.

"It was very sad," said Amy. "And very beautiful." Amy felt Tim's fingers interlace her own at her words. Her heart felt as if it had grown larger, swollen by the warm hand embracing her palm.

"It's about my mother," he said. He bit his lip. "She died when I was ten."

"I'm so sorry," said Amy, feeling awkward. She wanted to say something that would help, that would provide comfort. But she had nothing. She squeezed his hand instead.

Tim squeezed back. "I haven't told anyone else that's what the song's about."

He turned to her and Amy found herself staring into eyes the color of chestnuts.

"I feel like I can trust you," he said. "Already." Tim released her hand and wrapped his arms around her back.

"You can," said Amy. She felt the bottle he was holding brush against her as she closed her eyes and leaned in.

"Zombie alert!" shouted someone. Tim quickly released the embrace as a drunken crowd of Halloween revelers stumbled by, pulling scary faces at the two of them and laughing.

They watched them go, then walked on themselves, the moment gone. His hand found hers again. "I think there's a corner shop up here," said Amy. "They probably sell corkscrews."

"We don't really need one," said Tim. "I'm afraid I got you alone on false pretenses."

"Oh," said Amy. He must have seen her hide the corkscrew in the kitchen. She let go of his hand, feeling embarrassed.

"It's nothing sinister," he added quickly. "Although, lying to get a pretty girl on her own in the cold, dark night surrounded by zombies . . . maybe it does sound a little on the creepy side."

"Lying?" queried Amy, although inside she was busy being delighted about the "pretty" comment.

He sheepishly held up the bottle. "Screw top."

Amy laughed. "There was a bottle opener in the kitchen," she confessed.

"I know." He smiled. "Is that a little park?" he asked. "It looks nice."

"That's a bit of grass in the middle of a roundabout," said Amy.

"Care to join me for a swig of cheap red wine from my screw-top bottle in the middle of a roundabout?" he offered with a small bow, proffering his hand.

Amy took the hand and smiled again. "That's the sort of offer I don't get every day," she said. "At least not from a rock star with pumpkin in his ears."

"And wine," he replied, twisting open the bottle as they sat on the rough grass. "Don't forget the bottle of wine." He handed the bottle to Amy. It felt cold in her hand, but the wine warmed her throat. She passed the bottle back to him and watched as he drank. The bottle caught the moonlight and glowed a deep, beautiful green.

Chapter Two

Amy nestled the pieces of the mug between two embroidered silk cushions on the sofa and spent a long time searching for her glue. It was frustrating; she must have at least twenty tubes of the stuff, accumulated over the years, but now, with the mug sitting, scared, incomplete, she couldn't find any of them. She rummaged through her kitchen drawers. Didn't the glue want to fulfill its sticky destiny? She pushed a collection of spare paper napkins to one side and stopped.

There was a photograph. Of the three of them together: Amy, Chantel, and Tim. Taken outside this house, on the day they'd moved in, more than fifteen years ago. Amy was carrying a single oversize rucksack that contained all her worldly possessions. She was smiling. But back then, of course, she couldn't have known what those two would do to her.

The doorbell rang.

Amy put the photograph back in the drawer and covered it with the napkins again. Unless whoever it was had a delivery of glue, Amy could do without a visitor. But hiding hadn't done her much good so far. Checking she had her keys, Amy made her way carefully through the hallway, opened the door just wide enough for her to squeeze outside, then swung it closed behind her.

A man stood in front of her. He looked strangely familiar to Amy, but she couldn't work out why. He had a gentle attempt at a beard and wore a ratty old T-shirt in a shade of brown that matched his coffee-colored eyes. He smiled at her and held out his hand. Amy was surprised that she could still make out dimples through his beard. She hesitated, then took his hand. After clutching the cool mug, his hand felt hot to the touch.

"I'm Richard," the man told her. "From next door. I think you met my partner and sons earlier?"

Amy looked past him into her front garden. Both boys were stroking Smudge, who was lying between two of her potted plants with his ears pushed back. He was giving the children a suspicious look as they showered him with unexpected affection. Of course— that's where she recognized the man from, she realized. He was a bigger, bearded version of his elder son.

"The mug isn't fixed yet," said Amy quickly. "So I'm afraid you can't have it back now."

"What?" asked Richard, looking confused.

"I can't track down my glue," elaborated Amy. "And once I do, it will need some time to set."

"I'm sorry," said Richard. "I don't know what you're talking about. What mug?"

"Oh," she said. "Nothing." They stood in silence for a moment.

"Lovely front garden you have," he said. "I don't think I've ever seen so many pots."

"They are very fragile," warned Amy. She felt herself flush at the compliment nonetheless. There was another moment of silence. Richard turned to check on his children, then looked back at Amy.

"My sons have taken quite a liking to your cat," he said eventually. "I heard she took a bullet for them?" He smiled again, like a co-conspirator. "Thank you."

"It's a he," replied Amy. "Smudge. And he's not mine. He belongs to Rachel next door. Your wife met her earlier."

"My girlfriend," corrected Richard.

"I can't keep a cat," continued Amy. "Because I have birds." The harm that animal could do if he ever got inside. Smudge looked at her, then lazily stretched out and closed his eyes, enjoying the children's caresses. But there was no fooling Amy. She knew the carnage he could cause.

"The boys would love to see the birds sometime," said Richard. Then he turned and called to his two sons, "Wouldn't you, boys?" Charles clambered to his feet, pulling his smaller brother up too, and they started walking towards the door. Smudge opened his eyes and began licking his foot. He seemed annoyed at his massage ending.

"No!" said Amy, stepping backwards and banging into her own door. Three sets of surprised brown eyes looked back at her, and she realized she'd shouted. Suddenly Amy wanted nothing more than to be inside her house again—but she'd have to step closer to her neighbors, turn around, and fiddle with her key. Instead she pinned herself to her door and tried to breathe.

"No worries," said Richard breezily, stepping backwards to give Amy more room. He put a hand on Charles's head. "Small birds are easily startled. I wouldn't want the boys to scare them. We'll be off." He smiled at her. "Thanks again. Pop over for a drink sometime, you're always welcome."

Amy breathed a sigh of relief as they left through her gate, then turned around and let herself back into the house.

AMY HAD BEEN nervous about getting her train home on Monday after what happened last time, but a glance around the carriage reassured her that no one was even looking in her direction. She'd bought a new tube of glue on Sunday, and now the mug was setting underneath a small pile of open cookbooks on a box in her living room. She'd managed to refrain from checking on it that morning. The extra hours would make all the difference; she knew from experience that impatience would only make the recovery process longer.

Her commute seemed to fly by, as it often did when she was distracted, and she hopped off the train and walked home. She heard voices coming from the new neighbors' house as she walked past. Raised voices. She hurried her pace, hoping that their shouting wouldn't be a regular thing. It was bad enough listening to Rachel's arguments, let alone being assaulted by domestic anger from both sides.

Moving was a stressful time, she decided generously. They'd soon settle down.

Smudge wasn't lurking by her potted plants in the front as he usually did, so Amy popped her key straight in the lock and entered her house. She'd restacked the newspapers at the weekend, and her hallway felt positively empty as she edged past the bottles. It had been a muggy July day, the kind that often ended in thunder, but the ground floor of her house had remained cool as a cave. She paused. It was as she feared; she could still hear the shouting. It was muffled and she couldn't make out the words (thank goodness), but it wasn't exactly a relaxing backdrop to her evening either. She found herself hoping that they wouldn't have the loud makeup sex that Rachel and her husband indulged in. That would be more than she could bear.

It couldn't have been very nice for Scarlett, listening to the sounds of arguments all day. Amy rested her hand briefly on the robin's back, then peeled her own blazer off and draped it over a box with the others. Remembering her patient, she went to the box it was sitting on to investigate. Very gently she lifted off the books, one by one, then unfurled the bubble wrap she'd used as a bandage. "Excellent," she said, lifting the mug. It had a thin and wobbly line running down it, like dry cracked earth, but it was structurally sound once again. She picked up the mug and put it against her face. She felt an exchange of energies: warmth from her cheek heating the mug, and the cold china cooling her in return. The line where she'd mended the break made a little indentation in her own face. A mirrored wrinkle. Amy felt a moment of completeness. She imagined drinking from it, the glorious exchange of fluid. It was time. She went to the kitchen to make tea, taking the mug with her.

It was a shame she had to give it back, she decided. It would be a great new addition to her collection. Even stacked as high as she could reach, her mugs took up most of her countertops, but they were such beautiful colors she didn't mind at all. It was like having a lovely but fragile rainbow in her kitchen. And it wasn't as if it was worth cooking anything complicated anyway. At least not just for her.

She glanced out the window, listening to the bubbly hiss of the kettle.

Then she froze.

She blinked, then looked again.

Although she rarely went out there, Amy loved to admire her back garden through her kitchen window. It was very different from the front, which was well ordered and full of her beautifully potted plants. The back was a private little nature reserve: untidy but ruggedly beautiful. Not through neglect, she told herself, but through generosity to wildlife. She stored her empty terra-cotta pots out there, stacked on top of one another like the turrets of a tower. Some of her pots were large—big enough to house a modest olive tree—and others were more petite, just right for herbs such as sage or lavender. A few of the larger ones were on their sides, making small caves that Amy imagined the squirrels would enjoy. While each pot had been waiting for its perfect plant, the opportunistic ivy had taken hold, concealing some in a rich green disguise. Even Amy had to admit she'd amassed rather an impressive collection over the years.

Nettles had sprung up, and she'd let them thrive. She was sure she'd read somewhere that they were good for caterpillars, and she did love seeing butterflies fluttering around her space.

But her favorites were the brambles. They'd overtaken about a third of the garden, creating a small, prickly forest. Now they were covered in modest white blossoms, but by the end of summer they'd bring forth an abundant crop of blackberries. Amy always resisted the urge to pick them, instead allowing the birds to feast. There was nothing more joyful than watching a family of blackbirds gorging on juicy berries, their yellow beaks stained purple.

But it wasn't a family of blackbirds in her garden. It was two small boys and one large black cat.

Smudge was sniffing around one of her towers and studiously ignoring Daniel, who was stroking his back, emitting the occasional shriek of delight at the softness of his black fur. Charles, the older child, was busy inserting himself inside a blackberry bush. Already all she could see was the backs of his legs: the rest of him had been swallowed by the bush. He'd probably knock off some of the flowers, thought Amy, and they would never become berries. Plus he'd rip his clothes, not to mention the scratches that would befall his skin.

The gaps in her fence had a lot to answer for.

Amy leaned over her sink to tap the window and warn them off, but they didn't notice. She called out, but again to no avail. Smudge must have heard, because he suddenly leapt to the top of one of the green towers of ivy-covered pots, which wobbled precariously. Perhaps she should move the pots inside, she thought, and looked around for where they might live. But of course, towers of mugs lined every surface of the kitchen, and boxes and a couple of stray clocks took up most of the floor space. It had been a while since she'd seen the floor properly, let alone cleaned it.

Really, her house was too small, she decided. The pots, beautiful as they were, would have to take their chances outside.

Charles had been swallowed completely by the bush, and it shook as if possessed. Daniel was dangerously near a large patch of nettles, his eyes fixed on Smudge. Amy wished for a large wall between the two gardens, rather than the rickety fence that clearly couldn't contain the curiosity of the children. This had gone far enough. Amy went to open the kitchen door and go out to shoo them away.

It was easier thought than done. Her kitchen was small, and since she rarely went into the garden, she'd started to use the area in front of the door for extra storage. She heaved down a box, glancing briefly inside. It contained a rather beautiful tea set: cups and saucers with elegant gold rims, and roses and strawberries meandering across the fine bone china. She'd found it in a charity shop, complete but for the milk jug, which she'd trawled the internet for in the vain hope of finding a match. She really must use the set, she thought. Maybe to drink Earl Grey tea, then she wouldn't need milk. She had a box of the stuff somewhere. She glanced around her kitchen. Perhaps she'd just buy a new packet.

A crash.

So loud that Amy jumped and the little teacup she was holding flew in the air, and it was pure luck that she caught it again. She rushed to the window.

Smudge dashed across the garden, his tail fluffed up short and fat in fear as he fled up a tree.

Charles staggered out of the blackberry bush. Even through the grimy kitchen window, Amy could see that he was scratched by the thorns.

She looked at a heap on the ground, not recognizing it. Then she realized.

Her pots. A tower of pots had fallen.

Amy wondered why Charles was so panicked. He was screaming as he pawed at her garden. It wasn't as though the pots were his. They were hers.

Amy felt sick with guilt and worry. She couldn't remember the last time she'd been out to check on the pots, couldn't even remember what each one looked like. She didn't deserve them; they had a right to a better life. She'd been imagining them to be happy under the ivy, but what if they'd felt starved of attention, of sunlight, of the plants that should have made them complete?

Neglect.

That was what it was. And now, perhaps, she would lose them.

Amy put the teacup back in the box and moved it to one side. There were more boxes underneath, and she hurried to slide them across the floor to give her access to the door. Charles was frantic now, tugging at her pots. He'd do more harm than good; she needed to get out there and stop him.

He was shouting. Amy paused and listened. Then she realized why he was so upset. Who was missing from the scene in her garden.

His brother.

The tower had fallen on Daniel.

February 1999

"I can't believe I missed out on meeting a handsome older guy in a band because I was busy snogging bloody Dean Chapman!" It was Saturday afternoon, and Chantel and Amy were lounging around in Chantel's bedroom. Her mother's flat was much smaller than Amy's parents' home, but the girls preferred to hang out there. It felt warmer somehow. Amy's house always felt empty. Perhaps it was because her parents were always working at the hospital.

Cursing Dean Chapman had become a familiar refrain from Chantel over the past four months as Amy and Tim had grown closer.

"I think you like Dean really," said Amy, looking up from a magazine she'd been flicking through on the bed. "If you don't, how come you always end up kissing him?"

"Because he's always got weed. And I always have booze." Chantel paused. "And he is a good kisser," she admitted.

"Chemistry," said Amy. "That's what you've got. I reckon you'll end up getting married and having loads of little Chapmans."

Chantel shuddered. "Talking of little ones, have you guys still not done the deed?"

"Not yet," admitted Amy.

Chantel had been lying back, but sat up at this news, her eyes bright. "Do you think he's gay?" she asked.

"Do I think my boyfriend is gay?" repeated Amy, incredulous. "Of course not."

"Think about it," continued Chantel, warming to her theme. "He's nineteen, he hasn't slept with you, and you're tall and elegant and flipping gorgeous. And he uses coconut-oil conditioner. I don't want to stereotype, but—"

"I wish I hadn't told you that," said Amy. She could smell coconuts even now, and could almost feel Tim's silky hair between her fingers. It reminded her of stroking Samuel, the rabbit her grandmother had bought for her birthday one year. That was until her mother had forgotten to close the cage, of course, and she'd found him squashed next to a zebra crossing on the high street.

"We're taking our time," said Amy. "I want it to be special."

"Sunsets and rose petals?" asked Chantel, miming throwing up. "He does know you're not a virgin?"

"We haven't discussed it," said Amy. "And what happened doesn't really count." Her mind went back to a brief drunken encounter on top of a pile of coats with Eric Townsend at a party he'd thrown while his parents were in Tenerife. She'd been sick on the coats shortly after and had crept out while he was snoring contentedly.

A knock on the bedroom door announced Toyah, Chantel's mum. "I'm popping to the shops," she said, poking her head round the door. "You girls want anything? I could pick up some of those fish cakes you like, Amy, if you fancy staying for dinner?"

"Tim's cooking for me tonight," said Amy, a little proudly. "Spaghetti Bolognese."

"A handsome musician who can cook," said Toyah. "I don't suppose he has a single brother?"

"Mum!" exclaimed Chantel.

Toyah laughed. "I was thinking of you. Although a toy boy does sound rather appealing. . . ."

"He's an only child," said Amy. "Sorry to disappoint."

"Probably for the best," said Toyah. "We can't have the Smith girls fighting over a man." She smiled. "Right, I'll be off. I'll stock up on pineapple juice for you, Amy. I'm sure you'll be back tomorrow to give us all the details."

"Thanks," replied Amy, as Toyah disappeared.

"So Tim's cooking you dinner tonight?" prompted Chantel. "Maybe tonight's the night."

Amy looked down. She'd been thinking the same thing.

"Oh, I bet it is," said Chantel, reading her face. "What are you going to wear?"

"That blue velvet dress," said Amy. "With my wedged boots."

"Good call," said Chantel. "You look hot in that." She paused. "And underwear?"

"Of course," said Amy, a little shocked.

Chantel laughed. "No, I mean which underwear? You can't have those white cotton knickers with the flowers on that you insist on wearing, with that awful beige bra. You need something sexy." She went over to her chest of drawers and began rummaging through it. "Ah-ha," she said, triumphant. "This is what you want." She pulled out a lacy black bra and a matching thong.

"I couldn't—"

"I've never worn them," said Chantel. "Never had the chance. Bloody Dean Chapman, cramping my style. And it's not like I'd waste them on him."

"But then he'd know. . . . He has seen my bra already," she admitted. She imagined her embarrassment if things did go further and he saw that underwear. He'd think she'd been planning it. For some reason, even though she wanted to, the idea of him thinking she'd dressed up specially made her feel mortified.

"He's seen that monstrosity and he's still interested?" said Chantel. "Maybe he isn't gay after all. In which case . . ." She opened another drawer and began to rummage. "Here we are," she said, then frowned at the box. "Only a month till they go out of date. How tragic is that. The Chantel of a year ago was clearly overoptimistic." She chucked the condom box to Amy, who immediately buried it deep in her handbag, coloring at even the idea of such things being in her possession.

"Thanks," she said.

Chantel came over and gave her a hug. "I know I tease you," she said. "But it's just jealousy. He's a great guy and I'm really happy for you. You're brilliant and he's very lucky."

Amy hugged her back. "Thanks," she said again. "You're the best."

"And I want to know every detail," continued Chantel. "No fobbing me off this time with excuses about being too drunk to remember."

"I won't be drunk," said Amy. But Chantel had given her an idea. "I've got to get going," she said, kissing her friend on the cheek. "Wish me luck."

"Like you need it."

AMY STOOD IN the wine aisle at the small supermarket, wishing she'd saved the bottle from the night they met. Now all she could remember was that it had been red wine with a screw top and that the bottle had a lovely soft green glow to it from the moonlight once they'd drunk the wine. She could hardly tell the bored-looking assistant stacking shelves that and expect any help.

It would be more romantic if she could remember what it was, but the thought would still count if she bought any nice bottle of wine. Her eyes scanned the shelves, but she knew nothing about wine and the only criterion she had to go on was price. She had a ten-pound note in her purse from when she'd babysat Teresa next door. That would buy something good. Something special.

She selected a bottle with a pretty line drawing of the Tuscan hills that was reduced from £11 to £6.99. It had a cork, so she picked up a corkscrew too, just in case. He'd laugh at that; it was even better than a screw top. She'd not been to Tim's flat before, but his flatmates had gone away on a lads' trip to watch football in Manchester and he'd invited her. He'd cook, he said. She'd rarely been cooked for before by anyone other than her grandmother or Toyah. And she didn't count the hurried meals that her parents provided between shifts, or the microwaved cheese and ketchup on toast that was Chantel's specialty.

She took the bottle to the till, feeling very grown-up. She was going to have dinner at her boyfriend's house and she was bringing wine. *Boyfriend.* Even that sounded sophisticated. She had been too shy to use that word herself, but then he'd introduced her as his girlfriend to his bandmates, and she'd glowed merrily. After that she used the word as often as she could, feeling a little echo of that glow every time.

The woman at the till pursed her lips at the bottle. She was about the age of Amy's mum but wore large gold hoop earrings that Amy could never imagine her own mother wearing. "ID?" she asked.

"What?" said Amy. "I'm eighteen." It was true. She'd celebrated her birthday last month.

"Course you are, love. You need to prove it."

Amy rummaged in her handbag. Her student card for art college hadn't arrived yet. She didn't have a driving license. Since she'd turned eighteen she'd started taking her passport with her when she went to pubs, but she wasn't going to a pub tonight and it hadn't occurred to her. "Please," she said. "I'm going for dinner at my boyfriend's house and I want to bring a bottle of wine." She hoped that made her sound older.

"Nope," said the woman. "It's policy."

An older woman from the next till looked up at Amy. "Get some chocolates, love," she said. "Or how about a nice bunch of flowers? Not just for girls, you know."

Amy turned away, taking her wine back to the shelf. She put it with the other bottles, turning it so the labels lined up. Her ten-pound note was scrunched in her hand. Tim didn't really like choco-lates, though she felt like some right now. She wandered over to the flowers, but the limp bunches of freesias and carnations didn't feel right. A few houseplants sat next to the flowers: an out-of-season selection of Christmas cactuses and a few small African violets.

Then she saw it: a gorgeous fern, large and luscious, its leaves unfurling like tentacles. It looked as though it belonged on the rain-forest floor, not in a small supermarket. She bent down to check that she could afford it, and saw that it came in a glazed pot the color of pumpkins.

It was perfect.

Amy's embarrassment dissipated as excitement mounted. She picked it up, feeling like a jungle explorer as she took it to the till, this time choosing the older lady who'd helped. "He'll be pleased with that, love," the woman said. "Pretty pot too."

Amy nodded. "He'll love it," she said.

AMY LAY IN bed. Tim's arm was draped over her and his eyes were closed. She listened to him breathing. The fern was on the table next to his bed and the outline of his head was silhouetted against the orange pot like a cityscape in a sunset. The leaves were so close to his head that she saw them softly move as he breathed in and out.

She heard the hum of her phone vibrating with a text message, and carefully rolled over and leaned out of the bed to grab it from the floor. Tim's arm remained on her body, soft and warm.

She nuzzled her head closer to Tim's coconut-scented hair as she read the message. It was from Chantel. Of course it was. Amy smiled. She typed a quick reply before turning off her phone.

He's definitely not gay ;)

* * *

BEETHOVEN'S FIFTH RANG out again and again, accompanied by fierce banging on Amy's front door. It wasn't helping. "Let us in," shouted Nina, for the umpteenth time. "What's happened out there?"

"Climb over the fence," snapped Amy.

"Open the front door," replied Nina.

"The fence will be quicker," shouted Amy. She finally pushed the last box out of the way. She breathed a sigh of relief that the key was in the lock, or else she'd never have found it. She turned it and pushed her back door open, running into the garden. She ignored the nettles that stung her legs with their acidic hairs as she went to join Charles searching through the pots. He was attempting to heave over an upside-down pot that was bigger than he was. Amy forced herself to ignore the other pots looking at her mournfully from the ground, their injuries unassessed. They would have to wait. Instead she gripped the pot and pulled with Charles. They turned it over.

Nothing.

She saw the boy's father wrestling with a loose fence post and pushing his way through. "Daniel!" he shouted.

A giggle. "Daddy, find me," said a voice.

"Over there," said Richard, pointing to a large pot on its side covered in ivy.

Amy reached it first. She pushed the ivy aside.

Daniel blinked at her and grinned. The tension dissipated. "Hide-and-seek," he said. He saw their worried faces and frowned. "Ice cream?" he requested.

Richard pulled his son out and enveloped him in a huge hug. Amy saw Nina watching them through the gap in the fence. It was all too much for Charles and he started to cry.

"They shouldn't have been in my garden," said Amy, before anyone could accuse her of anything. She surveyed the damage caused by Smudge. The larger pots were okay: they'd been at the bottom of the tower and were made of terra-cotta almost an inch thick. She gathered up more pots, rescuing them from the nettles. Her arms got stung, but it was what she deserved. Everything seemed intact.

Then she saw it. The fragments of it, to be more precise.

Amy remembered when she had discovered that pot in a local thrift shop. It had caught her eye immediately, sitting in an inconspicuous place on a shelf next to a pile of beads and a well-worn black leather handbag. She'd kept it by the front door for years, using it to store her umbrellas, before her hallway got too crowded and she'd moved it outside. It had a beautiful white glaze peppered with daisies, their petals the color of lapis lazuli. In the center of each flower was a brilliant dot of pumpkin orange, and the flowers seemed to dance around the pot.

No more.

It must have landed on a rock, because it had shattered into many pieces. Amy gathered up the fragments as best she could, but they hid from her in the long grass as if scared of what she might do to them.

"The pot," said Amy, feeling tears pricking her eyes. "It's beautiful and it's broken."

"Are you kidding me?" said Nina, clambering through the hole in the fence. "Daniel Joseph could have been hurt, and you're upset about a pot?"

"Ice cream, please," said Daniel.

"Can Daniel have a Mini Milk?" asked Charles, starting to calm down. "It will help."

"You were meant to be looking after your brother," said Nina. "You should have been paying more attention."

Charles was silent.

"Easy, Nina," said Richard. "Can't you see he's upset?"

"We're all upset," muttered Nina.

"It's not your fault," Richard told his son. "We just want you both to be safe." He held Daniel with one arm, the boy's arms and legs wrapped around his father, and used his other hand to ruffle Charles's hair. "And everyone is okay."

"This garden is a death trap," said Nina. "I'm minded to report you to the council."

"It's private property," said Amy, feeling defensiveness mix with her shock and grief. "Your children were trespassing."

"We're not her children," said Charles.

"Ice cream, PLEEEASE," demanded Daniel.

"I've had enough of this," said Nina. She turned around and squeezed herself back through the fence. They all heard her slam the back door behind her.

"I kicked my ball over the fence by accident," explained Charles. "I was looking for it in the brambles. Daniel followed me. He was playing with the cat."

"No harm done," said Richard, with an apologetic look. "Sorry about your pot, Amy." Amy looked up. "I'll get that fence mended too," he added. He glanced around, taking in her garden. "I can see that this space isn't really designed for little monsters." Richard went over to the fence and encouraged both children through. He followed them.

Amy sank to the ground. In spite of the shock, she was determined to use what little daylight there was left to find the pieces of the pot. If she found them all, perhaps she'd be able to repair it. Already she'd gathered about eight pieces, but she was sure it amounted to less than half of what she needed. She squeezed the largest piece in her hand, feeling the shard digging into her palm, then set it down and balanced the others inside it as she used her whole hand flat on the ground, feeling for more fragments.

Then she stopped. Something was glinting at her in the last of the summer evening's sun.

She pushed an ivy leaf aside and reached out to pick up the object. It was a ring. A pale blue aquamarine was set in the center, framed by two tiny diamonds.

Beautiful.

And familiar.

Chapter Three

"**D**amn it," said Amy as a heavy recipe book landed on her big toe and sent little waves of pain all the way up her leg. She glanced down at the book. *The Joy of Slow Cookers*. She'd never even used it, but she had a couple of slow cookers too, somewhere, probably still in their boxes. She rarely even fast-cooked. She decided to get rid of the book, and the cookers too, if she could find them. She looked for a place to start a rubbish pile, but there wasn't an inch of space in the spare room. Later, she told herself, and kicked the book out of the way.

Except there was no out-of-the-way. She could barely even get into the room. Amy felt she'd been pretty disciplined in the rest of the house. There were walkways to help her reach the key areas of most rooms: doors, windows, vital furniture. She had a bed she could sleep on, most of the sofa to sit on, enough kitchen to grab food and make tea, and she could almost always get to the toilet.

The spare bedroom was different; it was where it had all started. Amy had decided long ago not to beat herself up about it. People kept stuff they didn't often use in spare rooms. Everyone did.

At first, she'd just had a shoebox. It had been the counselor's idea, a memory box to help her accept what had happened. And it had helped. She'd stopped hassling Tim's friends and Chantel's mother for news, stopped writing down everything they told her in her diary in an attempt to make sense of what had happened. In fact, she'd cut them off entirely. People were not what she needed: they could always leave. Instead she'd collected her memories and put them neatly into a box.

The shoebox had grown too small, or perhaps her memories were too big. She stopped seeing the counselor and instead found a large box that had once carried oranges to the supermarket. She filled it; it felt good. Even now, just the smell of an orange made her think of him.

She picked up more boxes, ones that had transported bananas from Peru, mangoes from Pakistan, and carrots from Shropshire. Once she'd filled these, she gave up using boxes and started piling her treasures on the bed. No one was sleeping there, as of course Chantel was gone too.

Now, facing a wall of stuff, Amy found herself regretting her decisions. Why couldn't she at least have kept the original box somewhere accessible? She looked at the objects, piled up. She caught the eye of a china magpie, staring at her accusingly from between two bottles and a broken clock. Spines of more cookbooks mocked her. She hadn't made a single crumb from *101 Breads and Batters,* nor experienced *The Taste of India.* The saucepans she'd need were probably at the back of that room somewhere, underneath more newspapers spanning the last decade.

She would get rid of it all, she decided, immediately feeling better. Anything she didn't need would go in the rubbish. She'd find the box in no time. Amy grabbed the china magpie, and felt its cold vulnerability in her hands. She'd keep just this one thing. She reached for a cookbook, but made the mistake of glancing at the title: *Pie Night.* She had to keep that one; she did love pies. A wooden spoon caught her eye—it would be wasteful to throw that away. But she could put it down in the kitchen. That would help.

Amy carefully made her way down the stairs, holding her spoon. Perhaps she didn't have too much stuff, she decided. It just needed to be better organized. Redistributed throughout the house. She popped the spoon on the kitchen counter and trotted back up the stairs. She'd find that box in no time.

AMY SAT ON the floor, just inside the spare room doorway. She'd forgotten that the carpet was green in there, a light shade like lichen creeping over a tree. She'd been working for an hour and she'd cleared a space that not even Smudge could sleep in. She was acres away from finding the box. A bottle cork sat next to her, the one item she'd decided to get rid of. She chucked it back into the room; it wasn't worth bothering with. Amy leaned back against her piles and closed her eyes.

That ring.

Maybe she didn't need to find the diary that was in her box. Memories drifted back to her like waves lapping at her feet. She remembered the first time she'd spotted the ring in the window of the small antiques shop. The shop was in what was the center of town, before the modern high street had been created to service the new flats and houses. The old town center was a bus ride from her family home, but seemed a world away. Cobbled and crumbling, it was built around a meandering river inhabited by swans.

Of course that area would house that shop, and of course that shop would house her perfect ring. She remembered the window display still, the ring nestled between a peacock brooch and some beads cut from Venetian glass. Every time she'd walked past that shop, she'd looked to see it sitting there, as if it were waiting for her. She'd know it anywhere. Even resting in the nettles in her back garden, years later.

How had it got there? Amy asked herself the question again. It seemed impossible. Tim wouldn't just have abandoned it in her garden, not back then, and not now after all this time.

But there it was, and now it was sitting in her living room next to Scarlett, who would guard it faithfully.

The ring changed everything.

Amy hadn't believed it when they'd disappeared. She had searched and searched for her lifelong best friend and boyfriend of ten years, convinced something terrible had happened to them. They wouldn't betray her.

But eventually she'd been worn down. No clues, no leads, and nothing but pitying looks from everyone she'd asked. Even the police believed they had run away to be together. Eventually Amy had accepted that as truth. She couldn't face anyone from her past, couldn't bear to see the people who'd known the three of them together. They must all think she was so stupid not to have seen what was going on.

And now the ring. The ring from Tim. The ring that told her he loved her.

Except he wasn't here. What had happened?

She pulled out recipe books from the clutter in front of her, chucking them behind her into the hallway haphazardly. She pulled out another box and pushed it out of the room without even pausing to see what was inside.

She was making headway. She'd find something. A clue. Something she'd missed in the haze of grief and anger all those years ago.

Behind the box was a large wide-necked vase, made from a beautiful cut crystal. Inside it lazed a china carriage clock. The clock ticked at her; it was one of the few that still worked, and had lovely little honeysuckle blossoms painted on it. Really it should be somewhere she could see it more often. The vase too; it was the perfect size to house roses cut from the garden. Or honeysuckle, she thought. Then she could put the vase with the honeysuckle next to the carriage clock and have a little honeysuckle corner in the living room. The birds would appreciate that. She pulled at the vase, but it was stuck— more boxes were wedged on top. She tugged harder, thinking again of a honeysuckle corner. Scarlett was particularly partial to the scent of that gorgeous flower.

The corner of a box was caught just inside the vase, causing the jam. Amy pushed it up, but it was heavier than she thought. Using a bit of force, she shunted it up with the base of her hand, and the vase came free at last.

The boxes swayed. Amy hurried to steady them, but it was too late.

She felt a hard, sharp stab of pain right by her eye.

Then nothing.

"WHAT HAPPENED TO your face?" asked Rachel, falling into step next to Amy.

Damn, thought Amy. Tuesday morning and she'd mistimed leaving her house, and now she'd be stuck with her neighbor on her walk to the station. Perhaps on the train too, if she couldn't shake her, all the way to London Bridge. She considered feigning having forgotten something and going back inside, but she was already heading for the last train that would get her to the office on time. She hated being late even more than she disliked Rachel's company. All she really wanted to do was think about her ring and what it meant, ideally with an ice pack on her injury.

"I walked into a door," she lied.

"It's a big bruise," said Rachel.

"It was a big door."

Suddenly Rachel's hand was on her arm and Amy was pulled to a halt. "You can talk to me, you know," said Rachel in an urgent whisper.

"Hurry up, we'll miss the train," Amy said. Rachel was getting weirder, she thought. Shaking off her hand, Amy started off again at a brisker pace. Rachel's shorter legs meant that every third step turned into a funny little half skip to keep up as she bobbed along beside her.

"I didn't know you were seeing anyone," said Rachel, a little breathless already.

"I'm not," said Amy, wondering where that had come from. Then she realized what Rachel was getting at. Talk about jumping to conclusions. She couldn't help but laugh: those TV soaps had finally addled Rachel's mind. "I'm not," she said again.

"It's not funny," snapped Rachel. "I'm just trying to help. I worry about you."

Amy spotted a bright flash of color on the ground and her heart leapt. She bent to pick it up. "I've never seen you smoke," said Rachel, watching her.

"I don't." Amy pocketed her treasure.

"So why did you pick up that lighter?"

"Lighters aren't just for cigarettes," snapped Amy. "Are we getting this train or not?"

They reached the station. Amy dawdled, fiddling inside her bag to give Rachel a head start, hoping they wouldn't have to travel together. She needn't have bothered. Rachel had charged through the gate and was headed for the far end of the platform. Amy went in the opposite direction. The carriages at the back were often emptier, although it did mean a longer walk once the train pulled into the station at the other end.

She was just in time; the train arrived as she reached her favorite spot to board. She chose to stand, rather than to sit in the only unoccupied seat next to a man sleeping with his mouth open, a small trickle of dribble running from the corner of his mouth to his collar. Holding on to the handrail with one hand, she reached the other to touch the tender area around her eye. She flinched. It was very sore and she could tell that it was still swollen.

After the attention from Rachel, Amy was half expecting people on the train carriage to cast her some enquiring glances, but no one gave her so much as a second look. This was a big city after all, she reminded herself. She thought of the old man she'd seen last week on the train with no shoes, his gnarled feet black and bloody. And the woman who took the train every Wednesday morning and sang "All Things Bright and Beautiful" for the duration of the journey in a warbly soprano. A woman with a small bruise on her face was nothing compared to some of the people who boarded the train. It was one of the things that she loved about living in London. The anonymity.

"Oh, Rachel," she sighed, thinking of her neighbor's overactive imagination. The man standing next to her subtly shifted his weight to put more distance between them. She hadn't meant to speak out loud. Rachel's reaction had tickled her, but it made her realize something.

It wouldn't be so funny at work. She couldn't have her colleagues at Trapper, Lemon, and Hughes coming to the same conclusion as Rachel. Carthika and Zoe were just as silly as Rachel, if not more so. She couldn't deal with pitying glances, and it didn't exactly go with her carefully cultivated image of controlled competence. She needed to hide her injury and makeup was the answer.

Fortunately there was a Boots chemist at the station. Amy popped in and leafed through bottles of foundation in various shades that all reminded her of clay. Her current beauty regime was pretty nonexistent, and she couldn't imagine her skin being any of those colors.

"I see you've found our soft matte range," said a voice. Amy turned to see a young woman modeling the foundations so efficiently not a patch of her natural skin was visible. Blusher made a diagonal line from her cheeks to the tops of her ears, and she had on a pretty shade of lipstick that reminded Amy of a maraschino cherry adorning a sundae. Her name badge informed Amy that she was called Joanna. "Oh," she said as she saw Amy's injury.

"I've been in the wars," said Amy, pleased with that explanation. Suitably vague and a little lighthearted. Not the type of thing a battered woman would say at all.

Joanna frowned at her, leaving temporary cracks in her own foundation that made Amy think she could be older than she'd at first thought. "Hmm," said Joanna. "Ivory blush, I think. Give me your hand." She put a stripe of the makeup on Amy's hand and rubbed it in a little, and they both admired it. "Right every time," said Joanna with a satisfied smile. "Unless you want to go a shade darker to bring a bit more color to your complexion?"

"I just want to cover the bruise," said Amy. "Please."

"Sit down." Joanna gestured to a rather unsteady-looking stool that Amy had to hop backwards to mount. "A concealer is what you need first." She took a small sponge and began dabbing at Amy's eye.

"Ouch," said Amy.

"It might sting a bit, but once I'm through no one will notice a thing. Foundation next. And maybe some blusher, right along here. You've got such lovely cheekbones," she added admiringly. "All they need is a tiny little bit of color to bring them out."

Amy sat, feeling like a chocolate-covered child having her face wiped by her grandmother, while Joanna fussed around her. "There," Joanna said eventually, standing back and admiring her work. "Not bad at all. You have beautiful skin. You'll only need a very light foundation once that bruise has healed."

She handed Amy a mirror, and Amy inspected her face. Her eye looked a little puffy, but it was nothing that a bit of water retention and a bad night's sleep couldn't explain. The bruise itself was gone, hidden beneath a mountain of concealer. Her cheeks looked flushed, as if she'd been for a run.

"I'd love to get some eyeliner on you, bring out those beautiful gray eyes, but it's probably not a good idea right now. Come back and see me when it's healed, and I'll do a proper makeover."

"Excellent work," said Amy politely. "It will do nicely."

Joanna smiled at the compliment, then took Amy's hand. Amy waited to see what she'd apply. But instead she just squeezed it.

"If you need anything else, you just need to ask me," she said, looking straight into Amy's eyes.

"Thank you," replied Amy. "But you've done a great job."

"Anything at all," added Joanna, with her hands still holding Amy's. "My cousin . . ."

Amy took her hand away. Why couldn't anyone mind their own business? "Where's the till?" she asked. "I'm in a hurry."

Joanna gestured to the front of the shop. "It's three for two on makeup," she added in her business voice again. "If you want to get the blusher too." She lowered her voice. "And I'd recommend arnica, to help the healing."

Amy waited in the queue, clutching her foundation, concealer, a small tub of arnica, and the pale-pink blusher. It sparkled like powdered gemstones under the fluorescent lights.

AS AMY ENTERED the office, she had a sudden urge to turn around and go home again. She could call in sick. Although she'd eaten nothing but a few crackers once she came to last night, it wasn't just her eye that hurt. She felt sick to her stomach.

She couldn't skip work, she decided. In all the years Amy had been an administrator, she'd barely ever called in sick. Except for when it happened, of course, and she didn't count that. Sometimes, perhaps she should have stayed at home. She still remembered the rather unpleasant train ride into the office the day after she'd experimented with some discounted shrimp from the station deli. That was a day that should have been spent within easier reach of a toilet.

Amy made her way to the kitchen. The smell of sour coffee from the machine was making her stomach worse, and a cup of the stuff would do her no favors. She perused the tea bag selection and chose an organic-looking bag of chamomile tea.

"Bright and early again, Amy." Trevor Trapper smiled at her as he came into the kitchen. He said that every morning, and had done so for the past seventeen years. Amy passed him his favorite mug, a large white one that even Amy didn't care for. It declared his support for Nottingham Forest Football Club. He took the mug, then frowned. "Not having your usual coffee this morning?" he asked, looking at her selection.

"I'm feeling a little under the weather," replied Amy, hoping he wouldn't notice her eye. "I thought chamomile tea might be softer on the stomach."

"Ah, yes. You do look a little . . . Mrs. Trapper swears by the stuff when it's her time of the . . ." He paused, and suddenly seemed very interested in the inside of his mug. "Let me know when the papers come in from the Apex family," he said over the whir of the coffee machine as it spat out foam for his cappuccino. "I'd like to deal with that estate personally."

"Of course, Mr. Trapper," replied Amy.

She took her tea to her desk and settled down, the pile of post in front of her. Most of her communications were by e-mail now, but physical documents still played a large role in this financial advice firm. She'd had the same swivel chair since she'd started here, and years of sitting in it meant the contours perfectly matched the shape of her body. She was determined not to keep any of her treasures at work, tempting as it was to make use of extra storage space. Instead she kept her desk tidy and anonymous. She didn't even have a special mug in the office, choosing whichever of the generic office mugs happened to be free. Colleagues had adorned their workstations with pictures of children, partners, and holidays, but Amy didn't have anyone to put there. Not anymore. She could put up a picture of Scarlett, but she didn't think the others would understand.

She closed her eyes, but it wasn't Scarlett's image that came into her vision. It was the ring again, seemingly imprinted on the insides of her eyelids. She lifted her right hand and massaged the base of her left ring finger. She felt as if there was an absence there, as though her finger missed the ring it had never worn. "How did it get there?" she mused. "I don't understand."

"What don't you understand?" Amy opened her eyes to see Carthika frowning at her.

"These Apex papers," said Amy quickly. She must be more careful—speaking her thoughts out loud was beginning to get embarrassing.

"No wonder you don't understand them," said Carthika. "You haven't even opened the envelope."

Amy looked down. Carthika was right. A large white envelope sat in front of her, unopened.

"How do you know it's from Apex?" asked Carthika. Zoe, Emma's replacement, stopped typing and listened.

Amy found to her embarrassment that heat was creeping up her neck into her face. She must be blushing. And she was meant to be the head of the team—it hardly instilled confidence. She glanced down again. "When you've been working here as long as I have," she said, trying to will the color from her face, "you start to recognize handwriting." The address was written in a large, clear hand, with little circles instead of dots on the *i*'s. She inserted her letter opener, shaped like a small dagger, opened the envelope, and scowled. The documents weren't from Apex after all. "Oh," she said to herself, and put it in the pile to be processed.

"Maybe you're losing your touch?" enquired Carthika, sounding rather more amused than the situation warranted. Amy looked up and noticed Zoe staring at her.

"You look different today," declared Zoe. "Are you wearing makeup?"

"She is," agreed Carthika, as though Amy couldn't hear them. "And she's distracted." She paused. "I know! She's got a crush!"

"It's probably Liam from marketing," agreed Zoe. "She likes his shiny suits." They both laughed.

"It is not Liam from marketing," snapped Amy.

"So it's Tony from the post room then?" said Carthika. "I knew it."

Amy made a humphing noise that she hoped communicated that they'd discussed the subject long enough and it was time to get back to work. She began tapping at her keyboard in case the message was not clear. It worked. The others turned back to their own screens, still sniggering, and Amy listened to the reassuring rhythm of keys being pressed. Work being done. She breathed deeply and found her eyes closing again.

The ring floated into her vision. She'd left it at home, guarded by Scarlett, but now she wished she had it with her. She wanted to feel it. To squeeze it in her hand. To check that it was really there and she hadn't imagined it.

Amy felt the sick feeling inside her belly rising up, until it was level with her heart. What did it mean?

She put her hand on her heart, trying to quell the sensation. Then she realized what it was.

Hope.

AMY FOUND SHE couldn't think about anything else. Not while she processed papers, not while she ate her cheese and pickle sandwich, not even while she attended the team meeting that she was meant to minute. As it concluded, she realized all she had were doodles of concentric circles, like hundreds of little rings that fitted neatly inside one another.

Finally the day ended. Amy caught the train home on autopilot; it was lucky the platform hadn't been changed or she could have ended up anywhere. She got out at her station and walked slowly home.

"Amy!" To her dismay, she saw Rachel and Nina lingering by her front gate, the midpoint between their houses. They were deep in conversation. That was all she needed. "Nina told me what happened."

"Your cat broke my pot," said Amy, hoping they'd get out of her way. That incident felt like years ago now.

"We both know that's not the issue here," said Rachel, standing her ground so she blocked Amy's path. "Now, I've been very patient, but there are children here . . ." She paused, made a funny little sound, and Amy saw Nina uncross her arms to place a steadying hand on Rachel's shoulder. "Children," repeated Rachel. "And it's not a safe environment."

"They shouldn't have been in my garden," said Amy.

"We all know that," said Nina. "I've told them. But that fence is your responsibility. Richard was very generous to offer to replace it."

"There's help for people like you," said Rachel, in that sanctimonious voice that Amy felt that Rachel reserved for her.

Amy had a vision of Rachel and Nina trying to pave over her beautiful wilderness. "I like my garden," she replied. "And it's good for the local wildlife. Now, if you'll excuse me . . ." She pulled open the gate, and the women finally stepped aside.

"It's not just the garden," added Rachel, as Amy put her key in the lock. "You need help."

"You need to mind your own business," said Amy. She was torn. She wanted to get inside, but she could feel Rachel's eyes on her back, waiting to have a peek at Amy's hallway.

She breathed a sigh of relief. The women were retreating, both back to Rachel's house. "I do my best to be compassionate," she heard Rachel say. "But it's just getting worse."

"You've got enough to deal with," agreed Nina. Amy looked around. They were out of eyeshot. She opened her door and quickly stepped inside, pulling it shut behind her.

AMY SELECTED A mug adorned with a meandering honeysuckle and made herself a cup of tea. She went to the living room and sat with Scarlett and the ring. The tiny diamonds glittered back at her.

It still sparkled in her inside light, but not with the same intensity as it had outside when it greedily gobbled the light of the sun and spat it back as rainbows.

She would put the ring on, she decided. For safekeeping. She paused. For some reason it seemed not quite right to wear it. Like putting on a dead person's clothes.

She took a deep breath, ignored her misgivings, and slipped on the ring. It felt like a tiny hug, wrapped around her finger.

But cold.

Amy admired her hand, then got up, feeling the weight of the ring on her finger, and went into the kitchen. She saw the broken pot, forgotten in the excitement of the ring, and felt a pang of guilt. Collecting the pieces, she tried to fit them back together, like a three-dimensional jigsaw.

It was hopeless—too many were missing. Amy looked regretfully at her bin, and picked up the shards to dispose of them. One of the pieces caught her eye. A complete flower gazed back at her.

She stopped.

Even broken, the shards had beauty. She turned away from the bin and put the pieces back on the kitchen counter. There would be some use for them still, she decided. She didn't paint anymore, of course, but they could become tesserae for a craft project. She was warming to the idea. Maybe she could make a mosaic to frame one of her mirrors. Or she could set them into her front path. Or, if she bought a fish tank, they could live inside as lovely little decorations.

For the moment, they could live on the kitchen counter. She had other fish to fry, so to speak.

She looked at the pieces again, remembering the pot. It had sat by her front door for so long. She felt a wave of excitement.

Could that be how the ring had arrived in her garden?

Amy pictured the scene. Tim, standing outside the door. Wanting Amy back. Clutching the ring, ready to propose. Getting scared.

Posting it through the door instead, knowing that Amy would know what it meant.

Not knowing that Amy's house was already filled with treasures.

But then why did he not come back? That pot had been in the garden for . . . Amy didn't know how long. Years. It must be. Why hadn't he rung the doorbell? Why hadn't he come back for her?

The doorbell rang, and Amy jumped. She hurried to the door and swung it open, half hoping that Tim would be there, ready to explain.

Richard. Only Richard. Looking embarrassed.

"Sorry to disturb you," he said, clearly uncomfortable. Amy stepped out and pulled the door almost closed behind her, feeling disappointment flooding through her. "Rachel told Nina that something had happened, and . . ." He paused and glanced behind him. They both watched Smudge, who was taking a leisurely stroll across the road. "And the women thought that maybe, if you needed someone to, you know . . ."

"What?" asked Amy.

"A bit of muscle," said Richard, shrugging.

Amy laughed, feeling the tension dissipate as she did so.

"I have muscles," insisted Richard with mock offense. "It's not that funny."

"Of course you do," said Amy, trying not to look at him so she didn't laugh again. "It's just Rachel. One bruise and she thinks I'm being beaten. Something fell on me, that's all."

"It's your own business how you keep your house, but if it's not safe—"

"I dropped something on myself," insisted Amy, wondering how he'd guessed the truth. "My house is fine."

Richard held his hands up in a gesture of surrender. "I'm sorry. I shouldn't snoop." He smiled. "We can leave that to Rachel."

"Thank you," said Amy. She waited for him to leave.

He lingered for a moment, looking as if he might like to be invited in.

"Good-bye," said Amy.

"Bye then," he replied. Amy waited until he turned to leave, then went back inside.

She looked around. Her hallway *was* a little cluttered, she thought. Richard must have caught a glimpse of it, to have jumped to the conclusion he had. She laughed at the memory of his face, when she'd made the muscle comment. He had a sense of humor, and it was a while since she'd shared a joke with someone. It felt nice.

Amy went back to the living room, carried her tea into the kitchen and left it by the sink, and made her way up the stairs. She took a deep breath at the sight of her upstairs hallway. Last night, when she came to, she'd not even attempted to pass the mess and had just made her way downstairs. She'd fallen asleep on the sofa with a bag of frozen peas that must have been ten years old slowly defrosting on her face. In the morning, she'd just about managed to scramble over the fallen boxes into her bathroom to have a quick shower, but she hadn't even looked at the damage. Now was the time.

She'd been lucky: the box that hit her in the eye was fairly light. It could easily have been full of cookery books. That would have been dangerous. Or a mirror could have fallen and smashed into sharp shards. Amy made another resolution to sort through her things. At the very least, she should make sure everything heavy was at the bottom.

She opened the fallen box and carefully rummaged through, looking for signs of damage. She felt a flood of gratitude to the Amy who'd packed this box. It was full of mugs, each one encased in thick bubble wrap the way a spider would wrap a fly. Everything seemed intact. She unwrapped one of the mugs, just to check. It had a handle in the shape of an electric guitar and was inscribed with a motto: *Keep Music Live.* Tim would have loved it, she decided, and she put it on the carpet. She'd use it for her tea in the morning.

The morning. That was when she'd sort out the rest of this mess. Amy yawned, and looked at what was in front of her. Clocks, mirrors, boxes, cookbooks, lighters. They'd all been piled in that room, and now they were strewn over the hallway, blocking her route to the bathroom. Luckily, she had a small toilet downstairs. She couldn't face clambering over all this tonight. Amy went back downstairs. Maybe she'd be best off sleeping in the living room again.

She wasn't used to wearing makeup, or needing to wash her face in the evening. She went to the kitchen and splashed herself with water, then wiped her face with a dishcloth. Even "ivory blush" looked orange on the cloth, but after three washes the same amount still came off each time. She grabbed a bottle of washing-up liquid, squirted a tiny amount of the emerald-green gel onto the palm of her hand, lathered her hands together, and then, with her eyes tightly shut, spread it onto her face. She rinsed, shuddering at the soapy taste that managed to sneak into her mouth even though it was clamped shut. She rinsed again, and dried her face with another dishcloth.

Her skin was so dry that it felt too tight for her face, and Amy wondered if this was how her mugs felt after she'd washed them. She applied a bit of hand cream from one of several bottles of the stuff on the counter, but it was little match for the dryness. She dabbled on some arnica and decided that tomorrow she'd visit Joanna again to buy some proper cleanser and a face cream. This injury was proving expensive.

Amy went into the living room. It was nice to sleep here, among her birds. Like the sleepovers she used to have at Chantel's house as a girl. She turned out the light and carefully felt her way to the sofa, where she sank down and pulled a blanket up to her chin.

She'd need to clean up the upstairs hallway, she knew that. But maybe she didn't need to find that box. She closed her eyes and visualized it. It might have been ten years or so since she'd looked inside, but Amy knew its contents by heart. It wouldn't help.

Her fingers went back to the ring. She needed to confirm that Tim had bought it. And she needed to know when.

The answers wouldn't be in that box. She needed to go back. Back to somewhere she hadn't been for a very long time.

December 1999

"Where am I going to sleep?" Tim chewed the edge of his fingernail and looked out of the train window.

"In a bed," replied Amy with a laugh.

"Yes, but where?" asked Tim. "In your room? On my own? How will it work? Maybe this wasn't such a good idea. Maybe I should just head back home."

"You are spending Christmas with my grandma and me," insisted Amy, with the weariness that came from a conversation repeated over and over. "She's looking forwards to it."

"Being onstage in front of hundreds of people is much easier than this," complained Tim.

"Hundreds?" queried Amy, raising an eyebrow.

"Tens," corrected Tim. He laughed. "On a good night. But, hey, we're building a reputation. It takes time."

Amy reached out and touched Tim's arm. "You'll be sleeping in my room with me," she said, her voice gentle. "How's that?"

"Perfect." Tim put his hand on her arm. "Don't expect any action though," he added, his voice falsely light. "I don't think I could perform knowing your grandma is next door."

"Thanks for warning me," said Amy. The train pulled into a station, and she smiled. "This is where that gorgeous little antiques shop is. Remember, the one I was telling you about?"

Tim stood up. "Let's go."

"I didn't mean now," said Amy. "We'll be late."

"Come on." He took her hand and pulled her to her feet. "Be spontaneous."

"I suppose we can get the bus from here," she said. "It goes to the end of her road."

"Serendipity," replied Tim.

They got off the train, and Amy led the way to the shop. "I can get a present for your grandma," said Tim.

"She really doesn't need anything," said Amy.

"She must like presents though," Tim insisted. "Everyone likes presents."

"She's got too much stuff already. You'll see what I mean when you get to her house."

"Let's go see this shop. Arnold's. That's it, right?"

"It is," said Amy. They lingered by the window. Amy wondered if he'd remember.

"That's the ring you like?" he asked, pointing to it. It had a pale blue stone with a tiny diamond on each side. "The one you told me about?"

Amy smiled. "Yep," she said. "It's pretty, isn't it? The color reminds me of the sky early on a summer morning."

"You and your skies," replied Tim, squeezing Amy's hand.

The owner, a gentleman in his seventies, greeted them. "I'm Arnold," he said, and to both their embarrassments reached out to shake their hands. "All this is mine," he said, gesturing around the shop as though it were a vast empire.

Tim nodded politely. "Very nice," he said. "Cool deer head."

"He's an elk," replied Arnold proudly. "Handsome beast, isn't he? He's traveled all the way from Canada."

Amy breathed in deeply. The shop had a musty scent that reminded her of the university library. She used to walk by this shop all the time and gaze in through the window. But she didn't often allow herself in and had never bought anything. It felt more like a museum than a shop: everything was just too beautiful to own.

Tim was peering at the tag on the ring. "Oh," he said. "It's not cheap."

"It's an aquamarine," said Arnold. "Emerald cut, framed by two baguette diamonds. Art Deco." He smiled. "Your sweetheart has lovely taste. Would she like to try it on?"

"No, it's okay," said Amy, blushing at the old-fashioned term. "I don't actually want the ring," she lied. "I just like to look at it as I walk past. It's been here for years."

"It's waiting for a special home," said Arnold, and winked at them.

"Very special at that price," said Tim. "You wouldn't buy that unless you were going to propose." The words hung on the air. Amy picked up the closest thing to her, a small vase, feeling strangely awkward. They'd never discussed marriage; as she was not yet twenty, it seemed an abstract and rather taboo subject.

"Do you like that?" asked Tim. He took the vase from her.

"Vintage Bohemian glass," said Arnold. "Gorgeous iridescence to it, and only a tiny chip."

Tim glanced at the price tag. "It's lovely," he agreed.

"It is," said Amy, barely noticing it. In her mind she was picturing their wedding, and it made her feel vaguely guilty. She glanced at her watch. "We'd better get going. We'll be late."

"I'll get the vase for your grandma," said Tim.

"She said not to get her anything."

"No one ever means that," replied Tim. "Does she like vases?"

"I suppose," said Amy.

"Can you wrap it?" he asked Arnold.

"Merry Christmas," said Arnold, flamboyantly shaking out a bright-red piece of tissue paper and dexterously wrapping it around the vase.

They both returned the greeting. Tim took the package, and Amy shepherded him from the shop.

"YOU WERE RIGHT," said Tim, shuffling uncomfortably on the floral sofa before reaching back to remove an unfortunate china doll he'd been sitting on. "Your grandma does have a lot of stuff."

Amy looked around the room. School photos capturing various awkward stages in her childhood lined the mantelpiece, coupled with Plasticine figurines she'd created at primary school. A teddy bear that had belonged to her father before her sat with them on the sofa, and her A level art projects occupied most of the wall space.

"It's nice," said Amy. "My parents didn't save anything from when I was younger. They gave it all away for the needy."

"This house is like a shrine to Amy," said Tim, leaning over and giving her a little kiss.

"I think it might be a shrine to you too soon," said Amy, gesturing to where the vase sat, pride of place, next to a rather humble attempt at a parrot the young Amy had crafted from macaroni, glue, and a liberal sprinkling of glitter. "She loves that vase."

"I'm glad I got it for her," said Tim, "after all the trouble she's going to."

Amy's grandmother had shooed them from the kitchen while she finished with the turkey, insisting they sit and rest. Two of her grandmother's best china teacups sat in front of them, the sweet tea gradually cooling.

"She loves Christmas," said Amy. "But my parents never come.

They always volunteer for extra shifts at the hospital—plenty of people get sick in the holidays too, they say." It wasn't much of a loss: her dad didn't like turkey, and her mum always asked for a donation to Amnesty International instead of a present. Amy preferred just being with her grandmother. Her parents were good people, ridiculously good people. And yes, they loved her. But they loved everyone else too. She always had the feeling that when they were with her, they would rather be somewhere else. Somewhere they could be helping people on a grander scale than just their daughter.

"Did I tell you Dad invited me to spend Christmas with him and Roberta?" asked Tim all of a sudden.

"Maybe you should meet her?" ventured Amy. "They are getting married."

"I don't want to. Dad might think he can replace Mum, but . . ." He stopped and bit his lip. "I can't spend Christmas with them," said Tim finally, "with someone else sitting where Mum should be."

"Let's go in the garden," said Amy, keen to keep Tim cheerful. "We can see if there are any flowers we can pick to go in your vase. And there's something else I want to show you."

It was cold outside, and the muddy grass felt soft and squidgy under their feet. The garden was scant compared to how Amy knew it from the spring, but still some flowers braved the cold. "Winter honeysuckle!" she exclaimed, and proceeded to cut a couple of stems of the sweetly scented flowers from the bush that grew up around the shed. She hesitated for a moment, her hand on the shed door. "Would you like to see inside?"

"I'm not that into lawn mowers," said Tim, stamping his feet to keep warm. "Let's get back inside."

"It's not just a shed," said Amy, suddenly feeling unsure of herself. "My gran cleared it out. It's where I paint, when I come here. There's something for you in there."

"A present?" asked Tim. "What are we waiting for?"

Amy fished a key from her pocket and opened the padlock on

the door. "It's not much. . . ." she said, switching on the light. She was hit by the smells she loved. Oil paint, turps, and the gorgeous scent of pine that emanated from the wooden walls. "Just a project I was working on last time I was here, but wasn't ready to share. . . ."

"Amy!" Tim stood motionless in front of a large canvas. "I knew you were talented, but . . ."

Amy looked at the painting. She'd always loved colors and had often been inspired by the sky, but in the past she'd always felt compelled to limit the sky to the background, the top of a more figurative scene of houses, trees, people.

But in this painting she'd let herself go. Giant swaths of vibrant oils traveled confidently across the canvas. Purples and oranges and reds, the paint so thick that sometimes it cast a shadow of its own. In the bottom corner, the purple so dark it was almost black, she'd woven in a coiled guitar string—one of Tim's, which she'd saved when it snapped at a rehearsal. Above it was a piercing blast of yellow, brighter than a field of sunflowers.

Tim's eyes didn't leave the painting, but his hand found her own.

"I hear the song when I look at this," he whispered. "But more beautifully than I've ever played it."

Amy squeezed his hand. "I didn't know if I'd managed it. I didn't know if you'd understand. . . ."

"Of course I do. It's love and hurt and regret . . ."

"And hope," said Amy.

"Yes," replied Tim. "And hope."

"Merry Christmas," said Amy.

"Merry Christmas, Amy Ashton," replied Tim. He took his eyes from the painting and directed them towards Amy. "And thank you."

Chapter Four

Great fields of yellow stretched out, bright even through the train's dirty window. Rapeseed wasn't as dramatic as the fields of sunflowers that she remembered from her school trip to France, but it had a magic of its own. And it reminded her of home. Amy shuddered. It was a long time since Amy had been home.

She wasn't actually going home. Now that the weekend had finally arrived, she was going to the old town center. To the shop where the ring was from.

Amy reached for the ring, now dangling from a silver chain around her neck. She kept it under her shirt. She preferred to wear it on her finger only in private.

So now the ring sat with her, a cold circle near her heart.

The train pulled into her station. Amy sat still, unable to move. An elderly woman made her way to the door, pushed the button, and stepped onto the platform. Amy closed her eyes for a moment, unsure what to do. She felt the ring against her chest, and after a moment jumped up and ran for the door. She bumped into a woman

carrying heavy shopping, apologized, and then stepped out. The
doors slid shut behind her.

She was here.

The platform felt different. The signs were new, the typeface
unfamiliar. There were digital posters now, replacing the old paper
ones. They advertised blackberry gin and elderflower tonic. Outside
the station, everything looked more familiar: cobbled streets, a small
river. Even the swans looked the same, gliding along gracefully as
if fully aware of their beauty. She'd loved this area when she was
younger, and had longed to live here instead of the modern little
development her parents had chosen.

Amy felt a flutter of excitement as she approached the shop. It
was still there. The same white sign with black lettering declaring the
shop to be ARNOLD's. The same jangle of a bell as she pushed the door
open. Even the same elk's head, mounted on the wall. Still waiting
for a final resting place.

"Can I help you?" Amy turned. A young man wearing glasses and
a nervous smile looked at her.

"I'm just browsing," she said, casually picking up a china orna-
ment. If the ring had sold recently, this man might remember it.
She'd just have a little wander round first. Then she realized what she
was holding and gasped.

It was a china sparrow: a plain enough bird, but its feathers were
exquisitely rendered. She could almost feel their texture. The shades
of brown were rich and deep, like a chocolate cake laced with cara-
mel cream. And its eyes. Alert and inquisitive. Friendly. And fearful.

Amy had to have it.

She handed it to the man without even asking the price. He
nodded at her choice as if he approved. Amy felt her excitement
mounting as she perused the shelves. They were laden with treasures. She found an owl made from tiny shells, each one in the perfect place to replicate its feathers. There was a beautiful china cup,
shaped to look like a bulbous purple tulip. Amy felt her lips tingle

at the thought of drinking from it. There was even a glazed ashtray in the shape of a lemon, so perfect that Amy couldn't help but bite her lip. She presented each item to the man, with strict instructions to guard her would-be purchases at the till. Although she was the only customer in the shop, she couldn't risk someone else gazumping her. The mere thought of losing one of these treasures made her feel sick.

Adding a silver cigarette lighter, a handheld vanity mirror, and a heavy carriage clock to her haul, she beamed at the shopkeeper. "You have so many beautiful things in your shop," she said, feeling friendly. "I could buy it all."

"You've got a fair bit of it," he said.

"I have something else too," she said. "Something to show you." Amy put her hand to the ring at her throat, then lifted her arms to fiddle with the clasp of the chain. She removed it and slid the ring off, bringing it to the man's attention. "This came from your shop. I was hoping that you might remember selling it?"

The man frowned at the ring. Amy felt a small wrench in her heart as he took it from her, and she already longed to be holding it again. "It's lovely," he said. Amy nodded. She knew that. "But before my time."

Amy felt her heart sink. "When is your time?"

"I took the place over four years ago," he told her.

So Tim hadn't been to the shop in the last four years. Disappointment welled up inside of her. Amy grabbed a small china vase, the action feeling vaguely familiar. She looked at the vase. It was white with a blue Greek meander pattern winding round the neck. She added it to her pile for purchase and felt a little better. The ring was still more of him than she'd had for a long time. And it could still help her.

"Do you keep sales records from earlier?" she pushed. "Could you find out who bought it?"

"It wasn't you?"

Amy paused, not wanting to share too much. "It was a gift," she said. "But it got lost for a long time, so I don't know who it's from."

"Too many admirers?" the man said with a laugh. Amy frowned, unsure if he was making fun of her. "Sorry," he continued, seeing her expression. "We keep sales records now, but they don't date back to before my time."

"And you're sure it wasn't sold more recently?" Amy held her breath, willing the man to sound uncertain.

"We stopped selling jewelry when I took over," he said definitively, handing her back the ring. Amy threaded it through the chain and fastened it around her neck as the man began carefully wrapping Amy's selections in tissue paper. "Never sold much of the stuff anyway," he continued. "We don't have a proper security system here, and a few bits went missing. Installing CCTV was too expensive. So I stopped stocking it." He paused to admire the shell owl. "Arnold picked this for the shop, maybe fifteen years ago. He'll be pleased it's found a good home." He paused and looked at Amy. "I don't suppose you want a stuffed elk head?"

Amy blinked, thinking of the name over the door and the old man she had met. "Arnold? Could I talk to him?" Perhaps he would remember.

"He's gone, I'm afraid," said the man.

"Dead?" asked Amy. "I'm sorry."

"No chance, tough old beggar." He chuckled. "He's ninety-five now. Doesn't look a day over eighty. He's retired, handed the business over to me. I'm his grandson." The man smiled, looking proud of his lineage. "He still likes to keep tabs on what I'm selling though. I think he's worried I'm going to turn the place into a trendy gift shop. As if." He looked around his musty empire. Amy could sense a kindred spirit.

"I wonder if I could visit him?" asked Amy.

The man smiled back at her. "He'd always like to see a good customer," he said. "He'll probably try to sell you something though.

You can take the man out of the shop . . ." He winked at Amy. She decided that perhaps he wasn't a kindred spirit after all.

She would never wink.

"I WAS JUST about to give up on you." Amy looked in surprise at the man standing in her front garden as she arrived home, clutching her bag of purchases. He'd articulated a thought she'd had so many times. "I thought maybe you didn't get the letter."

"The letter?" asked Amy.

"Don't tell me the letter didn't come through," he said. "The office is usually pretty good, but every now and then. Never mind. I'm here. You're here. Shall we get it done anyway?"

"I'm sorry," began Amy. "I don't—"

"Of course not," said the man. "You didn't get the letter." He held out his hand, and after a moment's confusion Amy took it and found her own hand engulfed in a vigorous handshake. "I'm Bob," he said. Then he inexplicably laughed. "The kids love it, but I was Bob the builder before there were any cartoons or that catchy little song." Amy looked at him blankly. "Anyway," he continued. "I'm from Partners in Weysham. We look after the council's freehold properties. You own the leasehold, correct?" He glanced down at a clipboard. "Miss Amy Ashton?"

"Yes," said Amy, feeling overwhelmed.

"Great," he said. "You'll be pleased to know I've come about the chimney. I might not look like Dick Van Dyke, but here I am."

"The chimney?" enquired Amy.

"You must have noticed the stack is loose. I can see a piece of it in your garden over there." He gestured, and Amy saw what she now realized was a stray piece of tile. That was good: she'd thought it must have chipped off one of the pots.

"You need to get on the roof?" Amy asked, feeling dread creep up inside her. "My pots, I don't think it would be safe—"

"No worries," said Bob cheerfully. "I can look from the inside. If the stacks come loose, I'll need to check the whole thing. You can't be too careful with chimneys."

"Inside?" repeated Amy.

"Yes," said Bob. "And a nice cup of tea wouldn't go amiss." He winked at her, and Amy wondered when everyone had starting winking all the time. "I could grow a handle and spout. Love the stuff." He stood to one side to let Amy pass to the door. She stayed put.

"You can't come in," she said.

"Fair enough," said Bob, looking a little miffed. "Since you didn't get the letter." He turned to another page in his clipboard. "When suits?"

"Never suits," said Amy. "You can't come into my house."

Bob looked at her. "I have the relevant identification," he said with a sigh, rummaging through his bag.

"It's not that. You can't come in." Amy thought for a moment. What did people say? "The place is a bit of a mess," she said, finding a phrase she'd heard.

Bob laughed. "No worries, you should see the way the kiddies leave our place. Like a bomb went off. I've seen it all before, don't you worry."

"Thank you very much for your time," said Amy. "But I'm happy with my chimney. Just tick it off your list."

"It doesn't work like that, I'm afraid," said Bob, his voice hardening a little. "This has been called in by a concerned neighbor. Bits of the stack are falling—it's a hazard."

"Which neighbor?" asked Amy. Rachel sticking her nose in again.

"A concerned and anonymous one," said Bob. "Listen, it won't take me long to check it out. I won't look at the mess, I promise. But I need to make sure it's structurally sound. We've got a duty of care." He sniffed at the official-sounding words, then smiled again. "We can't have your house falling down now, can we?"

"Falling down?" echoed Amy.

"Worst case," said Bob with a friendly laugh. "But even best case, you've got pieces of chimney loose up there. It's not safe. If it's falling here, it will be in the back too. What if one of the kiddies from next door was in your garden and got hit by something?"

"The next-door children are not allowed in my garden," said Amy.

Bob referred back to the clipboard. "There's a note on that too," he said. "Falling pots?"

So that was what all this was about. "No one but me will be in that garden," said Amy. "And I'll take my chances."

"Twenty minutes for me to take a quick look, and I'll skip the tea."

"This isn't a negotiation," said Amy stiffly. "It is my house and you can't come in." She looked at him again. "And I'd like you to leave my garden please. It is private property."

"Takes all sorts," muttered Bob, backing out of the garden with his hands held up as if Amy had pointed a gun at him. "I'll need to call it in to the office." He looked at her again. "You do know you're breaking the terms of your leasehold? You will have to let us in eventually."

"Good-bye," said Amy. She watched until he was back in his van before she finally turned to her door and slipped inside her house.

AMY STOOD IN her kitchen, looking out of the window. It had been a hot summer's day, and now the setting sun had painted the sky a shade of violet that echoed the buddleia growing in the far corner of her back garden. A solitary tortoiseshell butterfly, still awake, fluttered haphazardly in the breeze before pausing to drink from the cluster of scented blooms. Amy had restacked the fallen pots and they looked solid again, silhouetted against the sunset. There was a time when she would have been desperate to paint that skyline, but now it just made her feel empty.

She couldn't have anyone inside her house. They wouldn't be able to find the chimney in any case. She couldn't remember the last time she'd even seen her fireplace.

What she needed was a wall. A wall would keep the children out of her garden. It would protect the pots, protect the children, and, she hoped, would mean that Bob left her alone. The chimney stuff was nonsense. She glanced at the hallway, sure that the local newspapers she'd amassed were full of stories about the council being underfunded and overworked. If she made sure the children couldn't get in, then the council could worry about real issues instead.

But how? The idea of builders made her shudder. It would be as bad as Bob—stomping through her house, getting dirty footprints on her newspapers, knocking over bottles and pots, crushing her nettles as if they didn't house precious butterfly cocoons. She'd be obliged to make them tea, which they'd drink from her delicate mugs in their big, careless hands.

No.

She didn't know much about building walls, but how hard could it be to do herself? Some bricks, some concrete, a bit of elbow grease, and a how-to video on YouTube. That was all she'd need.

She paused. The materials were heavy. Awkward. Her house was terraced; she'd need to get them through her house to reach the garden. Amy stepped out of her kitchen into the hallway. However careful she was, something could still be broken as she heaved sacks of cement and bags of bricks through. That's if they'd even fit.

She heard a noise from next door. The voice had a scolding tone, it was probably Nina telling off one of the children.

Of course.

Richard had said he'd fix the fence.

A wall could be put up from his side. They'd just moved in, so their house was bound to be relatively empty; it would be easy to bring the materials through. It was his children that were the issue, after all. It was officially her side to maintain, so she'd offer to pay for the materials and the labor.

Amy hated asking for help, but as she looked around the house she realized that she needed to. She had a responsibility to keep her beautiful possessions safe. They trusted her.

She'd do it now.

Amy stepped past her bag of shopping, saving up the pleasure of unpacking her new treasures for later, and opened her door. By now the violet sky had faded to a papal purple and the world looked as though it were cast in shadows.

"There you are, Amy," said Rachel, making her jump. Rachel and Nina were standing outside Nina's house, both with cigarettes lit. Amy watched the lit ends, which seemed to dance in the night air like fireflies.

"I've started smoking again, okay?" said Rachel. "I've been under a lot of stress."

Nina put her hand on Rachel's arm. "You deserve a break," she said.

"So do you," replied Rachel. "It's a big responsibility you've taken on. Not everyone would do that." Both women sucked on their cigarettes, then puffed out smoke that swirled around in the breeze before disappearing up into the night air.

"I've come to see Richard," said Amy, suppressing a cough.

"Oh?" said Nina, looking amused. "What do you want with Richard?"

Both women were looking at her, and Amy found herself uncomfortable under their scrutiny. She pulled at her loose black T-shirt.

"I just want to ask him something," said Amy.

"He comes with two kids, you know," said Nina. "Before you get any ideas."

"What?" said Amy.

"Sorry, just teasing," said Nina. Rachel laughed.

"What did that man say?" asked Rachel, before Amy could get past her. "Was he here to get rid of your mice?"

So she had been watching. Of course she had. "The mice do not come from my house," insisted Amy.

"Okay," said Rachel. She tapped her cigarette until ash fell to the ground. "If you say so."

"Can I go through?" Amy noticed that the door was ajar.

"Be my guest," said Nina, stepping aside. "It's past eight, but he's in the garden, not putting the kids to bed." She dropped her cigarette and ground it into the earth with her shoe.

Amy walked past them, feeling their eyes on her back. There was something about the new friendship between her neighbors that reminded her of school.

Nevertheless, she felt a little pang of excitement. It had been a long time since she'd seen the inside of a house that wasn't her own, and she'd never been inside Mrs. Hill's place before.

She almost gasped as she entered. The hallway was huge. The house was a mirror image of her own, it must be, but it felt enormous.

Cavernous.

Empty.

A small bike and a tricycle leaned on the wall, and shoes that seemed impossibly small for a person to wear littered the floor. But she could see the floor, and the walls. She glanced up the stairs. The whole width could be used. Nothing to clamber over.

For a moment she imagined her life in a house like this.

Simpler. Safer.

Emptier.

She almost turned back, keen to have her possessions around her again.

No. She had to protect them. She had to ask Richard to help her with the wall.

Amy had a quick glance in the living room. Again, it seemed huge. A smattering of toys and balls adorned the floor, but they must be lonely. It felt sad to have so few possessions. She hurried on through to the kitchen, where she noticed a few dirty pans and a gorgeous smell of roasted vegetables that made her think suddenly of her grandmother. Amy hadn't cooked for herself in years. The kitchen led to the garden; no boxes blocked the path to the French doors.

Mrs. Hill had been a keen gardener in her time, but had done less and less as she got older. The light was fading fast, but Amy made out a couple of large rosebushes covered in pink flowers, lavender in full bloom, and an apple tree laden with abundant, inchoate fruit that would ripen come autumn.

Amy stepped into the grass, unmowed and at ankle height. No sign of Richard. "Hello?" she queried.

Three heads appeared from the grass. "It's Amy!" exclaimed Charles.

"Amy!" repeated his little brother, sounding excited.

"Amy?" said Richard. "From next door?" He got to his feet and started brushing grass from himself. "Welcome. Can I get you a drink?"

"Amy Amy Amy," chanted Daniel.

"No," said Amy, feeling flustered at the sudden attention. "I'm not staying."

"Stay!" ordered Daniel, wrapping his small sticky hand around hers and squeezing. "Ice cream?"

"No ice cream," said Richard firmly. He looked at Amy. "Unless you'd like some?"

"No," said Amy. "Thank you." She tried to extricate her hand, but the toddler's grip was surprisingly strong. She glanced at him and saw he was wearing a T-shirt featuring Mickey Mouse winking merrily at her.

"We're waiting for the stars," Charles told her. "Lie down and you can watch them appear. What's your favorite juice?"

Amy felt a little dizzy at the non sequitur. "I don't know," she said, remaining standing.

"If you had to pick one or else you'd die?"

"Pineapple, I suppose," said Amy. "I need to talk to your father."

"That's mine too!" exclaimed Charles. "Daniel's is apple. Dad's is orange. Nina likes grapefruit." He crinkled up his nose in disgust. "But you and me like pineapple. It's the best." He grinned at her. "I like you."

Amy took a step backwards.

"You're a bit of a hero round these parts," explained Richard, "since you stopped the boys getting into trouble over that broken mug."

Amy thought of the mug with a flash of guilt. It was still sitting in her kitchen. "I'll bring it back," she offered reluctantly.

"No rush," said Richard.

"I'm sorry about your pot," added Charles. "Was it a special one?"

"They are all special," said Amy.

"Like my JCBs," agreed Charles. He grinned at her again. "I'll show you."

"No thanks," said Amy quickly.

"I see one star!" said Daniel. He released Amy's hand and flung himself backwards so he was lying down facing the sky.

"Bit of a Saturday night tradition," explained Richard, lying down himself. "I'm enjoying it so much that I've already designed a conservatory so we can stargaze year-round. Maybe even catch a few sunsets."

"Dad's an ar-chi-tect," explained Charles, pronouncing the word carefully, as if it might break.

"Want to join us, Amy?" asked Richard, lifting his head again. "There's plenty of room on the blanket."

"No," said Amy, feeling a bit thrown by the allusion to sunsets. "I just wanted to ask you something." She hesitated. "A favor, I suppose." All three were lying down now in a little circle, their heads close to each other and their bodies fanning out like the spokes on the wheel of a bicycle. After an awkward moment watching them, Amy crouched down. Her knees clicked in objection.

"Come on," said Charles. "Lie next to me."

"And me," said Daniel.

Amy didn't feel right lying in a neighbor's garden, but she did have to talk to Richard. She sat down on the blanket next to him, clasping her arms around her knees. Richard had his hands folded under his head, and when he breathed out she could feel the rough skin of his elbow gently grazing her ankle. She shifted farther away. "About the fence . . ." she began.

"There are billions of stars," Charles told her, sitting up and wriggling closer to her. He turned towards her as he spoke, and she could smell chocolate raisins on his breath. He thrust his head backwards to look up.

"Squillions," said Daniel.

"That's not a real number," said Charles. He smiled at Amy. "He's too little to understand. Not like us."

Amy looked up. More stars were appearing as the light faded. The sky was vast and surrounded them, like a giant salad bowl over their heads. She tried to bring up the wall, but found it harder than she expected to talk of a divide when they were all sharing the same sky. Instead she blinked and looked back at the stars, feeling tiny. She used to do this a lot when Tim first went missing, finding comfort in the fact that he could be looking at the same sky.

"Shh," said Richard, although none of them had said anything. "Listen."

Amy obeyed. There was a gentle rustling sound in the leaves. "That could be a hedgehog," said Richard.

"Or a frog," said Charles.

"Or a dinosaur," contributed Daniel.

"Rachel has mice," said Amy, feeling wicked. "It could be one of them."

Birdsong rang out. "That's a robin," said Richard. "Out past its bedtime."

Amy listened, and her mind went to her own birds. "The fence," she said. "I was thinking perhaps a—"

"I've already bought a new fencing panel," Richard told her. "I'll put it up next weekend."

"Maybe something sturdier?" began Amy. "I was thinking that a wall—"

"Oh, the fence will be fine," said Richard. "It will keep the monsters out." He reached a hand out and tickled Daniel, who chortled with delight.

"We can ring the front doorbell if we want to visit Amy though, can't we, Dad?" asked Charles.

"You'll have to ask her," Richard replied.

"Can we? Please?"

Amy stood up. "I don't really think—"

"I'll bring pineapple juice," said Charles.

"And ice cream too," added Daniel.

"And JCBs," continued Charles. "A digger and a crane. The excavator is special so it stays in my room."

Amy didn't have the strength to fight back. She'd just have to spend more time pretending not to be home. "We'll see," she said as she made her way back inside, blinking in the light.

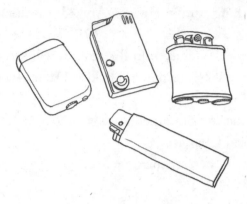

August 2000

"I can't believe they've put us on at the same time as Blur," complained Simon, the bass player in Tim's band. He looked out of the train window at the gray skies.

"I know who I'm going to choose," said Chantel. "Damon Albarn is fit."

"No one is going to come see us," said Simon, tragedy in his voice. "Our first gig at a festival will be a disaster." He leaned forwards, resting his forehead on his camping bag in a pose of dejection. "And it's raining," he muttered. "Course it is."

"I can't believe my mum is sunning herself in Dubai with Aunt Laura and I'm stuck here in the rain," complained Chantel.

"I thought your mum hated the sun?" asked Amy.

"Not as much as she hates her brother-in-law." Chantel laughed. "I think Aunt Laura bought her the ticket just to torture her. Mum would probably rather be at this gig."

"I know where I'd rather be," replied Amy loyally, taking Tim's hand. "Because this gig will be the best thing there ever was." Tim leaned in and nuzzled her ear gratefully.

"You two are disgusting," declared Chantel. "I can't believe I have to share a tent with you."

"Me neither," said Tim. He'd complained about it to Amy a lot, but she'd been adamant. Chantel had never been camping before and was terrified—and there was no way Amy would make poor Chantel share a tent with Simon. "Couldn't you buy a plane ticket?" continued Tim. "You're working now."

"Minimum wage on reception," replied Chantel. "Hardly the stuff of long-haul dreams."

"Cheer up," said Amy, glancing out the window. "The rain has stopped."

They all perked up at the sight of the sunshine cutting through the clouds, and Amy felt a little wave of excitement. Most of the people on this train looked just like them: young, scruffy, and with enormous backpacks presumably full of camping equipment, wellies, and weed.

The train finally pulled in at the station, and they followed the throngs of people through the town, across the bridge, and to the fields, joining the huge queue to get in. "Can't we line-jump?" asked Chantel. She didn't have a backpack and was hauling an out-of-place wheelie suitcase. "'Cos you guys are IN A BAND." She said the second half of the sentence loudly, but no one looked around.

"We're hardly the Chemical Brothers," said Tim, sounding rather embarrassed. "I think we wait like everyone else."

"Spoilsport," said Chantel. "What's the point of being a rock star if you don't get special treatment?"

"The music," said Tim.

"Whatever," said Chantel.

"You girls are festival virgins, right?" asked Simon. Chantel and Amy glanced at each other and nodded. "A few tips from an expert," he continued, as they finally made their way into the fields. "One. Travel light. You've already failed that one, Chantel, by bringing that ridiculous suitcase."

"I need somewhere to keep my hair straighteners," she replied.

"Course you do," said Simon with a laugh. "And where are you planning to plug them in, genius?"

"There must be plug sockets," said Chantel. "How do you plug your guitars in?"

"She's got a point," said Tim, laughing. "I can just see Chantel at the corner of the stage, straightening her hair while the Red Hot Chili's are playing."

"Got to look my best," said Chantel with a smile.

"Number two," continued Simon. "Provisions. The food on-site is overpriced and shit. Once we've dumped our stuff, we go to the Tesco in town and stock up. Sausage rolls, beer, sausage rolls. No one is eating poncy quiches and hummus near my tent. I'm looking at you, Tim."

"One time," said Tim, "and you'll never let me forget."

"Number three. Where to camp. You think you want near the loos in case of nighttime pees, but you don't. These are festival toilets and they stink. You think you want near the bushes for shelter. You don't. Bushes are makeshift loos for the lazy. They stink too. You think you want near where the bands are playing. Wrong again. People get drunk while they listen and vomit on their way back. You don't want to be on the vomit trail. It stinks."

"So where do you want to be?" asked Chantel.

"High ground," said Simon. "You want all the crap running somewhere else." Both girls pulled a face. "Midway, midfield. Minimize the risk of anyone pissing on your tent."

"I can't believe you talked me into coming to this," said Chantel. "I wish I was with my mum in Dubai."

"Just think of Damon Albarn," said Amy. "It will all be worth it."

*   *   *

"YOU, ME, AND a druid wedding at Glastonbury next year," Spike told Chantel. She giggled. Amy rolled her eyes, but Chantel was lapping it up. "I'll be back from Ibiza by then."

"I'd love to go to Ibiza," said Chantel. The girls were sitting in the chill-out tent a bit the worse for wear, and Spike had zoned in on Chantel. Handsome, probably fifteen years their senior, and with dirty blond dreadlocks and a sunburn that had faded to a deep browny-red, he exuded confidence and stank of weed. Chantel was smitten.

"Tell me your business plan again," said Amy.

"T-shirts," replied Spike. "With slogans. Clubbers will love them. I'll make my fortune." He paused. "But it's not about the money," he added, as quickly as his slow drawl could manage. "It's about the experience."

"I think it sounds amazing," said Chantel. "I've never been abroad."

"Yes you have," said Amy. "We went on that school trip to France when we were eleven. We saw the Bayeux Tapestry, remember?"

Spike laughed, and Chantel scowled at Amy. "I'd love to go to Ibiza," said Chantel again.

"Come with me," said Spike. Chantel giggled again, and Amy saw that his hand was wrapped proprietorially around her friend's thigh.

"We should find the others," said Amy, standing up.

"I'm happy here," said Chantel.

"It's getting late," argued Amy.

"You go," said Chantel. "I'll be fine."

"I'll stay," said Amy.

"No, you go," Chantel said, her voice insistent. "Find Tim."

"I'll take care of your friend," said Spike, fishing a silver tin from his pocket.

Chantel grinned. "Catch you later, Amy. Don't wait up."

BY THE TIME Chantel got back to their tent the next day, it was gone noon. She grinned at Amy again. "You smell weird," said Amy.

"Let's find the showers." But when they saw the showers on offer, they decided they were not that desperate. Then at Tesco, Chantel had a brain wave, and now here they were, enacting their plan.

"You guys are worse than Tim and his quiche," complained Simon. Amy poured water over Chantel's hair from a giant Evian bottle and massaged in shampoo. "This is not the festival spirit. You're meant to be roughing it."

"It's shampoo and conditioner in one," replied Chantel. "We are roughing it."

"You're meant to have greasy hair and stink," insisted Simon.

"I think it's hot," said Tim. "I'll wash the rest of you, Amy."

"We've got wet wipes for everywhere else," Chantel told him through a mop of wet hair. "Before you get excited."

"Mouth closed," said Amy as she dowsed Chantel's head in water. "All done. Salon-perfect."

"Maybe I should have left my hair dirty," said Chantel, producing a towel from her suitcase. "I could get dreadlocks, like Spike."

"And eight piercings, like Spike?" asked Amy.

"Nine piercings," corrected Chantel. "There's a secret one." She grinned.

"Spike smells funny," said Amy.

"We all smell funny," said Chantel. "It's a festival."

Tim glanced at his phone. "The rest of the band are checking out the audio. Come on, Simon." They got up to leave. "Not sure if we'll make it back before the gig. Nine p.m., Bacardi tent."

"We'll be there," said Amy.

"With clean hair," added Chantel. "And straighteners."

"And Spike," said Amy, rolling her eyes.

AMY STOOD AT the very front. It was a good thing that she and Chantel had got there early: it was packed. She'd barely heard the acts before Tim's band, she was so nervous on his behalf. She glanced at the sea of people behind her. This was the biggest gig Tim's band had ever had.

The boys came onstage to screams from the audience. They were unlikely to have heard these guys before, so it must be generous anticipation and festival fever. She saw Tim scan the audience, his eyes wide at the size of it. Then he spotted her and smiled. Chantel squeezed her hand.

When the band started playing, Amy realized something. All these people, but it was her he was singing to. Only her. She felt happiness well up inside her.

They played the upbeat tracks first, then slowed it down with Amy's favorite song, "Already Dark." She broke Tim's gaze for a moment to turn around and take in the crowd. The jumping had stopped, and people stood, mesmerized. Then someone got out a lighter and began waving it in the air, in time to the music.

Suddenly little flames appeared everywhere. Amy's eyes went back to Tim. He'd never looked so happy. For once Amy found herself wishing that she smoked so she could join in.

"This is worth braving those toilets for," said Chantel, who'd got out her own lighter and was waving it. Even Spike was swaying in time to the music, his arm wrapped around Chantel.

Amy nodded, her eyes locked on Tim. "It's perfect," she replied.

Chapter
Five

"**G**ood morning to you, madam. Fine day we're enjoying today. Good westerly breeze." Amy nodded politely at the elderly man who had swung the door open for her as soon as the buzzer indicated the lock was released. He wore a captain's hat and navy blazer. He stood to one side and made an elaborate sweeping gesture with his arm. "Ladies first, of course. Enjoy your visit." He saluted her, then slipped out the door as soon as she'd entered. Amy turned to see he'd begun a jaunty trot down the driveway of the Lockhart Care Home.

"Captain's gone again," shrieked an elderly lady sitting in a chair by the door, banging her hands on the armrests excitedly. Amy stepped aside as two women in white uniforms appeared and gave chase to the captain.

Amy looked around. The building was modern, with beige walls and carpets the color of smoked salmon. It smelled of disinfectant, with a hint of boiled cabbage. The reception area spilled out from what she imagined was the main sitting room, and there were a number of residents sitting in chairs. Some were clearly in their own worlds, a few were asleep, but the rest looked at her curiously. All wore slippers. It made Amy think of her grandma, determined to stay in her own home, surrounded by her memory-infused possessions till the end.

The lady who had raised the alarm waved at her. "Not your fault, dear," she told Amy. "He tries it every time. Regulars are onto him, but you weren't to know."

Amy nodded, looking out through the glass door. The captain was returning, with a staff member on each arm as if they were going for a friendly stroll on the deck of a ship. "Sea's a bit choppy," he said, nodding to Amy as he came back inside. "Set sail tomorrow." He continued on the arm of one of his escorts, while the other released him and greeted Amy.

"Sorry about that," she said. "Someone is meant to be on reception to stop that kind of thing happening, but if residents need us, we get called away. We're short-staffed. He never gets far. Now, how can I help?"

Amy hesitated. "I'm here to visit Arnold Putney," she said. She put her hand in her pocket and clutched the piece of paper on which his grandson had written the name and address of the care home.

"Ah yes, his grandson called to tell us you were coming. Lovely old gentleman. He's just finished lunch, I believe, and will be back in his room." Amy glanced at her watch. Noon.

"We feed them early," the staff member told her. "Room twenty-four. Along that corridor and up the stairs."

Amy followed the instructions. She paused outside his door, wondering what she was doing here. There was no way a ninety-five-year-old man would remember selling a ring more than four years ago. And if he did, what did it mean? Tim was still gone. She was clutching a small bag of shopping, and glanced inside it to steady her nerves. She could see a small wine bottle peeking back up at her, as if to ask her what she had to lose. Nothing, she decided, and knocked on the door.

"Come in, love," said a voice, presumably Arnold's. Amy obeyed.

The room was small but bright, with a single bed, a couple of chairs for visitors that had the institutional feel of a headmaster's office, and a coffee table with a little lamp. One shelf was covered in framed family photographs, including several Amy recognized as the man from the shop as a small boy. A luscious ficus sat in one corner. The pot was a nice rendition of the willow pattern.

Arnold was sitting in a chair that faced the window, but he slowly started to stand up when Amy entered and was twisting around to see her. "Oh, don't go to any trouble," she said, visualizing a nasty fall and broken hip.

He ignored her, and successfully got to his feet and maneuvered himself to face her. "Not at all," he said. "Lovely to have such a beautiful visitor. What gorgeous chestnut hair you have. And those eyes." He paused, and Amy felt his eyes inspecting her. "You look familiar. Have we met before?"

"Not really," said Amy.

"No matter. Come, pull up a chair next to me."

Amy carefully put her bag on the bed, then lifted one of the chairs and placed it a healthy distance from Arnold's. "It's good of you to see me," she said. He tottered a little bit, and Amy realized he was reaching out a hand for hers. She hurried to take it, alarmed at his unsteadiness. He grabbed her hand and lifted it to his mouth, placing a long, wet, and rather gummy kiss there. Amy did her best not to grimace, then reclaimed her hand and sat down. Arnold began the process of sitting down too, and Amy jumped up to help him.

"Thank you, darling," he said, then looked at her expectantly. She sat down and looked back. "Did you bring me a little something?"

"Of course," she said, jumping up again and going to her bag. She removed the half-size bottle of red wine that his grandson had told her to buy.

Arnold grinned. "There's an empty black currant juice bottle in the bedside drawer," he told her, his voice an exaggerated whisper. "Be a love and fill it up, will you?"

Amy obeyed, careful not to spill any on the pink carpet, then gave the bottle to him. He lifted it to his lips and took a shaky swig. "It's not a bad place, this," he said, wiping his mouth and breathing out a satisfied sigh. "Proper cooked breakfast and hot lunch. Just sandwiches at dinner, mind. But they've got a ridiculous no-booze policy. Like anyone would notice if us lot were drunk." He laughed and offered her the bottle. "Half of us are off our rockers anyway."

Amy shook her head. "It's yours," she said.

"So, what can I do you for?" Arnold beamed at her, clearly in a good mood. He took another swig of the wine and Amy watched a drip escape from his mouth and make a run for it down his chin. He reached his tongue out and caught it, frog-like and surprisingly quick. "Sure you don't want any? You look like you could use a drink."

"I'm fine," said Amy. "Thank you for meeting with me."

"My grandson said you had something you wanted to show me, from the shop?"

Amy removed her necklace, then slid the ring off and held it out to Arnold. He took it, then reached into a pocket and popped on a pair of glasses. He peered at it carefully. She watched him, looking for a sign of recognition on his face.

"I liked stocking jewelry," he told her. "I never had much of it and it always took a while to sell, so I remember every piece. It was Dave who stopped it, in the end. My grandson. I think he was worried we'd be robbed. But I liked seeing the expression on people's faces when they buy something special like this. Some women bought jewelry as a treat for themselves. Sometimes men came in to buy stuff as an apology. God knows what they'd done."

He looked at Amy, who nodded patiently. "Do you remember this ring?" she asked.

"I liked to imagine who'd buy which piece, and why. I wasn't always right, of course. I remember, I picked out a lovely brooch, Art Deco it was, silver filigree in the shape of a dainty little beetle. Citrine for eyes. I was sure that one would be bought by a man who had a wife who loved gardening. But then this woman came in, must have been about your age, and got it for her twelve-year-old son. He liked bugs and jewelry. Strange world, eh?"

Amy nodded again. "And this ring?"

"My Dave sounded quite taken with you," Arnold said. "Said you bought that owl?"

"It's lovely," said Amy. Her thwarted longing to know about the ring was curdling in her throat.

"Ah yes, I can tell you have a good eye. Artist, are you?"

"Yes," replied Amy, taken aback. "Well, no. Not anymore."

Arnold took another sip, then looked down at the ring again. "This ring," he said, his voice affectionate. "I always knew it would be bought for love."

"You remember it?" Amy leaned forwards. She could smell wine and black currants on Arnold's breath. "You remember who bought it?"

"I picked it up at a car boot sale," he continued. "Got it as part of a job lot. Some junk, some fun costume stuff, a rather lovely malachite bracelet. But really I bought it all for that ring." He frowned at it. "Lovely Art Deco piece," he said. He handed it back to her. "Aquamarines aren't the priciest of stones, and the diamonds are tiny, but it is very elegant, don't you think?"

The ring felt warm from Arnold's grasp, and Amy allowed herself to slip it onto her finger. "But you don't remember who bought it," she said eventually.

Arnold looked up. "Of course I do," he said. "I'd been imagining who'd buy this for years, and the lad fitted the bill perfectly. Tall chap. Dark hair. Handsome. Bit fidgety. Hummed under his breath a lot."

Amy squeezed the ring. That was Tim.

"I thought he was sure to propose," said Arnold. "That the ring was for an engagement. I can tell when someone is in love."

"No," said Amy. "He didn't."

"Shame," said Arnold sadly.

"I haven't seen him in over eleven years," she added.

"Eleven years," said Arnold. "That's about the time I sold the ring, give or take a year or two. Maeve was still alive, because I remember telling her about it. It was the most expensive thing in my shop at the time. I remember wondering how a lad like that had found the money." He grinned. "Not crazy money, like some of those rings in the Hatton Garden stores, mind, but more expensive than a china bird. Higher margin too." He winked at her, and Amy was reminded of his grandson.

"Thank you," she said, wanting to think about the significance of what she'd discovered. Tim had bought the ring around the time he'd disappeared. "You've been very helpful."

"Not a problem, darling," he said. "My grandson visits, but it's good to have the company of a pretty young lady like yourself." Amy certainly didn't think of herself as young anymore. Everything was relative, she supposed.

"Look after that ring," he told her. "It's a lovely piece, very much of its time. Understated. But still beautiful." He looked up at Amy. "Like you."

THE RING COULDN'T talk. It could only hint, and Amy could infer. But hearing the words from Arnold—*love, engagement, propose* . . . She had to try again. She had to try to find Tim again.

What if she'd been wrong all these years? What if she hadn't been betrayed at all?

Amy shivered. If he hadn't left to be with Chantel, what had happened? And where was Chantel?

Amy's hands flew over the keyboard on Monday morning. Of course she wouldn't find him online; she'd tried that many times.

But perhaps she could track down his old friends. It had been eleven years. Perhaps someone had heard something.

"Are you looking at Facebook?"

Damn Carthika and her constant nosiness.

"You told us we shouldn't be on there, even at lunchtime. No place in the office for social media, you said."

"There's every place for social media," said Liam, approaching their bank of desks. "Twitter is the future of marketing."

Carthika rolled her eyes behind his back, and he sat down on Amy's desk. She pulled the Apex file to one side just in time. "Can I help you?" she asked reluctantly.

"I hope so," he replied, smiling at her. His teeth looked brighter than they had the last time she'd seen him, and she wondered if he'd been whitening them. He didn't elaborate on his hopes, and remaining seated on her desk, blocking her access to her keyboard.

"Well?" she prompted.

"Ah yes," he replied. "I'm doing an internal communications piece, and I need someone to sound out reactions."

What a waste of time, thought Amy. "I'm sorry, I'm very busy," she said.

"You were on Facebook!" said Carthika unhelpfully. "After you told us not to, even at lunch."

"That's not true," said Amy, although that did sound a little bit familiar. "What you do in your lunch hour is up to you."

"It's not lunchtime now," said Carthika, taking an exaggerated look at her wrist. Amy noticed she wasn't even wearing a watch. "Tut-tut."

"If you must know, I was in at half seven and am taking an early lunch break," said Amy. She gestured to a cheese and pickle sandwich she'd picked up from the supermarket. "Not that I need to justify myself," she added, starting to feel annoyed. "I've never taken a cigarette break. Unlike some."

"Chill out." Carthika laughed. "I won't tell. And for your information, I've cut down to ten a day. Practically a nonsmoker."

Liam smiled again at the exchange. "So you'll help?" he said.

"I'll nominate Carthika," said Amy.

"I really think you would be—"

"Carthika it is," said Amy. "Would you mind . . ." She gestured to him to get off her desk.

"Of course," he replied. He dismounted with a disappointed thud and walked back to his desk.

"Back to work," said Amy. Carthika was staring daggers at her. "I need to get back to my research."

"Facebook research?" said Carthika. "And all that makeup last week." She grinned. "Are you tracking down an ex-boyfriend—" She stopped short, then said quickly, "I'm sorry, I didn't mean . . . Of course, I'm so stupid, I shouldn't—"

"It's fine," said Amy, discovering her jaw was clenched. She'd never discussed what had happened with Carthika, but clearly she'd been the subject of office gossip. "The Jessop accounts need filing."

Carthika went back to her work, uncharacteristically quiet. Amy took a minute to swallow her emotions, then allowed her gaze to return to the screen. She just wouldn't think about it. That was best. Perhaps a little distraction would help.

Amy opened a new window and went to the ceramics section of the Oxfam website. She bought an ashtray in the shape of an upturned tortoise. Feeling better, she opened her packet of sandwiches and took a bite.

She was interrupted by an instant message popping up. Liam. She chewed her sandwich and frowned. She'd suggested to Mr. Trapper that instant messaging be turned off. Her team seemed to use it to chat to one another while appearing to be working, occasionally betraying themselves with a guffaw of laughter.

Perhaps Liam was using the system appropriately, thought Amy generously. For a message more urgent than e-mail but less intrusive than the phone or another visit to her desk. She read the message.

Nice to chat to you today.

Hardly important. She deleted it without replying.

Another appeared. If you won't help me with my research, maybe you'd like to join me for a drink?

Flakes of Amy's half-chewed sandwich launched themselves from her mouth onto her screen. She coughed and took a gulp of water.

"You okay?" asked Carthika.

"Fine," stuttered Amy. She minimized the message and went back to the Oxfam site. Her fingers hovered over the image of a porcelain canary perched on a gnarled branch. She added it to her basket, then chose a pretty yellow cup and saucer set adorned with a pink lily.

Another message. How about it? The words were followed by an image of a fat little face indulging in what Amy guessed was meant to be a wink.

She wouldn't normally reply to instant messages, but Amy decided this time she must. No thank you, she typed. For any further research questions please liaise directly with Carthika via e-mail.

Feeling a little better, she went back to Facebook. Of course, she didn't really go in for social media. Meeting people in person was bad enough, without having to see pictures of people's kids, dogs, and dinners. But she'd kept her profile open all these years. Just in case.

She had a surprising number of friend requests from people she used to know. Some of them she barely remembered, but other names brought back vivid memories. George Matthew. She'd doubled over in laughter when he'd got a sunflower seed stuck up his nose in primary school. Mary Cook. She'd solemnly told Amy that her dog had got pregnant by sniffing a baby. Georgina Pewter. She'd deliberately wet herself, age eleven, in PE when the teacher refused her a toilet break. Georgina had giggled while she did it and dropped her hockey stick in the puddle.

Amy ignored the requests. Another message popped up from Liam. This one was only a face, and it seemed to be crying. Amy felt a pang of pity; then she saw the face was also smiling. Crying with laughter, she realized. Whatever next. Amy deleted the message and did a search on Facebook. There he was.

Simon Oaks.

His profile picture showed him onstage clutching a bass guitar. Amy scanned his other photos and found a few shots of his band. She didn't recognize any of the members from the old days—presumably more "artistic differences." He and Tim used to have them all the time, though they'd stuck together.

Until they hadn't.

Amy looked and saw that he had a little green circle next to his name. He was online now.

No time like the present, she told herself, and took the plunge.

AMY ENDURED A long hug. "I can't believe it's you," he said, as if Simon were expecting someone to have hacked her Facebook account, arranged a meeting, and then impersonated her. "You look the same. As gorgeous as ever."

Amy knew that wasn't true, and she couldn't bring herself to return the lie. Simon had the look of a shoe even Amy would decide was ready to be retired: well-worn and less than fresh. But his smile was the same, taking over his whole face until his eyes crinkled. She was surprised that he seemed genuinely pleased to see her.

"It's good of you to meet me at such short notice," said Amy. She'd been a little taken aback when he'd turned out to be in town and proposed getting together that very evening. She'd fished around for an excuse, but found none. And here they were, hugging outside a pub on a quiet street near the station.

Amy extracted herself from the embrace with the excuse of buying him a drink. He settled down on a green leather sofa near the door, and Amy marched to the bar, trying to compose herself. She ordered a gin and tonic, ignoring the barman's suggestion to make it a double. She bought a pint of "whatever's on tap" for Simon that came, to her relief, in a rather sturdy and unattractive vessel. At least she wouldn't have to worry about something more fragile in Simon's always rather shaky hands.

She delivered the drinks and graciously clinked glasses with him. Simon took a long draft of beer and grinned at her again. "It's good to see you," he said. "Course it is."

Amy nodded.

"The band is going strong," Simon volunteered. "Did you meet Tony? Best drummer we've ever had."

"No," said Amy.

"Oh yes," continued Simon, warming to his theme. "You should hear us now. Completely different sound. More cosmic. Hoping to get a gig soon at the Sheep and Goat. You should come."

"Maybe," said Amy, who couldn't think of anything worse. They sat in silence for a moment.

"So I saw on Facebook that you're single still," said Simon. "Never settled down myself either. Had a few goes, but you know how it is. Never found the right woman." He looked at her expectantly. Amy nodded noncommittally. "Phil married off, couple of rug rats. And Idris too. He had twins with Sandy, remember her?"

"Of course," said Amy. She felt in her pocket for the ring. "I have to admit," she began, "I have an ulterior motive for inviting you here."

"I thought so," said Simon, smiling at her. "We always did have a connection. Course we did."

"What?" said Amy.

"Chemistry," continued Simon. "Wouldn't have been right back then, of course, but now . . ." He paused. "It's really nice to see you. You look great." Amy started to wish she'd not applied that blusher Joanna had given her. She took a sip of her gin and tonic, feeling the ice cube clink against her teeth.

"Let me stop you there," she said. He frowned at her. "There's something I need to show you." She took the ring from her pocket and held it out to him.

"You should wear that on your finger," he scolded, leaning back in his chair and taking a swig of beer. "It's just rude, leaving it off. Gives a guy the wrong idea."

"I didn't mean to—"

He leaned forwards again, and enclosed her ring-free hand in his own. His hand was a surprise, warm and rough. "Sorry," he said. "I'm happy for you. Course I am. I'm glad you've found someone. After what happened, we all thought you might—" He stopped himself.

"You misunderstand me," said Amy. "This ring"—she popped it onto her finger—"I haven't met anyone else. It's from Tim."

Simon raised an eyebrow. "From Tim?" he repeated.

"Yes," said Amy. She paused.

"You've seen him?" he asked. He narrowed his eyes at Amy, and she could tell he thought she'd lost it.

"Of course not," said Amy. "He's been gone for years."

"That's right," affirmed Simon.

"I found it," she continued. "In my garden. I don't know how long it's been there, it was buried under . . ." She paused again. ". . . a few bits and pieces. But he knew I liked this ring. He was the only one who knew. So he must have . . ." She stopped.

"I always thought he loved you," said Simon. "Course I did. I was as shocked as anyone when it happened."

"Did he ever mention to you . . ."

"Never," said Simon. "Not the ring, not Chantel. Nothing. We were having some creative differences at the time though. You remember."

"Yes," replied Amy.

"So I was surprised when he told you he was meeting me that night," said Simon. "He wasn't, course he wasn't. But it was nice, in a way, being the cover story. I always thought it meant he still considered me a friend, even when he was planning to leave."

"And he hasn't been in contact, all these years?"

"Nope," said Simon. "If he contacted anyone, I think it would be you."

"Not if he left with Chantel," said Amy, bitterness creeping into her voice.

"I don't believe that," said Simon. "Never did. Tim needed you. You were his rock. Chantel couldn't be a rock, she was adrift at sea herself." He smiled. "Sounds like that would be a decent line for a song, don't you think? I might write that down."

Amy watched as Simon grabbed a pen and started scribbling on a beer mat, ignoring a scowl from the barman. "You were all of our rocks," added Simon when he was done. "Tim, Chantel. And me." He hesitated, and Amy saw a cloud of hurt drift across his features. "I think it was you that I missed the most," he said. "When they went missing."

"I've been here," said Amy.

"You were at first," he said. "When you thought I might be able to help you find them. But when you found out I didn't know anything, you stopped calling too."

"I was upset," said Amy, feeling the need to defend herself.

"Course you were," said Simon. "I was too. You guys were my best mates. When those other two went, I thought maybe we'd get closer. But it was like you went missing too."

Amy hesitated. She had never thought of herself and Simon as particularly close, but they had a lot of shared history, shared experiences. Even a shared flat for a long time. She supposed they had been friends too. And she'd left him—just like Tim and Chantel had left her.

"I'm sorry," she said.

"Water under the bridge," said Simon, his voice falsely light. He held his beer up to Amy and they chinked glasses again, the sound of glass on glass making Amy flinch.

"Anyway," babbled Simon, clearly wanting to lighten the maudlin tone, "I hadn't seen him for a little while before he was off for good. He'd fallen in with some others, a bad crowd."

"What others?" asked Amy, her ears pricking.

"House music fans. Up to no good. Wouldn't know decent music if it hits them in the earhole. He even went to a few 'gigs' with them. Not that you can call that stuff a gig."

"Right before . . . it happened? I don't remember that."

"It was probably while you were away in Florence."

Amy nodded. "Do you have names?"

"No chance. Only met them once myself. Seemed nasty." He stood up. "Another drink? We've got a lot to catch up on."

"No thanks," said Amy. "I need to get home." She hesitated. "But another time," she added. "I've missed you." As soon as she said the words, Amy realized she meant them.

Simon smiled at her, his face brightening. "For sure," he said. "Course you have."

SHE HEARD IT before she saw him. *Boing boing boing.* Irregular, arrhythmic. Sure enough, Charles was bouncing his ball outside her house. "I'm being careful of your pots," he preempted. "Look, the ball is under control. That's fifty-six bounces now." The ball rebelled and bounced away from his hand at an acute angle just as he said that. Charles gave chase. He bent down to coax it out from under a parked car. "You put me off," he scolded her.

Amy nodded and walked past him to go into her house.

"It's okay," said Charles. "I don't mind. I've finished now anyway." Amy turned and realized he'd followed her up her garden path, his ball fitted neatly under his arm.

"Isn't it a bit late for you to be out?" she asked.

"I'm eight and a half now," said Charles. Amy looked at him blankly. "That's almost nine," he explained, then added, "You're late too. Where have you been?"

"Nowhere interesting," said Amy. She wanted to open her door and go inside, but she'd much rather the boy and his ball were at a safe distance first.

"Was it a date?" asked Charles.

"That is certainly none of your business," said Amy, surprised. "Now, if you don't mind—"

"Would you like a pineapple juice?"

Amy found she was rather thirsty after that gin and tonic and would like a pineapple juice, but she wasn't going to admit it now. Not when she needed to go inside and plan her next steps. "No thank you," she said. "Won't your parents be worried about you?"

"My dad knows where I am," said Charles confidently. "And Mum is dead."

He said it so matter-of-factly that Amy didn't know what to say.

"Is Nina home?" she asked finally.

"She's at Rachel's house," said Charles. "They are besties now." He grimaced.

"Maybe I will have that juice," she said, remembering Richard's invitation to pop in. "Just quickly."

Charles let out a whoop of joy. "You're the first friend I've had to visit here," he told her, taking her hand in his own clammy one and leading her to his front door, where he released her hand again to struggle with the key for a moment. "Do you like diggers?"

"Not particularly," replied Amy. She followed him. He turned around to shush her as they walked past the living room. She glanced inside. Richard sitting on the sofa with Daniel curled up on top of him, with a little stream of dribble running from his mouth onto his father's T-shirt. Richard waved and put his finger to his lips in a gesture of silence. Amy crept past. They both looked so comfortable, so relaxed. So happy.

"Excavators?" asked Charles, when they reached the kitchen.

"What?"

"Do you like excavators? I've got a really good one. Fully to scale, just like the one they use on real-life building sites. Dad gave it to me for my eighth birthday, because I've been so good."

"Not really," replied Amy. Charles took the juice from the fridge. He filled a glass to the very brim with the bright-yellow liquid, and some swilled out onto the floor as he walked over to where she'd perched awkwardly at the small breakfast bar. He lifted her glass to his mouth and siphoned some up before passing it to her.

"Cranes?"

Amy thought a moment. "I suppose they are all right," she said. "For lifting stuff up high."

"Great choice," said Charles enthusiastically. "Cranes are awesome. They are my third-favorite heavy vehicle, after diggers and excavators. Do you want to see my collection?"

"Maybe later," said Amy, sipping her juice. It was wonderfully cold and made her think that she should get her fridge seen to. Nothing ever got this cold at home. Then she thought about having a repairman in her house, and changed her mind.

"I like your ring," said Charles all of a sudden. "Are you married?"

"No," replied Amy. She paused, trying to think of something else to say.

"Good," said Charles. He paused too. "My dad isn't married to Nina."

Amy nodded, and took another sip of her juice.

"The ring is a bit of a mystery," she confided. It felt weird to talk about it to this little boy, but once the words were out it was a relief. "I found it in my garden. After the cat knocked over the pots."

"Finders keepers," said Charles approvingly.

"I think it was meant for me," said Amy. "From my boyfriend."

"You have a boyfriend?" Charles picked at a scab on his knee.

"No," said Amy. "He left, a long time ago." She paused. "Disappeared."

"My mum's gone," said Charles. "That's pineapple juice and losing people that we have in common. And cranes." He paused. "So where is he now?"

"I don't know," replied Amy.

"Did you call the police?" asked Charles, looking excited.

"Of course I called the police," said Amy. "As soon as he went missing."

"Police cars are my seventh-favorite vehicle," Charles told her. "After diggers, excavators, cranes, fire engines—"

"They searched for months," interrupted Amy. "Nothing."

Charles paused. "What do they think happened?"

Amy took a sip of juice. She didn't like talking about their explanation. "Someone else left at the same time as he did," she said slowly.

"The murderer!" said Charles. "It's obvious."

"No," said Amy. "It was my best friend. The police thought that they'd run away together, and I thought that too, eventually. But now I've found the ring, and it makes me think that maybe they didn't run away together after all. . . ."

"Oh," said Charles. He frowned.

"What's going on in here?" Richard stood in the kitchen doorway. His hair was even messier than usual, mirroring the shape of the couch cushions. Daniel stood next to him, thumb in mouth.

"It's private," said Charles. "Go away."

"No, I'll go," said Amy. She hesitated. "Thank you," she said to Charles.

"You should go back to the police," said Charles. "Tell them you've got a new clue."

"Police?" asked Richard. "Amy, are you okay?"

"*Nee-nor nee-nor*," contributed Daniel.

"It's nothing," said Amy. "I need to get going." She turned to Charles. "Thank you," she said again. "The pineapple juice was lovely."

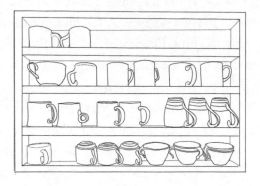

July 2002

"Great to have you on board, Amy. It's nice to have a younger face around. Freshens the place up." Mr. Trapper smiled at Amy, and she felt her glorious summer slipping away.

"Thank you," she said. "It's only for a month," she added, more for her benefit than his.

"Of course. Fine arts student, your gran said. Maybe you can brighten up the office. In between photocopying, I mean." They both looked at the drab gray office, the only color a framed photo of Mr. Trapper's baby daughter, her head encased in a candy-floss-pink hat as she stared accusingly into the camera.

"I can try," said Amy. "But I'd better get going now." She bent down to pick up her bag, keen not to spend longer here than she needed to until she was being paid her seven pounds an hour.

"I'll introduce you to Margery," said Mr. Trapper. "She can show you the ropes, that way you can hit the ground running on Monday." He stood up, and Amy reluctantly followed him down a staircase to a drab-looking elderly woman sipping coffee and critically examining her fingernails. "Margery, this is Amy. Her gran sings with Mrs. Trapper in the church choir. Fine soprano."

Margery looked up, seemingly unimpressed by the familial connection. "She'll be helping you over the summer," continued Mr. Trapper. "Photocopying, typing, deliveries, and the like." He smiled benevolently, ignoring the fact that Margery was still scowling. "I'll leave you two to get acquainted," he said, heading back to his office.

"It's nice to meet you," said Amy, holding out her hand.

"We're very busy here," said Margery, taking another sip of coffee and ignoring the proffered hand. "You'll hardly get a moment to yourself. Slave driver, that Mr. Trapper."

"Really?" said Amy politely.

"Oh yes," replied Margery. "Get yourself a coffee now, while you still can. Then you'll need to load the photocopier. It's out of paper. I'm rushed off my feet." She glanced at her shoe, then back at Amy, as if to prove her point.

"I don't actually start till Monday," said Amy apologetically. "I think Mr. Trapper just thought we could meet and, you know, you could tell me a bit about the job—"

"Monday it is," said Margery, turning back to her computer. "Coffee's gone cold," she added, scowling again. "It's a madhouse here."

AMY TOOK THE mug of tea from Tim. They were sharing; it was Simon's turn to do the washing up, and he was in his room sleeping off a hangover. The others, Tim included and by proxy Amy, were refusing to clean a single item in protest.

Amy didn't mind. Sitting cross-legged on his bed, she took a sip and passed it back, enjoying the simple intimacy. The painting she'd given him hung on the opposite wall, making the room feel as if it were in a constant state of sunset. "It was awful," she continued. "The room I'd be working in is in the basement so there's not even any light. And the photocopiers make this weird whir and blow out hot air, and Mr. Trapper said to watch out if I put my hand in there to unblock a jam because the last girl burned herself."

"Welcome to the world of work," said Tim. He'd taken some shifts stacking supermarket shelves to supplement his income from the band. "It's shit." He raised the mug to her in a mock cheers. "At least you'll be getting decent money."

"It will be worth it," said Amy. "It means I can stay in town over the summer." She looked at him, hoping he'd take the hint. They'd been together almost four years now. Surely it was time. "And see more of you."

"About that," said Tim. He passed her the mug back, and Amy gripped it in anticipation. It felt smooth and hot, and Amy realized her palms were sweaty. "I was thinking, you'll be here most nights anyway. I know it's not the Ritz or anything, and there are always piles of washing-up around, but maybe if Simon knew there was a lady here, he'd get his finger out—"

"Yes," squealed Amy. She squeezed the mug, then put it down and flung her arms around Tim, burying her face in his neck. "I'd love to move in with you. Thank you." She released him and beamed up.

"I didn't expect you to be quite so thrilled," he said, smiling back at her. "You have seen our bathroom? Four guys sharing a place, it's not exactly—"

"I don't care," said Amy, her summer taking shape again in her mind. A flat share in Camden. Every night with Tim. Waking up with him each morning and not worrying about whether she'd remembered to pack clean clothes. "It's perfect."

"You're perfect," said Tim. He leaned forwards and kissed her. "Let's celebrate," he said, gently nuzzling her ear. "I think I'm going to like sharing a room with you."

*   *   *

THE AFTERNOON SUN spilled through the flimsy pink curtain, casting Tim's sleeping face with a glow that reminded Amy of strawberry ice cream on a hot summer's day. She couldn't resist.

Amy grabbed the mug that sat on the bedside table and took it to the bathroom to add a little water. On the advice of her art professor, she didn't just carry a sketchbook with her anymore. She had a small watercolor set, a few brushes, and a pad with thick, coarse paper just waiting to be painted on. She knew now that color was at the heart of her art, and pencils, though convenient, would never do that justice.

Amy settled herself on the carpet, ignoring the biscuit crumbs and tobacco shag that kept her company, and, dipping a wide brush into the mug of water, she started to paint. Not Tim's features, but the color of his skin as the sun poured through the curtain. The color of his dark hair, shining almost blue in the light. He snored, and she took a finer brush, using it to create tiny flecks of movement above him.

It wasn't perfect, but it gave her the memory she needed. She'd use it as a base for something in oils next time she was in the studio. But she'd need texture. Amy stood up, stretched, and a pouch of tobacco caught her eye. She pocketed it: she'd mix tiny flecks of tobacco with the paint. Perfect.

She looked back to Tim. His eyes were open and he was watching her. "If you wanted to start smoking, you could just ask for a rollie," he said, rubbing his eyes and stretching luxuriantly. "You don't need to wait till I'm asleep to snaffle it."

"Sorry," said Amy, removing it from her pocket and perching on the edge of the bed. "I was going to use it for an art project—"

"Take it," said Tim with a laugh, sitting up. "I've got plenty. I knew it would be something like that. I was only joking." He noticed the sketchbook. "Let me see."

"It's just preparation," said Amy, feeling embarrassed as she always did revealing a picture that wasn't finished. She moved it out of his reach and glanced at her watch: it was 2 p.m., so Mr. Trapper would likely be back from lunch. She jumped up to get her phone. She should let him know as soon as she could that she wouldn't need that job after all. He could find some other poor unfortunate to spend her summer burning herself on photocopiers.

"Where are you going?" asked Tim.

"I'm going to tell Mr. Trapper where to stick his job," she said. "Politely, of course."

"What? Why?"

Amy looked at Tim in confusion. "If I don't have to find a place for the summer, I won't need to work the whole time." She smiled. "Maybe I'll do a little bar work and still be able to do that trip to Florence. . . ."

"Oh," said Tim. "Yes, of course." He smiled at her, then glanced at his watch. "Right. I have to get going. I've got a double shift at the supermarket, then we've got that gig tonight. You're coming, aren't you?"

"I wouldn't miss it," said Amy.

"Great," Tim replied. "I'm on an early tomorrow though, so I can't stay up late. Enjoy telling Mr. Trapper where to go."

"Yes," said Amy. She watched Tim pulling on his trousers. She realized he had bags under his eyes and his skin, always rather fair, had an unhealthy gray pallor when he was out of the sunlight. Perhaps it wasn't just cigarettes and alcohol. Perhaps it was exhaustion. "You are working hard," she said, "with the band and the supermarket."

"It will be worth it," said Tim. "When we get signed. There's a scout coming next week, did I tell you? Then all our money problems will be over."

"Money problems?" repeated Amy.

"Shitty jobs and crummy flats," said Tim. "It won't be for much longer." He smiled at her. "It's given me an idea for a new song, actually. I just need to work out the harmonies. Perhaps I'll have time to play around with it after the shifts tomorrow. Who needs sleep anyway?"

"I'm taking that job," declared Amy suddenly.

"What? It sounds horrible."

"I want to help," she said. "I'll take that job and we'll share the money. You can cut down your shifts and spend more time on your music."

"No, Amy," said Tim. "What about Florence?"

"Florence can wait," said Amy. She closed her eyes a moment, thinking of the colors she'd miss. The pink, green, and white marble outer panels of the cathedral basilica, the orange of its dome. The vibrant reds of the pasta sauces, even the murky greens of the Arno. She opened her eyes again. None of that compared to Tim, looking at her with concern as he took a sip from the mug.

The mug she'd used for her brushes.

"Stop!" cried Amy. "Don't drink that!"

He spat the water back into the mug. "And I thought Simon was disgusting," he said, pulling a face. "Has my tongue changed color?" He stuck it out for Amy to inspect.

Amy started to laugh—a giggle that grew out of control, until she was laughing hysterically. Suddenly Tim was laughing too, and she found his arms encircling her and his face buried into her neck. "What have I let myself in for, living with you?" he muttered as he kissed her.

She felt the cold china of the mug press against her cheek and Tim's hot breath by her lips. "I needed somewhere to rinse my brushes," she managed to say between laughs and kisses.

"Once I've got a recording contract, you won't have to pay a penny," said Tim. He leaned back, and his face was serious again. "I'll even buy you some proper brush-washing pots, whatever they are called. And if they give me an advance, you might even be on your way to Florence before the summer is up."

Amy watched as Tim reached over, grabbed his tin, and started to roll a joint. "What are you doing?"

"I'm a kept man," joked Tim. "I'm having a smoke and then I'm calling in sick and later I'm going to write you a love song like you've never heard." He grinned at her and lit up, using the empty mug as an ashtray. "I'll make it up to you, Amy Ashton," he said merrily. "Just you wait."

Chapter Six

The police station hadn't changed much in eleven years, on the outside at least. It had been brand-new at the time, the pride of the borough. Amy remembered the smell of freshly dried paint and newly laid carpets. Back then, some of the windows still had a layer of plastic to be peeled off, as if the police were putting it off until the last minute to keep the glass from scratches, the way Amy liked to do with the screen of a new phone. The trees outside, once scrawny little sticks with barely a leaf, had flourished into fine specimens, reminding Amy that time had passed.

A lot of time.

Amy took a breath and entered the revolving door, getting out as quickly as she could on the other side. She remembered disliking the doors then too: they sucked you in and spat you out like the currents of the ocean.

She'd phoned ahead and discovered that Chantel's ex-boyfriend Jack still worked there. Amy still couldn't believe that Chantel had ever been in a relationship with a policeman—such a contrast to

Spike. And now Jack was no ordinary policeman: he was Detective Chief Inspector Hooper.

Jack hadn't been on the case back then; it would have been a conflict of interest. It was his girlfriend, after all, who had disappeared. But he had always seemed to know what was going on. And at least Amy could rely on him to remember what had happened. The special constable on reception guided her through a corridor with heavy fire doors every few meters, which he diligently held open for her. He led her through a busy open-plan office to a large glass door. He knocked, a friendly "enter" was given in reply, and Amy found herself through the door.

Jack stood up to greet her, reaching out a tanned hand. He'd aged well. He'd been strong and muscly eleven years ago, but had always struck Amy as hungry. The last decade had filled him out with a softer twenty pounds that he wore like an expensive jacket. He smiled at her, and Amy found herself feeling uncomfortable in his presence. "Amy Ashton," he said, greeting her like an old friend. "It's so good to see you."

Amy nodded. "Congratulations on . . ." She gestured at the surroundings.

"Thank you," he agreed. "I've been lucky. Take a seat. Tea? Coffee?"

Amy felt a hot drink was too much of an imposition for the suddenly important-seeming DCI Jack Hooper. But she could feel the insides of her mouth drying out, as if filled with cotton wool. "Water?" she requested.

Jack pressed a button on his phone and ordered a still water for Amy and a cappuccino for himself. "I don't think we'd even had the coffee machines installed last time you were here," he said conversationally.

"No," said Amy. Sweet tepid tea sprang to her memory so vividly she could taste it. "You didn't."

"Things have changed," he said with a smile. "And how are you?"

Amy was saved from answering by the arrival of the drinks. His coffee was served in a surprisingly elegant bone china mug that looked rather vulnerable in his large hands. Amy found herself worrying for it even as she sipped from her own rather ordinary glass. She took the opportunity to change the subject.

"I found something. In my garden," she told him. She paused. "It may seem like nothing, but I thought it might have a bearing on what happened to Tim. And Chantel."

"Eleven years ago?" Jack looked surprised.

"I'm still in the same house," explained Amy. "Where we all lived together."

"Go on," he said.

Amy pulled the ring from her handbag. She'd grown tired of constantly sliding it on and off the chain or in and out of her pocket, but had felt it didn't look much like evidence when she wore it on her finger. At Charles's suggestion, she'd placed it inside a sandwich bag. He'd assured her that was how the police liked to look at clues. "Fingerprints and DNA," he'd said, unperturbed when she told him she'd not only handled it constantly but also polished it. She handed the bag to Jack.

"It's a ring," she explained. He peered inside the bag and nodded agreement. "Tim bought it," continued Amy. "Before he disappeared. That's been confirmed by the owner of the shop. I think he was going to give it to me. To propose."

Jack nodded again. "Very possibly." He gave her a sympathetic smile and handed the bag back. "It's good that you have this," he said, his voice gentle. "You need memories. Thank you for showing it to me."

Amy frowned at him. "But this is significant, don't you think?"

"How so?"

"I know you always thought that because they disappeared at the same time that they'd left together. On purpose."

"We don't know what happened. That is one of several explanations, and it did seem the likeliest to me. You agreed, eventually. Remember?"

"But why would he leave with her if he wanted to marry me?"

Jack took another sip of his coffee. "We both got our hearts broken back then," he said, his professionalism fading to softness. "I was devastated when Chantel left me. They must have just wanted to be together, and we were collateral damage."

"That's what you always said," said Amy. "But the ring—it suggests otherwise. Tim was the only person who knew I liked this ring. We'd looked at it together in the old antique shop near where I used to live. When we saw it, Tim even said that it was right for an engagement. And then, all of a sudden, it appears in my garden." Amy thought of what Charles had said. "It's a clue."

"I'm sorry," said Jack, shaking his head. "But discovering this item is not going to help us find Tim. Not even if we'd found it back then, and certainly not now."

"It changes things," insisted Amy. "It means he didn't just run away with Chantel. Something might have happened to him. To both of them."

"It doesn't change anything," said Jack. "Not as far as the police are concerned. It's a lovely keepsake for you—"

"No," said Amy, "that is not what it is. It is proof he didn't want to leave me."

"People change their minds all the time," said Jack, his voice a little less soft now. "I'm sorry. We couldn't find him a decade ago. If he doesn't want to be found, he won't be. Neither of them will be. A piece of jewelry doesn't change that." He looked at Amy, who had put the bag between them on the table. "Even Chantel's mother has accepted that they are gone now."

"Toyah?" It had been years since Amy had spoken that name.

"She's moved to Dubai. A fresh start. That's probably what you need too."

"Dubai?" queried Amy. It didn't sound right. Not for Chantel's mum. "With her sister?" she asked, a little incredulous. "And her brother-in-law?"

"Toyah came to give me her number before she left, in case there were any developments in the case. Would you like it? I'm sure she wouldn't mind."

Amy hesitated. Once she'd accepted that Tim and Chantel had left together, she'd cut herself off from Toyah, feeling she was tarnished by her daughter's betrayal. But if there were another explanation? Amy nodded and scribbled down the number that Jack gave her.

"But in terms of the case," continued Jack, "I don't see what more we can do. Not after all this time. I'm sorry, Amy, I wish I could help."

Amy picked up the bag with the ring and put it in her handbag. "I understand," she said. She did. If she wanted to find the truth, she wouldn't have the help of Jack or the police. She'd be on her own.

Amy found herself staring at his hands, mainly to avoid eye contact. She noticed a thick gold band on his own finger. She glanced around the office, seeing framed photos documenting a pretty wife, two children, and several exotic holidays. He'd moved on with his life. Of course he had.

It was just her, longing for a past that perhaps had been a lie anyway.

"Thank you for your time," she said, standing up. "You must be busy."

He shook her hand. "Wear the ring," he told her, his voice kind again. "It's very beautiful."

Amy nodded, then turned around and left the office.

AMY LEANED FORWARDS over the small potted geraniums, trying to pick the best one from the selection in the garden center. She'd taken the ring out of the sandwich bag, feeling rather ridiculous. Now it dangled around her neck on a chain again and caught on the flowers. Amy untangled it and tucked it back inside her shirt, doing up another button to keep it safely inside. This ring had got her nowhere. Tim was still gone; the ring couldn't tell her where he was or why he'd left. Maybe Jack was right. It was nothing more than a pretty piece of jewelry.

Amy bit her lip and tried to focus on the flowers. She'd managed for all these years without him. Without knowing. She'd just have to continue like that. It hadn't been so bad, once she'd found her rhythm. And she'd made sure that no one would ever hurt her like that again. Her precious things certainly wouldn't.

Amy picked up a geranium plant covered in buds, then walked past the selection of terra-cotta pots with barely a second look. They were nothing special, she told herself, and she had plenty already. In fact, that was the point of this expedition. She had chosen one of her pots and she was going to plant it up to give to Richard and the boys as a thank-you for agreeing to fix the fence. She didn't like the idea of relinquishing it at all, but at least it would be close to home. She hoped they'd put it in their front garden so she could still admire it each day.

The pot she'd chosen from her collection had a beautiful wide neck and lovely curves down to its dainty base. It was a deep blue, like lapis lazuli, with little white stars etched into the glaze. The geraniums would have small white flowers, like little clusters of stars itself. The boys would love it. At least, she hoped they would.

And if they didn't, they could always give it back. It would look rather fetching in her own front garden.

Amy fought the urge to buy a second geranium to keep—she had several already—but did allow herself a little browse through the assortment of seasonal plants. Strawberry plants were on special, with dainty white flowers and little berries ripening. She selected three healthy specimens, one for herself and one for each boy, wondering if she could spare two more small pots to plant them in before she gave them away.

Of course she could, she decided, feeling generous. Maybe she'd even give them one of her small watering cans. She couldn't bear to think of the strawberries going thirsty, the plump red fruits shriveling like raisins.

"No pots today, love?" The man at the garden center till grinned at her.

"No," she said firmly, then hesitated. Panic began to rise up in her throat. One pot had been broken. She was giving away one more with the geranium and two small ones for the strawberries. Her stock was dwindling.

The man saw her hesitation. "We've got some lovely pots on special," he said. "Three for two."

That was a good deal.

Her hand went back to the ring, dangling around her neck.

"I've got enough, thank you," she replied. She paid for her purchases and carefully put them in bags, hurrying towards the bus stop in case she changed her mind.

AMY USED A pair of scissors to slice into a sack of topsoil in her back garden. Picking up a small shovel, she lined the selected pot with earth before carefully turning over the geranium and shaking it free from its plastic pot. She planted it carefully in its new home, topping up the sides with fresh soil and patting it down. The strawberries were next, each going into one of her small pots: a red one for Daniel, white for Charles. Some stems already had small berries protruding, others were still in blossom. The plants were wilting, so Amy lifted her watering can and gave the thirsty plants the drink they longed for.

Amy wiped her hand across her forehead and found she was sweating. She'd already changed from her usual uniform of black leggings and a loose T-shirt into an old pair of denim shorts that she'd found and a vest top. But she was still far too hot. And as thirsty as the plants had been. When she used to help out in her grandmother's garden, her grandma would bring her fresh lemonade to cool her down. Even when grandma was suffering from arthritis, she still insisted on squeezing lemons by hand. Amy remembered helping, the sour juice sometimes escaping and stinging her eyes. Her grandmother would always kiss them better.

"Hello!" Charles poked his head through the gap and grinned at her. "Dad is putting up the new fence this afternoon."

"That's good," said Amy.

"But there's still time to change your mind," he told her. "If you'd like to keep a gap."

"No," said Amy. "I think it's for the best."

"Okay," said Charles. He watched her as she poured more water from the watering can onto her newly planted pots. "Can I help?"

"All done," said Amy. She picked up the geranium. "This is for you," she said. "For all of you, to say thank you for the fence." She passed it through the gap, feeling a little wrench as she let go.

"I have strawberry plants for you too," she continued, determined to follow through with her plan. "One for you and one for Daniel." She lifted the pots, one in each hand, and passed them through the gap.

"To keep?" asked Charles, sounding incredulous as he reached out to take one. "Forever?"

"For as long as you can keep them alive," said Amy, feeling concern rising up in her. "You must water them every day. Not too much though—"

"Daniel!" Charles was shouting to his brother. "Come and see what Amy got us."

"That's lovely." Richard's head appeared over the fence. "How kind of you, Amy."

"It's nothing," said Amy.

"It's the best present ever," said Charles. "After my digger and my fire truck and my—"

"We get the idea," said Richard with a laugh. "Amy, I thought you might like to inspect the fencing I've chosen."

"I'm sure it's fine," said Amy, secretly hoping it would be tall enough that he wouldn't be able to see over it.

"It's your side really, so I thought you might like to make sure it's to your liking."

"Oh," said Amy. She paused. "I'll pay you for it, of course."

"That's not what I meant," said Richard. "Sorry, I didn't mean for it to sound like that. I'm the one with little escape artists chasing down your cat."

"Smudge is not my cat," said Amy again. She found herself blushing. He probably kept getting it wrong because she was a woman living alone and therefore he assumed she was a little old cat lady. "I'm probably younger than you think," she muttered to herself.

"What?" asked Richard. "Listen, pop on through while you still can. We can chat over here. Maybe you'd like some lemonade?"

Amy started at the offer. The family next door seemed to have an uncanny ability to read her mind. "Okay," she said, unable to resist, and made her way to the gap in the fence.

Amy was disappointed at the other side. The lemonade was not in a glass jug with fresh lemons and clinking ice cubes like her grandmother used to make; it was a rather warm can of 7UP that Richard tossed in her direction and she failed to catch.

"She likes pineapple juice," Charles scolded his father, picking up the can, brushing off the grass, and handing it to her.

"Sorry," said Richard.

"I like lemonade too," said Amy. She held the can awkwardly, aware that if she opened it she ran the risk of spraying them all with sweet wasp bait. She looked up from it and glanced at Richard for the first time.

"Oh," she said. He was wearing denim shorts, flip-flops, and that was it. She quickly looked back to the can of 7UP.

Charles looked at her, then at his father. "Dad," he said. "You're so cringe." He passed his father a T-shirt.

"Sorry," said Richard, putting on the T-shirt. "Sun's out, guns out, and all that."

"You don't have guns," said Charles.

"It's fine," said Amy, trying to quell her blushes. "It's your garden, you've a right to . . . I'm not an old lady, you know."

"I can see that," said Richard, then he looked down and up again. His eyes lingered for a moment on Amy's long legs, so rarely on display. She caught his eye, and they both looked away. She looked back. Color was creeping up his own cheeks, only partially hidden by his beard. He made a funny sound that Amy thought was probably an awkward attempt at a laugh. "I mean, we're all old to these tykes." He ruffled Charles's hair.

"I'm three and a half," piped up Daniel.

"That's almost four," explained Charles.

"Indeed," said Amy.

"Good maths," agreed Richard. He laughed, more naturally this time. "So, what do you think of this fencing panel? I went for a plain wood."

Amy found she had nothing much to say on the subject of fencing panels. "I expect my ivy will cover it in no time," she said.

"You hate it," said Richard, with another laugh.

"Dad, you're being boring," said Charles.

Nina came into the garden wearing a little white dress and huge sunglasses. "Gorgeous weather," she said. "Oh, hello, Amy," she said, glancing at Amy's legs. "Here again? Making use of the hole in the fence, I see."

"Amy said we can still visit whenever we like," Charles told her. Amy frowned. She didn't remember saying that.

"You too, Richard?" asked Nina, putting her arm around Richard's waist. She let out a small peal of laughter that was probably designed to be pleasant.

"Dad likes Amy," said Charles. "We all do."

"I have to get going," said Amy. "Thank you for your hard work." She paused a moment. "And the lemonade." It was still unopened, and she dithered, wondering whether it was more polite to hand it back or take it with her.

"That's yours now," said Charles. "Next time you come there'll be pineapple juice. I promise."

"Good-bye, Amy," encouraged Nina, waving. Amy slipped through the gap in the fence.

Amy looked at the piles of pots, lopsided now she'd given some away. She picked up a small pot that sat inside a large one near the ground, causing panic among a family of wood lice who'd been sheltering there, safe from the elements. They scurried this way and that, bumping into each other several times before fleeing down a drainage hole to the safety of the earth below.

She almost gasped with joy.

There they were. Two large fragments of her broken pot, lurking inside this one. Perhaps she had enough to fix it now. She lifted them out.

Something else was underneath.

An envelope. It was muddy and had been nibbled around the edges, probably by one of Rachel's mice, or perhaps a snail, and there was a hole in the corner. It had clearly been wet at some point, and the ink had run. But she could still make out her own name and address, printed on the front in block capitals.

Amy sat back and ripped open the envelope. Inside was a photo. She frowned at it.

It made no sense. A bit of park, or woodland perhaps, at sunset. It could have been anywhere. She looked more closely. Some sort of big car or truck at the edge of the picture. It meant nothing to her.

There was something else in the envelope.

A letter.

The writing was smudged. It must have been hiding inside that pot for a long time. Rain had leaked in, mud was smeared over it, some sections were missing completely. She could make out very little of it.

But that handwriting.

She'd know it anywhere.

July 2003

"Are you sure that's a good idea?" suggested Amy tentatively. "You're onstage in five minutes."

Tim knocked back another shot of tequila. "It's just what I need," he replied, wiping his mouth. "Where's my pint?"

Amy passed it to him, then took a sip of her white wine from a clear plastic cup and looked at the tequila bottle. They'd bought it on the way to the gig and it was already half-empty.

"It's buzzing out there," said Chantel, storming into the dressing room—really a glorified closet. She turned her back and stripped off her office uniform of a blazer and shirt. Underneath was a sparkly low-cut top. "Oh, and in here too," she said, turning back round and spying the bottle. "Some for me?"

"Course there is," replied Simon. "Pretty thing like you." He refilled Tim's shot glass and passed it in Chantel's direction

Chantel downed the shot, holding out her glass for more. "Where's the rest of the band?" she asked.

"Idris and Phil couldn't make it," said Tim.

"Artistic differences?" joked Chantel.

"Something like that," muttered Simon. "Twats."

"Oh," said Chantel. "But don't you need a drummer and another guitar player?"

"We'll manage," said Tim. "We'll have to."

"You'll be brilliant," said Amy. "You always are."

"Come on, Tim," said Simon. "Let's get out there. Take your pint with you. The fans are waiting."

"THE EQUIPMENT WAS faulty," said Amy through the door of the cubicle in the men's loos. "It wasn't your fault." She tried to peer under the door, but she could just see a pair of mucky trainers. She straightened again, keen to avoid the anonymous fluid on the toilet floor.

"We're shit," said Tim. "We've always been shit. It just didn't show so much when Idris and Phil were being shit too."

A man came in, and for a brief moment the open door allowed the noise of the club in. Just as suddenly the volume fell again. The man glanced at Amy, then undid his flies and used the urinal anyway. She tried not to look.

"People shouldn't have been so rude," said Amy. "And that bottle. That's assault."

"It barely touched me," said Tim. "And I'm pretty sure it was aimed at Simon."

"You sounded brilliant," said Amy loyally.

"They were rubbish," said the urinal man, zipping his flies and failing to wash his hands. "Total dogshit." The noise rose again as he opened the door, then faded.

"Ignore him," said Amy, hearing a wail from the cubicle. She paused. "I think it was just the microphone. It must have been faulty. Shall I go talk to the manager?"

"For God's sake, no," said Tim. "Amy, stop telling me I'm great. I have ears. It drives me crazy when you try to wrap me in cotton wool like I'm a delicate little flower. Respect me enough to be honest, at least."

"But you're so talented—"

"Stop talking, Amy," said Tim. "And listen." He paused. "If we can't be honest with each other . . ."

His voice trailed off. Amy stood still. She felt as though she'd been punched in the gut. "You don't mean that," she said.

The noise rose again and his answer was lost. Chantel appeared. "There you are. I've been looking everywhere." She glanced at the cubicle. "Is he in there?"

"He won't come out," said Amy. "I've been trying for ages."

"I've got half a bottle of tequila with your name on it, Timmy-boy," said Chantel. "So get out of this piss-drenched hole and come with me."

The door opened and Tim stepped out. "Come on then," he said, head hanging.

"Don't you think you've had—" began Amy.

"No," said Tim. "You coming?"

"No," said Amy. "I've had enough."

AMY WAS CURLED up in bed. Wide-awake. She glanced at her phone—3 a.m. She shifted her position, but it wasn't the bed that was making her uncomfortable. It had been happening more and more recently. Tim drinking and smoking while Amy looked on nervously. She was annoying him. He was annoying her.

Perhaps it was over.

Amy took a sip from the glass of water next to the bed. It couldn't be over. She loved him.

She closed her eyes, but it was just a performance for herself. She knew there'd be no sleep.

She listened to the pipes. Someone somewhere in the building had flushed the toilet.

The noises became jangly, and Amy realized that now someone was at the door. Simon and Tim both lived here, and she wished intently for it to be Tim coming home. And at the same time she didn't. She closed her eyes, ready to feign sleep. She couldn't face an argument. Not now.

The bedroom door opened, and she couldn't help but peek. Tim stumbled in the darkness.

"Hello," said Amy, feeling a current of love overwhelm her as he bent down and gave her a kiss that smelled of smoke and tequila and something sweeter. "Come to bed."

"Chantel's here," he told her, standing up again. "We're just going to have a little smoke first. Maybe a nightcap. There's some rum in the cupboard."

"Really?" asked Amy. "It's late."

"Just one. About tonight . . ." he began. The sweet smell grew more intense and Amy felt something brush her face. "I wanted to buy you flowers," said Tim. "To say sorry. But everywhere was shut."

"It's three in the morning," said Amy.

"That would be why," he said. "So I picked you these."

Amy took what he held out and flicked on the bedside lamp. Tim crinkled his eyes in the light, and it took Amy a moment for her own eyes to adjust. She was holding several stems of honeysuckle, covered in elegant white flowers that made her think of ballerinas. She breathed in deeply, enjoying the scent.

"I hope the neighbors don't notice they've gone," said Tim.

"They are beautiful," said Amy, feeling some of the stress of the night melt into the fragrance. "Thank you."

"I told you she'd like them." Amy saw Chantel's figure in the doorway. "Hi, Amy," she said. "Sorry for leading Tim astray."

"It doesn't take much," said Amy. "But the flowers are lovely."

*   *   *

AMY DREAMED OF her grandmother's garden. Honeysuckle and roses and fresh lemonade. But when she woke up, the flat stank of rum and cigarettes and weed. Amy coughed as she entered the living room, partly from the fumes and partly to wake up Chantel and Tim, both fast asleep on the sofa, gently snoring. It didn't work. One cigarette had turned into another party—albeit just for two. She'd known it would.

Amy went into the kitchen to make herself a coffee, but the meager collection of mugs had all been used for drinks the night before. Amy longed for a world where she could fill her kitchen cupboard with mugs. Beautiful mugs in all the colors of a sunset. But for now, she made her way back to the living room and grabbed the closest one. It smelled worse than just rum and Coke, and Amy peered inside. The butts of cigarettes and joints floated in the drink like tampons in a toilet.

Amy put it back down and decided to buy a coffee on the way to the studio instead. She shared the studio with a collective of other artists, and this was her one chance of the week to get some painting done. But she wasn't feeling inspired.

Tim was stirring but Chantel was still fast asleep. "It's nice having her stay over, isn't it?" said Tim, his eyes opening. "Livens the place up. Any coffee going?"

"There's no coffee because you two have turned all the mugs into ashtrays," said Amy.

"Really?" said Tim. "I thought we just used the orange one." He leaned forwards and grabbed a blue mug. "Oh, and this one too. Sorry."

"We can't carry on living like this," said Amy.

Tim rubbed his head. "I'll sort it," he said.

Chantel opened her eyes. "I can hear nagging," she said. "It had better be after ten a.m."

"It's seven thirty," said Amy.

Both Tim and Chantel groaned. "No wonder I feel like shit," said Chantel. "I'm calling in sick."

"Ditto," said Tim. "Shelves can stack themselves."

"I've got the studio for two hours this morning because that's all I can afford," said Amy. "Then I'm going to the office. It would be really nice if this place wasn't disgusting when I get back."

"Sure, sure," said Chantel. She closed her eyes. Tim was already snoring. Amy slammed the door on her way out, hoping the sound reverberated inside both their heads.

AMY DIDN'T DO her best work at the studio. The colors felt subdued, the textures muted. She rarely painted anything she was pleased with these days. She sometimes wondered if it was partly her job at Trapper, Lemon, and Hughes that was to blame; it was meant to be just for a month, after all. That was a year ago now, but it had gone from filling university holidays to filling her life. She should curate a gallery perhaps, or work in an art supplies shop. Maybe she could even teach. Amy took a moment to imagine herself teaching life drawing to an enthusiastic and talented class. Then she'd go to her studio, full of ideas, and be able to paint the masterpiece that she hoped was still lurking within her.

But she needed to pay the rent. Tim still refused to get a better job than the supermarket, insisting that it was just an interim thing till his band made it. To him, getting a proper job meant accepting that the band didn't have a future.

Amy stewed like overbrewed tea all day, still feeling hard done by when she got home that evening. Tim came into the hallway and gave her a kiss.

"Come into the living room," said Chantel. "We've got something to show you." Amy obeyed, and gasped.

The room wasn't spotless: that would be impossible. But it was cleaner than she'd seen it before. Tim's guitars were neatly stacked in a corner, and a mug filled with honeysuckle sat on the coffee table.

But what really stood out were Amy's paintings. The one she'd given Tim years ago had always lived on the wall in his bedroom, but until now most of the others had been shoved unceremoniously in a cupboard. Now her three favorites adorned the walls. Each depicted the sky at a different moment. Sunrise, with little pieces of cracked eggshell worked into the paint. Midday, the rich yellow sun adorned with flecks of golden bottle tops that Amy had picked up from the pavement and ground down to powder. Twilight, the purple sky punctuated with dried buddleia that floated like clouds in front of the nascent moon.

"We thought it was time to display them," said Chantel with a grin. "Here, just until you get an exhibition."

"Which you will," said Tim. "I know you will."

"We had a spare mug after we washed them all up, so we put the honeysuckle in it," said Chantel. "Looks nice, eh? Arty."

"It looks amazing," replied Amy, looking at her two favorite people. "Thank you."

Chapter Seven

"**B**right and early again, Amy," said Mr. Trapper as he ran the coffee machine. "That's what I like to see. Catching the worm."

Amy nodded, but she barely even saw him. She went to the stationery cupboard and took out a brown envelope with *Please Do Not Bend* printed on it. She slipped out the photograph and the remnants of the letter from a slender cookbook she'd been using to keep them safe, and made to transfer them to the envelope. She paused.

She could hardly make out any of the writing. Rain had seeped in, snails had left their glittery footprints, and Rachel's mice had nibbled much of the rest. The letter must have been inside that pot for years—the pot that used to live by her front door, holding umbrellas. The letter could easily have slipped inside, just like the ring had. Then when her hallway had become too crowded, she'd taken out the umbrellas and moved the pot outside. Others had been piled on top, protecting the letter from the worst of the elements.

And now here it was. Her name at the top. Typically, the first line was perfectly preserved, but said so little.

I don't know where to begin. I'm so sorry. I had to be selfish.

That handwriting. Gently slanted, oddly neat for a person often so careless. It made Amy remember countless notes passed to her in class. Uncontrollable fits of giggles. Hugs and shared clothes and laughter and Malibu rum. She hadn't had a friendship like it again.

After the first line, it was just the odd word that was legible. But it was enough for Amy to complete the heartbreaking jigsaw:

jealous
love
afraid
run
sorry

Amy shoved the paper into the envelope. Perhaps it was a good thing the letter was in that state. It was a confession she didn't want to read.

Just when hope was rising. Hope in the shape of a beautiful aquamarine ring. Hope that they hadn't betrayed her. And this letter came to tell her to believe what she so fervently wanted not to be true. It was as if it had happened all over again. As if they were rubbing her face in it still, years later.

She looked at the office shredder and wondered if that was why she'd slipped the letter into her handbag that morning. But shredding it would make it no less true.

Amy turned her attention to the photograph. Why had Chantel included it? Amy supposed the letter might explain, but she couldn't imagine what the explanation would be. *We grew up together, then I ran away with your boyfriend. Here's a pretty picture of a bit of woodland in the sunset to make up for it.*

She needed to find out where this place was. It was the only solid clue she had, with the letter illegible. If she found out where the photo was taken, surely that would bring her one step closer to the truth.

"Fancy meeting you by the stationery cupboard." Amy looked up and saw Liam grinning at her. "Thought any more about my offer?"

"Is Carthika not giving you the feedback you need?" replied Amy, slipping the photograph into the envelope.

"Touché," replied Liam. Amy smelled extra-strong mints on his breath. "You know what I mean." He winked at her, in case she needed an extra clue.

Amy took a step backwards. "I don't socialize with people from the office."

"Perhaps you could make an exception?" asked Liam.

"Sorry," said Amy.

"Offer still stands," he said, undeterred, "if you change your mind."

Amy went back to her desk without replying and sat down, the envelope in front of her. She took out the letter again, and read the words that she could: *. . . love . . . run . . . sorry . . .*

Everyone had thought it at the time. Jack had been convinced. The police said they couldn't say for certain, but she knew they thought he was right. She'd been betrayed.

And not just betrayed. Tim and Chantel had left everything to be together. Without her. And she'd not been on a date since.

A message popped up. Changed your mind yet?

Amy typed the words quickly, before she had a chance to think about it:

Okay. Let's have that drink.

*   *   *

THE SPARE ROOM in her house hadn't always been spare. Renting the house, the three of them, had been Chantel's idea. She'd viewed properties until she found a little two-bedroom place they could afford to rent. Amy and Tim were happy to oblige: their previous flat share had reached the end of its shelf life. It wasn't till years later, when their landlord wanted to sell, that Amy had bought the house. She felt like she had no choice: she couldn't bear the thought of having to move all her precious belongings. And she needed to stay in that house. If they came back, she wanted them to be able to find her.

Amy had kept Chantel's room as it was for several months after they'd gone, hoping Chantel would come back with a reasonable explanation and want her things again. Then Amy kept her shoebox of memories in the room, then larger boxes, until eventually it was uninhabitable. She stood in the doorway now and surveyed what was in front of her.

She'd barely made a dent in it the last time she'd tried to clear out, and she'd acquired a black eye in the process. Amy paused. It was as if Chantel didn't want her in there.

Chantel didn't have a choice, decided Amy, thinking of the letter. Amy wanted that shoebox with her diaries. Perhaps there was a clue there, something she'd missed all those years ago. A clue about what they were planning.

Amy clenched her teeth until she heard them grinding together and grabbed a large cardboard box. She wasn't going to sort through it and she wasn't going to throw anything away. All she needed was a pathway. Where was the shoebox? She closed her eyes for a moment, trying to picture it. Was it in the wardrobe? Under the bed? Only one way to find out.

She took a mirror and carefully leaned it against the box behind her. She'd block off her hallway again at this rate, but she had to find it. She hauled out another box. Out of the corner of her eye she thought she saw a tiny dark shadow darting across the room. Her imagination, she decided. Certainly not a mouse.

She could see the corner of the wardrobe now. She stopped putting boxes in the hallway and just began to pile stuff behind her. Finally she had one of the wardrobe doors clear. She opened it.

The wardrobe was full, every inch of the space used for storage. Amy remembered now, she'd hidden treasures in there at first, before she gave up and let belongings take over everywhere. Amy took out the possessions stored there carefully; it was like rediscovering old friends. She placed her finds on top of the boxes behind her. There were lots of shoeboxes in the cupboard. But not the special one. It had originally housed a pair of Adidas trainers that Tim had treated himself to. These boxes were all Chantel's.

As were the clothes. Amy looked at them, hanging there like ghosts. The sparkly top Chantel had worn to Tim's disastrous gig when he'd ended up in tears in the loo. Now that she looked at it, she noticed how low-cut it was.

And there was the vest top Chantel had worn to the festival. Glittery. And there was the tight red sweater Chantel had worn when she joined Amy and her grandmother at Christmas one year.

Amy rummaged through the clothes, wondering when it had begun. How long had they been deceiving her for?

Her hand stopped at a silky blue dress. That was hers. She'd not lent it to Chantel, she was certain of it. Chantel would have come into her room, their room, and taken it.

Suddenly Amy found herself pulling off her black T-shirt and her jeans. The dress was over her head. It was the color of the midsummer sky, full-length with short sleeves and a neckline that made Amy feel naked.

Amy pulled the band from her ponytail and leaned over, running her fingers through her dark hair. She flicked her head back and felt a momentary head rush. She turned around.

A dozen mirrors reflected her image.

This was how she used to look. Older now, much sadder, but for the first time in years she recognized herself.

Amy twirled around, the shoebox forgotten. She decided that she would force herself to clear a path to her own wardrobe. She used to enjoy wearing beautiful colors. The yellow of spring daffodils, purples reminiscent of the evening sky, the blue of a hazy morning. She'd painted with those same colors, plus the terra-cotta oranges of Florence and the green of freshly mowed grass. She had never liked black, perhaps that's why she'd started wearing it when they had gone. Joy had seemed wrong.

Amy clambered back over the boxes and went downstairs to experiment with Joanna's makeup. A healthy amount of foundation and blusher, and she looked even more like the girl she used to know. She was pleased she'd kept all these mirrors now: every time she turned around she was surprised by the pleasant-looking person who glanced back at her. She gave herself a tentative smile, testing how it felt to try to look happy again.

THE DOORBELL RANG, and for once Amy didn't mind its jaunty tone. She opened the door and saw Charles standing there. "You look different," he told her.

"I found some old clothes," she said.

"Your face looks different too," he said suspiciously.

"What is it?" asked Amy.

He smiled at her. "You said I could ring your doorbell when I wanted to see you." Amy didn't reply. "So here I am," said Charles. "I thought we could play in my room, so we don't break any more of your things."

"I'm actually quite busy—" began Amy.

"There's always time for a break," replied Charles brightly. "We have to be careful in my room too. No breaking things when we play."

"I'm a bit old for—"

"You're younger than my dad, I bet, and he plays with me sometimes. Nina never plays. She's too boring."

Amy thought about the mess upstairs. She should really clean up all the boxes she'd moved. But to where? She still hadn't found the shoebox she wanted, so she didn't want to put everything back in that room, but where else? She bit her lip and considered getting rid of some of her things. But which ones? The thought of it made her feel uneasy. Maybe it was a problem for later. "Okay," she said. "Just for a little bit."

"Come on then," said Charles, taking her hand. "We've not got all day."

Amy slipped on a pair of sandals and allowed herself to be dragged along into the house next door. She was beginning to get used to its emptiness now. Charles went up the stairs taking them two at a time. Amy lifted her long dress to keep it out of the way and did the same. "This is my room," Charles told her proudly as he opened the door. "I have to share it with Daniel," he confessed. "But the coolest toys in it are all mine."

Amy saw the little plastic car bed that she'd spotted when they'd first moved in. It had a blanket on top that depicted Mickey Mouse kicking a football. There was a bigger bed on the other side of the room with a blanket illustrated with every construction machine imaginable. "Take a seat," said Charles, gesturing to the building-site bed. She perched on it tentatively. "It's good for bouncing on," he told her. Amy nodded and looked around. There were two little chests of drawers, a smattering of bright plastic toys, and a few dinosaurs exploring the carpet. It was pretty tidy.

Charles dragged out a heavy red box from a corner and turned it over. Little yellow machines spilled out, covering the floor. "My collection," he said.

"It's lovely," said Amy, feeling a sense of kinship.

He rummaged through another box and produced a heavy book. "This book has more than you'll ever need to know about construction equipment, my dad says." He turned to a well-used page. "Look."

Amy obeyed. "Keep reading," instructed Charles, going to the cupboard. He came out with a box containing an excavator. "The JCB 220X LC," he told her. "Remote-controlled." He carefully opened the box and withdrew several pieces of tissue paper, then a small machine. He placed it on the floor. "My dad gave me this for my birthday," he said. "It's a to-scale replica of the ones they use on real construction sites like in this book." He pointed. "Except in real life they don't have remotes. People get inside to drive."

"It's very nice," said Amy.

"Do you want to drive it?" asked Charles. "You have to be very careful."

"You show me how it's done," said Amy.

"Good thinking," replied Charles. He switched it on, and a high-pitched whirring sound began as it explored the room. "It's best in the hallway," said Charles. She followed him as he drove it out. "It can really pick stuff up. Look, I'll show you." He pushed open a door, and they went inside. Amy found herself in an adult's bedroom. Charles grabbed a lipstick from a dressing table, which he threw to the floor. He frowned in concentration as the machine struggled to scoop it up. "Give it a minute," he said. "Lipsticks are tricky." He struggled some more, then tossed it a bottle of perfume with a poppy painted on. "That's a better shape," he said. They both watched as it picked up the perfume bottle and thrust it towards the bed. "Cool," said Charles.

"What's cool?" Richard was standing in the doorway. Daniel stood with an arm around his leg. "Oh, hello, Amy." He looked at her. "You look different."

"Like a princess," said Daniel.

"I found some old clothes," said Amy, feeling uncomfortable.

"Blue suits you," said Richard.

"Got it!" The excavator spun round in victory, clutching the lipstick.

"Nice skills," said Richard, dragging his eyes away from Amy and back to his son.

"Watch this." The machine dropped the lipstick and went up to the chest of drawers. Charles pursed up his whole face in concentration, as the excavator arm reached up, grabbed the drawer handle, and pulled. The drawer opened, and they all clapped. "Shush," he said. "I need to focus." The machine let go of the drawer and pulled out a handful of silky underwear. "Ta-dah!" he said.

They clapped again, and the machine spun around in victory, spreading underwear over the floor.

"What's going on?" The laughter stopped and they all turned to look at Nina, standing in the doorway. "What's that on the floor?"

"Sorry about that," said Richard, gathering up the panties. "Charles was just showing us how good he's gotten at using the excavator."

"Are those my underwear?" asked Nina. "And is that my perfume on the floor?" She looked around the room, and her eyes fixed on Amy. "Oh, hello again," she said. "You're all dressed up." Her eyes went back to Richard.

"I found some old clothes . . ." began Amy.

"Indeed," said Nina. "Richard, you didn't tell me we had company?"

"I'm actually here to see Charles," said Amy.

"Of course," said Nina. "Charles, you have a perfectly good room to play in without coming in here." She turned to Richard. "Tell him, darling."

"He didn't mean any harm," said Richard, shoving the underwear back in the drawer. Nina went over and took them out again.

"Silk needs to be folded," she said.

Amy saw the look in Nina's eye. "We're all sorry, Nina," she said. "Would you like some help folding?"

"Good-bye, Amy," said Nina.

"But Amy hasn't had any pineapple juice yet," objected Charles.

"I'm sure Amy is very busy," said Nina. "Aren't you, Amy?"

Amy slipped through the door and hurried down the stairs.

* * *

THE NEXT EVENING Amy saw a woman at her door as she walked home from the station. She felt a moment's annoyance and stood back to wait for the person to put whatever flyer she had through her door and leave. It was a large matriarchal woman wearing loose floral trousers. Amy felt herself coveting them, even though they'd be several sizes too big for her. After coming home the previous evening, she'd created a pathway to her old wardrobe and was enjoying wearing the odd bit of color again. It made every day feel a little more hopeful. To Amy's surprise, the woman bent forwards and peered through Amy's letter box.

"Can I help you?" said Amy, in a tone that told the woman she wanted her to leave.

The woman straightened. "Are you Amy Ashton?" she asked, with a jovial smile that revealed teeth of a shade suggesting she enjoyed tea and coffee. Or red wine.

Amy frowned at her. "Who wants to know?"

"I'm Leah Silverton," said the woman. "From the council."

Amy looked at her blankly. Leah waved an identity badge from a lanyard round her neck at Amy. Amy peered at it. A much younger Leah smiled back at her.

"I'm glad I've finally caught you," Leah continued. "Can I come in?"

"No," said Amy.

"That's quite a collection of stuff you have in your front garden," continued Leah, unperturbed. Amy looked at her, suspicious of the compliment. "What's it like inside?"

"What do you want?" asked Amy.

"I think it would be better for us to discuss indoors," said Leah. "In private."

Amy looked around. "Outside is fine," she said. "Why are you here?"

Leah gestured upwards, and for a moment Amy thought she was going to ask if Amy had found Jesus. "That chimney of yours," she explained.

"Who called you?" asked Amy, rolling her eyes. "Was it Rachel? She needs to mind her own business."

Leah ignored her question. "If we can't talk inside, let's have a seat on your wall," she said, sounding resigned. "I've been standing up for a long time and my back aches." The two women walked back up Amy's path and perched uncomfortably on her wall. Amy felt a flash of guilt as she heard Leah exhale loudly as she did so.

"I'm sorry not to be more hospitable," said Amy, relenting. "But I wasn't expecting you."

Leah raised an eyebrow. "I understand you refused a visit from my colleague Bob Hendricks, back on the ninth of July. That will need to be rearranged."

"I don't want anyone in my house," said Amy.

"There's another matter," continued Leah. "We've been sending you letters for months, but you haven't responded." She opened her bag and got out a brown envelope full of papers, which she shuffled through like a deck of cards. "Starting in October last year. Seven in total. I can give you the dates?"

"I haven't had any letters," said Amy.

"Could they have got lost?" asked Leah. "That does happen. Especially in these types of cases."

Amy thought about her hallway and didn't reply. "What do they say?" she asked.

"We've had a complaint," said Leah. Amy turned to look at Rachel's house, and saw the curtains flicker. "An anonymous complaint," added Leah. "Someone was concerned for your safety, and we wanted to check your living conditions."

"I'm fine," said Amy. "My house is fine."

"About that," continued Leah. "You do own the leasehold, but the council holds the freehold. We have a duty of care—"

"Thank you," said Amy, trying to quell the anxiety that rose in her throat like heartburn. "But it's my house and there is no issue."

"I'm not here to judge," said Leah, in the most judgmental tone Amy had ever heard.

"Everything is fine," replied Amy.

"And I understand there was an incident involving your back garden and the children next door? On the . . ." She referred to her notes. "Fourth of July, two weeks ago?"

Amy bit her lip. Maybe Nina had reported her. The letters dated back months, so Rachel must have started it off. She suddenly felt the brunt of her neighbors on both sides being against her. Fighting on two fronts. For a moment, she felt she wanted to move house, to get out of here. But she couldn't leave. Not now. What if he came back?

"It was nothing," said Amy, trying to sound breezy, a hard feat when she felt as if she couldn't breathe. "A cat. The kids shouldn't have been in the garden, but no one was hurt. We've fixed the fence now. The children can't get in." She realized she was talking too fast.

"Can I see the back garden?"

"No."

Leah made a little sighing sound and shifted her weight on the wall. "We're not getting very far, are we?" She made a note, but angled her paper so Amy couldn't read it. "I'm going to have to come back, I'm afraid," she said finally. "With some support. We need to get inside your house, for your own safety. You'll get a letter in the post with a date and time. Look out for it." Leah put her notebook away. "In the meantime, I'd suggest you have a clear-out, especially in areas that could be a danger to others. That 'garden' needs to be cleared, and we need access to your chimney, at a minimum." She put a hand on Amy's arm. Amy flinched. Leah spoke more softly. "We don't want this to be traumatic," she said. "But we need to think of everyone's safety, including yours. If you can make it better, even just a little better, we might be able to avoid any unpleasantness. Do you think you can do that?"

Amy nodded.

"Good." Leah got up and smiled, as if they were old friends catching up over a cup of tea. "I'll be in touch. Look out for the letter. We don't want it getting lost again."

Amy watched her walk away, and made sure Leah was right at the end of the road before she turned and walked back up her front path. She put the key in the lock and disappeared inside her house.

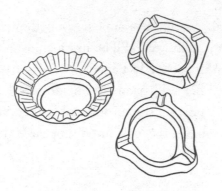

February 2004

Amy couldn't work out what the sound was. She opened her eyes. It was dark, except for a beam of light from her phone. That's what it was. Her phone was ringing. She rolled over and grabbed for it on the nightstand, instead finding Tim's china ashtray, shaped like a guitar. At least he'd bought one now, instead of using her mugs. She sat up and grabbed her phone, blinking the fuzziness of sleep from her head. Tim emitted a soft grunt and snuggled his head deeper into his pillow.

"Amy? Thank God you're there. I need your help." Chantel spoke quickly, as if she were on fast-forward.

"What is it?" Amy sat up in bed. It wasn't the first time she'd had a call like this in the middle of the night. "Tim doesn't have any weed," she said. "He's given up."

"Shush," said Chantel. She paused. "I've been arrested," she hissed.

"Arrested?" echoed Amy.

"It's all a big mix-up," she said. "I was carrying some gear for Spike, and then when the police turned up he chucked another bag at me, and you know I used to captain the netball team, I caught it like an idiot. He ran and I was left looking like some kind of dealer. But I'm not. You know I'm not."

"Where are you now?" said Amy, feeling around the floor for her clothes.

"Holborn police station," said Chantel.

"On my way," said Amy.

Tim rolled over and opened his eyes. "Chantel?" he questioned.

"I need to go to the police station," said Amy.

Tim looked at his phone. "It's one a.m.," he said.

"She needs my help."

Tim got up and flicked on the overhead light. Amy fumbled to get her jeans on. She could see Tim in the mirror, scratching at his pale chest and blinking in the light. "You're not going to the police station in the middle of the night," he said, talking to her reflection. Amy opened her mouth, ready to argue. "At least not alone," said Tim. "Give me a minute to find my trousers and I'll come with you."

"It's okay," said Amy. "She's my friend. Go back to sleep."

"No way," said Tim, pulling on a crumpled T-shirt. "I can always call in sick tomorrow."

"Again?"

"Emergency," he replied. He leaned forwards and kissed her, his breath tasting of the nighttime.

"Thanks," said Amy.

AMY BLINKED UNDER the harsh glare of the lights in the police station. She was grateful for Tim's arm around her shoulders as they stood together, watching a drunk man in a disheveled suit complaining to the female officer on reception.

"Sit down, sir," said the officer. "If I have to tell you once more . . ."

"I've been robbed," slurred the man again. "My wallet. My phone. My bloody house keys. It's all gone and you lot are doing nothing."

"I've given you a form," she said. "Kindly take a seat."

The drunk man turned to Tim. "We pay her wages with our tax money and she's telling us what to do?"

"Maybe just fill in the form," suggested Tim, pulling Amy farther away from the man.

"Formedy form form form," said the man, looking disappointed that Tim didn't share his outrage.

"Trouble, WPC Kelly?" A large, muscular man strode into the reception. He was in plain clothes, but his bearing showed that he was a policeman. "Perhaps this gentleman needs to spend some time in the cells for being drunk and disorderly?"

"I'm fine, officer," said the man, all talk of his taxes disappearing. "Just filling in my form." He sat down.

"Thanks, Jack," said WPC Kelly with a smile. She turned to Amy. "Can I help you?" she asked, her voice tired.

"My friend's been arrested," began Amy. "But it's all a misunderstanding—"

"Your friend's name?"

"Chantel Smith," said Amy. "She shouldn't be in here. It's her boyfriend's fault—"

"Fill in this form," said Kelly, handing her some paperwork. Amy felt a moment's affinity with the drunk man.

"Will she get out once I fill this in?"

"Fill in the form and I'll see what the situation is," replied WPC Kelly.

Amy sat down on the institutional plastic chair, leaving as much space as she could between her and the drunk man, who was now muttering under his breath about the contents of his lost wallet. Tim was standing up, looking uncomfortable. The officer who had threatened the drunk man leaned on the reception desk chatting quietly to

WPC Kelly. Every once in a while a short burst of laughter between the two of them punctuated the silence.

Amy finally completed the form and stood up to hand it back. The female officer was still smiling at something when she took the form.

Tim grabbed Amy's arm and she looked around to see Spike hurry past, his head down.

"Where are you going?" she asked.

"Home," said Spike, reluctantly pausing. "I've been released."

"You've been released?" repeated Amy.

"Yes."

"But Chantel is still here," said Amy, looking to the policewoman for verification. She nodded. Spike carried on walking.

"Stop!" commanded Amy. Everyone looked up. Even the drunk man stopped muttering. "This is all your fault," she said. "Have you told them that?"

"Keep your voice down," said Spike. "It's not my fault." He smiled at the muscular policeman and gave him a little shrug of the shoulders as if he didn't know what Amy was talking about.

"Chantel is in trouble," said Amy.

"She'll be fine," replied Spike. "She'll probably just get a caution."

"I can't believe you're letting her take the heat for this," said Amy, feeling anger mount inside her and spill out like lava from a volcano. "Actually, I can." She looked around. "He is a drug dealer," she declared, addressing the policeman. "He should be in prison."

"Shush," said Spike, trying to laugh it off. He hissed at Amy, "Cut it out. She was the one holding the drugs."

"Because you chucked them at her."

"Shut up, Amy," said Spike, squaring up to her.

Tim came to put his hand on Amy's shoulder. "Don't talk to her like that," he said.

"You can shut up too," said Spike. "It's not like you're squeaky clean." He turned back to Amy. "You don't know what happened. Are we going to have a problem?"

"Is he giving you trouble, ma'am?" The policeman had come to stand between them.

"Yes," said Amy. "He's the drug dealer and he's got my friend to take the rap for him."

"Interesting," said the policeman.

"She'll go along with it and he'll get away scot-free. It's not fair."

"Amy doesn't know what happened," said Spike, turning to the policeman. "This is libel."

"Amy!" Chantel rushed into the middle of them all and flung her arms around Amy. "Thank God you're here."

"This is the friend you were talking about?" asked the policeman, looking Chantel up and down.

"Yes," said Amy.

"Get out," he said to Spike, giving him an encouraging steer towards the door. Spike didn't need to be asked twice. The policeman looked at Amy and Chantel. "Wait here a moment," he said, and went for a word with WPC Kelly.

"I hope you told the police what happened," said Amy.

"I've just got a caution," said Chantel. "It wasn't worth making a fuss."

"I'm glad you're okay," added Tim.

"Right," said the officer, returning. "A quick word with you, ma'am"—he looked at Chantel—"and then you can all go."

"Thank you," said Amy. She took Tim's hand and watched as the policeman spoke with Chantel, handing her a small piece of paper. "I can't wait to get to bed," said Amy.

"I need a little something to calm me down," whispered Tim. "It's been quite a night."

TIM WENT STRAIGHT to the Beatles tin in the living room when they got back to the flat, removed a tiny clear plastic bag, and gave it a little shake. "Just enough left," he said.

"What are you doing?" said Amy. "You've given up."

"Special situation," said Tim. "Tonight was pretty stressful." He fetched the guitar-shaped ashtray from the bedroom before settling down to roll up.

"Brilliant idea," said Chantel, watching him.

"Terrible idea," said Amy. "Chantel, drugs got you into this mess."

"Spike got me into this mess," countered Chantel. "Can you believe him?"

"Yes," said Tim. "He's an arsehole." He lit up and inhaled deeply.

"He's got some making up to do," agreed Chantel, reaching for Tim's joint.

"You can't be thinking about taking him back?" said Amy. "Chantel, you need some self-respect."

Chantel took a deep drag and watched herself blow smoke rings in the mirror. "We're not all Little Miss Perfect with fine arts degrees and bright futures," she said. "Some of us are massive screw-ups." She passed the joint to Tim. "Aren't we?"

"Speak for yourself," said Tim. He leaned back on the sofa and closed his eyes. Amy grabbed the joint from his hand and stubbed it out in the ashtray before it singed the cushion. Chantel calmly picked it up and lit it again.

"No lectures," said Chantel, throwing herself down on the sofa too. "I can't face it."

"You need to break up with Spike," said Amy. "You'll have a criminal record now."

"They just gave me a caution," said Chantel. "It's no big deal."

"It *is* a big deal," said Amy. "And can you please put out that joint? It's making me feel sick." She reached out to take it, but Chantel held it out of her reach.

Tim's eyes opened. He grabbed the joint from Chantel and stubbed it out in the ashtray. "Amy was meant to be painting tomorrow morning and then going to work, but she still got up in the middle of the night to come to your rescue."

"We both did," said Amy. She reached out and took Tim's hand, still holding the ashtray. His hand felt warm and comforting under her own.

"I wasn't going to let you go alone," said Tim. They both watched as a small wisp of smoke danced upwards. Tim used his other hand to stub out the joint completely, twisting it against the ashtray. He leaned over and gave Amy a kiss.

"You were the one who lit that joint," grumbled Chantel. "And seeing you two coo over each other like lovebirds is not what I need right now."

"What you need is to leave that drug dealer," said Amy, turning her attention back to Chantel but leaving her hand with Tim. He gently stroked her thumb.

"He's not really a drug dealer," said Chantel. "You're exaggerating."

"He deals drugs," replied Amy.

"Yes, but it's not like he's a gangster," protested Chantel.

"He set you up," said Amy.

"True," said Chantel. Amy could sense victory was close. "But I don't want to be alone," she added.

"He's not the only option," said Amy. "There are plenty of nice guys out there."

"Like Tim?" asked Chantel. He'd nodded off on the sofa, his mouth open.

"Easy, tiger," said Tim, briefly coming back to life. "I'm a catch."

"I was joking," said Chantel. "You're great. Everyone is great compared to Spike. Even bloody Dean Chapman."

Amy laughed. "He's married now," she said. "Did you hear?"

"No way," said Chantel. "He was my backup. Now even he's taken and I'll be sitting on the bloody shelf with a criminal record."

"It's just a caution," said Amy. She smiled at her friend. "What did that policeman say to you?" she asked, curious.

"He gave me his number," said Chantel. "In case Spike gave me any trouble."

"He fancied you," said Tim, eyes still closed.

"No he didn't," said Chantel.

"He did," said Tim. "A man knows."

"He was hot," admitted Chantel. "Bit square for me."

"Square is what you need," said Amy.

Chantel paused. "Perhaps you're right." She sat up. "I fancy starting over," she said. "Somewhere new. I've always liked the sound of Wales. Rolling hills, sheep. I might get a job in a quaint little pub and flirt with the local farmers."

"I like the sound of that," said Tim, surprising Amy. "No bloody drummers throwing tantrums, no supermarkets with shelves to be stacked, no loans to be paid off. I could be one of the farmers in your pub. I rather fancy myself shearing sheep."

"You two wouldn't last five minutes," said Amy. "You need the city. The buzz."

"Spike said the countryside is heaving with drugs," said Chantel. "Nothing else for people to do."

"Count me out," said Amy. "I like it here."

"Just you and me then, Timmy," said Chantel.

"And the sheep," said Tim. "Don't forget the sheep."

AMY TRIED TO ignore the unwelcome light of dawn creeping in through the curtains. Instead she turned over in bed to snuggle up closer to Tim. She rested her head on his chest and felt the regular thud of his heartbeat, echoing her own.

"Do you think she'll break up with him?" asked Tim. Amy was surprised at the question. She'd thought Tim was asleep.

"I hope so," she said. "I've never understood what she sees in him. And now he does this to her."

"Dangerous bad boys," explained Tim. "Women can't resist us."

"Us?" questioned Amy with a laugh.

"Of course *us*," he said. "I'm the epitome of danger: a hard-drinking rock star."

"You haven't been drunk in ages," said Amy proudly. She didn't mention that the band hadn't had a gig for ages either. "And you like coconut-scented toiletries and giggle like a baby if I tickle your belly," she added, running her fingers teasingly across his stomach.

Tim emitted a shrill squeal at her touch and sucked his stomach away from her hand. "Point made," he said.

"And I bet you wouldn't throw a bag of drugs at me if the police showed up."

"If I did, would you catch it?" asked Tim, turning on his side and looking at her. "Would you take the rap for me?"

"I've always been terrible at netball," replied Amy. "I'd probably drop it."

"I hope so." Tim's voice was serious. "I hate the idea of dragging you down with me."

"Don't become a drug dealer and we'll be fine," joked Amy.

"I mean it," said Tim. "I sometimes think you'd be better off without me. You could really go places, Amy. Maybe I'm bad for you."

Amy stared at him. Even in the dim light she could see concern clouding his features. "You're no Spike," she said. "You're talented, funny, and kind. And the love of my life." She leaned forwards and kissed him. "And you even stub out joints when I ask you to, into an ashtray shaped like a guitar."

"I am rather wonderful," said Tim, sounding happier. "And you're the love of my life too." He grinned at her, then snuggled down into the pillow, one arm resting comfortably across her chest. "Even if you can't catch."

Chapter
Eight

"Two visits in a week, Amy," said DCI Jack Hooper. "After eleven years with barely a word." He was sitting at his desk, but a hand rested on the mouse of his computer and his eyes were flicking back and forth to the screen as if the answers were to be found there.

"I'm sorry to bother you again," said Amy, feeling like he wished she'd leave. She hadn't even been offered water this time.

"I am very busy," he said, typing something on his keyboard.

"It's just that I've found something else," said Amy. "It's a letter. From Chantel." His eyes finally left the screen, and Amy felt as though he'd jolted a little. "You are busy," she said. "Maybe I should take this to someone else."

"No, no, it's fine," said Jack. "I've sent the e-mail now." He turned away from his computer properly and gave Amy his attention. "What . . ." He paused, with uncharacteristic hesitance. "What does she say?"

Amy got out the letter and passed it over to him. "See for yourself."

He grabbed the letter and studied it. "It's not in great condition," he said finally.

"It's been in a pot for rather a long time," said Amy. "It must have fallen in when I kept it by the door, and I didn't notice it in there when I moved the pot into the garden."

"All sorts have been eating at this," he said. "I really can't make out what Chantel is getting at. Can you?"

"Just the odd word," said Amy. "But I think perhaps it is a confession."

"Confession?" echoed Jack.

"That she and Tim did run away together. Look. *Jealous, love, run.*"

"I see," said Jack. He looked at the letter again. "Yes," he agreed. "It must be that. I always told you." He smiled at her. "Perhaps this is the closure you need."

"There's more," said Amy. She passed him the photograph. He took it and stared at it for a long time.

"Do you know what this is?" he asked finally.

"No idea," replied Amy. "I thought you might recognize it?"

"No," he replied. "Sorry." He looked again. "I don't see any landmarks either. It could be anywhere. Impossible to find out."

"I'm going to investigate," Amy told him. "Ask around the people we used to know. Someone must recognize it. Surely if I can find out where the photograph was taken, I can find out more about what happened. It must be linked."

"I can take care of that for you," said Jack, his hands on the photograph. "I am the professional, after all."

"I'd rather do it myself," said Amy, grabbing the photo back. "If you don't mind."

"Of course," replied Jack. He paused. "A word of warning though." Amy looked up at him, surprised. He leaned forwards. "I didn't want to tell you this," he said. "But Tim came to me, before he left." He sighed. "He was having money trouble. You know what he was like."

"He came to you?" queried Amy.

"Yes," replied Jack. "He needed my help."

"He asked to borrow money?"

"No," said Jack. "He'd already borrowed money, from people he shouldn't have."

"Who?" asked Amy.

"People he met through Chantel. Anyway, these people wanted their money back, and Tim was worried about what they might do to him if he didn't pay."

"You've never said," replied Amy, her voice careful. "Could these people have been involved in what happened? In why he went missing?"

"I spoke to my colleagues at the time, and it was one of the avenues they explored," said Jack. "But it didn't lead anywhere, so I never bothered you with it."

"So he might have left to escape the debt?" Amy hesitated. "Or could they have . . . ?"

"Like I said, my colleagues explored that avenue at the time. It was a dead end. I don't mean to worry you," Jack continued. "But I wouldn't go raking around in the past. No point digging up trouble for yourself."

He picked up a business card and scribbled something on the back, then handed it to Amy. "If you need anything," he said, "anything at all, you call me directly. That's my personal mobile number." He smiled at her. "Amy, I just want the best for you. Stay safe."

AMY SAT AT her computer screen wishing she had never agreed to go for that drink with Liam. She didn't have time this evening. Jack's warning had made her even more determined to find the truth. It was a new lead, and the most promising one she'd had for a long time. She needed to investigate.

Spike. That's who she needed to find. He'd know who Chantel knew. He might even have lent Tim the money himself. He did always have plenty of cash around.

Amy's stomach curdled at the prospect. She could almost smell him now, that strange stale aroma of weed, sweat, and the avocado oil he rubbed into his dreadlocks. Amy had never liked Spike, and it had made things awkward back then. She remembered how pleased she'd been that Chantel and Tim got on so well. Amy let out a short, bitter laugh. The irony.

What's so funny? Amy looked at the message from Liam. He couldn't see her desk from where he sat, so he must have seen her laugh and then hurried back to send the message. He followed up the note with a little animated image of a donkey snorting with laughter.

Charming.

Amy minimized the message and thought. Spike. She realized she didn't know his surname. He'd been a one-name person, like Cher or Madonna.

Simon. Simon might have his number. She remembered now. He hadn't liked Spike either at the beginning, but he'd warmed to him once he discovered his access to high-quality hash.

Amy got out her phone and sent Simon a quick message. Then she sat, staring at her phone. Ten a.m. Neither Simon nor Spike was likely to be up at this time if their pasts were anything to go on.

"Waiting for a call?" asked Carthika. Amy looked up from her phone to see Carthika looking amused. "A watched phone never rings."

"Thank you for that wisdom," said Amy.

"Anytime," replied Carthika, thankfully turning back to her own desk.

So drinks tonight. . . . What's your vibe? Another message from Liam, who seemed unperturbed that Amy had ignored his donkey.

Would no one leave her alone to get on with what she needed to do?

Sorry I can't tonight, replied Amy. She needed to focus on her investigations.

You promised, came straight back, with a picture of a cartoon bird with enormous oversized eyes brimming with tears. The bird reminded her of Scarlett, and Amy felt a pang of guilt, although she'd hardly consider that her agreement constituted a promise. LOL was the next message he sent.

Coffee instead? wrote Amy. She could do with some fresh air. A quick espresso to dispense with her Liam obligations.

Lunch? came the reply, swiftly followed by an image of an obese man devouring a rather magnificent-looking burger.

Fine, replied Amy, not wanting to continue a lengthy negotiation process. In the meantime she typed "Spike" into Google and watched the results appear. Hopeless. Nails, dogs, and a number of references to some kind of cactus computer-game character sprang back at her. No smelly drug dealers. She'd have to hope that Simon came through.

"THIS WASN'T REALLY what I had in mind," said Liam as they walked into the grab-and-go section of the tiny supermarket. "I told you I could get us a table at Sky Rocket."

"This is good," said Amy, selecting her usual cheese and pickle sandwich, and adding a rather fetching plastic bottle of still lemonade and a small bag of chocolate raisins to her haul.

"Shall we eat it in the park?" asked Liam, grabbing a triple-decker club sandwich with two bags of cheese puffs, a Mars bar, and a can of Diet Coke.

"Sure," replied Amy as they went to the checkout. Liam snatched her food from her and, despite her protestations, insisted on paying. She glanced at her phone. Still nothing.

"Hoping for a better offer?" asked Liam.

Amy felt dreadful. "I'm sorry," she said, putting her phone in her pocket. She tried her best to smile at him. "Of course not."

"You won't get one, you know," said Liam, rather ungraciously. "Oh," he said, as they came to the door. Rain was pouring down from the sky.

"We'll have to eat at our desks," said Amy, feeling pleased. "Still, this was nice."

Amy felt her phone beep in her pocket, and she couldn't resist whipping it out. It was from Simon and contained a number.

Spike's number. It must be.

"I've got to make a call," she said. She looked at Liam. "I'm so sorry. It's an emergency."

"Next time I'm planning the date," he said miserably. He lifted his jacket over his head and dashed back towards the office.

WHEN AMY ARRIVED at her street that evening, she discovered Rachel, Nina, Richard, and both boys staring up at the enormous tree outside Amy's front garden. Amy slowed her pace as she approached, wondering if there was a chance she could sneak past and into her house without them noticing. There always seemed to be someone lingering around the street now, waiting to make poor Amy's life more difficult. All she wanted to do now was sit among her things and think about what to do next.

A branch in the tree shook unnaturally, and Rachel reached her arms up towards it. "Come down now, sweetheart. There's a good boy."

Amy pushed her gate, which squeaked in an act of betrayal. They all turned towards her. "I told you about the vermin," said Rachel, her voice agitated. "And now poor Smudge is frightened out of his wits."

"He's not much of a cat if he's been scared by a mouse," said Amy, her patience already gone.

"Oh, Amy, it's a disaster," wailed Charles. "That poor mouse."

Daniel turned to her, his eyes full of tears. "Mickey needs help," he said.

"What's going on?" asked Amy.

"The boys saw Smudge playing with something," said Richard. "They went to see what it was, and he grabbed it in his mouth and climbed up the tree."

"He's never been that high before," said Rachel. "He'll be terrified."

"He had no problem jumping all over my pots," said Amy.

"He's practically level with the roof now," exclaimed Rachel. "What if he falls?"

"Rescue Mickey," squealed Daniel.

"Who?" asked Amy.

"The mouse," explained Charles. "We need to save him before Smudge gobbles him up."

Richard looked to the tree. "I'm not sure I can climb that," he said, sizing it up. "No low branches."

"It's probably not a mouse," said Nina. "It could be a rat, living the life of Riley in that house of yours, Amy."

"Rats are actually pretty clean," interjected Charles. "We were learning about them in school."

"Rats are filthy, vicious pests," said Rachel. She looked back to the tree. "Come down now darling." She paused. "Stuck up there with a dirty great rat."

Amy went to take a deep breath, but found her lungs wouldn't cooperate. Air wasn't getting into her at all. Rats in her house. She gulped again, feeling off-balance, and found black creeping into the edges of her vision. An image of Scarlett popped in front of her eyes, a rat crouched on the bird's beautiful back, its black eyes glinting in the light.

"I've got you," said Richard, as strong hands squeezed her arms. She leaned into him, feeling warmth and calmness emanating back. "Just breathe."

Amy obeyed, and the tightness in her chest started to release.

"She's fine," said Nina. "You can let go of her now."

"Take as long as you need." Richard's voice was soft, his breath warm in her ear.

"It was tiny," said Charles. "It wouldn't have been a rat. I think it was a baby mouse."

Daniel started crying, big dramatic sobs that overtook his whole body. Richard released Amy and went to his son. Amy found her strength returning as she looked at the tree. "I can climb that," she said, suddenly feeling confident as adrenaline pumped through her. She'd had plenty of practice scrambling over her piles of boxes. The tree would be easy. "Someone give me a leg up."

Richard tried to transfer Daniel to Nina, but his screams intensified. "I'll take him," said Charles, grabbing his brother round the middle.

Richard came over to Amy. "Are you sure?" he asked. "A moment ago you were faint."

"I just need to reach that first branch," she said.

"No problem," said Richard. "I can lift you that far. You're light as a feather."

Nina tutted. "I don't really think this is necessary—" she began.

"Save Smudge!" exclaimed Rachel.

"And the mouse," said Charles.

Richard grabbed Amy by the legs and heaved her up. She reached and caught the lowest branch, then used Richard's hands as a foothold. She swung herself up.

At the sight of her approaching, Smudge climbed up higher. But Amy was determined, clambering up until the branches could barely hold her weight and wobbled precariously. Amy reached out to the cat, and saw that there was something tiny, clutched tightly in his jaws. Just as she thought he was going to let her take hold of him, he leapt to a lower branch and then down to the ground, more worried by her than the height. He landed elegantly enough, until Rachel threw herself onto him, knocking him over. Charles let go of his brother, and Amy watched from the tree as boy, cat, woman, and mouse grappled with each other. This must be what the world looked like to Scarlett, she thought, rather enjoying the bird's-eye view as the action played out underneath.

"Got it," said Charles. "It's alive." Daniel immediately stopped wailing and ran over.

"Careful it doesn't bite you," said Richard.

"It's in shock," replied Charles. "And it is a baby."

"Let's take it inside and find a box," said Richard.

"Don't you take that animal into our house!" said Nina. "It's filthy."

"We'll get it to the vet," said Richard.

"What will that cost?" said Nina. "It's a pest!"

"Pet!" declared Daniel, the tears gone as quickly as they had come. "New pet!"

"We'll see what the vet says," said Richard, disappearing into the house and reappearing moments later with a shoebox.

"It's me or the mouse," declared Nina.

"The mouse," said Charles quickly.

"MICKEY!" shouted Daniel.

"We don't know if it is going to make it," said Richard.

"It's a pest," insisted Nina. "We should put it down."

"Nina!" exclaimed Richard. "A little compassion, please?" Nina disappeared inside the house, slamming the door with a dramatic bang. Richard ignored her and looked up at Amy. "Are you okay up there?"

"Fine," she replied. She carefully backed her way to the lowest branch and then hung there for a moment, rather like a monkey, before letting go and dropping to the pavement. "You get to the vet."

Going to his car, Richard handed Charles the box as he strapped Daniel into the car seat. A moment later they were gone, and Amy found herself standing on the road looking at Rachel, who was still fussing over Smudge.

"I love him like a baby," said Rachel, more to Smudge than to Amy. "When we couldn't . . . he was what we got instead. I love him so much." She buried her face in Smudge's fur. The cat was purring now.

"I'm sorry," said Amy.

"We're still trying," said Rachel. "It's amazing what they can do these days." She looked up. "But it's not been easy." Amy bit her lip. Rachel rubbed Smudge's ear, and his purr ratcheted up like the hum of an engine. "Thank you, Amy," said Rachel. "I know I've been a bit up and down with you. Mainly down. But thank you for saving my cat."

"He's tough," said Amy. "I don't think you need to worry about Smudge."

"He can't help it, you know," said Rachel. "He doesn't mean to hurt things or upset children. But hunting is in his nature."

"Of course," said Amy. "None of us can help who we are."

AMY SAT IN her hallway on a messy pile of post. She didn't like post—it certainly wasn't treasure. But somehow with all the newspapers and pots and bottles, it seemed to linger in her house too. Her mind went back to the letter from Chantel. It had been hidden by all her possessions. Perhaps, if she hadn't kept quite so much, she'd have found the one thing that really mattered.

She didn't want what it said to be true, but Amy realized the letter could have brought her closure. Closure, a long time ago. Even when things went wrong between Amy and Tim, they'd always come back together. He'd understood her better than anyone she'd ever known. At least, she'd thought he had. She remembered wanting to find Tim so much that at times it felt like even a body would be a relief. Before she'd finally allowed herself to believe she'd been wrong about him, perhaps from the start. She'd been betrayed.

And now all she was left with was a fraction of the story, a confusing ring, a picture of a sun setting over some trees.

And a mouse problem.

It was the bottles' fault. The bottles and the pots and the newspapers and the birds and the ashtrays. They'd hidden the truth from her.

Maybe Leah was right. Maybe she should have a clear-out.

She pictured the mouse, tiny and vulnerable in Smudge's jaws. It was a mouse, but could it have been a rat, as Nina had suggested? There were children here now. Maybe her house was a public nuisance.

The bottles on the hallway floor first, decided Amy, getting to her feet while she felt the urge. They were empty wine bottles. They were nothing special. They had been drunk from, they had served their purpose. The kind thing to do would be to get rid of them. Put them in the recycling so they could have a chance at a second life.

Broken down and remade. Reborn. Just because they didn't stay in their current form didn't mean that they wouldn't be happy.

Happy. Amy almost laughed at herself. They were bottles—inanimate objects. She was a sensible person. She worked in financial advice, for God's sake. So what if they reminded her of him? He didn't want to be reminded of her. He'd left, abandoned his whole life to be with someone else. Her best friend.

Where to start? Amy grabbed the nearest bottle, then a few more. As many as she could fit in her arms. She staggered to the door and pushed it open, almost flattening Richard, who was standing on the other side next to a deliveryman holding a huge bouquet of red roses.

"I was just coming round to see how the hero was," said Richard. "But it seems you're popular."

Amy looked at the flowers. "You must have the wrong address," she told the courier, trying not to drop any of the bottles. Richard sprang forwards and took several of them from her.

The courier lifted up the visor on his helmet and frowned at the label. "Are you Amy Ashton?" he asked.

"Yes," said Amy.

"Sign here," he said, thrusting out some kind of tablet. Amy scrawled on it with her finger, finding it oddly difficult to fathom writing without a pen.

"Those are rather spectacular," said Richard. "Who are they from?" The courier gave Richard a sympathetic look, then closed his visor and made his exit.

Amy didn't answer. Flowers. Could they be . . . ? Red roses weren't exactly his style, but still . . . She tore open the envelope.

"I'll leave you to it," said Richard, without leaving.

Amy read the writing. "Oh," she said, feeling disappointment flood her. "Just Liam."

"Who is Liam?"

"No one," said Amy. She forced herself to smile—otherwise she thought she might cry. "How's the mouse?"

"It will be fine," said Richard. "And the best bit is that the vet said it was just the right age to tame. So we're going to keep it." He lifted the bottles in his hands. "What's the deal with these?"

"Can I use your recycling bin?" she asked. "I never used mine . . . and then I needed the space for the pots, so . . ."

"Of course," said Richard. He looked at Amy, one eyebrow raised. "That looks as if it was quite a party. Invite me next time."

"It took me years to drink these," said Amy with dignity. "I didn't binge like some kind of teenager."

"I'm sorry," said Richard. "I was joking. It's not funny." He glanced at Amy's open doorway. "Those newspapers could be recycled too."

"Not the newspapers," said Amy. "They contain information," she explained.

"From how long ago?" queried Richard.

The newspapers were all the local papers, and some dated back eleven years. At first Amy had scanned for information, in case some keen journalist had found out something the police had not. Then, as she'd lost hope, she found she didn't have the energy to scour the pages. But she couldn't simply get rid of them. There could be a clue.

But still. Some stuff must go. "You can take the bottles you're holding," she told Richard, feeling decisive. "Just the ones you're holding. Will there be room for old post too?"

"Of course," said Richard. "Whatever you need." He smiled at her. "You know, you're brave in more ways than one, Amy Ashton."

Amy frowned at him. "Take those bottles before I change my mind," she said, confident that she still had plenty more left. He took the bottles, and Amy closed the door behind him.

Amy looked around, and chose the bottom step as the best sorting location. She grabbed the mail that still sat on the doormat and the letters that had spilled from her pile, like the bubbles overflowing from freshly poured Prosecco. She'd start there.

She put anything that had a marketing message on the cover straight into a pile for recycling. Printed envelopes got a cursory open and check, before being condemned to the same fate. She saw that Leah was right, there were a few letters here from the council, getting increasingly aggressive in tone. She put them in the recycling too.

Progress was quick, and soon Amy's recycling pile reached her knees, the papers gently caressing her legs. She thought about what would happen to the paper next. What would it be turned into? A book, perhaps, she decided. She looked at the envelopes. Several books, probably. That would be a nice second life for junk mail. She got up to go to the loo and had to wade through paper to move. She'd put the first load out now, she decided. Gathering it up in her arms in a giant hug, Amy opened the door and made her way to the recycling wheelie bin that sat outside Richard's house. She struggled to lift the lid, pulling a face at the smell that came out, of moldy baked beans and not completely clean cartons of yogurt. She tried not to look at the bottles, then dumped the papers inside. She went back into the house.

The hallway felt different already. Spacious. The floor was clear, at least by the doormat. Amy took a deep breath. It was lovely.

She almost felt like opening her door to show the world, then recoiled at the thought.

Was it lovely? Amy looked at the dirty floor. She'd forgotten how ugly the lino was. Maybe the bottles were better after all. She felt a draft. At least the post had provided some insulation.

It was Wednesday. The rubbish wouldn't be collected again till Monday. She had until then to change her mind. Nothing was gone forever.

Amy heard her phone beep and grabbed it from her pocket.

Spike.

And he wanted to meet.

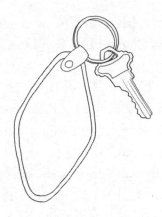

June 2004

"It's like *Little House on the Prairie*." Chantel was practically skipping up the garden path.

"It's a tiny two-bed house in a grotty suburb," replied Tim, "with bad lino and horrible green carpets."

"It's a clean start," said Amy. "I think that's what Chantel meant."

"No drugs in the house," said Chantel, smiling. "No crazy parties and no rum at three a.m. Tea and biscuits and the occasional sophisticated glass of wine."

"I've always been a sophisticated wine sort of guy," said Tim, giving Amy a little kiss. "You remember the night we met?"

"Always," said Amy, leaning in to return the kiss. "Screw tops and roundabouts," she whispered to him.

"I'll do the honors," said Chantel, ignoring them. She put the key in the lock. "New life, here we come."

"Wait," said Amy. "Let's get a photo." She balanced her camera on the wall, set the timer, and the three of them stood and posed, grinning like maniacs. She and Tim were clutching backpacks full of their possessions; Chantel had two large wheelie suitcases. "Say cheese," said Amy.

"Cheesy," said Chantel. She opened the door and breathed in. She turned to Amy. "Thank you for this," she said, giving her friend a hug. "Sometimes I just feel like I want to shed my skin and start all over again. And now I can."

Amy hugged her back. "Fresh start," she said. "I can't wait." She was excited. True, the higher rent meant she was stuck full-time at Trapper, Lemon, and Hughes for the foreseeable future, but she could still spend evenings and weekends painting.

"It's a pity there's no garage," said Tim.

"You don't have a car," said Chantel.

"For rehearsals," explained Tim. "We'll have to do it in the living room."

"We won't be popular with the new neighbors," Chantel said. "That couple next door already look pretty sour."

"Mr. and Mrs. Hill? I met them when I came to take the mattress delivery. They seem very nice—I bet they'll love Tim's music," said Amy loyally.

"It's a more mellow sound these days," agreed Tim.

Chantel opened up one of her suitcases and removed a small kettle and three chipped mugs. "Tea?" she said. "We should christen the new house."

"You're the perfect flatmate," Amy declared. "I never would have thought to bring a kettle."

"We'll have to shop for all the other bits and pieces we need tomorrow," said Chantel. "I left everything else at Spike's place. Pretty tragic, isn't it? All we've got to show for ourselves is in these suitcases. And those hideous backpacks."

"I've got my music," said Tim defensively. "And Amy has all the gorgeous art in her studio. You have . . ." He paused. "Does a criminal record count?"

"It's just a caution," said Chantel. "And you're an arsehole."

"Ignore him," said Amy. "He's very protective of those back-packs."

Chantel laughed. "I've dealt with worse," she said. "Right. I'm going out to buy milk and biscuits. And I'll get more keys cut."

Chantel left, and Amy and Tim stood looking at each other. "I forgot to carry you over the threshold," he said regretfully. "Shall we go out and in again, now she's gone?"

"I think we need to be married for that," said Amy.

"A traditionalist?" said Tim. "There are a lot of things we do that you're meant to be married for."

For a second, Amy thought he was going to propose. It would be perfect: a new start in the new house. Planning a wedding. She'd design the invitations. Tim's band would play at the reception.

If Tim saw that thought cross her mind, he didn't let on. "Come on," he said. "Let's christen the place properly." He tried to pick Amy up in a fireman's lift, and she let out a surprised scream. "Maybe not," he said, setting her down and kissing her instead. "Let's check out the bedroom."

AMY LAY NEXT to Tim. They hadn't bought a proper bed yet, just a mattress on the floor. They hadn't even taken the plastic wrapper off, and she could feel it sticking to her bare legs.

"I do want to, you know," said Tim all of a sudden. Amy glanced at him; she'd thought he was asleep.

"Want to what?" said Amy. Although she thought she knew, she wanted him to say the words.

"You know what I mean," said Tim. He clearly didn't want the words spoken. "But I want to be sorted first. So I can take care of you."

"It's not the fifties," said Amy. "I earn more than you do at my day job, plus I've had that gallery interested in my paintings." As soon as the words escaped her lips, she regretted them. Here he was, telling her he wanted to get married, and she was boasting about her own success.

"That's cool," said Tim, unperturbed. "But I'm a mess. You know that. I need to get the band sorted, or maybe I need to call time on it. Study law, like my dad said I should. Go back to him for a loan, tail between my legs."

"But music is your passion," said Amy, keen to make up for her earlier lack of empathy. "And you're so talented." Although even she had to admit, he'd earned almost no money from the band for the last few years. She'd wondered herself if it was time for him to look for alternative careers. He was smart; he shouldn't be stacking supermarket shelves forever.

"I love how supportive you are," said Tim, and Amy felt guilty again for her thoughts. He leaned over and kissed her, the plastic crinkling loudly underneath him. "And I just wanted you to know that one day, I'll do it."

"And one day I'll say yes," said Amy, wishing that was what she'd said at first.

They were interrupted by a loud bang on the bedroom door. "You guys decent?" called out Chantel.

"Just a minute," said Tim. They both hurriedly put their clothes back on as Chantel came through the door carrying a tray, clearly stolen from a pub, that held three cups of tea, a packet of shortbread, and a shiny pile of keys with enormous fluffy key rings. "Yuck," she said, staring at Tim's bare chest as he pulled a T-shirt over his head. "There is such a thing as a gym, you know."

"There is such a thing as privacy too," grumbled Tim, taking his tea from the tray.

Chantel popped the rest of it down on the floor and sat on the mattress. "Springy," she commented. "Nice."

"That's a lot of keys," said Amy, helping herself to a biscuit. "And quite a collection of key rings."

"A copy of the front door keys for you, one for me, and two for Tim, because he'll lose his," she said. Tim pulled a face at her. "And two copies of the back door key. We can keep one in the kitchen and you can keep the spare, Amy, because you're the most responsible. Great key rings, eh? My treat. Yours is the pink one," Chantel said to Tim, throwing his set in his direction. He caught it, spilling his tea in the process. "Yours is gray, Amy, to match your eyes. I've got brown."

Amy took her set in her hand and squeezed it, feeling the reassuring sharpness of the keys' edges against her skin. She stroked the key ring, a gray fluff-ball that reminded her of a curled-up mouse. "Thanks, Chantel," she said.

"Thanks, Amy," replied Chantel, her voice serious. "And you, Tim. I needed this." She reached out and gathered them both in a large hug. Amy hugged them back. Living with the two people she loved most in the world. She knew she was going to be very happy in this house.

Chapter
Nine

When Spike had suggested that they meet in his "office," Amy couldn't help but picture the word in quotation marks. Probably used ironically to describe a squat that doubled as an opium den. She'd counter-proposed a café nearby, but Spike was insistent. She settled by suggesting a meeting in the morning, when she imagined there to be fewer of whatever "clients" (also in quotation marks) Spike had around. He'd agreed, and surprised her by proposing 8 a.m. The "office" was in town, and looking at a map, Amy discovered that if she kept the meeting short and to the point, she wouldn't even be late for work.

And she wanted to keep it as short as possible. She'd stopped by the Boots at the station again on the way and Joanna had obliged with a generous four sprays of perfume that left Amy with a slight headache. Still, it would be better than Spike's fragrant alternative, and she couldn't risk the scent of cannabis lingering on her clothes in her office.

So Amy was rather surprised when she found herself standing in front of a large corporate building, rather smarter than the offices of Trapper, Lemon, and Hughes. She double-checked the address and then stepped inside, wondering if she'd somehow contacted the wrong Spike.

There were lots of companies in this building, and she filled in her details on a large book of lined paper. She hesitated at the name of the person she was visiting, feeling that to write "Spike" was somehow inappropriate. There was no alternative, so she scribbled it in a messy, hopefully indecipherable way. Apparently she was expected, and the receptionist solemnly handed her a lanyard and instructed her to take the B lift to the seventeenth floor. Amy obliged. She stepped out of the lift to a maze of offices with glass partitions and myriad logos and stood there, feeling lost.

"Amy Ashton?" A tall man with short gray hair and a smart suit was looking at her.

"I'm looking for Spike," she said, feeling like a little girl. "I'm sorry, I don't have a surname."

"You haven't changed a bit!" he exclaimed. Amy found herself encased in a hug. The man released her and held her back from him a little so they could better see each other. "You don't recognize me without the dreadlocks, do you?" he asked.

"Spike?" Amy peered into the face. Sure enough, he was starting to look familiar. His eyes were less sleepy, his skin was cleaner, and he was missing his trademark smell. But it was him.

"Gosh, that takes me back," he said with a laugh. "Michael Spikerton," he added. "No one has called me Spike in years. Come, come, we'll go to my office. I've ordered breakfast."

Amy followed him, feeling dizzy with his transformation. He led her into a small room with a desk, table and chairs, and a dazzling view of the city. "Mini Danish?" he asked her, gesturing to a very corporate-looking breakfast platter. "Or fruit skewers? Help yourself and I'll pour the coffee."

"What happened to you?" exclaimed Amy, unable to contain herself.

"I grew up," replied Spike. "A while ago now. Milk?"

"Yes," said Amy. She took a cinnamon swirl from the platter and sat down, staring at him. "When . . . ?"

"I'd always planned to become an adult when I hit forty. Have fun in my twenties and thirties, and, man, I did." He smiled at Amy, memories filling his eyes. "By then I'd built up enough of a nest egg"—he winked at her—"so I quit the drugs, invested the money, and cut off my dreads. They were starting to stink."

"What do you do now?" Amy gestured around the room.

"This and that," said Spike mysteriously. "Import-export. Bit of property development. Investments. All pretty legal." He grinned at her again. "It's actually much easier work. More sociable hours. How's the art?"

Amy picked up the pastry, then put it down again. "I don't paint anymore," she told him.

"That's a shame," he said.

She looked at the mug in front of her—white, bland, and corporate. "I don't remember you looking at my work back then," said Amy, suddenly feeling angry at this new Spike. Michael. "You were too busy getting high and getting Chantel in trouble with the police."

Spike looked nervous for the first time. "I hope we're not going to have a problem," he said. "I've changed." He looked at her, his face hardening. "But if it's trouble you want . . . ?"

"No," said Amy, alarmed at the turn the conversation was taking. Spike had seemed harmless enough when she first met him, but she remembered now that he had a temper.

"Sorry," said Spike, taking a bite of a miniature croissant. "Uncalled-for."

"That's okay," said Amy.

"So how are you?" asked Spike, his voice friendly again. "Are you still in that same house?"

"Yes," replied Amy, surprised.

"I've got a few properties in the area now," said Spike, the sales-man in him coming out. "I'd be happy to arrange for mates' rates. For old times' sake."

"I'm happy where I am." Amy paused. "I've come about Tim," she said. "And Chantel."

"Have you seen her?" Spike dropped the croissant back to his plate.

"No," replied Amy. "Not since she disappeared."

She took the photo from her bag and passed it across the table. Spike inspected it. "What's this?" he asked.

"Do you recognize the photo?"

Spike frowned at it. "Sorry," he said, passing it back. Amy swal-lowed disappointment and stared at the picture. It was a beautiful sunset, but why couldn't it have a landmark? A clock tower. A church. Instead it was just anonymous trees, the ubiquitous sun, and the cor-ner of some kind of vehicle. If only she could find out where it was.

"I blame Jack," said Spike, out of nowhere. "I never liked him. You know he's a DCI now?"

Amy ignored him. Of course Spike would be jealous of Jack. "Jack told me that Tim borrowed money. From a friend of Chantel's. I thought you might know something about that."

"Not a thing," said Spike quickly. "Tim wasn't my biggest fan."

Amy felt disappointment rise up her throat and mingle with the cinnamon pastry. "You're sure?" she said. "You had quite a lot of cash around. Perhaps—"

"I certainly didn't lend him money," replied Spike. "I'd never trust a musician to pay me back. Definitely not Tim."

"And you don't have any idea who might have—"

"None," replied Spike. He picked up his croissant again. He looked into the air, as if his memories were floating there. "I never thought Chantel would have done that to you," he said, his voice hushed, as if someone might be listening. "You guys were so close. I think if she'd have run off with anyone, it would have been you."

"Well, it wasn't," said Amy.

"That's what I'm saying," said Spike. He paused. "When Chantel and I were together, she still loved you the most. Not in that way," he added hurriedly. "But it was hard, that's all I'm saying. Always being second fiddle to her best friend."

"I didn't see much of her once she was with Jack," said Amy.

Spike shrugged. "Maybe it was different with those two," he said. "But I don't see her leaving you for a man. Not any man. Certainly not Tim. It just doesn't feel right. You must know that."

AMY SAT IN her house looking at Scarlett. The bird looked back. *Leopards can't change their spots,* thought Amy, *and robins can't change their red breasts.* But drug dealers? It was like the opposite of Samson; perhaps cutting off his hair had given him strength.

What he'd said about Chantel had made her think. Perhaps it wasn't just Tim she should be looking for.

She stood up and went to find her handbag. Inside was the piece of paper with Toyah's number. The country code made it feel long and complicated.

Dubai.

It seemed an unlikely place for Toyah to end up, but perhaps her dislike of the sunshine was overshadowed by her desire to be around family. And perhaps her brother-in-law had mellowed. People changed. Amy knew that.

She'd searched for Toyah on social media, hoping to be able to message her. But nothing. Amy was surprised. She also searched for Tim's father. He came up on Facebook instantly, and Amy fired off a quick message to him before she could change her mind.

Amy held the paper again, running her finger across the lettering. It had been years since she'd spoken to Toyah. Once she'd been like a second mother to Amy; she'd certainly felt closer to Toyah than she had to her own. But after the initial flurry of contact and panic when Chantel and Tim disappeared, Amy had stopped calling. Toyah had tried to get in touch several times, but Amy hadn't answered. If her daughter could betray Amy like that, she'd decided, she had no reason to trust Chantel's mother.

Unless she'd been wrong all these years.

Amy picked up her phone and dialed. She realized she hadn't even checked what time it would be in Dubai now, and decided to hang up and work that out first.

But before she could, a voice answered.

Not Toyah's.

"Is that Laura?" she asked.

"Yes," said a suspicious voice. "Is this a sales call? Because I'm busy."

"No," said Amy. She hesitated. She'd met Laura once or twice, and pictured her in her mind's eye. Dark-blond hair always partnered with a tan. An elegant array of white trousers and tailored jackets. A no-nonsense approach to life that Amy had found intimidating. "I don't know if you remember me," she mumbled. "It's Amy Ashton. I was friends with Chantel."

This was greeted by silence. "How did you get this number?" Laura asked eventually.

"Jack Hooper gave it to me," said Amy. "He was Chantel's boyfriend—"

"I know who Jack Hooper is," said Laura, her voice careful. "What were you doing talking to him?"

"Is Toyah there?" asked Amy, not feeling up to dealing with Chantel's rather aggressive aunt after all.

"She's out right now," replied Laura. "But I can take a message."

Amy hesitated for a moment, unsure how much to share. "Can you tell her that I found something, please? Something that I want to discuss with her?"

"That's rather cryptic," said Laura. "Care to be more specific?"

"It's a letter," said Amy. In for a penny, in for a pound. "I found it five days ago, but I think it's been there for a long time. From Chantel."

Silence greeted her again.

"I couldn't read it," continued Amy. "Not much of it. It's been outside awhile and it's all smudged by the rain. There was a picture there too. A photo."

"What was in the photo?" asked Laura.

"I don't know," said Amy. "A park maybe. Trees. A sunset. Some kind of car in the corner. But I can't tell where it was taken. I thought that Toyah might recognize it. She could help me understand what Chantel was trying to tell me."

"And did you show the letter to Jack?" asked Laura.

"Yes," said Amy. "And the photo. He didn't recognize it."

"There was no address on the letter, for you to contact Chantel?"

"Nothing legible," replied Amy.

"You're sure?"

"Of course I'm sure," snapped Amy. Then she felt bad. Laura must want to know where her niece was too. "Sorry," she said. "But the letter was in quite a state."

"Did you show it to anyone else? The photo or the letter?"

"Spike," replied Amy.

"Spike? How's that little scumbag?"

"Surprisingly well," said Amy. For a moment she felt an overwhelming urge to gossip about Spike's change in appearance with Chantel. But this woman on the phone was not her friend. Not even close.

"He didn't recognize the picture," said Laura.

"No," said Amy, feeling impatience rise up again. "When will Toyah be back?"

"Not for a while," replied Laura. "But I'll tell you what to do. Scan in the picture and the letter and e-mail it to me. I'll show Toyah, and she can get back to you if she recognizes anything. She's very busy though, so it might take her a while."

"Okay," agreed Amy, writing down the e-mail address Laura gave her.

"Amy?" said Laura, her voice a little softer. "It's been a long time since Toyah has heard from you."

Amy nodded agreement, forgetting for a moment that she couldn't be seen.

"I think that she'll be pleased that you've been in touch. Very pleased."

"I just want to find out the truth," said Amy.

"Of course," replied Laura.

"I can't imagine Toyah in Dubai," said Amy, her voice thoughtful. "It just doesn't feel right."

"What are you talking about?" snapped Laura. "She's here with me. Her sister."

"But . . ." Amy paused. She knew Toyah didn't get on with her sister or her sister's husband. But she couldn't say that. "It's so hot," she finished lamely.

"We're not camped out in the middle of the desert here, you know," said Laura. "There's air-conditioning and skyscrapers and sunscreen."

"Okay," said Amy, unconvinced.

"Listen, Amy. Toyah is fine here. But keep your thoughts to yourself."

"What?"

"You can't trust everyone."

"I'm well aware of that," said Amy. Belongings were what she could trust. People were not.

"Take care, Amy." She hung up.

The phone call reminded Amy how abrupt Laura could be. She remembered now that Toyah used to complain about her sister and was rather pleased when she moved abroad. She'd said that Laura was an easier person to love when there was a continent between them. Add in her dislike of sunshine and the fact she couldn't stand her snobbish brother-in-law, and Amy found it more and more unlikely that Dubai would be where she chose to move. Something didn't add up.

She'd lost her daughter, Amy reminded herself. Grief made people behave in odd ways.

Still, it left Amy feeling uneasy. She wished she'd had the chance to speak to Toyah herself after all. The unease mixed with another emotion. Sadness. She realized that it wasn't just Chantel she'd missed from that family.

It was Toyah too.

AMY PAUSED. SHE could hear a noise coming from outside her house. People talking. She made her way carefully through her little ravine to the window.

It was six o'clock, but still light in the middle of the summer. Three women and a man were standing just outside the gate to her garden. Amy peered at them. Rachel and Nina, loitering there as usual. The man she didn't know. He looked bored and was glancing at his watch. The third woman she recognized. Floral trousers again. It was the woman from the council.

The woman looked over and Amy tried to duck, but there was a box in the way. They locked eyes.

"She is home," said Leah loudly.

"I told you she would be," said Nina. "She's always in, of an evening."

There was nothing for it. Amy made her way to the door. She opened it. "This is a surprise," she said.

"It shouldn't be," said Leah, sounding cross. "We sent you a letter."

Amy found herself rather pleased that she'd cleared out her hallway, and left the door a little ajar. "Must have got lost in the post," she said, thinking of all the mail she'd dumped into Richard's recycling.

"I hope now is a good time," said Leah. "We know you are in full-time employment so we scheduled an out-of-hours visit."

"What for?" asked Amy.

"To look at your house," said Nina. "All that stuff, the pots, the mice. It's for your own good, Amy. I think I saw a rat the other day."

"A rat?" said Leah, making a note. "That's not good."

"Come on, Nina," said Rachel. "There was no rat. And just one very small mouse, and that could have come from anywhere." She smiled at Amy. "I have a cat," she explained to Leah. "He fetches them from all over."

Amy gave Rachel a grateful smile, but Nina was scowling at her friend. "It's a menace to the children, her being here," she said.

"Really?" said Rachel. "I thought the children were rather taken with her."

"That's not the point," said Nina.

"Quite right," added Leah. "This is about your house, Amy, not about your character." She paused. "Have you had a chance to clean up at all?"

"The hallway," said Amy. She opened the door a little more, and all three women peered in. The man stayed back, leaning on his van, his fingers twitching. He looked very much like someone who wanted a cigarette.

"That's quite a lot of stuff I can see on the staircase," said Leah. "Can I come in and take a better look?"

"No," said Amy, feeling panicky again. "There's no point. I'm going to clear the rest of the house," she lied. "But I've only done the hallway so far."

"Okay," said Leah, making a note. "That's a shame."

"But we've got a schedule, don't we, Amy?" interjected Rachel. "The hallway was this week's target, then next week we're going to do the living room, then the kitchen before we move upstairs in August. We've hired a skip."

Amy's heart sank at the thought of her beautiful belongings higgledy-piggledy in a horrible dumpster.

"Isn't that right, Amy?" prompted Rachel.

"Are you okay, dear?" asked Leah.

Amy pulled herself together. "Yes, I'm fine," she said. "And yes," she added, looking at Rachel, "I have help."

"Well, that's good to hear," said Leah. "But I do think we should take a little look now, just to know what we're dealing with."

"She clearly doesn't want us here," said the man. Amy had forgotten he was there. "And she's got a plan. That's all we need. Let's write that up and check back in, say, two weeks?"

"Three," said Rachel.

"Great," he replied. "Come on, Leah. The match starts in ten."

"We will be back," warned Leah, looking a bit miffed at being overruled. "To do a further assessment. And the chimney will still need to be repaired."

"You're just going?" asked Nina. "You're leaving it like this?"

"There's not much else we can do for the moment," said Leah regretfully. "But don't worry. The council's wheels are in motion."

Nina snorted and disappeared back to her house. Leah and the man got back in their van.

"Thank you, Rachel," said Amy.

"No worries. I used to be employed by the council, so I know how it works."

Amy waited till the van had driven off. "I'm not going to get a skip," she whispered.

"I know," said Rachel. "But I'm sure there's something we can do." She grinned at Amy. "I'm off to feed Smudge. We wouldn't want him getting an appetite for any more mice."

"I ALWAYS HOPED I'd meet you one day, but I thought it would be with my son on your arm." Amy found herself in a hug that lasted too long. It was a Saturday afternoon and she'd spent all morning traveling here, but she suddenly wished she could turn around and go home again. Eventually Tim's father released her. "We should have met years ago," he added. "All that time. Wasted."

"Thank you for seeing me, Mr. Carver," said Amy. He'd been easy to track down on Facebook; he was the generation that embraced the technology without understanding privacy settings.

"Call me Alan." They looked at one another, assessing the damage. Alan was in his late sixties. Tim had told her that he'd been young when he married Tim's mother. Love at first sight, apparently. And it had lasted until Tim's mother died, eleven years later. Alan had disappeared into his own grief, having little love left to deal with his devastated ten-year-old. Tim had never forgiven him for that, made all the more bitter when Alan eventually remarried. Amy hadn't met Alan or his new wife in all the years Amy had been with Tim.

"Come in," said Alan with forced joviality. "We've a lot to catch up on."

Amy entered the house. It was generously sized, one of many identical detached homes in what would be described by an estate agent as a luxury development. The walls were a pinky shade of cream with light carpets that felt thick and soft under Amy's feet. "Shoes off, if you don't mind," said Alan apologetically. "Roberta's at Pilates, but she'd have a fit if she knew we were walking around in our shoes on the new carpet."

"Okay," said Amy, slipping off her trainers and noticing the teddy bears on Alan's socks for the first time. Being without shoes felt overly intimate, and Amy felt strangely vulnerable in her black socks as she followed Alan to the living room.

The room was large, but there were one too many plump velour sofas in the room so it felt crowded. Amy almost laughed out loud. Who was she to criticize? She padded up to the mantelpiece. There was a family photo: Alan, Roberta, and twin boys in school uniforms a size too big gazed back at her. To the side was another photo: Tim in his own school uniform, scowling at the camera.

Suddenly Amy wished she hadn't come.

"Have a seat," said Alan. "Tea?"

"No," said Amy. She perched on the edge of one of the huge sofas, which did its best to suck her back into its depths. "I can't stay long," she added.

"Of course," replied Alan. They sat in silence for a moment.

"Each time the doorbell rings, I hope it's him," he said all of a sudden. He looked at Amy. She gave him an involuntary flicker of recognition. Then he looked back down at the bears on his socks. "I know. Ten years and we hardly spoke. I never even met you. His girlfriend. But I always thought we'd make up one day. I knew he'd come around. I was rather hoping the arrival of the twins would do it, but then that's when he disappeared." Alan paused. "I didn't have time to deal with it then. And I wasn't very helpful." He looked at Amy. "I'm sorry," he said. "I thought he'd be back."

"I hoped you might have heard something," said Amy finally. "From Tim. That's why I've come."

"He's been in touch?" Alan leaned forwards on the sofa.

"No," she said quickly. "Sorry. That's not why I'm asking. I just thought that maybe it was me that he . . ." Amy couldn't bring herself to say that perhaps it was her he didn't want to see. That maybe she was the reason he'd left.

"It would be you he called," said Alan, "if he's . . ." His voice drifted off too. He looked to his socks again. "But I don't think he's coming back. Not after all this time." Alan got up and went over to the photo. "He was handsome," he said. "I know the twins are fair, but they've got something of Tim about them, don't you think?"

Amy looked at the photograph of two smiling blond boys. "Maybe," she said doubtfully.

"Glad you think so," said Alan with a smile. "Although people always said Tim looked like his mother. . . ." His voice trailed off. "Are you sure you won't have that tea?"

"If you haven't heard anything—" started Amy, standing up.

"Have tea with me," said Alan. "Please. I didn't see my son for almost ten years before he went missing. Maybe you can fill me in?"

Amy stood still. It had been a long time since she'd spoken about Tim.

"Could you tell me about his music?" continued Alan. "I wish now I'd been more supportive. I'd kill to have been to one of his gigs. Not much use now." He picked at a bit of fluff on his sweater. "I wanted him to have a good job, not struggle as a musician. He was bright, he could have been a lawyer." Alan gestured round the house. "All this. Security. Everything I wanted for him came from a good place."

"He wrote the most beautiful songs," said Amy, sitting down again. "There was one, about a missed sunset . . ." She found she couldn't speak for a moment.

"I'll get the tea," said Alan. He stopped on his way to the kitchen and came back and squeezed Amy's hand. "Thank you for coming," he said. "Thank you so much."

IT HAD BEEN a long time since Amy had spent a night away from her house, but by the time she glanced at her watch that evening it was too late to make the long journey back. Alan had ignored her pleas to call a taxi to the nearest hotel and had insisted that she stay in their spare room. Roberta had put a shepherd's pie in the oven, and she and the twins, now eleven, chatted amicably about school and people Amy didn't know over dinner. Alan and Amy had eaten in silence, surrounded by an exhausted haze of memories. Eventually she'd accepted the fluffy towels Roberta pressed on her and slipped into a fitful sleep in a soft and overly hot bed.

Now she found herself with a belly full of bacon and eggs and smelling of Roberta's unfamiliar lily of the valley soap as her journey home was finally coming to a close. She'd fought back tears all the way. She could feel them now, brewing behind her eyelids and ready to escape as soon as she reached home. She turned the corner into her street. Alan hadn't been what she was expecting, and she found herself wishing again and again that she'd encouraged Tim to make peace with his father.

Alan Carver was what Tim had needed in his life. And he could have had his father back. If only his father had tried harder. Or if Tim had been able to forgive.

Amy felt a wave of forgiveness wash over her like Roberta's soap. If she had a second chance with the people she'd lost, she wouldn't waste it. She'd forgive them and at the very least have her friends again.

At least, she hoped that was what she'd do.

"Amy!" Charles bounded up to her, nearly knocking her off her feet. "There you are."

"I'm sorry, Charles," said Amy, feeling exhausted. "I can't talk today. I just want to go home."

"But that's it," said Charles. "Your home. Something's happened. Come see."

Amy felt the fatigue pushed from her body by adrenaline. And dread. She started to run after him and her mind ran too. A gas leak. An explosion. A fire. A burst pipe. A flood. A burglary. Her treasures burnt. Sodden. Stolen. Ruined.

"Amy!" said Richard, running up to her just as his son had done moments before. "Don't panic," he said, his words futile. "But something happened last night."

Amy pushed past him. She had to see for herself.

The building still stood. She couldn't see smoke, nor water.

Then she saw.

Her hand clapped over her mouth so hard it hurt. She felt Richard's hand on her shoulder. "I'm so sorry," he said. "I heard noises in the night, but I just thought it was foxes. I should have done something. . . . I didn't realize you were . . ." He paused. "Staying elsewhere last night."

Her pots.

Amy could barely take in the damage. She put her hand on her gate, unwilling to go inside. Richard's hand was still on her shoulder.

"We didn't know whether to clear up," he said, his voice quiet, "so we've left it. Do you want the police?"

Amy shook her head, in a daze.

"I expect it was just kids," he continued, as if that made it better. "Vandals. Your house hasn't been broken into, we've checked."

"I'm sorry, Amy," said Charles, close to tears himself. "The pots were awesome. And the flowers. Almost as awesome as diggers."

"Can I call someone for you?" asked Richard, as if she'd had a bereavement. She felt as though she had. "Your boyfriend perhaps? Liam, is it?"

"What? No." Amy found that a small, sticky hand had intertwined itself with her own. She looked down. It was Daniel. His other hand was to his face and he was sucking his thumb. "Ice cream for Amy," he said, the words barely intelligible through his hand.

"Good idea," said Richard. "Come to our house and I'll make you a cup of tea." He looked at her again. "Maybe something stronger is needed."

"I just need to . . ." Her voice trailed off.

"Of course," said Richard. He shepherded his kids away from her gate, and Amy felt the little hand release her own. "We'll be right over here. When you're ready."

Amy opened her gate and heard it swing shut behind her. She stood and looked at her garden.

All of her pots. Smashed. She bent down to the nearest one. It had a green glaze, but she could see the terra-cotta orange within, its true color exposed. She traced the break line with her finger, and more soil fell from the broken pot to the ground. The rose bush that had sat within it was draped on the ground. Its thorns had offered no protection.

She moved to the next. A family of crimson pots. The geraniums had been turning brown for a while, but the pots had kept their color. Brighter than blood.

Things were worse farther in. Shards of colors were scattered around until it was unclear which piece came from what pot. The plants were strewn about the garden like fallen soldiers after a battle. Roots exposed, leaves wilted, petals scattered.

Amy started to collect the pieces. She gathered as many as she could carry and clutched them to her chest, pressing them into her. She hurried, unable to abide seeing them so disparate. So broken. There were too many: shards started falling to the ground as she gathered more. She felt panic flood through her. She had to get them inside. To safety.

A hand on her back. "Come on, Amy," said Richard. "This can wait. You've had a shock." He took the shards from her and set them gently down. "We'll help you," he said. "But you need a moment to recover first. I'll get you a brandy."

Amy allowed herself to be led from her garden to the house next door and settled onto a sofa. A boy sat on each side of her, and Amy found herself being hugged by them both. She closed her eyes and felt the warmth from their little bodies.

Her pots.

What had she been thinking, keeping them in the front garden? She'd enjoyed looking at them as she arrived home each evening, but it had been selfish. She knew the terrible things people could do, and she'd just abandoned them to whoever was walking past.

Walking past. Or walking to her house. She remembered DCI Jack Hooper's warning. Could this be connected to the questions she'd been asking?

"Here you go," said Richard. He handed her a brandy in a heavy cut-crystal glass. She took a sip and felt the alcohol burn a path down her throat. She clutched the glass, feeling its solidity against her hand. She sipped again.

Richard scooted Daniel onto his lap and sat down next to Amy. "I mean it," he said. "We'll help. I thought I could pop to the garden center and get some plastic pots and a few bags of soil, and we'll replant everything. The plants will be fine. And then when you're ready, maybe you can put them in some of those spare pots from your back garden. We can even pass them across the fence and bring them through our house, if that would be easier."

"Thank you," she managed eventually. "That's very generous." She put the glass down, wondering why Richard was being so kind to her. Then she heard Charles whisper to his brother, and Daniel wriggled off his father's lap. Both boys slipped away.

"I can't believe anyone would do something like this," said Richard. His hand had reached around her shoulders. Amy allowed herself to nestle her head in the nape of his neck. She breathed in deeply. He smelled of freshly cut grass. She remembered sitting like this with Tim when her grandmother died. Tim had smelled of cigarette smoke, but the warmth of his neck felt the same as Richard's. She closed her eyes, and pretended that the last eleven years hadn't happened. That this was Tim sitting next to her, his arms around her. That he loved her. That she didn't need pots. Or mirrors. Or mugs.

"What on earth?"

Amy's eyes flung open. Nina was standing in the living room doorway. Richard uncoiled himself from Amy. "Oh, hi there," he said. He stood up. "You saw what happened to Amy's front garden? I was just—"

"I can see that," said Nina.

"'Scuse me," said Charles, banging into Nina's back. He was carrying something heavy and set it on the floor with a thud.

"What's that dirty thing doing in my house?" exclaimed Nina.

"It's not a dirty thing," said Charles. "It's the lovely pot Amy gave us, with the pretty plant inside."

"Geranium," said Amy.

"Exactly." He looked at her. "I know it was a present, but since yours were smashed I thought you might like to have it back for a bit."

"That's very kind of you," said Richard, grinning at his son. "Sometimes I think I haven't done such a bad job of parenting after all." He laughed and tousled his son's hair.

"Strawberries too," said Daniel. He followed behind his brother holding the little potted strawberry plants Amy had given them. Strawberry juice trickled down his chin. "Saved you one," he said, solemnly handing the plants to Amy.

"Touching," said Nina, her face twisted.

"We all like Amy," Charles told her. "Dad too."

"Charles," said Richard.

"But it's true," said Charles.

"I can see that," said Nina.

"Nina, you know that . . ." Richard's voice trailed off.

"I should be going," said Amy.

"Amy is very upset, after SOMEONE broke her pots," continued Charles. Even Amy noticed the glacial look he gave Nina as he spoke.

"What are you saying?" asked Nina, her voice rising.

"Nothing," said Richard. "Were you, Charlie?"

"Nothing," repeated Charles, his voice as sweet as strawberries.

"I have some clearing up to do," said Amy. "I'd better be going."

"We'll help," said Richard.

"You've done enough," said Amy.

"Quite," added Nina.

Amy got up to leave. She hesitated as she walked past Nina, then placed a hand on her arm. "You're lucky to have such lovely boys," she said.

Nina scowled at her. "I am," she replied.

Amy couldn't help but feel she'd said the wrong thing.

AMY LAY ON the sofa. It felt better, sleeping down here. Not that there was much sleeping going on. But if something happened, if whoever it was came back, she'd be better able to protect her things.

Not her pots: they were beyond repair. Richard had been true to his word and had replanted her plants in plastic containers. The boys had diligently watered them with the little watering can she'd given them. She didn't have the heart to tell them that really, it was not the plants that mattered to her. It seemed strange that some people could be so kind while others destroyed beautiful objects for no reason.

No reason. Amy let those two words echo around her mind. No one else's garden had been targeted. The cars on the street were untouched. What had she done to deserve this? Amy wondered if maybe she should have phoned the police. But if they weren't interested in tracking down Tim, she doubted they'd have time to investigate some broken pots. Jack's words circled in her mind again. Was it possible she'd brought this on herself?

It was ridiculous, she decided, to think it was anything other than vandals. Vandals breaking garden ornaments. She'd collected the pieces and they were stacked on the hallway floor, in the space vacated by the mail and the bottles she'd cleared out.

The bottles. They would still be sitting in Richard's recycling, waiting to be taken away. Taken away forever. Broken down. Smashed.

Amy realized she couldn't bear to lose any more. She sat up and glanced at one of her few working clocks. The face shone in the moonlight and Amy saw that it was past midnight. That didn't matter. The recycling would be collected in the morning. She still had time.

Amy got to her feet and put on her slippers. She made her way carefully through the living room path and grabbed a coat that hung on a hook in the hallway. The pieces of pots she'd collected were piled on the floor, framed by little halos of dirt. There were still lots of bottles and several stacks of newspapers, but all Amy could see was the space where the other bottles had been. She needed to have them all. She needed to save what she could.

She slipped her keys into her pocket and opened the front door. A noise.

Amy froze. Were the vandals back, intent on finishing the destruction of her treasures? She almost closed the door again, but the image of the bottles flooded back to her. They would think they had been abandoned. She couldn't bear it.

She stood at the door, listening. She heard a sound again, but it was soft. Foxes sniffing around the bins, she decided. Nothing to be scared of.

Amy stepped outside and closed the door behind her. Her things would be safe. The moon was bright, and Amy walked down her garden path trying not to look at the wilted plants lined up against the wall in their ugly plastic pots. She opened her gate and stepped onto the pavement. Her view of Richard's front garden was obscured by a privet hedge, but Amy knew he had two large wheelie bins that he kept there. One was dark gray, for rubbish. The other was a mossy shade of green and for recycling.

Amy stopped again. She heard another noise, a gentle creak. She stood by the hedge, peering through the leaves.

A pair of eyes peered back, shining in the moonlight. This was no fox.

October 2005

"What shall I wear?" Amy stood in the bedroom in her mismatched bra and pants.

"That's Chantel's department," said Tim. "I think you look great as you are."

"But she's not here," said Amy. "She's never here anymore. I miss her."

"You've got me," said Tim. "And we've got the place to ourselves." He winked at her, and Amy cringed. "How about your silky blue dress? That's pretty."

"I can't find it," said Amy, rummaging through her wardrobe. "Besides, it's a bit low-cut. I want to look respectable."

"He's a policeman," said Tim, "not a Quaker. And besides, he's going out with Chantel. He can't be that square."

"How about this?" said Amy finally, holding up a brown turtleneck sweater dress. "With opaque tights?"

"Sure," said Tim. "I love my tights opaque."

"You have no idea what opaque tights are, do you?"

"Not a clue," replied Tim. "But you look great in everything." He reached his arms out to her and she gave him a quick kiss.

"I should go shopping," she said. "Now I'm the senior secretary at Trapper, Lemon, and Hughes I should look the part." Margery in the office had finally retired, and Amy had been offered a promotion. She'd been in two minds about taking it: she was still hoping to be able to spend some time on her art, and more money came with more work. But she hadn't felt inspired for a long time. She'd taken the promotion and spent the extra money on the household items she'd been craving. She wanted to work on her art. But she also wanted a proper dining table. A matching set of cutlery. A Le Creuset pan in which to make casseroles. Perhaps even a suit to wear to work.

"What if he doesn't like me?" asked Amy, her mind going back to the task at hand.

"Then you don't have to marry him," said Tim. Amy glanced at him. They hadn't mentioned the M-word since the day they'd moved in. "Chill out," said Tim. "Spike never liked you and that wasn't an issue."

"He did!" objected Amy. "I just didn't like him. And besides, Jack is different. I think Chantel is really serious about him."

"I'll buy a hat," said Tim. "Come on, let's get going." He heaved himself up.

"You're not going like that?" said Amy.

"Like what?"

"Put a shirt on. A proper one, with buttons."

"Buttons, eh? The big guns."

"And clean trousers," she added, looking at the rather dubious spots on his jeans. "Chantel said the restaurant is fancy."

"I don't see why we couldn't just go for a beer," said Tim, pulling off his T-shirt and replacing it with a white buttoned shirt.

"You look gorgeous in that," said Amy.

"A pillar of the community," he remarked as he stripped off his jeans and stood in his boxers and socks, searching for a clean pair of trousers. "Okay," he said, finally dressed. "Will I do?"

"Always," said Amy.

AMY WAS RELIEVED she'd made Tim change. The restaurant was in town, and there was no denim in sight. It was busy and a waiter with an exaggerated French accent that Amy was pretty sure was fake showed them to their table. Chantel and Jack were sitting there already, staring into each other's eyes.

Jack Hooper stood up to greet her, and Amy found herself in a strong handshake. The last time they'd met had been in the police station late at night. She remembered him as muscly and a bit of a hero, but she hadn't noticed just how handsome he was: he had chiseled features and piercing blue eyes, and his shirt could barely contain the muscles underneath. Tim looked malnourished by comparison, and she gave him a reassuring smile just in case he was feeling inadequate. He didn't seem to notice.

"Great to meet you both properly," said Jack. "Chantel talks about you all the time."

"And you," said Amy. She leaned forwards and gave Chantel a quick kiss on the cheek, then went to sit down. To her surprise, the waiter was hovering behind her chair waiting to push it in for her. Amy sat down self-consciously.

"Isn't it lovely here," said Chantel. "It's Jack's favorite restaurant."

"The steak tartare is to die for," he said.

Amy glanced at Tim, who had recently become a vegetarian. He was scanning the menu.

"I remember the first time I met you guys," said Jack. "In the police station." He smiled at Amy. "You were standing up for Chantel."

"You did too," said Amy, grinning back at him.

"I told Chantel you fancied her," said Tim.

"Don't tell the bosses," said Jack. "But I even slipped her my number. I was heartbroken she never called." He smiled at Chantel, and put his hand on hers.

"I've said sorry," said Chantel, laughing.

"You've made it up to me," he said, giving her a big kiss. "Haven't you?"

"Of course," said Chantel.

"We bumped into each other at the gym," explained Jack. "Chantel didn't recognize me, but I knew it was her."

"At the gym?" queried Amy. She'd never known Chantel to visit such a place.

"Well, just outside," added Chantel. "I was thinking about going in and joining, when out he came, looking like a Greek god."

The waiter appeared again and filled their glasses with red wine. "The Pinot here is excellent," said Jack. Tim and Amy nodded, and Tim reached for a slice of baguette, then struggled to smear a swirl of hard butter over it.

"I thought beer would be more the copper's tipple," said Tim, giving up and taking a bite of dry bread. Crumbs sprinkled the table-cloth like snow.

"I like the odd beer too," said Jack. "But I do enjoy the finer things in life." He squeezed Chantel's hand, and she looked ready to burst with happiness.

"Jack isn't just a policeman," said Chantel. "He's on the fast track." Amy and Tim nodded again, trying to look suitably impressed.

"And you are in retail?" Jack said to Tim.

"What?"

"The shop you work in," explained Chantel.

"I'm in a band," said Tim, looking annoyed. "We're just looking for a new drummer, and then we'll be gigging again. I do a bit of casual work in a supermarket, just to tide me over."

"Before you hit the big time," said Jack.

"That's right," replied Tim, his voice a little too loud. "Why didn't you tell Jack about the band?" he asked Chantel.

"Chill out," said Chantel. She put her hand on Tim's briefly, then took it away. "It's just that you haven't had any gigs for such a long time. . . ."

The waiter appeared and took their order. Jack had the steak tartare, Amy ordered an innocuous-sounding fish dish, Chantel a salad, and Tim an omelet. "You're not having chips?" Amy asked Chantel.

"Watching my figure," replied Chantel.

"She's perfect just as she is," said Jack, then added, "We've been working out together." He looked at Tim. "You could join us sometime, if you like?"

Amy laughed. "Fitness isn't really Tim's thing."

"I'm fit," said Tim. "Just in a more subtle, relaxed sort of way."

"Right," said Amy. They sat in an uncomfortable silence for a minute; then thankfully the waiter came and topped up their glasses again. "How's your work going, Chantel?" asked Amy. "I've barely seen you since you started at Opco."

"It's good," said Chantel. "I do some admin now, not just reception work."

"That's great," said Amy. "I miss you in the house." Chantel didn't say anything.

"We wanted to say, actually . . ." started Jack, looking at Chantel, who in turn looked to the bread basket. "It seems a bit of a waste, Chantel spending most of her time with me and paying rent for her room at your place too. I've got plenty of space."

Amy looked at Chantel, who seemed fascinated by her napkin. Jack continued. "Of course, I wouldn't charge her rent. She could save up, get herself out of debt."

"Debt?" echoed Amy.

"Just a bit," said Chantel. "A few credit cards here and there."

"But she needs her room," said Amy. "With us. You guys have just met. Isn't it a bit soon?"

"We've been together three months," said Chantel. "And it's time for me to have my life too." She looked from her napkin to Amy. "I can't be the third wheel to you two forever."

"You're not a third wheel," objected Amy. "You're the best wheel."

"Maybe it's a good idea," said Tim. Chantel glanced at him and then down again. "Some space for everyone."

"I don't want space," said Amy. "I want my best friend."

"You'll still have me," said Chantel. "But I've got Jack now too." Jack took her hand and squeezed it tightly.

The food arrived. Amy moved her fish around her plate miserably. Chantel picked at her salad, and Jack wolfed down his meat. "Most expensive eggs I've ever had," commented Tim.

Chantel put her fork down. "I need to go to the loo," she announced. "Amy, come with me?"

"Girls and toilets," said Jack. "Always need to go in pairs."

THE LADIES' ROOM was beautiful. Soft jazz music was playing, and there was a funny little anteroom with sofas and mirrors and little pots of hand cream. "I don't need the loo," said Chantel. She sat on one of the sofas and picked up the bottle of hand cream, dispensing some onto her palm. "Damn, I've taken too much," she said, spreading it over her hands and up her arms. "Want some?"

Amy held out her hand, and Chantel smeared cream onto her. It smelled like the roses in her grandmother's garden. Chantel didn't let go of Amy's hand when she'd finished, and they sat, hand in greasy hand, until Amy started to cry.

"I really like him," said Chantel, tears forming in her eyes too. "He's different. He's the first guy I've been out with who's not a mess. You know the losers I usually go for. I can't believe I've finally found a good one."

"He seems nice," sniffed Amy.

"He is," said Chantel. "You've had Tim forever and I've had no one. I want to make a go of this. God knows I've screwed up enough in my life."

"You're okay," said Amy. She let go of her friend's hand and hugged her instead, her lotion-coated hands smearing the back of Chantel's top. "And you know you're always welcome back, anytime you want."

"Of course," said Chantel. She laughed. "I'll not be too far away, you know. Just a ride on the three-eighty-three bus. You must visit all the time."

"Try to stop me," replied Amy.

Chapter
Ten

"God, Amy, you gave me the fright of my life. What are you doing creeping around our front garden at night?" Nina was using one hand to push aside the branches of the hedge. The other she used to quickly close the lid of the gray bin. The movement turned on the sensor lights, and Amy suddenly felt as if she were onstage.

"I'm sorry," said Amy. "Richard said I could put some stuff in your recycling bins."

"At midnight?" questioned Nina. "Where's your rubbish?"

Amy felt herself grow braver at the mention of the word *rubbish*. That was not what it was. She stepped into the garden. "Actually, I put some stuff in there the other day, but I've changed my mind. I want it back."

"You know you've got a problem," said Nina. "You should get help."

"Can I just get my things?"

"Be my guest," said Nina, stepping aside. Her hand still rested awkwardly on the gray bin.

"What were you doing out here?" asked Amy, watching Nina's hand on the bin.

"Not that it's any of your business," said Nina, "but I was taking out the rubbish."

"It's late," said Amy.

"I've been busy," said Nina.

"Can I see?" asked Amy. There was something in Nina's face that worried her.

"Can you see my rubbish?" queried Nina. "You want our junk as well as your own?"

"Maybe," said Amy.

"Well, you can't," snapped Nina. "Get out of here."

"I need to see what's in the bin," said Amy, feeling determined. "If you don't show me now, I'll wait till you've gone to bed and then look."

"Fine," said Nina, stepping aside and muttering something under her breath.

Amy opened the bin and was greeted by a typically rancid smell. She peered inside, then leaned in farther and grabbed something yellow. She pulled it out.

"This is Charles's excavator," she exclaimed. "His favorite one."

"It's broken," replied Nina. "Now, will you go back to your house please? I need to get to bed. Richard will be missing me."

"Does Charles know you've thrown it away?" asked Amy.

"Of course," said Nina. "Is that all?"

Amy paused, thinking of her own possessions. How upset she'd be if something had been thrown away that she'd wanted to keep. How often she'd changed her mind about letting a treasure go. What if he regretted it later? The binmen would come tomorrow: he'd have no second chance. "I think I'll look after this for him," said Amy, dusting off the toy. "Just in case he changes his mind."

"For goodness' sake, Amy, let it go!" said Nina. She reached out to grab the toy.

Amy stepped back, holding the excavator out of Nina's reach.

"Give me that," commanded Nina, her voice rising.

"No," replied Amy.

"Why can't you just keep your nose out of our business and leave us alone!" Nina was shouting now, her voice echoing around the empty street. "It's not like you haven't got problems of your own. Look at you."

"I just want—"

"What's going on?" A sleepy-looking Richard was standing in the doorway. Daniel was in his arms peering at them. "You've woken up Daniel."

"And me," said Charles, following behind. He blinked at them, then frowned. "What are you doing with my excavator?"

"I thought you might change your mind," said Amy. "Broken things can be fixed, if you keep them."

"Broken?" queried Charles. He rushed forwards into the garden, bare feet on rough stone. He snatched the excavator from Amy's hands.

"You told me he knew," said Amy to Nina. "That he said it was okay to throw it away."

"Throw it away?" said Charles. "Never." He examined the toy. "It doesn't look broken."

Nina grabbed the toy back from Charles. "I've tripped over this piece of junk one too many times!" she said. "I told you that if I found it on the floor one more time . . ." Nina opened the bin again and dropped the excavator inside.

"Nina!" exclaimed Richard. He opened the bin, removed the toy, and handed it back to his son, who grabbed it from him and cradled it to his chest like a baby. "How could you do that?"

"See what she's like!" declared Charles. "She pretends to be all smiley but she's mean."

"Nina," said Richard again. "How could you do that?"

"I've had it," said Nina. "I've had it with all of you." She looked around. "I'm getting the car keys. I'm not staying another night in this house."

Silence greeted that announcement. Charles was focused on the excavator. "The wing mirror is loose," he said.

"I can fix that with some glue," said Amy quietly. "It will be good as new."

"Thank you, Amy," said Richard. He put Daniel down and stroked his elder son's head.

"No one cares that I'm leaving?" asked Nina.

"It's the middle of the night," said Richard, after a beat. "Let's talk about it tomorrow."

"That doesn't sound like an apology," said Nina.

"Why would I apologize?" Richard's voice was strained. "It looks like you are in the wrong here."

"I knew you'd take their side," said Nina. "It's always everyone else before me. Even this head case." She gestured towards Amy, who took another step back.

"There's no need for insults," said Richard.

"See what I mean?" said Nina. "You're on everyone's side but mine." No one answered. "Fine." She pushed past Richard and went inside, returning moments later with the car keys. "I'll be back tomorrow for my things," she said.

"We'll pack them for you," said Charles, rather smugly.

Nina jumped in the car, slammed the door, and sped away.

Richard stood still a moment, tiredness wrinkling his face. Then another expression passed over his features. Amy wasn't sure, but she thought it could be relief.

"Right, everyone," he said. "It's late. Back to bed."

He encouraged the boys back inside. "Good night, Amy," he said. "Sorry about . . ."

"Not at all," said Amy. "Sleep well." She watched them go back inside. The lights turned off. Amy waited for her eyes to adjust to the moonlight again, then opened the recycling bin.

She gazed inside, then reached in and pushed the papers to one side. The bottles lay there. Peaceful. Beautiful. She reached her hand in to pull one out, then stopped. It had been a hard day, and the conflict with Nina hadn't made things any easier, but at the same time she could feel a gentle sense of peace, emanating from the resting bottles. She'd saved the excavator for Charles. Perhaps that was enough for tonight. Perhaps it was time to let these bottles go.

She closed the lid, and realized that she felt a little bit lighter. Amy turned back towards her own house and walked home in the moonlight.

AMY SAT ON her hallway floor early the next morning with her front door open for extra light. It felt weird to her, having the fresh air flood her house, and she could see particles of dust dancing in the sunlight as if in celebration. She was sorting the fragments of pots into piles, trying to work out which piece went with which pot. It reminded her of doing a jigsaw puzzle; blue with the blue, flowers with the flowers. The edges were the easiest.

Some were not too bad. A few big pieces that could be easily glued back together. They would never be as strong as they once were, but they would be whole again. She could keep the plants in the plastic pots Richard had bought her and put them inside the repaired ones: that would keep the pressure off. An extra support system.

Others were beyond repair. She kept the pieces anyway, remembering her ideas for reuse. It had only been three weeks, but it seemed like forever since a single pot had been smashed in her back garden, revealing the lost ring to her.

And then the letter. And the photograph.

The ring was still around her neck, though of course now its meaning was less obvious to her. Had Tim intended to marry her, then found the pressure too much? How had it found its way to her garden? And when had the letter from Chantel arrived?

She glanced up to her hallway shelf. The large envelope with *Please Do Not Bend* firmly printed in authoritative red sat there, watching her as she worked. She sorted the last of the pots, then stood up and opened it again. Inside was the letter, its envelope, and the photograph. She looked just at the envelope for a moment, stepping farther into the sunlight flooding in from her front garden. The stamp was still there, but the postmark had long since been worn away.

She paused, then looked more closely. There was a very subtle raised shape, an out-dent. It made a gentle shadow, only visible in the bright July sunshine. She took her fingertip and felt the shape. It was familiar. Instinctively her hand went to her chest where the ring hung.

She removed the ring and held it next to the envelope.

It matched, stone for stone.

There was no doubt. This ring had been inside the envelope.

AMY TRIED TO process the information. Chantel had put an engagement ring from Tim, presumably intended for Amy, together with the confession letter. Why?

Not to taunt her. Chantel was not a cruel person, no matter what she might have done. She wanted Amy to have that ring.

Amy could see no explanation. A ring, a photograph, a letter confessing Chantel and Tim's love for one another. She lined up the items next to each other and stared at them until her vision went fuzzy.

"I've collected my things." Amy looked up. Nina stood in front of her, surrounded by several suitcases. "Bye."

"You're not really going?" asked Amy, hurriedly putting her clues back in the envelope. "I'm sure you guys can work it out. Wasn't it all a big misunderstanding?"

"It's not just that stupid digger," said Nina. She made no secret of peering into Amy's house. "God, you've got a lot of stuff," she said.

"Thank you," replied Amy.

Nina let out a reluctant laugh, then came and leaned on Amy's porch railing. "I don't like how I've become," she said. "I did some not very nice things. That's not me."

Amy looked at her.

"I didn't smash your pots, Amy," she said, in response to Amy's gaze. "I fell in love. I thought I could take the boys on too, but it's too much. I was angry all the time. I wanted Richard, but not with his baggage."

Richard appeared at Amy's gate.

"We all have baggage," replied Amy. She glanced back into her house. "No one travels lightly anymore."

Richard nodded. "Come talk when you're ready," he said, addressing Nina.

"Losing someone you love isn't easy," said Amy quietly. "If you have a choice . . ."

"Staying isn't easy either," replied Nina. "It's time to go."

"Just a minute," said Amy, remembering. She left Nina standing in front of her house and hurried to the kitchen. "Here," she said, handing her the yellow mug that had been broken the first day they met. "I've fixed it."

Nina looked at the mug, then up at Amy. "Keep it," she said. "It's yours now."

"Thank you," said Amy, relieved that the mug could stay with her. She smiled at Nina. "Good luck."

"Good luck to you too," replied Nina. "I think you're going to need it."

AMY HAD ENJOYED her trip to the supermarket. For so long she'd eaten whatever provisions the corner shop provided for dinner and a ready-made salad or sandwich from the places near the office at lunch. Wandering around the supermarket with an empty trolley that could be filled with possibilities had been a pleasure. What a vast array of food was available, if you had the space to store it.

Amy still didn't have much space, but she'd cleared away a few of her least favorite mugs from the kitchen counter and dug out a slow cooker. A single-pot meal, the recipe book declared, that would be wholesome and delicious was within the skill set of even the least accomplished cook. That was what the boys and Richard would need with Nina gone. Preparing a meal in times of trouble was what her grandmother would have done, and Amy chopped carrots contentedly. A packet of sausages, a couple of onions, and a few small potatoes sat on top of a box next to her, patiently waiting their turn. She'd brought Scarlett into the kitchen to watch her newfound domesticity, and the bird looked on, surprised and curious.

AMY HAD LEFT the meal to do its thing all day while she was at work—slow cookers were aptly named. But opening the lid and breathing in the rich aromas, Amy decided it was worth it. She emptied the contents into a rather elegantly curved stew dish that she'd picked up at a charity shop some years ago. It had a cream-colored interior and a dark-blue glaze on the outside that had made Amy think it could be a relative of one of her mugs. When she'd got it home, she'd found that the blues didn't match, but she'd kept it anyway.

Amy realized she'd got stew on her black trousers and went upstairs to change. She selected an orange dress from the wardrobe, which was now permanently accessible. The color reminded her of an egg yolk, warm and rich.

Wrapping tea towels around the dish to protect her hands, she made her way outside to knock on Richard's door. It was harder than she'd anticipated with both hands occupied, so she set the dish down for a moment to knock and was bending down to pick it up again when the door swung open.

She stood up, feeling a little light-headed. "Amy?" said Richard.

"I thought that since Nina had gone, you might need . . ." She picked up the dish and thrust it forwards.

"What's that?" he asked, then smiled as he realized. "I can cook, you know," he said with a laugh. "It's not the fifties."

"Oh," said Amy, suddenly feeling foolish. Perhaps acting as her grandmother would have was rather outmoded.

"I'm sorry," said Richard. "I shouldn't laugh. That was very thoughtful of you."

Charles appeared at the doorway. "Amy!" he said. "My excavator savior and mouse rescuer." He smiled. "That's what Dad said you were." He turned to his father and whispered something.

"Of course," said Richard. "Amy, would you like to join us for dinner? We've just sat down. Will what you've made save till tomorrow?"

"I'm busy tomorrow," said Amy, wishing again that she hadn't accepted that date with Liam.

"Not a date?" asked Charles, his ears pricked.

"Well . . ."

"Amy's private life is her own," interjected Richard. "Sorry, Amy."

"The stew will keep for two to three days," replied Amy, pleased with what she'd read in the recipe book. "If kept refrigerated."

"Perfect," said Richard. "Then maybe join us again in two to three days." He smiled. "Come through."

The table was set with a wooden bowl containing salad, a smaller wooden bowl full of fresh garlic bread, and a plain Pyrex dish with a steaming lasagna. The boys had already been served, and Richard went to the kitchen to get an extra plate.

"Look how happy Mickey is," said Charles. "We bought him a proper tank with sawdust and a wheel and food and a water bottle of his own." Amy peered into the tank. A tiny mouse barely the size of her thumb peered back at her. Something in his expression reminded her of Scarlett.

"He is exquisite," she said.

"I love Mickey," agreed Daniel.

Amy took a seat. "Wine?" called Richard from the kitchen. "A nice glass of Merlot is the perfect accompaniment to lasagna à la Richard."

"Thank you," said Amy, helping herself to garlic bread.

"Nina didn't eat garlic bread," said Charles. "Because of the carbs."

"Oh," said Amy. She looked at the bread in her hand and took a giant bite. "She was missing out," she said. Charles grinned at her. Richard filled her glass, and Amy admired the wine bottle. It appeared black and opaque when full, but as Richard filled her glass she saw the familiar translucence develop. It really was lovely.

Amy was distracted when Richard served her up a hearty portion of lasagna. She tried not to look at the bottle again as the four of them tucked in. It felt weird to Amy hearing the sounds of others eating around her. She was used to dining with only Scarlett's company.

"That's a pretty pendant," said Richard. "Is it a ring?"

"It's from an ex-boyfriend," said Charles. "But Amy isn't going to marry him because he's disappeared." Amy suddenly found the mozzarella in her lasagna hard to swallow, and took a gulp of her wine to assist.

"Charles," said Richard, "Amy might prefer it if you didn't reveal aspects of her private life at the dinner table."

"But you already know," objected Charles. "I heard Nina tell you after Rachel told her." There was silence for a moment, then the reassuring clatter of knives and forks on plates.

"It's okay," said Amy.

"Done!" announced Daniel. "Cartoons?"

"Okay," said Richard. The boy slipped off. "Charles, do you want to join him?"

"I'll stay here with Amy," replied Charles. "More wine, Amy?"

"I'll pour, thanks, Charlie," said Richard with a laugh.

Amy allowed her glass to be refilled. The glass was simply shaped but effective. She'd seen something similar in the supermarket and had managed to resist. In fact, she'd bought nothing more than she needed for her slow-cooker meal. Maybe when she went back she'd buy a bottle of wine to repay Richard for his hospitality. The thought sent a judder of memory through her so fierce that her wine glass shook. An inexplicable need to talk about what had happened rose up like heartburn.

"Are you okay?" asked Richard, placing a steadying hand on her arm.

"I found this ring in the garden," Amy blurted out, words escaping from her like rats running from a sinking ship. Or mice escaping her house. "And I didn't know what it meant, but I did know it was from him. Then I found a letter from my best friend who went missing at the same time, and a picture of a bit of woodland or a park or something but I can't work out where, even though I feel like perhaps that's the key to the whole thing. And now I know the ring was inside the same envelope. It all fell into the pot I used to keep for umbrellas by the front door, and sat in my garden for God knows how long, and the letter is all but illegible." Amy paused for breath. Both Richard and Charles were staring at her.

"Was it a nice park?" asked Charles.

"I don't think that's the point," said Richard, his voice soft. "Amy, have you taken this to the police?"

"That's what I said," said Charles, looking pleased. "When she told me about the ring *ages* ago."

"I took the ring and they weren't interested," said Amy. "I think they'd need more evidence than this—" She cut herself off.

"They need a dead body," guessed Charles, grinning darkly. "Maybe the letter tells you where the body is. It would just be a skeleton by now," he added, his eyes shining. "The worms would have eaten—"

"We get the idea," said Richard. He paused. "What did the letter say exactly?"

"I can't make out much of it," said Amy, trying not to think about skeletons.

"I'm a very good reader," said Charles. "I can even read Miss Gillingham's writing."

"I could look at it for you?" suggested Richard. "If you'd like a second opinion?"

"And a third," said Charles.

Amy hesitated. The letter felt private—but then, it was predominantly illegible. What harm could it do? "I'll go and fetch it," she said.

Back inside, her house felt quiet. For a moment she closed the door and shut her eyes. She could smell the dust and hear the silence. The letter was sitting in the kitchen now, protected by its *Please Do Not Bend* envelope. She didn't have to obey that writing, she realized. She could rip the whole package into tiny pieces, throw it away, and carry on living as she had been. She didn't even need to go back to Richard's house. She owed nothing to the neighbors, nor they to her. They could move at any point, and she'd have no right to ask them why or where.

Her things wouldn't leave. Scarlett would always be with her. Her mugs. The remaining bottles.

But not the pots. Things could be destroyed too, just like relationships. Her hand went again to the ring. The ring that could not tell her the truth.

Amy opened her eyes. It was unlikely that Richard would be able to decipher more of the letter than she had, but it was worth trying. She grabbed the envelope from the kitchen, blew Scarlett a quick kiss, and made her way back to the neighbors' house.

"There you are," said Charles, opening the door for her. "We're going to have ice cream as a special treat since we have company." He smiled at her. "That's you."

Daniel was back at the table, spoon in hand. "Ice cream," he said merrily.

"Would you like some, Amy?" asked Richard. "It's from Cornwall, apparently."

"Sure," said Amy. Perhaps it would settle the nervous feeling in her stomach. They all sat around the table again, the envelope in the middle. Charles reached out for it.

"Finish your ice cream first," said his father. "Then we'll look when Amy is ready."

Daniel beat them all in finishing his ice cream and wandered back to the television. Amy ate hers slowly, but eventually took a final lick of the spoon and set it down. It had been a long time since she'd indulged in ice cream. She reached for the envelope and emptied the contents. She could see Charles itching to grab the letter, and passed it across to him. "Do you want to look at the photo?" she asked Richard.

He took it and frowned. "Trees, grass, hills. Some kind of machine on the edge. I can't see any landmarks."

"Let me look," said Charles. "I know all the parks. You take the letter." Richard looked to Amy, who nodded assent. They switched papers, and Amy took another sip of her wine. There was only a small amount left in the bottle now, and the emptiness glowed a brilliant green in the light.

"That isn't just any machine in the corner," said Charles finally. "It's a digger." He looked excessively pleased with himself. "Look, you can see the edge of it here." He pointed. "It's a JCB 5CX, I think. But that's odd. It has tracks." He paused. "Can I take this photo upstairs?" he asked. "There's something I want to check in my room."

"I suppose that's fine," said Amy. Charles took the photo and scurried away.

"I don't know what to make of the letter," said Richard finally. "There's not much to go on. I don't want to pry," he added, "but did they say anything to you before they left?"

"No," said Amy. She hesitated. "Chantel was my best friend. We grew up together. I still can't believe that they would do that to me. If I could find out where this photo was taken, perhaps . . ." Amy stopped and took another sip of wine. "It's been so hard," she said. "Not knowing what happened and having to believe that they betrayed me. I've lost them, but not in a way I can mourn. Not properly."

"At least you have hope," said Richard. "I'd give anything to have that back." He drank from his glass, then put it down. Amy realized they were both staring at the bottle.

"It must have been hard," said Amy. She thought of Tim and his father, Alan, lost to each other in their separate griefs. "To be there for the kids when you were trying to deal with your own pain."

"They were what got me through it," said Richard. He looked at Amy. "I'm not sure I'd have made it, without them." For a moment Amy thought he was going to cry. Instead he smiled. "I stopped working, I had to. I needed to be there for Daniel. He was so little. And for Charles too. Best thing I ever did."

"How did you manage?" asked Amy.

"I had my own architecture firm, and I sold it. Now I freelance there part-time. I spent as much time with the kids as I could, never went out of an evening." He took another sip of wine. "Then I met Nina, and she seemed lovely at first. I wasn't sure, you know, that I'd be able to be with anyone else. But you move on. Sounds like we both have. You can't live in the past."

Amy nodded, although she wasn't sure that was true.

"You've been through a lot," she said.

"We all have," said Richard. "But we've plenty to be grateful for too. Join me for another glass?" He rose and went to the kitchen. "I'll open a new bottle."

"Thank you," said Amy. She rested her fingers lightly on the empty bottle in front of her.

"Things with Nina had been bad for a while," confided Richard, returning. "I could tell she wasn't great with the kids, but I thought I was being too hard on her. I was comparing her to their mother and that wasn't fair. But our relationship wasn't how it should have been either. I can see that now."

Charles bounded back in, holding a book. Amy glanced at the title: *The Encyclopedia of Diggers and Big Machines.* "I've found something!" he said.

"I think that's enough detective work for tonight," said Richard. "Why don't you keep your brother company watching cartoons?"

"No," declared Charles. "Amy, look." He waved the open book in her face. "The 5CX model has wheels, not tracks," he said. "But in this picture, it's got tracks. Look."

Amy looked. "Okay," she said, not understanding.

"It's been modified," said Charles.

"Let me see that," said Richard. "You're right." He grinned at his son. "Nice work."

"What does it mean?" asked Amy.

"Sometimes the builders request that machines be modified for specialist tasks."

"So?"

"A modified machine is possible to trace," said Richard. "We'll need to call the JCB head office and hope they cooperate. But they might be able to tell us where it was, even eleven years ago." He smiled at her. "It's not definite," he said. "But thanks to Charles, there's a chance we can find out where this photograph was taken."

October 2006

"It was a lovely service," said Tim, holding a small plate of sand-wiches for Amy that they both knew she wouldn't eat. "She would have liked it."

"I keep thinking she'll walk through the door," said Amy. They both looked at the door to the church hall. Suddenly it opened. Amy watched it, filled with a pointless hope.

"Sorry I'm late," said Chantel, walking straight over to Amy and hugging her. "The train in front broke down."

"You're here now," said Amy.

Chantel took a sandwich and wolfed it down. "Jack thinks carbs are the enemy of fitness," she explained, "so we don't keep them in the house. I bloody miss bread." She looked at Amy. "I'm sorry, Amy," she said. "But your grandma was always feeding me egg salad sandwiches."

"She'd want you to have them," said Amy, attempting a smile.

Chantel took another one. "In her memory," she said, taking a bite.

Amy's parents came over and Chantel gave them each an awkward hug. With Amy's grandmother gone, they were finally going to make the move to El Salvador that they'd been talking about for years. Her mother told them all about the community they'd be helping, but Amy found she couldn't focus. Tim wrapped his arm around her shoulders. She leaned into him, letting his body carry both their weights.

A WEEK LATER, and Amy still found herself close to tears whenever she thought about her grandmother. Everything seemed to remind Amy of her, from an egg sandwich to a framed photo to a child clutching a teddy bear. She still couldn't bring herself to sort through her grandmother's things, though her parents were keen to get the house on the market before they left. Amy just wasn't ready.

The doorbell rang, and Amy dragged herself up to answer it. A motley assortment of children stood on her doorstep with smudged face paint and witches' hats. "Trick or treat!" they declared in unison, thrusting a bucket towards her. An apologetic-looking adult stood behind them.

"Oh," said Amy. She'd forgotten all about Halloween. "I might have some oranges." The children looked disgusted. Fortunately Tim chose that moment to return home, clutching a large object covered in wrapping paper and a giant bag of lollipops. He put the package down and grabbed a generous handful of lollipops and dropped them into the bucket.

"Oranges!" he exclaimed as they left. "The kids would be within their rights to cover our house in toilet paper!"

"What's that?" said Amy, looking at the package.

Tim grinned at her. "It's Halloween. Do you know what that means?"

"You're not dressing up, are you?"

"Get inside the house," he said, picking up the package. "I'll reveal all."

Amy sat on the sofa and Tim put his package down with a clink. "Well, open it," he said.

Amy obeyed. Inside was a small palm tree in a pretty lilac pot. "What's this for?"

"Our anniversary," said Tim. "You forgot, didn't you? It's okay. I know you've got other things on your mind."

"It's lovely," said Amy, admiring the plant.

"Houseplants in terra-cotta pots always get me in the mood," said Tim, leaning in to nuzzle Amy's neck.

"Weirdo," she teased.

"You don't remember," said Tim, sitting back. "Do you?"

"Remember what?" asked Amy.

"The first night we were together. Properly together."

"Of course I remember," said Amy. "You cooked me dinner. Spaghetti Bolognese."

"And you bought me a potted fern," replied Tim, "in an effort to seduce me."

Amy remembered. Then she laughed, the first time she'd been able to since her grandmother died. "It worked," she said.

"It did," replied Tim. He took her hand. "I couldn't keep the fern alive," he said. "Back then. I was young and irresponsible." He looked at Amy. "But I'm not anymore. I'm going to make you my new vegetarian Spaghetti Bolognese recipe and get some water for our new green friend here. After dinner I want to talk."

"I'VE BEEN THINKING," said Tim. They were sitting on the sofa together with a glass of wine each. Plates smeared with the remains of the pasta sauce sat on the coffee table next to their new houseplant. Amy caught a glimpse of the two of them in the mirror she'd hung on the wall, and she realized how comfortable they looked together. Like an old married couple. Except they weren't married, she reminded herself.

"Always dangerous," she joked.

"Money is tight," he said, "without Chantel's rent."

"Do you want to get a new flatmate?" asked Amy, her heart sinking. She shifted away from him a little, almost involuntarily. The image in the mirror changed. If she couldn't have Chantel in that room, she didn't want anyone.

"No," replied Tim. "But I want you to be able to spend some time on your art. It's your dream."

"I can't afford a dream," said Amy. "I have to work full-time to pay the rent."

"It's time for me to pull my weight," Tim said. "Actually, it's well past time. The supermarket pay is shit. The band is going nowhere. I should give up on the music. Get a proper job."

"Music is *your* dream," said Amy, sitting back. She looked at the Tim in the mirror, and he looked back at her the same way, talking to each other's images as though they were at the hairdresser.

"You're my dream, Amy Ashton," said Tim. "And you've indulged me for years. If I was going to make it, I would have by now."

"You still could. . . ." Amy stopped. She realized she didn't really believe it.

"I have good A levels," continued Tim, "but no degree and no experience. I'm not going to make loads of money anytime soon, but I'm going to start trying. Media sales, I was thinking. Simon's brother does it, and he's going to get me an interview. What do you think?"

Amy didn't really know what media sales involved, but it didn't sound like stacking shelves at the supermarket. She turned away from mirror Tim to look at the real thing. He looked back at her, his face earnest. "It sounds great," she said. "You know I'd love you whatever you did?"

"You've proved that," said Tim with a laugh. "No one can accuse you of being with me for the glamour."

"You can still write songs?" suggested Amy.

"Of course," said Tim. He smiled at her. "Songs about selling adverts in *Batteries International.*"

"Sounds like a hit," said Amy. She leaned in and kissed Tim, glancing at the mirror again. This time she saw two people who would love each other forever.

Chapter
Eleven

"I was starting to think you'd changed your mind." Liam stood up as she entered the bar. Amy had very much changed her mind. But she'd already canceled once, and to do so again seemed too unkind.

He went to kiss her cheek, but Amy couldn't face that so she held out her hand. He shook it, and Amy found his hands damp and clammy. She was surprised. He didn't strike her as the type to get nervous. She found that endeared him to her a little bit more, and she smiled at him. "It was worth the wait," he said, looking her up and down. She was wearing something she hadn't worn in years: a silky red shirtdress the color of a cranberry. "Lady in red," he said, with a little half wink. "This should be a fun evening." The endearment fizzled away. "Take a seat," he said awkwardly, as if he realized he was on the back foot again. He gestured to a smart velvet-covered sofa. "I thought you'd like it here. It's classy. More romantic than a supermarket sandwich."

"It's a bit near the office," ventured Amy, looking around.

"It's fine," replied Liam. "None of the others would come to a nice place like this." He sat down next to Amy and rested his arm on the back of the sofa behind her in a studiously casual manner. Amy looked to the table. Two flute glasses sat beside an ice bucket, concealing most of what was probably a very beautiful bottle. Liam followed her gaze, then leaned forwards, removing his arm as he filled her glass and refilled his own. "I remember you drank Prosecco at drinks after work that time," he told her, looking pleased with himself. Amy found the shape of the bottle less appealing than wine. Its curves felt exaggerated, like a wine bottle that had had too much plastic surgery. "I got started without you," he added.

"Sorry I was late," said Amy. "I had some paperwork to finish."

"It's fine," replied Liam. "I hope you liked the flowers?"

"They were lovely," said Amy, remembering the roses that had turned up at her house. "But how did you get my address?"

Liam tapped the side of his nose, and Amy realized he must have been through the personnel files. "Beautiful roses for a beautiful woman," he said.

Amy took a deep swig from her glass. They sat in silence for a moment. Amy realized that although Liam might be nervous, she wasn't at all. That couldn't be right. She hadn't been on a date in more than a decade. She must be feeling something. Amy searched through her mind, looking for emotions.

All that registered was sadness.

She sipped her drink. Although she had accepted a glass of Prosecco at the work drinks, she didn't really like it. In fact, she didn't like bubbly drinks at all. Fresh homemade lemonade, red wine, pineapple juice, they were her taste. Tim never used to order for her. Even when he knew her so well, he'd always let her make her own choice.

But Tim wasn't here, she reminded herself. There were worse things a man could do to you than order you Prosecco when you'd prefer a glass of red wine.

Much worse.

She smiled at Liam, trying to behave like someone on a date might. "So you are new to the company?"

"I've been there three months now," he replied. "And you?"

"Seventeen years," she said. "Off and on." He looked startled. "It was meant to be a summer job, while I was at university," she explained. "Then things happened, and I kind of . . . got stuck."

"Lucky for me," he said with a wink.

Winking. Ordering for her. He wasn't making it easy for her to like him. She looked at him, searching for something to find attractive. He wasn't a bad-looking man; he had nice hair, had all his teeth, even if they were a shade too bright. It wasn't as though she was much of a catch herself, she thought. Middle-aged, emotionally drained, house overflowing. The personals ad didn't write itself.

Did people still have personal ads? She'd heard the girls in the office talk about online dating and apps. Swiping right. It sounded hellish.

Liam was right here, refilling her drink and saying something. He laughed at whatever joke he'd made, and Amy forced a polite little titter. His shirt buttons were pulling slightly around his stomach. He wasn't fat, but he wasn't in shape either. Good. Amy didn't like muscle-bound men. Chantel had always gone crazy for muscles, but Amy preferred her men a little softer, a little more delicate. She'd always found Jack's ostentatious strength unnerving—why would you want a partner who could so obviously overpower you with his bare hands? Tim had been perfect. Lean and slender, like a willow tree blowing in the breeze.

Tim isn't here, she told herself again, taking a swig of her drink. She looked back to Liam. He had nice eyes, she supposed, though they were rather small and close-set. His face was pleasant enough, though his cheeks were on the flabby side. Porcine.

"What was that?" asked Liam, his voice surprisingly sharp.

Damn. She'd spoken out loud. "Pour time," she said, her voice overly bright, like a highlighter over newsprint. She downed her drink and refilled Liam's glass, then emptied the rest of the bottle into her own.

"I'll get another," said Liam, clicking his fingers at a waitress and pointing at the bottle. The waitress winced and went to fetch the drinks. "Two bottles," said Liam, more to himself than to Amy. "It's going well."

Amy passed no comment. She sipped a fresh glass of Prosecco and discovered she was starting to enjoy the taste. Liam continued to talk, and she found her glass was almost empty, as if there were a leak somewhere. He refilled it for her.

"Have you ever been betrayed?" interrupted Amy, her glass suddenly almost empty again. She held it up and examined the bottom for the leak. The room was too bright, and she blinked hard to stop it spinning.

"What?" said Liam.

"Be-trayed," repeated Amy, more slowly. "My best friend and my boyfriend ran away together," she said, letting the words out without thinking.

"That's awful," said Liam.

"Bastards," said Amy. She gestured with her glass, and Prosecco swilled out over her hand. Liam refilled her glass again.

"You know the best way to get over someone . . ." said Liam.

Amy leaned forwards. "What is it?" she asked.

"Well, you know . . ." Liam looked uncomfortable.

"No," said Amy, "I most certainly do not know. It's not by collecting mugs." She laughed at herself, and Liam looked confused.

"Get under someone," he said eventually. Amy looked at him blankly. "It's just an expression," he said.

"Oh, I get it," said Amy, finding it very funny. She stopped laughing and looked at him. "You mean sex."

Liam coughed awkwardly, and a little Prosecco escaped his lips and flung itself at Amy.

"Let's get another bottle," said Amy.

"Do you want to have something to eat, maybe?" said Liam. "There's a little place I know—"

"No," said Amy. She waved at the waitress, who nodded an acknowledgment. "Just drink." She looked at Liam. "I haven't been this drunk for years," she said. "It's good."

Something was on her leg. She looked down. It was Liam's hand, his porky little fingers resting on her knee. She felt suddenly sick. "I need to go home," she said, standing up. "Scarlett needs me."

"But you've just ordered another bottle," said Liam, sounding annoyed. "I'll have to pay for that."

"Good-bye," said Amy. She grabbed her bag and hurried outside. What she needed was fresh air. She breathed in deeply outside the bar. It was dark already—perhaps this date had lasted longer than she thought. Amy decided to treat herself to a taxi; she didn't fancy trying to get the train home in this state. She looked around, but couldn't see one. She took a step forwards, but lost her balance.

"I've got you," said Liam. She didn't remember him coming out, but there he was, his arm around her waist.

"Don't touch me," she said, shying away at the contact.

"But I thought . . ."

A taxi drove past and Amy waved at it. It stopped for her and she climbed in.

"Great date, anyway," said Liam, peering through the window. "Are you free Friday?"

Amy pressed the button and the window closed. The taxi took her away, into the night.

"EXPECTING A PHONE call, Amy?" Carthika was sitting across from her in the office the next day, grinning. "After your hot date?"

"What are you talking about?" said Amy, putting down her phone. She realized she had been staring at it for rather a long time.

"He'll probably text," continued Carthika. "Or send a message on social. Although he could just surprise you at your desk."

"I don't know who you're talking about," said Amy. Her head was pounding. Surely Liam hadn't told Carthika? She must just be being her usual annoying self.

"More than one on the go?" asked Carthika. "You're a dark horse, Amy Ashton." Zoe giggled.

"Don't you have work to do?" asked Amy. Of course the phone chose that moment to finally ring, and Amy found herself scurrying away to an empty meeting room, to the amusement of her colleagues.

Richard had bumped into her that morning outside her house. Amy had only just held it together while he told her that he and Charles had spent the previous evening delving through layer upon layer of Google to find out what they could about the model of JCB that Charles had identified. He was right. It had tracks, and should have had wheels. It had been modified.

Richard had said that he'd contact the manufacturer for her today to go through the records. It felt strange to Amy to have someone help her like that, but also rather nice.

"Hello?" said Amy, a question in her voice although she could see it was Richard calling. She closed the door to the meeting room, which was really just a corner of the office sealed off with glass. It always reminded her of a large shower cubicle.

"Don't ask me how," said Richard. "But I've found it. In fact, ask me how."

"You've found it?" asked Amy. She felt a little sick and sank down into a chair.

"You could call me the Sherlock Holmes of the construction world," continued Richard merrily. "I rang the JCB head office and described a modification that I wanted, delineating just what Charles noticed in the picture, and they passed me around a bit, and eventually I got through to the right department. And I was able to get a history of where that machine had been, and then with a search dating to around the time that Tim went missing, I was able to locate the most likely location for the photo. It's here in the city. Abletree Park. Mean anything to you?"

"No," said Amy. All she could think was that when Richard rambled like that, he reminded her of his son. She traced the pattern of the wooden tabletop with her finger. Concentric circles, as unique as a fingerprint.

"Anyway, I've even found out that the three-eighty-three bus goes there."

"The three-eighty-three?" she queried.

"Yes," he replied. "So, go on."

"Go on what?" asked Amy.

"Call me the Sherlock Holmes of the construction world."

"Thank you, Richard," said Amy, a little stiffly.

"I'm sorry," said Richard, the brightness fading from his voice. "I've been treating it lightly. I should have been more sensitive."

"It's fine," said Amy. "I appreciate your help."

"Good. I thought we could go there later today. Can you get out of work early?"

"Today?" asked Amy.

"I think it's best that we just do it," said Richard. "So you don't have time to worry. Rip the Band-Aid off."

"Um . . ." Amy could see the wisdom in that; even so, she'd have several hours of worry to get through, as well as this hangover. Maybe a bacon sandwich would help.

"The boys and I will come with you," said Richard, "for moral support. That digger, by the way, was being used to build a playground. I've seen pictures online, and it looks awesome. Meet outside your house at four?"

"I'll check with my boss," said Amy, feeling strangely relieved to be railroaded instead of having to think it through. "But it should be fine."

"Great," replied Richard. "See you there." He hung up.

Amy would need to leave two hours early. She went back to her desk and fired a quick e-mail to Mr. Trapper, asking permission. He replied instantaneously with a single cryptic letter.

"What does 'K' mean?" she asked Carthika.

"Is that what your man wrote?" replied Carthika, who seemed unable to let it go.

"No," snapped Amy. "It is what Mr. Trapper wrote to me, and before you start, it isn't him, as he is a happily married man and twenty years my senior."

"Okay," said Carthika.

"I know it is okay," replied Amy. "What does 'K' mean?"

"Okay," said Carthika again.

Amy was just about to lose her temper when she realized. Okay. OK. K. She supposed being a partner at even a medium adviser firm like Trapper, Lemon, and Hughes left you bereft of time, but surely typing an *O* wasn't too much to ask.

"Mr. Trapper reckons he's down with the kids," added Carthika. "Didn't you see his leather jacket yesterday? Not that kids wear leather anymore—they are all vegans."

"Thank you, Carthika," said Amy. "I'll be leaving early today." Carthika opened her mouth. "And it's not to meet a man," continued Amy, realizing that wasn't strictly true. "Before you get excited."

"I was going to ask if you wanted help with the Apex document?" said Carthika.

"Oh," replied Amy. "Yes, thank you." She handed the weighty file across the desk.

"Good luck," said Carthika. She smiled at Amy. "I'm going to the greasy spoon. Want a bacon roll?"

Amy instantly forgave Carthika everything. "With brown sauce," she said, gratitude spilling into her voice.

"IT'S A BUS," announced Daniel as it pulled up at the stop. "It's got wheels."

"And they go round and round," replied Charles. "Chill out."

"No squabbling," said Richard, helping Daniel onto the bus. He promptly ran to the steps and started climbing up. "We'll sit downstairs," called Richard, but it was futile. The three of them followed Daniel up, arriving at the top deck just as the bus pulled away.

"I'll sit next to Amy," said Charles, pushing his dad out of the way. Richard shrugged and sat in the seat in front next to Daniel, who had pressed his face to the window like a suckerfish.

"What do you think we'll find out?" asked Charles, turning to Amy. She'd eaten the bacon roll, followed by two bags of crisps and a liter of Coke, and was feeling human again.

"I don't know," said Amy. She didn't. She couldn't work out why Chantel would enclose a picture of a park they'd never been to together. No matter how much she looked at it, she always felt she was missing something.

"Maybe we missed something," said Charles, reading her mind. "Let's look at the photo again."

Amy pulled the envelope out of her bag, and they both studied the picture intently. It was taken in the evening, and the sky was a hazy shade of violet with stripy clouds picking up the last orange rays of the sun. The trees were silhouetted against the skyline, the leaves abundant. It was the kind of scene she'd have painted, what seemed like a lifetime ago.

"It's like a painting," said Charles, and Amy almost jumped. "But if I was painting it, I'd have put the digger in the center," he continued. "Because that's the best bit."

"I like it at the edge," said Amy. "It's more unusual than the tradi-tional one-third one-third one-third composition. It's subtle where it is. A mystery."

"You're into art?" asked Richard.

"I used to paint," said Amy, feeling heat rising up her cheeks and realizing, to her embarrassment, that she was blushing. "Now I'm an administrator at Trapper, Lemon, and Hughes."

"I'd love to see your work."

"My paintings are the one thing I didn't keep," said Amy. "I sold the ones I could and got rid of the rest." After it happened, she couldn't bear to have her art in the house.

"You can always paint more," said Richard.

"No, I can't," said Amy. She looked at the window, noticing the layer of dust that had accumulated there. The husk of a tiny green-fly rested there too, its wing gently swaying from the force of her breathing.

"Ring the bell?" asked Daniel.

"Not till our stop," said Richard. "I'll tell you when." Amy looked up from the fly and out the window, relieved that the line of ques-tioning was over. "It's meant to be a lovely park," said Richard. "And it's a gorgeous day, so I've packed a change of clothes and towels for the boys in case they want to go in the paddling pool."

"Big splash," said Daniel. His hand reached up. "Ring the bell?"

"Not yet," said Richard. Charles handed Amy her picture back, and she slipped it into its envelope.

"Not yet," repeated Richard, at the small hand reaching up. "Patience."

Patience, thought Amy. She wondered what would be her reward.

THE TREES HAD grown and the season had changed. There was a playground where there had once been just the corner of a dig-ger. But as Amy stood, contemplating the view, she knew this was the right place. It was still several hours from summer's sunset, but there was no mistaking the skyline, the contours of the hills. This was where the picture had been taken.

She sat on the park bench that looked out onto the view and closed her eyes. It might have been peaceful here once, but now the sounds of children frolicking in the pool filled her ears.

"I've walked around," said Richard. Amy opened her eyes. "But I can't see anything. Any idea why the picture would be of this place?"

"None," said Amy. "I've never been to this park with either of them. I thought I might recognize something, a statue, or a plaque. . . ." Her voice trailed off. She didn't know what she'd been hoping for.

Yes, she did. Tim, standing there, waiting for her. Waiting in this spot for eleven years.

She knew he wouldn't be, of course she did. She clutched at the ring around her neck.

"Maybe the letter explained it," said Richard. "Perhaps if we have another look, now we're here? I feel like there should be instructions to dig somewhere. Or something hidden in the third rock from the great oak tree."

"I know every legible word by heart," replied Amy. "There's nothing like that."

"I suppose not. Maybe I've seen too many movies."

"Maybe."

"How was your date last night?" asked Richard suddenly. Amy turned to him, surprised. He was picking at the edge of his fingernail.

"Terrible," replied Amy.

"I'm sorry," said Richard. But he was smiling.

They sat in silence, watching the boys. Charles was hanging precariously from a tall rope structure that looked to be designed for a giant spider. He swung his leg up and made his way higher. Daniel was in the paddling pool, apparently doing an impression of a snapping crocodile to shrieks of delight from his would-be victims.

"You have very lovely children," said Amy, words she'd never thought she would utter to anyone.

"I'm very proud of the boys," said Richard.

"You should be." Amy watched Charles swing himself across the ropes and slide down a pole. He looked around, then ran to the paddling pool to join his brother. He received a huge splash of greeting.

"I always thought we'd have more," said Richard, his eyes also on his sons. Amy realized it felt easier for them to talk this way, without looking at each other. Like a confessional box. "I wanted a big family. We both did. I was an only child, and I'm glad the boys have each other. It's no fun being lonely." Richard glanced at Amy, who felt his gaze on her ear. She looked farther in the opposite direction to avoid eye contact, which she felt could break this confessional spell. "Nina said she wanted kids," he added. "One day." He paused. "But that was before she met the boys."

"Have you heard from her?" asked Amy.

"No. Maybe I should let the boys decide who I date next," Richard said. "I've not done well on my own."

"Me neither," said Amy, realizing that was an understatement. She glanced at him just as he looked back at her, and their eyes locked.

Amy thought she felt a moment pass between them. Maybe she hadn't. She looked away. Both boys were being crocodiles now, crawling around on their bellies at the edge of the pool. "So what now?" asked Richard.

Amy wasn't sure what he meant, so she took the easy option. "The ring was a dead end," she said. "I know Tim bought it, before he disappeared, but that's it. The letter is illegible. The photo led me here, but I don't see why. There's only one other thing I can think of, but there's a problem."

"What's the thing?" asked Richard. If he was disappointed in the turn the conversation had taken, he didn't show it.

"A box," said Amy. "When they first went missing, I kept press clippings and my diary and notes about what people said all together. But it didn't lead me anywhere. I was wondering whether it might shed some light on the ring, or the letter, or even this place."

"Does it?"

"I can't find it," admitted Amy. "It's somewhere in my spare room, but . . ." She hesitated.

"Spare rooms can be crowded," finished Richard gently. "How about I help?"

"What?" said Amy.

"Help you look for it? We could sort through, maybe clear out—"

"You can't throw any of my belongings away," said Amy quickly. In the early days various people had suggested they could "help." They couldn't.

"I wasn't going to," replied Richard. "Amy, I know you keep what you need to. That you've got a reason for collecting what you do. I was just suggesting another pair of eyes."

Amy hesitated. It had been a long time since she'd allowed anyone into her home.

"I don't think you realize—" she began.

"Let me help you," said Richard. "Maybe, once you've found this box, you'll be ready to move on?"

"I'll think about it," said Amy.

"Great," said Richard. "In the meantime, join us for dinner tonight? I know the boys would love it, and we can have that stew you brought over."

"Slow-cooked sausage and vegetable cassoulet," said Amy.

Richard laughed. "That's what I said."

Daniel came bounding up to them. He was soaked through and shook water off himself like a dog.

"Ice cream," he said, just before they even heard the tinny tones of the van in the distance.

"I swear he can smell an ice cream van a mile off," said Richard. "Come on, then. Ice cream once we've got you dry. Anything for you, Amy?"

"No thanks," Amy replied.

"Not even strawberry?" questioned Daniel, unconvinced.

"Actually," said Amy, "you know what? I will. Chocolate."

MR. TRAPPER WALKED past her desk the following morning, then walked back, and past again. "Can I help you, Mr. Trapper?" asked Amy.

"Oh, Amy, just the person," he said, as if surprised to see her. "Yes, actually, I was hoping to catch you."

"What is it?"

"Nothing important," he said. "Nothing at all, really."

Amy frowned at him.

"Maybe come to my office for a minute, just if you've time."

Amy got up and followed him.

Mr. Trapper's office was the opposite of Amy's empty desk. Framed photographs of his wife and kids littered the walls and surfaces. His two girls smiling at Disney World. Holding up the Leaning Tower of Pisa. More recently, as teenagers lazing on a beach somewhere. It reminded her of DCI Hooper's desk. Happily married men taking happy family holidays. She hadn't used her own holiday allowance in years.

"So," said Mr. Trapper. He had his Nottingham Forest mug on his desk in front of him, and he picked it up and put it down, though Amy could see it contained nothing but coffee stains. "This is rather awkward."

"Is it?" asked Amy.

"Yes," he said. They sat in silence. Amy looked at him. A bead of sweat was escaping from his hairline and making a dash for it down his cheek. It lingered on his chin before finally leaping onto his desk.

They both looked at it for a moment, before Mr. Trapper wiped it away with the cuff of his shirt.

"Have I done something wrong?" asked Amy finally.

"What? Wrong? Certainly not," he replied. He picked up the mug, then set it down again. "Listen," he began. "What you do on your own time is your business."

"Agreed," said Amy. The council must have been in touch with him: perhaps that was what Leah meant when she said the wheels were in motion. Mr. Trapper knew about her house. "It doesn't affect my work," said Amy. "Not at all."

"Of course not," replied Mr. Trapper. "But it's just . . ." He paused. "I feel I have a duty of care."

There it was again. *Duty of care.* Why couldn't people just leave her alone?

"You've worked here a long time, Amy," he continued. "Before and after it, you know, happened. I know it affected you. Of course it did."

"My work hasn't suffered," said Amy.

"No, it's not that at all. It's just . . ." He paused again. "I don't want you to get hurt."

"I'm perfectly safe," said Amy. "I'm very careful."

Mr. Trapper looked horrified. "I wasn't suggesting . . ." he began. "Maybe this whole conversation was a bad idea."

"Thank you for your concern," said Amy. "But I think you'll find my desk is always clear."

"What?"

"I keep my house one way, the office another."

"Your house?" Mr. Trapper looked at her, confusion piling onto his features.

Amy frowned. "What were you talking about?"

"Liam Salter," he said. "Apparently he's told a few people in the office that you two are seeing each other."

"Oh," replied Amy. If anything, she felt more mortified than ever. What had she said about being safe? "Oh God," she muttered.

"You're, of course, welcome to have . . . um . . . relations with colleagues," he began again. Amy felt as though she were getting a horrifying birds-and-bees chat from her father. She felt color rising in her cheeks. Mr. Trapper was already crimson, and sweat continued to run down his face. "But I thought you should know something."

"I'm not having relations—" she said.

"Good," said Mr. Trapper, clearly wanting the conversation over. "Because I have Liam Salter's CV here. There's something on here. It's a bit 'old-school' to include this sort of detail." Mr. Trapper made exaggerated quotation marks to communicate that he himself was not "old-school" at all. Then he paused again and looked down as he said the words. "Liam Salter is married."

IT HAD TAKEN Amy a while to find, but here it was, rescued from the depths of her kitchen cupboard.

A small vacuum cleaner named Henry.

She didn't often bother vacuuming; there didn't seem to be much point when there was so little floor space available. But Amy was allowing a visitor into her home, and she didn't want to let the side down. And her hallway was already a great deal emptier than it had been.

She started there, dusting off the remaining bottles with an old but freshly cleaned sock. Dried honeysuckle flowers fell from their stems as she went, drifting gently to the floor. Amy fought the urge to collect them together and save them. No. She would simply vacuum them up and get some fresh flowers.

But not red roses.

The very thought of it made her seethe. It wasn't as if she had even liked Liam. But to know that he was trying to betray his wife. With her. After everything.

It was too much.

More dried flowers fell to the lino, and Amy realized she'd been dusting the bottles way too vigorously. She had to be more careful or something would break. Amy switched on the vacuum and watched the flowers disappear. The lino was still stained, and had always been ugly, but at least it was clear of debris.

Amy went into the living room. She couldn't vacuum in here, it would be too dangerous for the birds. She straightened a box that was askew instead. Scarlett looked at her, and Amy gave the bird a gentle wipe with the sock. "Good as new," she told her. "Better, in fact." Amy smiled at Scarlett, but the bird looked nervous.

Perhaps allowing Richard into her home was a bad idea. She had a lot of belongings and a lot of responsibility. What if something were to be broken? Richard wasn't his sons, but he was a man. And men couldn't be trusted. Not with her things. And in fact, not at all.

She'd cancel. Amy went back to the hallway and pulled the vacuum cleaner along behind her to the kitchen, where with no little effort she was able to squeeze it back into the cupboard. It had been a foolish idea to try to clean, and she was lucky the only casualty was the withered honeysuckle. Amy made her way to the front door, looking regretfully at the empty stems poking out from her bottles. She opened the door to go to tell Richard she'd changed her mind.

"I was just about to press your bell," said Richard, smiling at her. "Let's go memory-box hunting."

"I'm sorry," said Amy. "Something has come up."

"I know it's hard," said Richard, "letting people in. But I can help."

"No," insisted Amy. "It's . . ." She paused, searching the recesses of her mind for an excuse. None came.

"I won't come in if you don't want me to," said Richard. "But a fresh pair of eyes could really help you find this box you're looking for." He smiled at her. "Let me help."

Amy took a deep breath. She did want to find that box, and she'd had no luck alone. After all, she'd even vacuumed.

"Okay," she said, opening the door and stepping to one side before she could change her mind. "Come in."

"IT'S NOT THAT bad," said Richard. His eyes, pupils dilated and slightly glazed, said otherwise as he peered up the staircase. This wasn't even the worst of it.

"Maybe this wasn't such a good idea," said Amy. She was still feeling angry at Liam, and was trying not to take it out on Richard.

"No, I'm here. Let's do it." Richard looked again at her staircase. "How do you get up there?"

"I have a technique," said Amy. "Here, let me show you." She plotted her special route up the stairs, making liberal use of the banisters when she had to skip a step.

Richard hesitated for a moment, then followed. "It's like that climbing frame in the park," he said. "Charles would like it."

"The boys can't come in," said Amy quickly. "They might break something." She paused at the top of the stairs, then watched Richard ascending. "Miss that step," she said, seeing him doubting his route. "And swing your leg over that box. That's right."

"No wonder you were so quick up that tree," said Richard, struggling. "Plenty of practice. Okay, I'm here."

"The spare room is this way." They edged past boxes, avoiding the mirrors that leaned on them. "Ouch," said Richard, banging his head on a protruding cookbook and almost knocking over a tower of mugs. "What was that?" he exclaimed, as something crunched underfoot.

"Be careful of the cigarette lighters," said Amy. "And the key rings."

"I thought it was a cockroach," said Richard. "And I didn't know you smoked?"

"I don't," said Amy.

Richard was silent as she opened the door to the spare room. She'd carved a path to the wardrobe, which she slid through and waved at him to follow. He stood still.

"In there?" he queried. "It looks pretty treacherous."

"Just be careful," said Amy. "Don't knock into anything and you'll be fine."

"Okay," said Richard. He stepped forwards, placing his feet tentatively as if trying to avoid hot coals. "If you say so."

"Here," said Amy. "I've made a clearing just here. I think it must be in one of the boxes in the wardrobe, or near it. It's where . . ." She paused. "Where I kept stuff at the beginning."

"Okay," said Richard again, his back bending in an exaggerated fashion.

"There's no need to stoop," said Amy, feeling judgment in the way he carried his shoulders. "You're not in a cave."

"So what's in the boxes?" asked Richard, standing a little straighter but still looking as if he expected an avalanche.

"I'm not getting rid of stuff," said Amy.

"That's not what I said," replied Richard. Amy watched him examine the pile next to him. Boxes, interspersed with stacks of mirrors that she didn't have room to display. A few cookery books slotted in between like cement. One poked out farther than the others, and Amy had adorned it with a rather fetching kingfisher, proudly clutching a small fish in its beak. Probably a minnow or a sardine. "Is that one of the birds you were talking about?" he asked. "When we first met?"

"Of course," said Amy. "I mainly keep them in the living room, but some have fluttered up here."

"I thought you meant real birds," replied Richard, staring at the kingfisher.

"Are you helping or not?" said Amy. "Here, I'll pass you things, and you can put them out of the way."

"Where out of the way?" he asked.

"My bed is clear," she said. "It's the next door along." She handed him a stack of books and opened up a box. He inched his way out.

The box mainly contained ashtrays. Amy smiled at one near the top. It featured an elephant lying on its back, holding the tray over its tummy and peering up. The next one was so different: cut crystal that even when dusty and in the dark room caught the light and reflected it back as rainbows. Gorgeous.

But no shoebox. She passed the box to Richard, warning him to take care with it. He glanced inside, then hoisted it under his arm. Amy tensed as she heard the ashtrays clink against one another, elephant on crystal. She moved on to the next box, and resisted the urge to check the time on each clock. They'd all stopped ticking as they ran out of battery, and she liked to see at what moment each had chosen to pause indefinitely. One, a classic carriage clock set into a mahogany frame, came back to life and ticked at her, but she realized it was just a twitch from being moved.

No shoebox. Amy continued, starting to enjoy herself. Richard stood watching as she went through the boxes, waiting to carry each to the next room. He no longer made conversation or commented on her belongings. It was nice to rediscover things she'd forgotten, like picking up a conversation with a friend she hadn't seen in years.

The thought sobered her and the smile she'd barely noticed developing fell from her face. "We're running out of room on the bed," said Richard. "Is there anywhere else . . . ?"

"The bathroom," said Amy. "I've kept the shower free. Make sure it's completely dry though. We don't want anything getting ruined."

"Indeed," said Richard. Amy chose to ignore the sarcasm in his tone. He was helping, after all.

"Maybe you would like a tea break?" she offered.

"Let's keep going," said Richard. "I don't fancy going up and down those stairs more often than I need to."

Amy assented, happy to get back to her boxes.

"Argh!" shouted Richard all of a sudden. "What the hell was that?"

Amy looked up. "Did you tread on something? Be careful."

"It moved," he said, pointing. Amy looked. She couldn't see anything. "I think it was a mouse—"

"It could have been a key ring," interrupted Amy quickly. "I have a few fluffy ones."

"That was no key ring," said Richard. He sighed. "Amy, how do you live like this?" he continued, the words escaping him fast, as if they'd been building since he entered her house. "It's no way to be."

"It's fine," said Amy.

"It's far from fine," he replied. "I have to admit, I thought that Rachel was exaggerating. Gossip, you know what people are like."

"Rachel has never been inside my house," said Amy with dignity.

"There's not really room for her," said Richard. "There's barely room for you."

"I'm fine," insisted Amy. "And it's none of your business."

"Listen, I get it," said Richard. "You've been through a lot. You need your things. But to have so many, all in your house? You can barely get up the stairs!"

"I manage fine," replied Amy.

"Can't you hire a storage room?" he asked.

"I need to keep everything here," said Amy. "Where it's safe."

"But it's not safe," said Richard. "It's not safe for your things. Or for you. Amy, there is so much more to you than all this. But your belongings are suffocating you."

Amy stopped what she was doing. She pulled herself up to her full height and turned to him. "You can leave now," she replied.

"Don't be like that."

"I can't have you getting injured by a clock or a newspaper," she said, her voice dripping with a sarcasm that didn't suit her. "Or bitten by a key ring."

"We can get you help," said Richard. "Counseling? I found it so—"

"Leave now," said Amy. She needed to be alone with her things, away from his concern. And his judgment. Instead Richard made to step towards her.

Before Amy realized what was happening, Richard was stumbling backwards. She'd pushed him. Quickly Amy put her hands behind her back, as if hiding a weapon.

Richard leaned hazardously against a mirror, which wobbled for a moment before both regained their balance.

"I'm out," he said, turning to leave.

"I'm sorry," muttered Amy, but she didn't ask him to stay. It was probably for the best.

Richard strode out of the room, banging his head on the protruding cookbook again. He swore under his breath. Amy heard irregular footsteps as he stumbled down the stairs, then the reassuring thud of the front door shutting.

She sank to the floor, leaning her back against the cold mirror. It had been a terrible mistake, letting someone in. No one else understood. A lighter sat on the floor, and Amy picked it up and flicked it on, watching the flame light up the air and feeling the heat on her fingers.

She flicked it off again. Fire was dangerous for her things. Instead, she leaned over and grabbed the nearest box, keen to see what beautiful treasures lay inside. Dried honeysuckle lined the box, and Amy shifted it carefully to one side.

Then she froze.

The memory box. Scattered with flowers like a coffin about to be buried.

She'd found it.

September 2007

"I'm not sure it's going to look like the picture," said Amy doubtfully, as she stirred the base for the supposedly green Thai curry from one of her new recipe books. "It's the wrong color."

"Isn't it meant to be a murky beige?" asked Tim. "All the best food is." Amy put down the spoon and reopened the page in the book. They both looked at the picture.

"I'm sure yours will taste good," said Tim.

"The photo in this cookbook is like a piece of art," said Amy. "Those muted greens, the pink of the prawns, the red of the chilis. I could cut it out and use it as a collage, maybe with some swaths of yellow running across the top."

Tim smiled at her. "I'd love to see you painting again," he said. "Actually . . ."

"What?" asked Amy.

"Nothing," said Tim. "I promised we'd wait."

"Wait for what?"

Tim didn't answer. He picked up a whole king prawn instead and held it delicately between his fingers. "I don't like the way this little guy is looking at me," he declared. "I told it I'm pescatarian and it counts as fish so I can eat it, but I'm not sure I can. Its eyes are so sad."

"You don't have to eat it," said Amy. "But don't we need to snap its head off before we cook it?" She looked back to the recipe book. "No," she said, relieved. "Apparently we can cook it like this and then people do that at the table." She shuddered. "Maybe we'll say we didn't have enough and just give them all to Chantel and Jack."

"Jack looks like someone who'd have no qualms about snapping the head off a prawn," said Tim.

"I'm glad they are coming over tonight," said Amy. "I've barely seen Chantel since they've been back together. Have you?"

"Why would I?" said Tim.

"I just wondered," replied Amy. "You have, you know, things in common."

"We haven't been on a secret drug-fueled bender, if that's what you're thinking," he replied.

"Of course not," said Amy.

"I've been clean for ages," added Tim.

"I know. It's just, I worry about her."

"Why?"

"Because I never see her anymore. Here," said Amy, passing Tim a carrot. "You can chop these instead. Julienne, apparently. From the picture I think that means like little matchsticks."

"That's some fine carrot cutting," said Tim, also leaning over the picture. "Good thing I have the skillful fingers of a guitar player."

Amy leaned over and gave him a kiss, then grabbed a large and angry-looking red chili. "Do you think she's okay? She seemed so sure when she broke up with Jack last time."

"She's like a cat," said Tim. "You have to break up with her nine times before it sticks. Look at Spike."

"Jack is better than Spike," replied Amy with a laugh. "I hope it does work out with them. She's definitely kissed her share of frogs."

"Jack is a bit of a catch," said Tim. "And he looks like He-Man."

"Maybe you should date him," said Amy, tossing her chilies into the frying pan and listening to them sizzle.

"Not my type," replied Tim. He leaned over her and gave her another kiss. "I like beautiful arty girls with spicy fingers who make me smoke outside even when it's snowing."

"I'll squeeze the lime juice in and see what happens," said Amy boldly, after giving Tim a kiss in return. "Did you buy fresh coriander?"

"I bought everything on the list," said Tim.

"This is nice," replied Amy, chopping the coriander. "Having a dinner party. We even have the right number of plates, and clean cutlery. It's like being a grown-up at last."

Tim put down his knife, and Amy noticed that the carrots were more like stubby little fingers than elegant matchsticks. So much for his musician hands. She didn't say anything.

Amy's phone buzzed. "It's Chantel," she said. "They are running late."

"What shall we do with the extra time?" Tim's hand slid suggestively around Amy's waist.

"Maybe you could have another go at the carrots?" she said. "Matchsticks, please, not fingers."

"I'm not sure about being a grown-up," he grumbled, picking up the knife again. "But your wish is my command."

AMY WAS JUST about to relent and let Tim eat the Thai curry when the doorbell finally rang. "I hate that ring tone," she said.

"It's Beethoven," replied Tim with a laugh. "A classic. And just the sound we needed. I'm starving."

Amy went to open the door. "Hello," said Chantel. "Sorry we're late." Her voice had a metallic quality to it, hard and mechanical.

"No worries," said Amy, going to hug her friend. Chantel winced a little at the embrace. "Are you okay?" asked Amy.

"Big session at the gym earlier," said Chantel. "I'm a bit worn-out and achy." She smiled at Amy. "But we're here now."

"This one took forever to get ready," said Jack, his voice bright and cheerful as he stepped in and gave Amy a warm hug. "Hope dinner's all right."

"Of course," said Amy. "We eat late anyway." She looked at Chantel, who was gazing at the empty wall. "I've missed you," she said.

"You too," replied Chantel.

"I'm always telling her she should come around more often," said Jack. "But what with work and the gym, she's barely got any time."

Tim poured them all a glass of wine, and they sat around the coffee table. Amy went into the kitchen and spooned rice into small bowls, which she upturned and removed to make little rice domes. She spooned curry onto each plate, adding prawns to Chantel's and Jack's. She sprinkled everything with the fresh coriander, and added a sliver of lime to each plate. It didn't exactly look like the picture, but it certainly seemed edible.

"Dinner is served," she said rather proudly, presenting the dishes to her guests. "Sorry about eating at the coffee table," she said, over her shoulder as she went back to the kitchen to fetch the other plates. "We're saving up for a dining table."

"You must come round to ours next time," said Jack. "We've got a six-seater."

"Very impressive," Tim told Jack, his mouth full of curry. "Amy, this is delicious."

"You should teach Chantel how to make this," said Jack, happily breaking the head from a prawn. "It's very nice."

"All I can make is cheese on toast," said Chantel, picking at the curry and ignoring the rice. "And since we've given up bread, that's not so useful."

"You should borrow one of my recipe books," said Amy. "I've got a few now."

"Nice plates too," added Chantel.

"Gosh, we're old." Amy laughed. "Sitting around dinner talking about plates."

"We'll have to pop some pills later," said Tim. "Prove we've still got it. No offense," he said to Jack.

"I know you're joking," replied Jack. He broke the head off another prawn. "Because if you weren't, I'd have to arrest you." There was a moment's silence; then Chantel laughed, the sound cutting through the room. The others joined in.

"Nicely cut carrots, don't you think, everyone?" said Tim.

"Did you do those?" asked Chantel.

"You can tell?" he said.

"Musician fingers," replied Chantel. She smiled at Tim. "Are you missing the band?"

"Turns out media sales is my calling," said Tim. "In fact, shall we tell her, Chantel?"

"Absolutely." Chantel and Tim grinned at each other.

"What's the secret?" asked Amy. "Tim, you were being weird earlier."

"You tell her," said Chantel. "You paid for most of it."

"You chipped in," said Tim.

"Just tell us," said Jack. "I hate secrets."

"We've booked you onto that art program, Amy," said Tim. "The one you've always wanted to do, in Florence."

"What?"

"It's all paid for," said Chantel. "And we've cleared the leave with Mr. Trapper." She let out a small squeal. "Are you happy?"

"I can't believe it," said Amy, stunned.

"It's time you worked on your art again, Amy," said Tim. "You're so talented."

"I haven't painted in ages," said Amy. "What if I'm not good enough?"

"Of course you are," said Tim. He grinned at her. "This is just the kick-start you need. And now that I'm making decent money, perhaps you can cut your hours at Trapper." He looked around. "Shall we open another bottle to celebrate?"

"Yes!" said Chantel.

"Better not," said Jack. "We're up early, training again. Aren't we, Chantel?"

"Oh yes," she replied. "None for me."

"You're looking very svelte," said Amy. "Isn't she, Tim?"

"No offense, Chantel, but I hadn't noticed." Tim leaned over to Amy and planted a kiss on her cheek.

"Eyes only for each other," said Jack, with a glance towards Chantel. "Adorable."

Chapter
Twelve

Amy sat in her bedroom, holding the box. It was as if she'd got the heart of her hoards in her hands, bloody and pumping. It was where it had all started.

Taking a deep breath, Amy opened the box.

Inside was her sketchbook. She'd taken to carrying it around with her when she worked at Trapper, Lemon, and Hughes and watercolors were not an option. She couldn't use it for the vibrant colors that she loved, but drawing at all had been better than nothing. She flicked through and found a line drawing of Mr. Trapper's second baby, its mouth wide open in an angry scream. Amy could almost hear the sound now, and remembered the afternoon when Mrs. Trapper had brought the baby in and handed her round to the cooing girls in the office, before the baby had decided enough was enough and started shrieking. The next sketch was of a rosebush in winter, its stems pruned so they just protruded from the ground. Then a picture of a robin, perched on a birdbath. Amy turned the page.

The drawings stopped and notes took over. That was when they'd disappeared. Scrawled ideas of where they could be. Hopeful at first. She remembered. Tim hadn't come home that night, and the next day she'd discovered Chantel was missing too. She looked at what she'd written: "Tim said he was meeting Simon." She remembered being angry; she was recently back from Italy and hadn't wanted him to go.

When he didn't come home that night, she was even more upset, thinking he'd broken his promises and gone on a bender. But when he was still missing the next morning, she'd started to worry. Tim didn't answer his phone. She'd called Simon, but he hadn't seen Tim for weeks and denied they'd had plans the night before. She'd tried Chantel, but couldn't reach her. Of course. And then she'd scribbled notes from her phone calls to everyone she could think of whom Tim might have been in contact with. No one knew a thing, but a few people hazarded guesses, which all included drugs and alcohol. She'd tried Chantel again, but still no answer. She'd rung their house phone, and Jack told her she hadn't been home either, but he wasn't worried. They'd had a row and he was sure she'd be back soon. Then she'd rung Chantel's mother, who had heard nothing from her. She called Jack again, worried for her friend. He'd told her not to be paranoid, she'd show up soon.

Except she never did.

Amy frowned at the notebook. Something didn't feel right. She left it open on that page and looked at the other documents in the box. Tim and Amy's shared calendar: it used to be pinned to the fridge and was illustrated with pictures of guitars from around the world. She'd bought it for Tim that Christmas. The day he disappeared was marked by Tim. *Out,* it just said. That was the understatement of the century. The next day was circled in red. The start of his new life, thought Amy, trying not to let bitterness spread throughout her body.

She shuffled through newspaper clippings. At the beginning,

she'd scoured the papers for relevant articles, and here they were, neatly trimmed with her kitchen scissors. She'd been saving them, hoping to discover more about what had happened. Of course, she hadn't. Once Jack accepted that Chantel was not coming home, he'd decided that she and Tim had run away together. With no leads to go on and no sign of foul play, the investigating officers seemed inclined to agree with him.

Amy found an interview with Jack in the local paper:

"Chantel and Tim had always been close," said Hooper. "But neither Amy nor I were suspicious by nature. Chantel and I had a disagreement and Chantel stormed out, saying she was going to stay with a friend. I thought nothing of it at first. It wasn't till days later when she didn't come back that I realized this was more than a tiff. She'd betrayed me with her best friend's boyfriend."

Stay with a friend, thought Amy. That should have been her; she was the only real friend Chantel had. But Jack knew Chantel wasn't with Amy. He knew she wasn't with her mother either—Amy had told him that. Why hadn't he been worried those few days earlier? Could that have made a difference? Amy got up, finding her legs had cramped where she'd been sitting on them. Gingerly she shook them out, carefully clambered over her things, and went downstairs. Jack's business card was sitting next to a pile of mugs, a little splattered with the sausage juice from the slow cooker. She dialed his number and left a message asking him to call her. She said she just wanted to check on a few details of when Chantel disappeared and when he raised the alarm. It didn't quite make sense to her.

Amy went back upstairs afterwards, back to the box. There must be more to it, she thought. Something that would give her the lead she needed.

*   *   *

AMY SAT AT her desk at work the next day feeling exhausted. She hadn't been able to face clearing the mess off her bed, and had slept on the sofa again. Not that she'd slept much at all, and when she had it was a fitful sleep filled with dreams of a robin trapped inside a guitar, flapping its little wings desperately in an attempt to escape. She sipped her tea from an anonymous office mug and tried not to think about it.

Another message popped up on her screen from Liam. It was the seventh this morning. Chirpy enough at first, they were getting a whiny, anxious quality, and the time between messages was dwindling.

Ignoring me? She deleted it.

You can't be that busy. Amy pressed Delete again.

Everything okay? Amy considered replying to this one with a simple no. Then she thought of his arm, snaking around her waist. Married. She couldn't bear to write back to him, but she needed the messages to stop.

"Carthika," she said, "is there a way to block someone from sending you instant messages?"

"Course," said Carthika. She leaned over, just as another message popped up. Amy deleted it as quickly as she could. "Getting too full-on?" she asked with a grin.

"It's nothing that concerns you," said Amy.

"Sorry," said Carthika. "I didn't mean to pry." Her eyes, however, were still on Amy's screen. Another message came up.

"Please make it stop," said Amy.

"Are you sure?" asked Carthika. She looked genuinely disappointed. "We all thought—"

Amy held up a hand to silence her. "We all?" she said, incredulous. How many people knew about the date? Amy felt anger and embarrassment rising up inside her, finding their outlet as a red flush on her face. It wasn't enough that a married man had pursued her, he had also told her entire team. She wondered what they'd heard.

"Don't look so upset," said Carthika. "Everyone wants you to be happy."

"I will be happy if I never see that man again," said Amy.

"Well, you won't get any more instant messages," said Carthika, pressing a button. She placed a hand on Amy's arm and whispered in her ear, "Just because he wasn't right for you doesn't mean that you won't find someone else. Don't give up."

Amy was just about to tell her to mind her own business and get back to work when she found Carthika's arms wrapped around her body, and she was drawn into a deep and warm hug that smelled of jasmine blossom. Amy lingered there a moment, breathing deeply. "Thank you," she found herself saying instead.

"Don't mention it," said Carthika, eventually releasing the embrace. "What are friends for?"

AMY STARED AT the clock on the office wall. It was charmless: a simple white face with black numbers and a hand that seemed to circle ridiculously slowly. Amy longed for the beautiful timepieces she kept at home, certain that even the ones that had long ceased to tick would move more quickly than this stubborn device. Finally the clock could resist the inevitable laws of space and time no more, and it struck 5 p.m.

Amy leapt up and grabbed her bag. With a half smile at Carthika and a nod that she hoped conveyed gratitude for her kindness, Amy hurried to the elevator. She wanted to be out of this office, away from Liam and back with her things. She felt as if there were more the contents of her box had to tell her, if only she could spend long enough listening.

A hand sneaked between the elevators doors as they closed and they opened again, revealing Liam. His face looked puffier than usual. "What a day," he said, getting inside.

Amy didn't reply. The elevator reached the ground floor. He waved to the receptionist and fell into step alongside Amy, who was walking as fast as she could towards the station.

"I expect you didn't see my messages," he said. "I sent a few."

"I saw them," said Amy, her voice icy.

"Good," said Liam, sounding uncertain as to whether that was good or not. He was a little shorter than Amy and practically running to keep up. "Can you slow down a bit?"

"I have a train to catch," replied Amy.

"I'll walk you to the station," said Liam.

"I'd rather you didn't."

"It's no trouble," puffed Liam.

Amy swung into the station, hoping to lose Liam in the crowds, but he stuck with her. She was pleased to see she was just in time for the five-oh-seven. She hurried towards her platform, Liam scuttling behind her like a determined dog.

"This is my train," said Amy, getting on board. "Good-bye."

Liam stood on the platform. "About the messages," he said.

Amy decided she had to be more direct. "I'd prefer it if you left me alone in the office," she said. To her surprise, he grinned at her.

"That's a relief," he said. He winked. "I thought you'd gone off me. Keep business and pleasure separate. Nice thinking."

To her further surprise, he hopped on the train. "How about we go for a drink now instead?" asked Liam. "We're not in the office."

"No," said Amy, stepping back. "Definitely not."

"Are you okay, love?" asked a man leaning against a pole near the train door. He stood up straight, and Amy saw that he towered over Liam. "This guy bothering you?"

Little beads of perspiration appeared on Liam's forehead, as if he were a mug covered in condensation.

"I'm fine, thank you," said Amy, feeling a spark of pity for Liam. "This man was just leaving."

Her protector grunted and turned away. The train doors shut before Amy could insist that Liam get off. Liam wiped the sweat beads across his face, leaving a wet trail.

"Looks like I'm coming to your house," he quipped.

"Absolutely not," said Amy. "You can get off at the next stop." She walked down the carriage and sat in the only available seat in a group of four. She glanced at the other passengers in her bank: a dark-haired woman reading an Italian newspaper, a young man playing some kind of game on his phone, and a teenage girl listening to music and staring out of the window.

"I was only joking," he said, following her and standing awkwardly in the aisle. "Listen, I just want to spend some time with you. That's all. No pressure."

"There will be no more dates," said Amy, her voice firm. She noticed the woman reading the paper glance up at her.

The train jolted, and Liam grabbed the top of her seat to avoid falling over. "But we had fun," he said. "Amy," he added, "I really like you."

"Liam," said Amy, "you are married." In exasperation, she'd spoken louder than she intended. The phone man was staring at them now, and the woman with the newspaper stopped pretending to read. Amy saw the girl with the earphones slip one out of her ear.

"Oh," said Liam. "You found out about that." The newspaper woman tutted.

"Yes, I found out," said Amy. "Because you told everyone in the office about our date, and Mr. Trapper, of all people, called me into his office to tell me about your wife. I have never been so humiliated in my life." She paused. "And I've had some pretty awful things happen to me," she added.

"Actually," he said. "I'm separated. I have been for over a year."

Amy looked at him. He seemed truthful.

"I know you probably think I'm some sort of smooth Casanova," he continued. The music girl made a funny snorting sound that she managed to turn into a cough. "But I'm not. You're the first person I've dated since my wife."

Amy took a breath. "I'm sorry about your marriage," she said. "But I . . ." Amy glanced around the train. Everyone was watching them. "Maybe we should talk about this another time," she finished, her voice gentle.

"That's a no, isn't it?" said Liam.

Amy nodded.

Liam looked crestfallen for a moment. Then he seemed to remember that he had an audience. "Plenty more fish in the sea," he said, his voice overly bright and a little too loud. He winked at the girl next to Amy. She turned away and put her earphones back in.

As if on cue, the train pulled into a station. "I'll get out here," said Liam. "Bye, Amy."

The passengers settled back into their phones, papers, and music as if they'd witnessed nothing.

AMY RELAXED INTO her sofa, the shoebox and a glass of wine in front of her. *In vino veritas* flickered into her mind, from somewhere in the recesses of her brain. *In shoebox veritas,* she thought. That was more likely. But she couldn't work out where in that box the truth was hiding.

The doorbell rang. Amy heaved herself up and went to open it. Richard was standing in the doorway. She felt awkward in front of him. It was the first time she'd seen him since she'd pushed him out of her house.

"Is everything okay?" he asked.

"I suppose so," replied Amy. "Why?"

"I saw a car I didn't recognize parked in front of your house," replied Richard. "What with the trouble with the pots, I just wanted to check. . . ." He trailed off.

"There's no car there now," said Amy, glancing past him.

"Yes," agreed Richard. He hesitated. "I wanted to see you," he confessed. "Can I come in?"

"Not really," said Amy. She didn't want to see his face react to her treasures again. She didn't like how it made her feel.

"Fair enough," he said, his face resigned. "Listen, I really am sorry. I just wanted to help, and you let me in before and I know that was a big deal for you, and I feel like I blew it. We all have our . . ." he gestured around. "Baggage," he finished, feebly.

"That's okay," said Amy. It felt nice to be apologized to. "I found the box I was looking for."

"That's brilliant," said Richard, with genuine enthusiasm. They stood in silence for a moment. "I'm pleased for you." He smiled at her. "What's next?"

"I haven't worked it out yet," she said.

"You will, Amy," he said. "I have faith in you."

"I don't know how you can," said Amy. "You've seen my house. It took me weeks to find a box."

"I know your secrets now, Amy," said Richard. He reached out and placed a hand on her arm. "And I'm still here."

AMY SAT ON her sofa again, but this time she was neither looking at the box nor her wine. Her eyes were closed, and she was thinking of Richard. She could still feel a small patch of warmth on her arm where his hand had been.

The doorbell rang again, and for once Amy found she rather enjoyed the sound. Daniel had interrupted their moment on the doorstep with an urgent request for apple juice, but Richard said he would return later. Amy smoothed her hair and glanced in one of the mirrors, liking the excitement she saw reflected back. She went to the door and swung it wide open.

But it wasn't Richard standing there.

"Hello, Amy," said a voice Amy had once known as well as her own.

Amy whispered a reply.

"Chantel."

April 2008

"I still can't believe you guys have done this for me," said Amy, opening up her suitcase.

"I can't believe it's come round so quickly," said Tim. "I'm going to miss you so much."

"Italy is not far," she said. "And it's only six weeks."

"I'll be watching the clock the whole time." Tim picked up the little alarm clock they kept by their bed and waved it in her face for emphasis.

"Please don't," said Amy. "Enjoy yourself. I will."

"That's what I'm worried about," replied Tim. "All those handsome Italian men. '*Ciao, bella,* oh, your brush is so sexy. Paint my muscly body and cover me in spaghetti.'"

"That sounds disgusting," said Amy with a laugh. "And you know I don't like handsome arty Italians. I like pale media-sales trainees who play guitar."

"And don't you forget it," replied Tim. He leaned forwards and kissed her. "Aren't you taking your backpack?"

"No, I bought this suitcase specially," said Amy, rather proud of it. Going on an arts program abroad and owning a suitcase. She felt extremely sophisticated.

"Well, I'm bringing the backpack when I visit," said Tim. "If I can get the bloody time off work. If I miss my stupid targets, I'm out."

"You won't," said Amy. "And I understand if you can't come." She didn't say it, but she was rather looking forwards to being by herself. She'd been with Tim her whole adult life. Living on her own for six weeks felt like an adventure.

"Is Chantel going to visit?" asked Tim.

"Jack can't get the time off either," said Amy.

"She can't come on her own?"

"Apparently not."

"He doesn't trust her around those spaghetti men either," said Tim. "And I don't blame him. You know how much Chantel likes her carbs."

"Not anymore," said Amy. The last time she'd met her friend, Chantel had ordered a salad again and barely touched it.

"It's good of Trapper to hold your job for you."

Amy looked up at Tim. She'd been carefully folding a purple dress. "Yes," she said. "A little sabbatical. He called it his way of supporting the arts." Amy was hoping that the program would go well and she would make some useful contacts. It was still her dream to quit that boring job in the little advice firm and make it as an artist. Perhaps now that Tim had a proper job, it would finally become reality.

"Then I suppose it's just me and the clock," said Tim. "Ticking away time until you come back."

THE STUDIO WAS beautiful. Large with high, ornate ceilings and exposed wooden floorboards splattered with the paint of artists past. In front of her was the life model, Antonio, confidently naked, reclined on a chaise longue like a lithe Roman emperor. Around her, her fellow students studied him with serious faces. Amy had done life drawing before, many times, but today especially she wished Chantel was with her. She longed for someone to make a joke. No one here was likely to oblige, and Amy knew that if she did it would be frowned upon and she'd be the subject of intense whispered criticism over large plates of pasta that evening.

And wine. Her stomach lurched at the thought. She'd lost her ability to drink since she'd been away, feeling the wine curdle inside her.

Her appetite had gone too. She'd nibbled on dry bread at most meals and moved her pasta sadly around her plate. Even the rich garlicky smell made her want to retch. It was homesickness, Amy decided. She hadn't thought that she could miss someone enough to put her off her penne, but she did. She wished desperately that Tim would hit his targets early and fly out to surprise her.

She glanced out of the window. The view was perfect. She could see the cupola of the cathedral in the distance, a round cone that reminded her of the hat she'd seen the bishops wearing in the paintings that hung in the Uffizi Gallery.

She'd dreamed of being in Florence many times on those long days spent filing suitability reports and investment recommendations at Trapper, Lemon, and Hughes. But now she was here, she just couldn't enjoy it. Not without Tim.

She'd call him tonight, she decided, from the pay phone outside the boutiquey little apartment she shared with two po-faced students. She wouldn't tell him she was off her food without him, he'd never let her hear the end of it. But she would tell him she missed him. That the clock was ticking for her as well.

AMY STARED AT the plastic stick. She was a couple of days late, that was all, and she'd bought the test just to set her mind at rest. She was so confident that she was not pregnant that she'd also bought tampons from the same small and fiercely priced little *farmacia* outside the studio. And here she was. Looking at the two little blue lines that she didn't need her limited Italian to interpret.

Pregnant.

Amy felt different already. A little life, growing inside her. A baby. Her baby. Tim's baby.

It wasn't planned, but Amy realized she wanted nothing more. They'd finally clear out Chantel's old room. Amy would paint little birds flying on the walls that the baby could gaze at from its crib. It would be a winter baby. She tried not to think about names already, but Robin popped into her head. She'd always loved those birds, friendly and festive and so delicate and beautiful.

She'd keep her job at Trapper for the moment—they were bound to have a maternity policy of sorts. Then she'd paint while the baby napped. Tim would soon start earning a decent commission. They'd get married. They'd be a family. Chantel would be godmother.

Amy longed to call Tim right now from the mobile in front of her, but international charges were extortionate and they needed to save their money. She sent him a text instead, asking him if he could speak. He replied with an instant yes, and Amy put the test in her pocket and carefully made her way down the dusty marble staircase to use the pay phone.

She hesitated before she dialed. She was happy; would he be? Yes, she thought. Of course he would. So happy.

Amy wished she could see his face when she told him. She heard his voice. "Hello?"

"Hello," she replied, then hesitated. There was only a week left of her trip. She'd wait and tell him when she got back. It would be worth it. "I've got something to tell you," she blurted out, then stopped herself. "But I don't want to do it over the phone."

"I have something to tell you too," replied Tim. His voice sounded odd.

"What?"

"You first," he said.

"No," replied Amy. "I'm going to wait and tell you in person."

"Me too," said Tim.

"I miss you," said Amy.

"The clock hasn't stopped ticking," said Tim cryptically. "I don't think it ever will."

Chapter Thirteen

"Is Tim with you?" asked Amy.

"Can I come in?"

Chantel was so familiar and yet a stranger. Her face was filled with nervous concern and she was picking at the edge of her thumbnail.

"No," said Amy.

"Please," said Chantel.

"Where's Tim?" asked Amy. "Are you two . . ." She trailed off. She found she couldn't say the words.

"Amy, we need to talk."

"We needed to talk eleven years ago," said Amy, finding the volume of her voice rising beyond her control. "But we didn't. You just left. Both of you." She leaned back against her doorframe. She felt pain in her head, then discovered that her fingers were pulling at her own hair.

"I don't want to shout about this in the street," said Chantel, her voice quiet as she glanced around nervously. Amy found Chantel's reluctance to make a public scene jarring. That wasn't the Chantel she used to know.

Used to love.

But that Chantel had gone. She'd gone forever when she betrayed Amy.

Amy shut the door and bolted it. Then she leaned against her hallway wall and closed her eyes.

"Please," said Chantel, her voice muffled through the door. "I need to talk to you."

Amy took a deep breath. She reached to the ring, still hanging from a chain around her neck. She needed the truth.

Amy stepped forwards and opened the door. Just a crack this time.

"Thank you," said Chantel. The women stood in silence, watching each other through the sliver of space that Amy had allowed. Chantel was dressed simply but neatly in jeans and a pretty lilac shirt, and she held herself straight. Straighter than she used to. Amy found herself staring at the white buttons on Chantel's shirt. Nothing else seemed real.

Amy peeled her gaze from the buttons and looked into Chantel's eyes. "What you did—" she began. Anger enveloped the rest of her sentence.

"Let me explain."

Amy's fingers hovered on her door. Part of her wanted to close it again. To sit with Scarlett and her mirrors and her mugs and never have to hear the words spoken.

"I want to tell you what happened," said Chantel. "Please, Amy."

Amy hesitated. Her things would still be there for her, no matter what Chantel had done. She put her hand to the ring again and squeezed it tightly. This was her opportunity to hear the truth. Afterwards she could shut the door again. Forever, if she wanted to.

"Five minutes," she said, opening the door and stepping back.

"Thank you," said Chantel.

Amy led Chantel to the living room and gestured for her to sit on the sofa. Amy ignored Chantel's concerned face at the state of the room and remained standing, her arms firmly crossed.

"Why now?" asked Amy, feeling betrayed by the tears that were starting to sting her eyes at the sight of Chantel in her house again. "Why do you suddenly want to see me now?"

"Aunt Laura called me," said Chantel. "She said that you wanted to speak to Mum, that my letter had been lost." Chantel looked up at Amy. "I'm so sorry," she said. "When you didn't reply to the letter, I thought it meant you didn't want to see me. That you blamed me for what happened." She looked down again. "God knows I blamed myself."

Amy found she didn't want to hear Chantel say the words. She didn't want to hear the confession. She picked up a green plastic lighter from where it lay on one of her boxes and squeezed it between her fingers. "Toyah wasn't in Dubai, was she?" she said.

"Dubai was a cover story," confessed Chantel. "Mum's been with me. She wanted to be near her grandchildren."

"Grandchildren?" The word felt like a knife in Amy's gut. Tim and Chantel had children.

It was too much.

Amy flung the lighter at Chantel. Chantel ducked, but there was no need: the lighter hit the wall far to Chantel's right.

"What the hell, Amy?" exclaimed Chantel, looking at a deep chip on the wall from the lighter. "Good thing you've always had terrible aim."

Amy ran to fetch the lighter. The plastic was cracked. "It's broken," she gasped.

"It's just a lighter," said Chantel, looking at the open box. "You seem to have plenty. Do you even smoke?"

"You don't understand," said Amy. "After what you did—"

"You don't know what happened," said Chantel. "Sit down. Let me tell you. Then if you want to, you can throw all the lighters in the box at me."

Amy found herself sinking onto the sofa. She held the lighter in her hands, gently now. The crack caught the light and she ran her finger along it.

"Your mum knew where you were," said Amy, without looking up from her hand. "And Laura."

"Aunt Laura didn't know," replied Chantel. "She just knew what she had to say if anyone called." Chantel paused. "I'm so sorry," she continued. "God knows what you must have thought, us both disappearing."

"So what did happen?" asked Amy.

"I saw the papers," said Chantel. "So I knew what the police thought, what Jack was saying. I couldn't bear you to think that was what we did. We'd never have done that to you. Never. Not me. Not Tim. That's why, eventually, I wrote to you."

"But you left together," said Amy.

"We disappeared at the same time," replied Chantel, her voice careful. "It's not the same thing."

"You haven't been with him?"

"No."

Amy looked at her friend. Chantel looked back, meeting her gaze. She was telling the truth, Amy was sure of it. She hadn't betrayed her. Neither had Tim. A weight lifted. Not from her shoulders.

From her heart.

Amy barely had a moment to feel relief. Worry flooded her.

"Then where is he?" asked Amy. "Where's Tim?"

Chantel broke her gaze and looked to the floor. Then she turned back to Amy. Still no words.

"Is he okay?" Amy pushed.

"No," replied Chantel finally. "He's not okay."

Amy didn't want to hear the words, but she needed to.

"He's not . . . ?"

"I'm so sorry," said Chantel. "Tim is dead."

Chantel reached to take her hand, but Amy was gone. She rushed to the kitchen and vomited into the sink, the lighter still tightly clenched in her hand. Chantel must have followed her, because she felt her stroking her hair. "Get out," said Amy, her head still over the sink. Chantel obeyed.

Amy lifted her head and stared out of the window. Smudge was in the garden assiduously cleaning his tail. He looked up from his work and stared at Amy for a moment, his gaze critical. Then he went back to his task. Amy opened her hand and looked at the lighter again, then she squeezed it tight.

Dead.

Amy ran the kitchen tap, then grabbed a mug, filled it with water, and took a sip. It was the yellow one, the color of butter, that she'd rescued from the neighbors only a few short weeks ago.

Amy took a deep breath and allowed the air to fill her body. Breathing while he couldn't. He hadn't betrayed her. But she would never see him again.

She had to know why. To know how.

Amy put the mug down and turned back to the living room. Chantel sat on the sofa, looking worried. "I'm so sorry," said Chantel.

"How?" asked Amy, feeling like the question took all the breath in her body.

"It's a long story," said Chantel.

Amy could feel grief creeping into the edges of her mind like a migraine, about to take over again. "Tell me now."

"Okay," said Chantel. "Here goes." She paused. "I don't know if I can do this," she said. "I've wanted to for so long, but now I'm here—" She stopped. "I don't suppose there's any more of that wine?" she asked, looking at Amy's wine glass still sitting there.

"You've been gone, without a word, for eleven years," said Amy. "And only now you come back to tell me that Tim is dead? No, Chantel. You can't have a glass of wine."

Chantel looked down. "Okay," she said. "That's fair." She paused. "Where to start?" Chantel took a deep breath. "You know I was rubbish at picking men." She laughed nervously. "A cliché really, the bad boy. Spike and his ridiculous white-man dreadlocks. Drug dealing. You remember when he set me up and you had to come and get me from the police station?"

Amy nodded. Her head felt disconnected from the rest of her body.

"Jack seemed different. He was respectable, going places. He even had a sensible haircut, for Christ's sake." Chantel began fiddling with a loose thread on Amy's silk cushion. "Well, it turns out he wasn't so different from the others after all. He wasn't as nice as I thought." She glanced up at Amy. Amy saw the pain in her friend's face.

"You should have told me," said Amy, alarm for Chantel forcing her grief to one side. "I could have helped."

"It wasn't so bad at first," said Chantel. "He didn't like how I dressed, and then he thought I should go to the gym more. I was a bit flabby."

"You weren't," said Amy.

"I thought it was a good thing," said Chantel. "Spike had helped me get drugs, and here was Jack helping me get in shape. I thought some of his clean living and drive might rub off on me. I was such a screw-up."

Amy opened her mouth to deny that, but Chantel held up her hand to stop her.

"Then one day I skipped a gym session. I'd been out with some of the girls from work and was a bit hungover, and I just wanted to watch telly. He was furious, called me a fat loser. Then he hit me."

Amy gasped.

"I tried to leave him," continued Chantel. "I broke up with him. Remember? I didn't tell you why, I was embarrassed. But then he was so apologetic afterwards and God knows I've made mistakes too. So I forgave him."

"You should have told me."

"I was ashamed," said Chantel. "And it was just the once. Until the next time. He didn't always hit me. I overslept one time and he held a pillow down on my face. I still have nightmares, gasping for air when there isn't any. I thought he was going to kill me, but he laughed it off, said I was overreacting. I told him I was going to leave him, and he said that if I did, he'd track me down. And that the next time it wouldn't be a joke."

Chantel looked at Amy. "Amy, I was terrified of him. And I was terrified to leave."

"You could have come to me."

"It was the first place he'd look. Your place and Mum's. I knew what he was like when he got angry, and I didn't want him coming near you guys like that." Chantel paused. "But enough about Jack," she said. "I need to tell you what happened to Tim."

"Did Tim know about Jack?" Amy found she was tapping impatiently on the lighter.

"No," said Chantel. "Jack despised Tim. Even though he saw how close you and I were, he still got it in his head that there was something going on with Tim and me. Then, while you were in Florence, Tim asked to see me. Alone."

"What for?" asked Amy, squeezing the lighter in her hands.

"He said it was important," continued Chantel. "I couldn't meet him straightaway—Jack would have gone ballistic if he'd found out. So I waited until Jack had a colleague's leaving do, the day after you were back. We arranged to meet in secret."

Amy felt sick. She looked up and saw Scarlett perched on a box, listening intently. "And Jack caught you together?" she said.

"It wasn't like that," said Chantel, her voice hurried. "It wasn't. Amy, you have to believe me."

"Tell me what it was like," said Amy.

"We met in Abletree Park," continued Chantel.

"The place where the photo was taken."

"I took that snap while I was waiting. I thought you'd like the colors of the sunset, it reminded me of one of your paintings. I printed it later, for you. I thought you would want to see where it happened. The last thing that Tim saw . . ."

"How kind," said Amy. She could feel years of doubt and frustration and anger leaking out as sarcasm.

"Just listen," said Chantel. "Tim wanted to talk about you. He was going to propose."

Amy sat back. It was what she wanted to hear, but it felt like she'd been hit by one of Charles's JCBs. "The ring," she said, reaching for it.

"Yes, the ring," replied Chantel. "He'd handed it to me to take a look at, and he wanted advice on how to ask you. Of course I tried it on. That's why I still had it after . . ."

"What happened?" asked Amy.

"Jack must have followed me," said Chantel. "I told him I was going to the gym, and like I said, he had a leaving do. But after I'd hugged Tim, I saw him. Standing there. Watching us."

Amy looked at her friend. She'd stopped fiddling with the thread and was gripping the cushion.

"He was silent at first," she continued. "Then he started running at me. Calling me a fat slag and saying he was going to kill me. Tim told me to run, and I did. I ran and ran. I knew that if he caught me, he could do anything. If he hit me for missing the gym, suffocated me for sleeping in . . ."

"What about Tim?"

"I thought he was behind me at first," said Chantel. "But when I looked back, he was shouting something at Jack. Then I saw Jack push him. Tim pushed him back. Next thing I knew, Jack punched him in the face. Tim fell backwards, I think he hit his head on the railings. Then he was on the ground. Not moving."

"And you carried on running?"

"Yes." Chantel's voice was a whisper. "I did. And I've never forgiven myself."

They sat in silence.

"I don't know what happened next," said Chantel eventually. "I kept running, like I said, and eventually checked into a B&B

for the night. I was just going to lie low for a bit, till everything had cooled down. Then I'd go back, get my things, and leave Jack for good. I thought Tim was okay, I really did. A black eye, maybe, and a sore head. It was me Jack was really angry with. Me he took things out on."

"But Tim wasn't all right," said Amy. Tears were brewing, but she needed to hear how the story ended.

"Jack phoned me, again and again. But I ignored him. There were calls from you too, but I thought you'd be angry at me, leaving Tim like that. So I ignored everyone. Eventually I decided I couldn't hide forever, so I answered the phone to Jack."

"He told you Tim was . . ." Amy couldn't say it.

"No," said Chantel. "He didn't tell me. He's never told me. But he sounded different. He cried down the phone. I'd never heard him cry before. He said he wasn't angry and just wanted to see me again. To make sure I was okay."

Chantel paused and looked at Amy. "You didn't meet with him?" asked Amy.

"No," said Chantel. "I told him I never wanted to see him again. But I asked about Tim, and he said Tim had run away like I had. But that wasn't true. I'd seen Tim hit the ground. He hadn't run. That's when I got worried."

Amy closed her eyes and held her hands over her eyelids to block out the light. She took a deep breath.

"I called my mum," continued Chantel. "She told me that Tim hadn't come home. You'd phoned her, looking for us both. I asked her not to say anything to anyone. If Tim wasn't okay, then I was the only person who could connect his disappearance to Jack. And Jack knew that. I was dangerous to him, which put me in even more danger."

Amy opened her eyes again. "He always told me that he believed you two had run off together," said Amy, the pieces falling into place. "He told the team investigating that too. And the local paper."

"I saw that," said Chantel. "If that was what he was saying, I was sure he knew Tim wasn't coming back. Jack had killed him. He was covering his tracks."

Amy felt the weight of years of not knowing crushing her. "You could have told the police," said Amy. "He would have been arrested."

"Would they have believed me over him?" asked Chantel. "Me? I'd been in trouble with the police for drugs. I hadn't even realized what happened for days. He was a distinguished officer on the fast track. And he could be so convincing, with his hero act."

"But there would have been evidence," said Amy. "DNA, prints?"

"Jack was smart and he was a policeman. If there was anything to link him to what happened, he would have got rid of it right away."

"The . . . body?" Amy hated to say the word. It felt so final. So unconnected to Tim.

"I figured Jack would have known what to do, where to hide it. It was already dark, and we were in a remote bit of the park."

Amy thought about the playground under construction, about the digger Charles had identified. Deep holes already dug in the earth. She shivered. "There was another reason," said Chantel, taking Amy's hand. "I told you in the letter."

"I never got that stupid letter," said Amy, snatching her hand away. "Why didn't you call?"

"He threatened you, Amy," said Chantel. "He said that if I went to the police, he'd get to you before they got to him."

Amy sat back.

"I thought by leaving, I was protecting you," continued Chantel. "Even contacting you put you in danger. Tim lost his life to that man, Amy. I couldn't let him hurt you too."

"Chantel . . ." began Amy. She couldn't finish the sentence. Wasted years, curdled by fears of betrayal. All down to a letter that slipped inside a pot.

No. All down to Jack.

Jack, who killed the man she loved and terrified her best friend into abandoning her. She thought of all the visits to the police station, the comfort he had offered her. The reassurance.

The lies.

She squeezed the lighter in her hand even more tightly, although she could feel the thin plastic strain under her grip.

"I know you're angry with me," said Chantel, looking at Amy's hands. "It was all my fault. I fell for Jack. I moved in with him. It was me who brought him into our lives. And Tim was the one who . . ." Chantel trailed off. "I'm so sorry, Amy," she said. "I had to get away. I thought you'd be better off without me." Chantel looked around the room, at the towers of boxes and birds and broken mirrors. "You were always so strong," she added. "I never imagined that . . ." She paused again. "I didn't realize . . ." She put her head in her hands. "God, Amy, what did I do to you?"

"Jack got away with it," said Amy, unwilling to talk about herself. "For all these years." She paused. "And you just disappeared."

"Mum gave me enough money to tide me over," said Chantel. "Everything she had. I was so careful. No credit cards, no mobile phones. Nothing that could be traced to me. It wasn't that much to leave, not really. My life was a mess, you know that. I was leaving behind a dead-end job that I hated. An abusive relationship. Half a bag of weed hidden in my sock drawer and a pile of debt. You and my mum were the only good things I had left. I thought I was doing the right thing by you. Keeping you safe."

"Where did you go?" asked Amy, her voice a little softer.

"Wales," said Chantel. "It was a fresh start, a clean slate. I got a job in a local pub, cash in hand, which came with a room upstairs. The landlord was a widower, and ever so kind. Things started to look up."

Amy looked at her. She knew Chantel well.

"Yes, we got together," admitted Chantel. "We've got two kids. I told Rhys everything, of course. More or less." She paused. "Can we have that wine?" asked Chantel. She was looking at Amy, and Amy realized Chantel didn't just want wine.

She wanted forgiveness.

"No," said Amy. "I don't think so." She paused, watching Chantel's face.

"I understand," said Chantel. "Perhaps I had better leave now?"

Amy hesitated. Part of her wanted to tell Chantel everything. That she'd been waiting for Tim all these years, a part of her always hoping he'd come back. She wanted to say that she didn't think she could love again after the betrayal she'd felt. That she'd never been able to completely let go because she could never be certain what had happened. That instead she'd collected her treasures and cared for them. Because they made her feel almost happy at times and they could never leave her. Like Chantel had left her. And like Tim had too, albeit she now knew it was not of his own volition. Perhaps if she'd known the truth, she would have moved on, instead of being fossilized inside this house, surrounding herself with belongings that made her remember a past long gone.

Chantel hadn't fossilized. Chantel had known the truth. She'd started a family. Even had a house in Wales, like she said she always wanted.

Amy was angry. Perhaps she always would be. But there was something else she felt too, her heart beating a little more fully, as if a vital component had been returned. Tim wasn't the only person she'd desperately missed over the past eleven years.

"Maybe you can have some wine," she said. "Just a glass."

Chantel beamed at her, but Amy found she wasn't ready to smile back. Instead she turned to the kitchen to fetch the wine. Chantel followed her.

"I like what you've done with the place," said Chantel, deadpan. It was so inappropriate for Chantel to criticize her and yet so intensely Chantel that Amy burst into something that was half a laugh, half a sob. "I don't know why I said that," said Chantel. "Sorry. There must be something wrong with me."

Amy poured the wine and handed a glass to Chantel. She refilled her own glass and took a nervous sip, wishing it were brandy.

"You live here alone?" asked Chantel, eyeing the towers of mugs doubtfully. "You've never . . . met someone?"

The doorbell rang before Amy could reply. "I can't believe you've kept that awful bell," said Chantel with an awkward laugh.

"I kept what I could," said Amy.

Chantel went to hug Amy, but Amy backed away. "No," she said. "I'll get the door."

Amy walked into her hallway and tripped over an empty wine bottle. She went to pick it up. It was perfectly ordinary. Glass, bottle shaped. She held it to the light. A pleasant enough shade of green, but nothing special. She hesitated a second, then went back to the kitchen and put it next to the bin. She'd take it to the recycling center tomorrow. It and about a hundred others. And some newspapers. And maybe even some of the clocks that didn't tick. It was just stuff, after all. Stuff that she didn't need and that weighed her down. Stuff that she would need to get rid of to make room for other things in her life. No. Not other things.

People.

Amy released the catch to the door. She knew the truth. It wasn't a happy ending, but at least it was an ending.

It would be Richard, thought Amy, remembering again the feeling of his hand on her arm. She needed to talk to someone, someone who wasn't Chantel. It was so much to take in.

She swung the door open, but it wasn't Richard she saw.

It was DCI Jack Hooper.

June 2008

Amy decided that she was glad Tim hadn't picked her up at the airport. Even as she heaved her heavy suitcase onto the train, she told herself it was a good thing. She'd be bound to blurt out her news, in front of the hubbub of people. It would be better to wait. Tonight, back home.

Or maybe tomorrow. Amy was tired and sweaty and didn't fancy a big conversation. She wanted a shower and then to curl up next to Tim on the sofa, feeling his warm body against hers. Then to go to sleep in bed next to him. She'd hardly slept since she'd found out, and had put it down to a mixture of excitement and hormones. And missing Tim. Being in bed and listening to his breathing was what she needed for proper sleep. Then tomorrow she'd make a special meal for dinner and tell him. Anything but pasta. That was the plan.

It was perfect.

The train ride seemed to take forever. She had to travel into the center of town and then catch her train out again. But finally, she arrived at her station. She'd told Tim which train she was on in the hope that he'd suggest coming to meet her at the station, but he had just replied with an X. The lift was broken, and Amy found herself lugging the suitcase up the endless flight of steps. She needed to get herself one of those little badges, she decided. BABY ON BOARD. Then someone would be bound to help her.

She wondered how she went about getting one, and decided to ask the station attendant. It would be quite a sweet way to tell Tim even, she thought. Just to present him with a badge.

"Congratulations, love," said the man in the ticket office. "We're all out. Apply online. Takes two to four weeks."

Never mind, thought Amy. It was a bit gimmicky anyway. She'd tell him properly. With words.

AMY JUMPED UP, wrapping her arms and legs around Tim when he opened the door. She buried her face in his neck and breathed in his smoky coconut scent and felt his warm body pressing against her.

Against them both.

"Easy, tiger," said Tim, gently shaking her off him. "You'll break my back."

"You think I've gained weight?" Usually Amy would be appalled at the suggestion, but she found herself excited. She was changing already. She half expected him to tell her she was glowing.

"Of course not," said Tim carefully. "I would never say that."

"What did you want to tell me?" asked Amy, releasing him and dragging her suitcase inside.

"Not now," said Tim. Amy frowned at him. He was being strange, but then again, she had a secret too. She probably seemed weird to him.

"Do I look different?" she asked, unable to resist.

"You look tanned," he said.

"I spent the whole time inside," said Amy. "Painting."

"Not eating spaghetti off naked Italians?"

"Only penne," replied Amy with a laugh.

"Fancy a drink?" asked Tim. "I'm having one."

"No thanks," said Amy. She paused. "I'm pretty tired tonight. But how about I cook us a nice dinner tomorrow?"

"I can't tomorrow," said Tim. "I'm busy."

"What?" exclaimed Amy. "But I've just got back."

"And I'm here now," he said, kissing the top of her head.

"You didn't even get me from the airport," muttered Amy.

"You told me not to!" Amy had, but that wasn't the point.

"Can't you cancel your plans?" she wheedled.

"You've been away six weeks, Amy, and you're complaining because I'm out one night?"

"Okay," said Amy. "Fine." She paused. "What are you doing, anyway?"

"Simon wants to chat band stuff," he said. "Think he's hoping I might join them for a gig. But it will just be a quick drink; shouldn't take long."

"I'm going for a shower," said Amy, feeling dirty and tired from her journey.

"Sorry, Amy," said Tim, giving her a little kiss. "We'll have that dinner on Friday. I'll cook. There's something important I want to talk to you about."

AMY SETTLED DOWN for a brief rest on the bed after her shower and fell fast asleep. When she woke up the next morning, Tim had already gone to work. She spent the day unpacking and even had a little look in Chantel's room. They could convert it into a nursery. Already Amy was imagining the glorious birds she'd paint on the walls. Maybe she'd create a real sky on the ceiling, complete with fluffy clouds and a bright rainbow that could extend to the walls.

Amy waited and waited for Tim to come home, but he didn't.

That quick drink must have turned into a long drink, then another, and then God knows what else. Eventually she gave up on him and went to bed, curling up on her own until sleep overtook her. She woke up in the middle of the night, assuming it was Tim who had woken her, but no Tim appeared in the bedroom. She got up and checked the living room to see if he'd come home and fallen asleep on the sofa, but there was no sign. She went to the loo, already a more frequent occurrence, then went back to bed. She hoped he wouldn't be hungover when she told him her news, but then he couldn't be blamed for that. He had no idea what was coming his way.

It was when she woke up Friday morning and he still wasn't there that she started to really worry. She phoned Tim, but it went straight to voice mail. They were probably passed out on Simon's couch, she decided. Or in a gutter maybe, she thought bitterly.

Amy went about her day, unpacking and doing laundry. She'd brought some of her paintings home in an art bag, and decided that she should put them up in the flat. Especially the painting of naked Antonio. That would serve Tim right.

She phoned Tim again and then Simon every hour or so, feeling worry building up inside her. Still no answer. She tried to stay calm; surely stress wasn't good for the baby. She was planning to go to the library later and get a book on pregnancy. Already she'd checked online and discovered that the baby was currently the size of a sesame seed.

Eventually, as she was picking the sesame seeds she couldn't bear to eat off a bread roll that she'd found in the cupboard for lunch, she got a call. Simon. She hurried to pick it up, sending her little pile of sesame seeds flying to the floor.

"Why on earth do I have seven missed calls from you?" asked Simon.

"Where's Tim?" asked Amy.

"Tim? How should I know?"

"He's not with you?"

"I haven't seen Tim in weeks," replied Simon. "The band broke up, remember? Course you do."

"You weren't with him last night?" Amy felt her heart fall into her stomach.

"It's been weeks," repeated Simon. He paused. "Have I landed him in it?"

Amy found she was too angry to reply. Why had Tim lied? She'd been away for six weeks. A lot could happen in that time. Amy couldn't help but leap to conclusions.

AMY DIALED CHANTEL again. She needed the moral support of her best friend. Chantel's phone went to voice mail too. Why did no one answer their bloody phones? She looked at her watch. It was lunchtime on a Friday, so Chantel would be at work. She didn't have the number, but Jack might. He worked shifts, so there was a chance he'd be at home. She scrolled through her numbers until she found the landline for Chantel and Jack. She didn't think Chantel would mind being disturbed at work. This was an emergency.

"Who's that?" Jack snapped.

"It's Amy," she said, then paused at the silence on the line. "Amy Ashton," she clarified.

"Why are you phoning?"

"Sorry," said Amy. "You sound tired."

"No," said Jack. "I'm not tired. Why would I be?"

Amy had no answer to that. "Sorry," she said again. "I was hoping to speak to Chantel."

"She's at work," said Jack. "Why would she be here?"

"I know she's at work," said Amy, thinking she'd never heard Jack be this rude before. "Can I have her number there? It's urgent."

"I don't have it," said Jack.

"Oh," said Amy, not really believing him. "I suppose I could try to find it online."

Silence greeted her on the line. "Actually, we've had a bit of an argument," said Jack. "If you must know, she didn't come home last night."

"Neither did Tim," said Amy.

"You don't think . . ." began Jack.

"Of course not," said Amy. But the seed had been planted.

AMY HAD NEVER been a big reader of newspapers. When she read, she liked novels. Beautiful books with stories where people made mistakes and learned from them and grew. The papers were full of people doing terrible things to each other and never getting any better. Not to her taste at all.

But after Amy reported Tim missing, the news was suddenly relevant. It wasn't some story about something awful that had happened a long way away and that would never affect her. There could be news in there about Tim. And about Chantel.

She found herself collecting all the papers when the story first broke. It was never headline news, even in the local papers. But there was something about the disappearance, at least at first. After a day or so the stories grew shorter, but still Amy bought all the papers, hoping for more. She carefully cut out any reference to Tim or Chantel, and she studied Jack's comments over and over.

Amy spent hours at the police station, making statement after statement. She had endless cups of sweet tepid tea, and was assured again and again that the police were doing everything in their power. Jack was a godsend, explaining the process to her and keeping her updated on every development.

Except there were very few developments. No one seemed to know anything. It was as if they'd vanished into thin air.

Eventually Jack sat her down and told her, off the record, what his colleagues believed: Chantel and Tim had run away to start a new life together. Jack and Amy were collateral damage.

Amy refused to believe it, and scoured the papers for more news. Perhaps even a message in the personals. She called Tim's friends again and again, and made a nuisance of herself in both of their offices.

She had to find them, and she felt sure that she would. She had to tell Tim about the baby.

No matter what he had done, he needed to know that he was going to be a father.

Chapter
Fourteen

"Hello there, Amy." Jack smiled at her. "I don't do house calls much anymore, but I thought I'd make an exception, seeing as how we're old friends." He went to move inside, but Amy stood her ground. "Can I come in?" he asked, clearly expecting her to say yes.

Amy slammed the door.

It wouldn't close. Amy looked down. Jack had his foot in the doorway in a well-practiced maneuver. She looked at him through the narrow gap and realized she was trembling.

"What's the problem, Amy?" asked Jack, his voice casual, although she could see beads of sweat on his forehead, betraying him. "I got your message. I'm sure I can clear it right up. Let me in."

Her message. Of course. She'd asked him why he didn't raise the alarm earlier when Chantel disappeared.

She knew now.

Because he'd killed Tim. And Chantel, the only witness, had fled.

The only witness, who'd escaped him for years.

And who was drinking wine in her kitchen.

"Not now," said Amy, trying to erase the terror from her voice. "Jack," she added loudly, for Chantel's benefit. Jack looked at her, suspicion registering on his face. She attempted a smile but her mouth wasn't cooperating.

"Have you got company?" he asked.

They both heard a noise from inside, the thud of something falling.

Jack didn't need a second prompt. He charged at the door, slamming into it with his shoulder. It flung open, its force pushing Amy into her hallway wall. Hard. She hit her head on the shelf and sent one of the bottles flying. It fell to the ground and smashed. She sank down next to it as Jack barged past her, crushing a piece of glass beneath his shoe. Amy stared at the shards for a moment, feeling dizzy.

She reached her hand to the pain on her head and felt a warm wetness. Then she looked at her fingers.

Blood.

Hearing Jack return from the kitchen, Amy looked up. He was alone; Chantel must have escaped through the back door. She took a deep breath and tried to pull herself together.

Jack was dangerous and she was alone. Now was not the time for confrontations. Amy tried to swallow down the fury she felt for him and ignore the pounding in her head.

He was looking at her, concern in his features. "God, Amy," he said. "I didn't mean to . . ." He reached out a hand to help her up, but she flinched away. "It's just when I heard the sound, I thought it might be an intruder," he said, clearly lying.

"I'd like you to leave now."

"Don't be like that," said Jack. "It was an accident. That shelf . . ."

"Please go."

"I really think I should stay," said Jack. "You can't be too careful with head injuries."

It was too much.

"Get out of my house," she said, unable to contain her anger.

"What's going on, Amy?" he asked. His voice was harder now, any concern he felt for her clearly dissipating. "Get up." He reached down again, but this time it wasn't an offer. He gripped her arms tightly, too tightly, and dragged her to her feet. She cried out in pain.

Chantel flung open the living-room door and rushed towards them. "Get your hands off her!" she yelled. Amy looked at Chantel. She hadn't run. Not this time.

"Chantel!" exclaimed Jack. He jerked backwards as if he'd been hit. For a moment Amy thought he might fall, but instead she felt his grip on her arms tightening further. He pushed Amy into the living room and Chantel followed.

"I mean it," said Chantel. "Let go of her now."

Jack looked at his hands, as if he'd forgotten he was still holding her. "Amy had an accident," he explained, releasing her. "That's all."

"Another accident?" asked Chantel. She pulled Amy behind her, shielding her from Jack.

"So you told her," he said.

No one spoke. The three of them stood together in silence, and Amy heard a clock ticking from inside one of her boxes. She glanced around and saw Scarlett perched on another box, watching the drama unfold. Amy longed to reach out and grab the robin, to hug her close to her chest.

"I looked for you, Chantel," said Jack finally, his voice eerily calm. "For a long time."

"I know," she said.

"Where were you?"

"I'd rather not say," said Chantel.

"Even now?" asked Jack, the calmness in his voice starting to evaporate. "What happened to Tim—it was an accident. You know it was."

"What you did to me wasn't an accident," said Chantel.

"I'm sorry." He paused. "It's different now. I'm married," he said. "Two little girls."

"I feel sorry for them," said Chantel.

"I've never laid a finger on a child," said Jack. "I'm not like that. Never was."

"That makes it all right?"

"The accident with Tim," continued Jack, ignoring her. "It changed me. It was the worst thing that ever happened to me."

"To you?" questioned Amy, incredulous.

"She told you it wasn't my fault, right?" he asked, turning to Amy. "It was an accident, that was all."

"You hit Tim and killed him," said Amy. The words tasted sour in her mouth.

"That's what she told you?" asked Jack. Amy nodded. "It wasn't like that. Chantel lied to me and sneaked off to see Tim. They were kissing in the park."

"We weren't kissing," said Chantel.

"What was I supposed to think?" continued Jack, ignoring her. "I was angry. You would have been too. Anyone in my shoes would have done what I did."

"Really?" questioned Chantel. "I don't think so."

"It was an accident," said Jack again. He looked at Amy, as if willing her to believe him. "I didn't even hit him that hard. But he fell backwards and hit his head on a railing. That was what killed him. It wasn't my fault."

"You hit him and now he's dead."

"But I didn't mean to kill him," said Jack, his voice rising. "It was a stupid accident that could have ruined my life."

"What about Tim's life?" asked Amy. Her head was throbbing.

"It was tragic," said Jack. "But there was nothing I could do. He was gone already."

Amy looked at him. Ruthlessly selfish, and he didn't even seem sorry. Just worried for what would happen to him.

"I could have got ten years in prison for manslaughter," said Jack. "And you know what they do to police in prison."

"You want us to feel sorry for you?" asked Amy.

"I couldn't let that happen," continued Jack. "Then I saw it. A hole. The machines. A way out. There was no one around. I had to take that chance."

"No you didn't," said Amy.

"I've been a model citizen ever since," said Jack. "A good policeman, a good husband and father. I've never lifted a hand to anyone." He looked at Chantel, then Amy. "Not really. And it was so long ago. There's no need to go raking up the past."

He'd said that to Amy before, and her pots had ended up destroyed. Amy wondered if Jack was responsible, trying to scare her into leaving things alone. She felt a cocktail of anger and fear well up inside her.

"Yes there is," she said. "Tim deserves justice."

"I'm sure we can work something out," said Jack, desperation creeping into his voice.

"No," said Amy. "We just need the truth. We all do."

"Chantel?" Jack turned to her. "I was heartbroken when you left. I thought you, of all people, would stand by me."

"You were wrong," said Chantel. "Jack, I was terrified of you. Of what you would do to me. To Amy. I don't want to live in fear. But I'm not going to hide away. Not anymore."

Jack seemed to grow bigger. Amy noticed him looking around the room. "You two are making this very difficult for me," he said. "I promised myself I wouldn't hurt anyone again."

"You already have," said Chantel. "Look at Amy."

"It could be worse," said Jack, menace in his voice.

Amy slowly sidestepped towards the window, pulling Chantel with her. Amy looked up at Scarlett, watching the action from her perch on top of a large stack of boxes. The top one contained cookery books, Amy was sure of it. The next one down had clocks, and she could see a heavy mirror, squeezed in between them.

"Are you threatening us?" asked Amy.

"I don't see what alternative you're giving me," Jack replied. He stepped backwards, bumping into a stack of boxes. "What the hell is wrong with your house, Amy?" he said suddenly. "Are you some sort of hoarder?"

Jack paused for a moment, then smiled. A nasty smile. Amy felt Chantel flinch next to her. "This place is an accident waiting to happen," he said, his hand on one of Amy's boxes.

Amy didn't reply. She looked up at Scarlett, the lovely robin who had stuck by her all these years. Why did she have to be there? She bit her lip. And the boxes. The boxes full of her lovely things. Her loyal possessions. Her delicate belongings.

Her heavy treasures.

Amy released Chantel's hand and lunged forwards. She pushed the tower of boxes from the bottom. It teetered for a moment, and she saw confusion flash across Jack's face. Then it toppled. A crash. Deafening. The sickening sound of breakages. A mirror smashed. Scarlett's china wings destroyed. Jack's bones broken.

Chantel's voice.

"Run."

June 2008

"No, Amy, there haven't been any new developments in the case." DC Jack Hooper spoke softly, but Amy could hear the edge in his voice. "Not the last time you came to see me, and not today."

"Still nothing from Toyah?" Amy squeezed the plastic cup of institutional tea tightly. The hot liquid spilled over the top and scalded her hand, but she barely noticed.

"She said that you'd been to see her again. Listen, Amy, her daughter is missing. You need to give her some space. She's heard nothing from Chantel." He paused. "Neither have I," he added.

"What about Tim?" Amy found desperation creeping into her voice again, although she'd asked the question over and over.

"No news. Not from Simon, not from Idris, not from his dad. As you well know. You've been in contact with all of them again, haven't you?"

"I need to find him," said Amy. "I need to find Tim. And Chantel. Something terrible must have happened."

"Must it?" asked Jack. Amy didn't answer, not wanting to hear what he said next. "Because you know what my colleagues on the case believe."

"Not my best friend and my boyfriend." Amy watched the skin on her hand turn an angry shade of red in response to the spilt tea.

"It's what it looks like," replied Jack. "Listen. I'm as hurt as you are. But we need to face the possibility that they don't want to be found. Not by us."

"They wouldn't do that to me," insisted Amy, though the days of hounding anyone she could think of had taken their toll. No one had seen Tim. No one had heard from Chantel. The worried looks and sympathy that she'd encountered when she first asked had turned to pity and annoyance as she went back to people again and again. "I don't believe it," said Amy, her voice less certain.

"Don't you?" queried Jack. "You might not want to. But I think by now you must."

"Maybe," admitted Amy.

"You leave things to me now," said Jack. "It's not good for you, hunting for them like this. I'm the professional. If they can be found, I'll do it. Promise you'll let me help?"

"I promise," said Amy.

"Good," replied Jack. "Leave it to me."

AMY SAT IN her garden, watching a bloated cigarette floating in an ashtray full of rainwater. It had been two weeks since Tim went missing, and she'd heard nothing. Chantel was gone too, and Jack was convinced that the two of them were having an affair and had run away together.

It wasn't possible. Not Chantel and Tim. Something had happened to them. Amy's mind raced through the possibilities, none of them good.

They were being held hostage somewhere by a violent psychopath.

They'd been in a car that had veered off the road into the sea, despite the fact that neither owned a car and they all lived miles inland.

They'd been abducted by aliens.

When she thought about it like that, Amy understood why Jack believed they had run away together. It was certainly more plausible than anything she could fathom. And yet, it seemed equally unlikely. There must be another explanation. An explanation that would help Amy find them. Every time someone walked by her house, Amy found herself at the window, but it was never them. Every time the doorbell rang, Amy sprang up and ran to it. Never them. She'd collected stacks of newspapers, desperate for news. Nothing.

Her back ached, probably from sitting in this plastic chair. It was her one piece of garden furniture, decorated with cigarette burns and speckled with bird poo. She stretched up, but the pain in her lower back intensified.

The baby was the size of a blackberry now, the book from the library had told her. Hard to believe that something so small could cause so much discomfort. It would be months before she could feel movement, but already Amy felt as if there was a gentle fluttering inside of her. Tiny legs attempting inchoate kicks. She hadn't had morning sickness yet. According to a forum on the internet, that could mean it was a boy.

A little Tim.

Tim would love a son. He'd be thrilled when he came home. Amy allowed herself a little fantasy, where he came back from . . . from where? An impromptu business trip, where he had met all his targets and earned a hefty commission. He'd be horrified that she had been worried; he'd written her an e-mail but forgot to press Send. He'd dropped his phone and it had stopped working, or he would have called. That sounded like Tim. So possible. Although Amy wasn't showing yet, in her fantasy she had a gently rotund stomach and her face glowed. He'd look at her, know instantly, and his eyes would fill with joy. "Yes," she'd tell him. "We're going to have a baby."

A robin flew down and landed on the ashtray. It perched at the edge, and lowered its beak to the water to drink, unperturbed by the cigarette. Amy held her breath, not wanting to scare the little bird away. It must be ten times the size of her baby, but it looked so delicate and vulnerable to Amy. A precious little life.

Amy felt a wave of optimism. Tim would come back. He had to. She had a part of him, growing inside her. A tie that couldn't be broken. A thread that would lead him back to her.

The pain in Amy's back intensified and she stood. Then she doubled over back to her seat, feeling a cramp spread across her stomach.

The robin looked at her, its beady eyes gleaming. Then it fluttered up into the sky. Gone.

Amy hobbled into the kitchen and grabbed her mobile phone, calling an ambulance. She rested her head on the kitchen counter. She took some deep breaths and ran through what the pregnancy books had said.

It was too late for implantation pain. Too early for Braxton-Hicks.

Amy tried to straighten up, and the pain shot through her again. Then she looked down.

Blood. Running down her leg.

Amy sank down to the floor and curled up, hugging her knees to her chest. The ambulance would be there soon. But she couldn't help but feel that there was nothing they could do. Amy rocked gently forwards and backwards, willing her baby to be okay.

Chapter
Fifteen

It was cold in the early August morning, and Amy held her paper cup of tea close to her, feeling the steam warm her chin. The horizon had an orange glow and it was getting lighter all the time; the sun was busy rising, almost white with the effort of turning the sky blue. Amy decided that if she painted again, she would no longer choose a sunset. She'd choose a sunrise.

Fresh starts.

She took a sip of her tea and turned around to look at the playground. Richard was staring at the hive of activity around what had been the paddling pool, but looked away from it to give Amy a reassuring smile. "It won't be long now," he said. They stood behind the police tape, with its strict instructions. DO NOT CROSS.

Amy had no desire to disobey that order. This was close enough.

It had been hard to get to this point. After what had happened in the living room, Chantel ran for help. Later Amy discovered it was Rachel who had called 999, but at the time all she could do was stare at Jack's hand, poking out from under her things. Twitching like a nervous spider, its movements reflected in the shards of a broken mirror.

Then stillness.

A flurry of confusion followed. An ambulance. The police. She heard Chantel's voice. "The boxes fell," Chantel had said firmly. "It was an accident."

Chantel continued talking to the police officer, her voice low. The officer's face changed and she called her partner over. Amy sat and watched while the paramedics tended to her head.

The boys had come out to see the emergency vehicles, but Richard quickly shepherded them back indoors. By the time the police car drove off with her and Chantel, only Smudge remained on the pavement outside their house, nonchalantly licking his tail.

Jack was in custody. He'd had a concussion and some bad bruising but would make a full recovery. His problems were only just beginning. Chantel had finally told the police what had happened, eleven years ago. They had taken her allegations seriously.

Now here they were, waiting to see if Tim's body was buried under the playground.

"What if he's not there?" whispered Amy.

"The police will find him," said Richard. "Now that they know where to look."

If only she'd got that letter earlier. The letter that told her Tim had not betrayed her. The photograph that showed where Tim had breathed his last.

And when.

Sunset.

Chantel hadn't wanted to come back to this place. Amy understood, but she felt she had to see for herself. Richard came with her. His arm rested comfortingly around her shoulders.

"It is different," said Richard. "Knowing that someone is dead. I know you've suffered loss already, but now it will feel final."

"I know what it feels like," said Amy. Without realizing, she'd put her hand to her stomach. Richard's eyes followed her hand.

"I'm sorry," he said, his voice soft. "I didn't know."

Amy looked back at the horizon. The orange line had vanished as if it had been an illusion. The sky was blue. She could feel the heat of the sun starting to warm the air. A shout sounded out, and Amy turned to see scene of crime officers in their white suits flock together like doves. Peering downwards.

"That's him," she said. "They've found Tim."

"THANKS FOR DOING this." Tim's father seemed incapable of letting go of her hand. "And that was such a beautiful speech."

"I think Tim deserves it," replied Amy. She looked around the small party at the memorial service. Tim hadn't been religious, so Amy hadn't been sure where to hold it. Then she remembered the festival where the band had played, all those years ago. The field was a little out of the way, but she remembered how happy he'd been.

"You'll scatter the ashes here?"

"We will," said Amy. She looked to the urn, surrounded by fragrant honeysuckle. Inside was what remained of Tim, mingled with the tiny pieces of Scarlett that Amy had had cremated with him. The bird was too badly broken to be mended this time. "After the concert. I think they are ready to start soon."

The remaining band members had reunited one last time. Simon, Idris, and Phil. Chantel stood next to her at the front as people gathered. She tentatively took Amy's hand. The two of them were gradually feeling their way back to friendship. Amy didn't think she could ever love Chantel like she used to, not after she'd left her for so long. But it felt good to have her back in Amy's life.

"This is a song about missing a sunset," said Simon, his face close to the microphone. "It was our signature song, written by the late, great Tim Carver. 'Already Dark.'"

Amy listened to the song, but she found her eyes wandering around the gathering. Erin, Chantel's elder daughter, had come to stand next to her mother and had taken her other hand. Daniel and Gwyneth, Chantel's youngest, were holding their arms out like airplanes and careering round. Charles was crouched on the ground, likely inspecting an insect. Alan stood mesmerized by the music he'd never heard his son perform.

And Richard was standing at the back, watching her. She gestured to him, and he came and joined her. It felt odd, listening to Tim's song with another man.

But she couldn't miss another sunset.

"SO WE'VE GOT three categories and I've brought labels," said Rachel, clearly relishing her role. "Green for keep. Red for throw away. Yellow for charity shop. Understood?"

Amy nodded miserably. "You don't have to do this yet," said Richard. "Not if you're not ready."

"I'm ready," said Amy. It had been weeks since Tim's memorial service. She had her friend back. She wanted the boys to be able to come into her house. She even wanted the council to be able to fix that stupid chimney. Rachel had arranged an extension with them after all that had happened, but it couldn't be put off forever. "Let's do this."

"Great stuff. Come on, team," said Rachel, punctuating her sentence with an enthusiastic double clap. "Hop to it. I don't want to see any slacking. No cups of tea till the kitchen is clear." She scowled at Chantel. "And no cigarette breaks."

"Did you really have to invite her?" whispered Chantel. "Just looking at her makes me want a smoke."

"She's okay," said Amy. "Give her a chance."

"Bottles," said Rachel, getting straight to work. "All rubbish. Agreed?"

"I'll need to check them," said Amy, feeling anxious. "But yes. Most of them can go. Recycling."

"Newspapers," said Rachel. "The local paper dating back God knows how long."

"Eleven years," said Amy.

"Red?"

Amy hesitated. She knew the truth now. "Yes," she agreed.

"I'll move them," said Richard quickly, grabbing a large pile. A puff of dust rose up and they all watched as the particles gleamed in the sunlight.

"I know what we need," said Rachel. She produced a box of surgical gloves and handed him a pair before pulling some on herself. "I can't take any chances on infection," she said with a nervous smile. "Not in my condition." The others didn't notice, but Amy took Rachel's newly gloved hand and squeezed it. Rachel squeezed back, then released Amy's hand. "Chantel and Amy, some for you too," she said.

Chantel reluctantly took the gloves. She sniffed them. "They smell like condoms," she said.

"Of course they do," replied Rachel. "They're latex. Are you helping or not?"

"Helping," said Chantel. "But I'll take my chances." She handed back the gloves and Rachel scowled at her.

"I don't need gloves either," said Amy. "Everything is perfectly clean."

"If you say so," said Rachel, carefully putting a sticker on a plastic bin. She looked around. "What about these smashed pots?" she asked. "Rubbish?"

Amy looked at the little piles of broken shards. She now believed that Jack had something to do with their destruction. "I need those," she said. "I thought I might use them for an art project. Keep."

"Really?" queried Rachel. "You've got a garden full of whole ones."

"Yes really," snapped Chantel. "Amy can keep whatever she wants." She smiled at her friend. "It's so exciting that you're doing art again," she said. "I can't wait to see what you create."

"Fine," conceded Rachel. "But we're still in the hallway and we've got the whole rest of the house to sort through."

"There's no hurry," said Richard, placing a hand on Amy's back. She smiled at the contact.

"Let's get started in the living room," said Amy. She went into the room and Richard followed her.

"Broken mirror?" asked Richard.

Amy looked at the mirror, the cracks spreading over it like a spider's web. "Okay," she said. "We can get rid of it."

"What about this clock?" he said, picking it up. "It thinks it's seven o'clock, but I know for a fact it's twelve thirty."

Amy looked at it. It was a pretty little clock face set into a gorgeous mahogany frame. "Keep," she said. "It probably just needs new batteries."

"And the lighters?" said Richard. "They mainly seem to be the ones you can buy from the corner shop. And I keep treading on them. And you don't smoke."

"Keep," said Amy. She closed her eyes and imagined being back in that field, listening to Tim sing and seeing the tiny flames dancing, waving from side to side in time with the music.

"This one is broken," said Richard, holding up a green plastic lighter with a crack.

Amy snatched it from him. "I need it," she said.

"They are a bit of a hazard for Daniel," said Richard gently. "I wouldn't want him here with this fire-starting equipment all over the floor."

Amy hesitated. He had a point. "Gather them up and we'll put them in a box," she finally said. "I'll put it somewhere Daniel can't reach."

She thought she heard a small sigh from Richard, but he obeyed, scooping up a handful of lighters. "Remember the council needs access to the house."

"A box of lighters won't stop them," said Amy. "They're little."

"There are hundreds of them. How about you keep your favorites?"

Chantel came in then. "Are you pressuring my friend?" she asked. "Because if you are, I owe her one tower of boxes crashing down . . ." She mimed pushing over the boxes and laughed.

"Don't joke about that!" Amy exclaimed. "Do you realize how many china birds were damaged beyond repair?" She thought again of Scarlett, her tiny body broken into too many pieces to count.

"I'm sorry," said Chantel. "I do want to support you. And I think putting the lighters in a box is an excellent idea. But those birds . . ." She shivered. "They are hideous and they give me the creeps. I don't like the way they are always watching me with their beady little eyes."

"You like them, don't you?" asked Amy, turning to Richard.

Richard suddenly seemed excessively interested in his shoe. Finally he looked up. "I don't," he said. "Sorry."

"I don't care what either of you thinks," said Amy. "I was happy with my birds for years. When neither of you were around, they kept me company."

"But I'm here now," said Chantel. "And so is Richard."

"I can't cope with this," said Amy. She began to shoo them out of the room. "I need some space."

Amy closed the door and sat with her back against it. She looked up and her towers of possessions loomed overhead. She wanted to get rid of her stuff; she wanted a normal house. A normal life, whatever that was. She imagined Chantel visiting with the girls. Richard and the boys coming over for dinner.

She got up and went to the box of recipe books. They were sturdy and, unlike the birds, had barely been scuffed in the fall. She needed these to help her cook for the children—that was only sensible. She got one of Rachel's green stickers and put it on the box. Keep.

There were some loose cookbooks too, so she labeled those. She opened a box and found it to be full of bottles of hand cream. She squeezed a small amount onto her hand and rubbed the silky lotion into her skin. The scent of honeysuckles flooded the room. She'd use the hand cream; it would be silly to throw it away. She put a green sticker on the box.

The next box was a miscellany. Key rings, a few vases just big enough for a handful of honeysuckle. A large number of clocks.

Amy took out a little travel clock. It was plain black and had an attached case that kept it from breaking and could be used as a stand. It wasn't particularly nice, and it didn't seem to work. Amy put a red sticker on the clock, then felt sick and ripped it off again. She returned the clock to the box.

This was harder than she thought. Even now.

Next, Amy took out a handful of key rings. One was a pretty amethyst with a metal hoop looped through it. She popped it into her jacket pocket, planning to use it for her keys. She found another, this one branded Nottingham Forest Football Club. She must have picked it up in a charity shop for Mr. Trapper and forgotten to give it to him. She put that in her pocket as well. She'd take it to the office on Monday for him. He'd been very amenable when she'd asked to reduce her schedule to three days a week to give her time to paint again.

Following that train of thought, Amy went back to her hand-cream box and selected a small tube of jasmine-scented cream. It was unopened and Carthika would appreciate it. She put it in her pocket too, feeling it bulge reassuringly. She'd let Chantel and Rachel take a few tubes too, to thank them for their help.

The birds next, decided Amy. Perhaps she didn't need quite so many. But which ones to give away?

Not the kingfisher, certainly. Amy put a green sticker on that one. Not the shell owl. And not the gorgeous parakeet, nor the friendly sparrows or the jay or the canaries. She wasn't ready to say good-bye to any of them.

Amy went to get another green sticker and discovered she had only one left. She went back into the hallway. "I need more stickers," she told Rachel.

Rachel frowned at her. "You've got loads," she said, looking at the pages in Amy's hand.

"I need more green ones," she replied.

Rachel sighed. "This is going to be a long day," she said. "I'll go find some more."

"Where are my bottles?" asked Amy.

"Recycling," said Rachel. "You agreed, remember?"

"But I need to check them first," said Amy, feeling panic sneak up inside her.

"They are in the front," said Rachel with another sigh. "Be my guest."

Amy went into the front garden and saw Chantel and Richard sitting on the wall next to each other, looking out at the road. Chantel had a cigarette in her hand, and they seemed to have found a comfortable silence that Amy didn't like. Amy went to the bottles and began to bring them back indoors.

"Amy!" From nowhere, Charles came hurtling towards her. "I'm playing hide-and-seek with Daniel," he said. "It's a little kids' game, and I'm too grown-up for it really, but my dad said if we play outside, he has to watch to make sure that Daniel doesn't hide anywhere dangerous while I have my eyes closed."

Amy smiled at Richard. That's what he was doing.

Charles lowered his voice to an exaggerated whisper. "We can all see Daniel behind that pot," he said, pointing to the back of Daniel's clearly visible head. "But I'm pretending to look for him anyway."

"That is kind of you," said Amy.

"I know," replied Charles with a smile, before asking, "How's your clear-out going? Is there room for us to play in your house now? We could bring Mickey over for a visit."

"Not yet," said Richard, getting up and putting a hand on Amy's shoulder. "I told you it takes time."

"I get it," said Charles. "I wouldn't want to get rid of any of my diggers. Or my fire engines."

"You'll grow out of them one day," said Richard.

"Never," declared Charles. "When I'm big enough, I'll be a digger driver and a firefighter and play with big machines all day long." He peered back into Amy's house, then looked up at her. "Maybe then I wouldn't need to keep all the toys," he said. "Because I could drive them in real life."

Amy nodded. Real life needed space to grow.

"I need to get back to work," she said.

Amy went back into her house and through to the kitchen. The towers of mugs loomed tall. Their colors were beautiful, but did she really need so many? She wouldn't be drinking tea in just her own house anymore. She had friends she'd visit.

Slowly, Amy started to deconstruct one of the towers. One by one, she put the mugs in an empty box and firmly stuck on a yellow sticker for the charity shop. She'd keep a few, she decided. Six.

Maybe ten.

But no more.

She took hold of the yellow mug that she'd rescued when Nina and Richard had moved in. She ran her finger down the crack. Not even the charity shop would want this, she realized. Perhaps she didn't either. Amy peeled a red sticker from her sheet. She had to let go of the broken things in her life. Some of them, at least. Gently, she affixed the sticker to the mug.

Going back into the living room, she was struck by the scale of what she still had to accomplish. Box after box after box.

She had to start somewhere. With a sigh, Amy pulled a box down from one of the piles and opened it. Ashtrays. She hesitated. She wasn't a smoker, but Chantel was. She'd need one when she visited. Amy's hands hovered over the box. She could keep one ashtray, she decided. But which? They were all so lovely. Perhaps she might take up smoking one day, she thought. Then she'd be justified in keeping the lighters too. Her mind went back to the only time she'd tried a cigarette, leaning out of Chantel's bedroom window. She'd coughed so much she was almost sick.

Maybe she wouldn't take up smoking, she decided. But once the house was clear she was planning to invite people to visit her again. Simon perhaps. What if he was there at the same time as Chantel and they were sitting far away from each other? She'd need to choose another ashtray to keep.

Or did she? Amy had always hated people smoking in her house. She thought again of Charles. She wanted him, his brother, and his father to visit more than anyone, and of course they didn't need ashtrays. Quickly, Amy peeled a yellow sticker from the paper and stuck it to the box. The whole lot could go to the charity shop.

Amy took a deep breath and pulled down the next box.

It revealed her mantelpiece, long hidden. Amy looked at it and smiled. She would put a single clock up there, she decided. One that worked. Perhaps a new painting. And one vase, for fresh flowers.

She opened the box and an array of bubble-wrapped vases peered back. Amy opened the top one, unable to resist the satisfaction of popping a bubble in the process. The vase was iridescent glass, probably Bohemian. The color of a sunrise. She had to keep that one.

The next was a sturdier construction, terra-cotta with a deep-purple glaze. Gorgeous. The following vase was Waterford crystal. She could still remember her joy at discovering it in a charity shop.

Amy took her last green sticker and placed it on the box of vases, then turned her attention to another box full of clocks.

She heard a soft knocking sound on the living room door, and Richard poked his head around.

"How's it going?" he asked.

"I've run out of green stickers," said Amy. "There's a lot I don't want to let go of."

"I know," said Richard. "In fact, I thought you might be feeling the house was a bit empty." He smiled. "So I brought you something."

"I'm not sure that's a good idea," said Amy. "More stuff is the last thing I need."

"Don't worry," he replied. "I got you something you can't keep."

"You'd be surprised what I can hold on to," said Amy. But she laughed a little, already feeling lighter.

He produced a bouquet of flowers from behind his back. Bright, messy, and wild. Daisies and buddleia and long trails of ivy. And honeysuckle. Lots of it.

Amy gasped.

"It's nothing fancy," said Richard. "The boys helped me pick it from the garden. Mrs. Hill had quite the green fingers, didn't she?"

"Honeysuckle," said Amy, disbelieving.

"We used lots of that," said Richard. "I know you like it."

"I do," said Amy. "Very much." She smiled back at him. "Wait here," she said. "I'll put them in water." She walked over to her vases, selected the iridescent one that reminded her of a sunrise, and took it to the kitchen to fill with water. She put the flowers inside and breathed in deeply.

She needed to make room for people. For a new man who brought her flowers. For little boys who understood her better than she did herself and threaded sticky little fingers through her own.

Amy went back to the living room and put the flowers on the mantelpiece. Then she unpeeled the green sticker from the box of vases, crumpled it up into a tiny ball, and put it in her pocket. She placed a yellow sticker in its place. The rest of the vases could go to the charity shop and find new homes.

"There," she said. "One less box."

Amy tried to smile, already feeling the loss. But she could feel the gain as well. She looked at the honeysuckle, the creamy flowers with their sweet scent and memories of the past. Then she looked at the daisies with brilliant white petals soft as a blanket, and the buddleia, tiny, modest blossoms coming together en masse to create something quite spectacular. Honeysuckle, yes, but so much more besides.

Amy looked to Richard. "You've done brilliantly today, Amy," he said. "You've let go of so much." He paused. "Perhaps . . ." He hesitated. "Perhaps there's more space now," he added. "In your life."

"Yes," said Amy. She hesitated too. "There is."

"I thought . . ." continued Richard. "That maybe you'll have room for us. For me and the boys, I mean."

"I hope so," she replied. And she did. She now knew the truth of what had happened. It was time to look to the future.

"And for me, especially?"

It seemed the most natural thing in the world to kiss him.

She did.

The kiss was warm and wonderful, scented of a summer's garden.

Amy broke away. "Are you sure? I still come with boxes of clocks, more cookbooks than I'll ever use, and flocks of china birds."

"I'll take you with or without the china birds, Amy Ashton," he said, reaching for her hand. Amy felt his skin against her own. Warm and soft. "No one travels lightly through life anymore."

Acknowledgments

Just as Amy collects bottles, I have collected an array of wonderful people who have helped with this novel.

My mother, Susan, who. has read this book so many times and has given brilliant ideas and valuable feedback with each read. She's amazing.

Philippa Pride, my insightful and kind mentor, and the members of the Next Chapter writing group. Thanks for the feedback and friendship.

Thank you to my agent, Euan Thorneycroft, and the team at A. M. Heath for the guidance, support, and belief, and for finding the book such perfect homes.

I'm so grateful to the fantastic team at Piatkus, with special thanks to my talented editors Emma Beswetherick, Anna Boatman, Amanda Keats, and Penny Isaac; their enthusiasm for Amy and her story has blown me away. Thank you to my publishers abroad: Cordelia Borchardt at Krüger, Kate Dresser at Simon & Schuster, and more I've yet to meet.

Special thanks to my baby daughter, Violet, for sleeping sweetly through the sound of keys tapping. And to my son, Teddy, for the treasures he collects and the diggers he loves.